Murder All Inclusive

by

Alastair Puddick

RAVEN
CREST
BOOKS
PUBLISHING

ISBN-978-1-7392592-3-5

DEDICATION

For Noah

CHAPTER 1

MONDAY

HOT, TIRED AND even more cantankerous than usual, Freddie Winters rolled his eyes as the angry woman loomed over him. Her breathing was ragged. Her face scarlet. Heat emanating from it. Her eyes were glazed with the start of angry tears and tiny specks of spittle flew from her mouth every time she spoke.

"But you can't just *stay* there," she said. "It's not yours."

"Look, I really don't see what the problem is," sighed Freddie, understanding exactly what the problem was. If the positions were reversed, he'd have been a hundred times as angry. "A mistake has been made. It would appear that I'm sitting in your assigned seat. I didn't know it was your seat when I sat in it. But I really don't see what the problem is. And there seems little sense in moving now. So, why don't you just shuffle along and sit in the seat I'm supposed to be in?"

"You really are the rudest man!" she said.

"So I'm told," said Freddie, grinning widely.

The woman made a strange squeaking noise, then turned and stormed off. Or at least she tried to storm off. But there was a queue of about 17 people blocking the aisle, so instead she had to slowly, angrily, squeeze and squirm her way back to the front of the plane, huffing and cursing as she went.

Freddie was in the wrong. He knew he was. And he didn't care.

When the angry woman had first approached him, smiling and saying, "Sorry to bother you," he had, naturally, mistaken her for an eager fan wanting an autograph. Freddie's latest book, *Death of a Mailman*, had recently been published to a certain amount of fanfare, and he was still getting used to being recognised.

The book was a fictional account of the real-life – and highly publicised – assassination attempt of his close friend and very famous author (national bloody treasure, if you want the truth), Dylan St

1

James. Not only had Freddie been instrumental in saving Dylan's life and catching the plotters, he'd then turned that story into a gripping psychological thriller – rushing it out in record time to capitalise on the notoriety he was already receiving.

Freddie had jumped at every newspaper and magazine interview they threw at him. He got a write-up in the Guardian. He was featured in the Times. He sat on TV couches being interviewed by the likes of Eamon Holmes, Lorraine Kelly and some annoying bearded twerp called Rylan.

It was all great publicity and helped with book sales. *Death of a Mailman* was by far Freddie's most successful book. Where his previous novels languished deep on the back shelves of bookshops, his newest had found itself in pride of place on the feature tables at the front of most stores. It spent several weeks in the charts. It sold a very healthy number of copies. And the publisher was desperate for a follow up.

Since then, Freddie had become a minor celebrity. And it wasn't uncommon for people to approach him in public asking for autographs, signed books, selfies and writing tips. Obviously, the last lot got short shrift. Why should he give advice away for free? Especially when colleges, universities and literary festivals up and down the country were offering to pay him to come and inspire the next generation of writers with his valuable knowledge and insights.

He was also not a fan of taking selfies with people. He couldn't see the point. Quite why people were so obsessed with themselves that they had to take pictures of their own face every 15 seconds, he'd never understood. As someone whose face could be best described as haggard, ghoulish and perpetually annoyed, Freddie had never particularly liked seeing it replicated in either print or digital format.

Despite this, Freddie was a realist. And if his adoring fans want to be photographed next to their literary idol, who was he to stand in their way? He was, however, selective about who he would take a selfie with. Especially after several uncomfortable experiences with large, sweaty men pressing their clammy bodies against him.

Also, as a newly respected author, he had to be careful about his image. He couldn't allow himself to be plastered across Facebook, Instagram and wherever else people post these things, grinning next to some toothless, ugly, dim-witted moron. People might think he was friends with these misfits. No, to get a selfie with Freddie, you had to possess at least a certain level of attractiveness. So, if your name was

Norman, if you were balding and if you bought your clothes in ASDA, you needn't even bother whipping your phone out.

No kids, obviously.

Attractive young women could, of course, have all the selfies they wanted.

And, naturally, Freddie always acquiesced to the little old ladies. As a crime writer, he knew where his bread was buttered. And with the old biddies being his primary audience, he needed to keep them sweet. Besides, they were so clueless about technology he'd lost count of the times he'd taken the picture with his own mobile, because the old dear wanted a selfie but didn't have a smartphone. God only knew how they thought they were going to get the picture. But if it made them smile for a minute and encouraged them to buy more books, then why not?

So, when this chirpy woman approached Freddie on a plane saying, "Sorry to bother you, but…" he naturally assumed she was after an autograph.

"No problem," he said, reaching into his pocket for the special autograph-signing pen he'd bought himself. "Do you have a book to sign? And who shall I make it out to?"

"Sorry, what?" she said, sheepishly.

"Your autograph," he said, slowly and clearly, assuming the woman was a bit slow. "What would you like me to sign? Do you have one of my books in your bag?"

"Eh… er… no, sorry. No… I think you're sitting in my seat," she said, waving a boarding pass in his face.

A smug, fat man across the aisle chuckled as he eavesdropped on the conversation. Freddie stared at him, a sharp stab of anger throbbing in his stomach.

"No, I don't think so," said Freddie, shoving the pen back into his pocket.

"Yes. 18C," she said, pointing to the number above his head, then the corresponding digits on her boarding card. "That's my seat."

Freddie knew he was in the wrong seat. He wasn't an idiot. When he first boarded the plane, he found his assigned seat to be far below his own personal standards. They'd given him an aisle seat, as requested. What he hadn't requested, however, was the mother and screaming baby located in the seat directly behind; the fat man in the middle seat with terrible body odour (so large he was spilling over into

Freddie's personal space); and the annoying-looking young boy in the seat across the aisle from him.

No bloody way I'm sitting there, he thought. So, he headed down the aisle, found a more comfortable seat several rows away, plonked himself down, and hoped to use his charm to convince the rightful occupant to switch. He then promptly forgot what he'd done.

A few moments later, she was back, flanked on either side by two stewardesses.

"What seems to be the problem?" Freddie asked, feigning ignorance.

"I'm sorry, sir," said Stewardess One, "but I have to ask you to return to your own seat." She was young and pretty, with a little too much make-up on, but seemed generally quite friendly.

Her colleague in the background was older, stocky and had her hair pulled back so tight it must have been cutting off the circulation to her feet. Her face was stern and grey. She looked down her nose at him disapprovingly. She'd clearly dealt with dickheads like Freddie before.

"Oh, is this not my seat?" he said, directly to the friendlier girl, pulling a boarding pass from his pocket and showing her. He thought he'd start with full-on ignorance and see where that got him.

The stewardess looked at the boarding pass, then smiled apologetically. "Sorry, no, this is 18C and you're supposed to be in 8C."

"Am I?" he said in his best confused voice. "Oh, gosh, what a silly mistake."

The stewardess smiled sweetly at him. He was winning.

"Well, I mean, all the seats are pretty much the same, aren't they?" Freddie said. "And I mean, I'm all settled in now." He pointed to the little pocket on the back of the seat in front and the Lee Child paperback he'd shoplifted from the airport WH Smith. "I don't want to cause any more disruption, so perhaps this lady could take my seat and I'll stay here?"

The nice-looking stewardess smiled sweetly, handed back his boarding card and said, "Nice try. I've asked you once nicely. Now you've got 10 seconds to move, or I'll call security and have you removed from the plane."

Sneaky cow. Pretending to be the nice one, then threatening to call the fuzz. The woman's bitter-faced colleague had a demented grin slapped across her lips. And the miserable cow whose seat he was in couldn't have looked smugger if she'd won the lottery three times in a row.

He thought about acting up. Shouting and screaming and giving them the famous Freddie Winters sulk. But then the image of him being dragged kicking and screaming from the flight flashed through his head – people laughing and cheering and filming it on their phones. So he bit his tongue, gathered up his belongings and, much to the amusement of the twat across the aisle, he sheepishly headed back to his own seat and squeezed in next to the smelly, fat git. He then spent the next 10 minutes muttering under his breath and cursing his agent for putting him in that position to start with.

What the hell was he doing here, anyway?

Following all the press attention he'd received after saving Dylan's life, Freddie had managed to find a new agent in the form of Alison. Compared with his previous agent – who would barely answer the phone to him, let alone secure him a decent book deal – Alison was a real go-getter. Still just a junior agent at her firm, she was feisty, ambitious, dedicated and a real force to be reckoned with. She was instrumental in securing a lucrative deal for *Death of a Mailman*, plus the new book he was supposed to be working on. The first draft was already due with the publisher, and Freddie still had little more than a title and a rough premise. And neither of those were very good.

Freddie owed much of his recent success to Alison. She was the one booking all the interviews and TV appearances. She organised blog tours, personal appearances at literary festivals, and teaching gigs at colleges and libraries. And thanks to her, his book signings were now very much sanctioned by the bookshop owners – and not down to Freddie simply turning up and surreptitiously setting up in a quiet spot at the back of the store.

When she'd first suggested attending a weeklong literary retreat, he'd baulked at the idea. Freddie could stomach a little face-time with readers every now and again (so long as they didn't get too close or ask him stupid questions). But a whole week in the company of budding authors? Fielding endless requests to read their manuscripts? Trying to pretend their shambolic offerings piqued his interest or showed potential? Or, worse still, reading something produced by one of these no-hopers only to discover it was better than anything he'd ever written? No, thank you very much. He'd rather cover his balls in honey and sit on a nest of green ants.

Alison had really sold it to him, however. Freddie was to be the guest star, she told him. He'd be there to sign a few autographs, hang out with literary fans, teach one masterclass on crime writing, and sit on a few panels to answer questions. Other than that, the time would be his own. And there was a decent appearance fee.

While he hated to admit it, Freddie could do with the money. While the initial advance for *Death of a Mailman* had been very generous – way more than anything he'd received for any book before – it didn't last very long. The sudden reappearance of Nina, Freddie's estranged wife, had seen half of it disappear before his eyes, like the worst magic trick he'd ever seen. He'd felt honour-bound – and legally obliged – to pay the several months of back rent he owed poor Mr Singh, his long-suffering landlord. And having spent the previous few decades living on scraps with barely a penny to his name, the sudden healthy balance of his bank account triggered in Freddie an urge to go on a very big spending spree, enjoying many, many nights out at fancy bars and restaurants.

After just a few months, his bank balance was back to its previously beleaguered state. He was still due royalties, but they always took their time trickling in. And while Alison had secured a healthy advance for his next book, the publishers were being real dicks and demanding to see the goods before they released the funds.

So, a week away from London, where he could get inspired and come up with his next literary masterpiece – while earning a few quid at the same time – seemed like a decent idea.

What really swung it, of course, was that the retreat was being held at a five-star, all-inclusive holiday resort in Malaga, Spain. He figured a few hours listening to whiny wannabe authors could be easily offset by spending the rest of the day lounging by the pool, eating and drinking as much as he could.

Crammed in next to Stinky von Fatberg, however, with a screaming baby behind him and a precocious young lad asking him questions from across the aisle, Freddie was wondering what the hell he'd let himself in for. And the bloody plane hadn't even taken off yet.

******

At the front of the plane, Marylin Sharpe was doing her best to ignore her client, Edward Cross, whine and moan as she rooted around in her

Hermes handbag. There was no way she was putting her beautiful bag up there in the overhead thingy with the common people's rucksacks, anoraks and carrier bags full of God knows what. A bag of this magnificence deserved its own locker. She'd have to hold the thing for the whole flight, and God help anyone who tried to stop her.

"Fucking Sleazyjet," muttered Edward, loud enough to ensure the people three rows behind him could hear. "Fucking tiny seats. No little TV to watch. Bloody cattle class."

He'd already delivered a four-minute monologue on the fact that there'd been no champagne to greet him as he boarded, no fluffy blanket and pillows, and no little bags of peanuts. And he'd been utterly incensed that the air hostess had spent more time helping an unattractive woman in a pink tracksuit, stuff an oversized travel bag into a tiny overhead compartment than she had tending to his needs.

"It's embarrassing," said Edward, taking his whining down to a conspiratorial whisper. "I mean, what if someone recognises me? Actually, no, scratch that, of course they're going to recognise me, aren't they? They'll be thinking: 'What the hell is he doing on this flying Day-Glo nightmare? Shouldn't an author of his fame be travelling by private jet? Or first class at the very least.

"God, they'll be thinking I've fallen on hard times. They'll be wondering if I'm going through another bloody costly divorce. Or what if they think book sales are suffering again, like… Oh, God, it's so depressing."

"Oh, hush, darling," snapped Marylin.

She was equally annoyed at travelling in such unaccustomed, low-rent conditions. But there was something far more vexing jangling her nerves. It had been 47 minutes since her last delicious puff of nicotine, and she was already feeling the chalkboard scrapes of withdrawal pulsing through her. And it would be at least another two hours before she could scratch that particular itch.

Quite how they expected people to go that long without smoking, she couldn't fathom. It was barbaric. Things were far better in the old days, when you could book a seat in the smoking section and sit there puffing away throughout the flight – and to hell with all the coughing, bleating whiners who didn't like it.

She'd tried the patches, of course. And the gum. But they were all useless. And now, as the tension pumped around her body with every heartbeat, she had to sit there listening to this man-child of a client crying about not getting special treatment. Life really was too short.

"I know it's not ideal," she said, adopting the sympathetic-yet-firm tone she found effective when dealing with blubbering authors, "but this was the best the organisers could do. Of course, I said to them: 'Do you really expect Edward Cross to travel in anything less than Business Class?' But they explained it was something to do with routes and time zones, and flying out of Gatwick rather than Stansted. And I knew you'd hate to go to Stansted… At least we're at the front with extra legroom."

"They could have stumped up for BA," sneered Edward. "All this puke-inducing orange. I can feel one of my migraines coming on."

"Believe me, I tried," lied Marylin. She'd taken the booking without a second's thought for her client's travel preferences. And if he didn't wind his bloody neck in soon, she was going to offer her extra legroom to the man several rows back with the dreadful body odour. That would shut Edward up. "I promise, this was the very best they could do. Besides, it's only two hours. And think of the publicity: *Celebrated author shuns the luxury of first class to keep it real with his readers.* I'll take a few photos on my phone and send them to the girls in PR. They can work their magic and we'll probably get a full page in *Grazia* or *Marie Claire*. Maybe even get something in the *Times Literary Supplement*."

Edward's eyebrows rose at the thought of it. He couldn't stop the slightest hint of a smile creeping onto his lips.

"In fact," continued Marylin, "maybe you could live tweet the flight. You could do with being more active on socials. We'll get you glad-handing with a few passengers, signing autographs… Great publicity. Really great."

"Yeah, okay…" said Edward. Then, as if suddenly remembering his previous gripe, he crossed his arms, slumped back in his seat and said, "But I'm still not happy."

"I know, darling," said Marylin, fighting the urge to poke him in the eye and tell him to bloody well grow up.

Honestly, when had he become such a bloody crybaby? She thought back to the eager young man she'd taken under her wing 20 years ago. The boy who was so full of promise, enthusiasm and sheer talent. The one who had been so keen for people just to read his books, he'd gladly travel the length of the country to do signings in even the tiniest bookshops. Now, with 20 books published, a cabinet full of awards and more than 30 million copies sold worldwide (none of which he could ever have dreamed of achieving without her help), he'd become one of the most privileged, whiny, constantly complaining authors on her books. And he expected her to do everything for him — as if she didn't have enough to do already.

Still, she thought, clutching her handbag a little tighter, his books were regular bestsellers, and that meant she could afford all the nice things in her life. The commission on his last book alone had been enough to cover the renovations on her little retirement cottage in Provence.

"Why don't we see if we can rustle you up a G&T?" Then she muttered under her breath, "I know I could do with one."

******

"What are you reading? What is it? Is it a good book? I like reading. My mum buys me lots of books. I've read all of David Walliams's books. They're funny. They make me laugh. Do you like David Walliams's books?"

The questions came rattling out, with barely a pause for breath between them. Freddie looked up from his stolen Lee Child and glanced at the young boy across the aisle, who was gazing eagerly back up at him. He was chubby with little round glasses and messy hair. The woman next to him — presumably the kid's mother — was gazing intently at her phone, and wearing a giant pair of headphones, presumably to drown out the annoying noise.

"We're going to Spain. We're going to a big hotel with three swimming pools and water slides. My mum says they do burger and chips and fish fingers and chicken nuggets for lunch. And there's a bar where you can get as much Coca Cola as you like. Although it might be Pepsi. I don't mind if it's Pepsi, but I prefer Coke. Do you prefer Coke or Pepsi?" The kid was incessant, like some kind of advanced Guantanamo Bay torture technique.

A crackly voice appeared on the plane's intercom. Freddie looked to the cockpit, squinted and tipped his head to the side, straining to hear the announcement.

Good afternoon, folks, this is your Captain speaking. I'd just like to welcome you onboard this flight to Malaga. Current conditions and travel times are looking good, aaaaaaand… you'll be pleased to hear that temperatures in Spain are a very toasty 38 degrees today.

A soft mutter of approval surged through the plane as people jostled enthusiastically.

The cabin crew have completed their final checks now. And we look forward to getting underway as soon as possible. Just to let you know, I've just heard from the tower that there's a liiiiiiittle congestion on the runway this afternoon. So, we've got aboooooooooout a 45-minute wait until we can take off.

All the passengers groaned in unison. Someone at the front of the plane let out an anguished howl. Freddie could have sworn he recognised the voice.

I'll let you know if anything changes. Until then, just sit back and relax.

"Fuck's sake," said Freddie.

"Ummm," said the annoying child across the aisle. "You said a swear."

This was going to be a long flight.

CHAPTER 2

THE HEAT HIT Freddie like a wave as he stepped down from the coach. The air-con onboard had been little more than a tiny overhead fan blowing warm air onto the top of his head. Compared to this, it had been a godsend.

Damn this hot weather. 24 degrees was as much as Freddie could take. Anything more just made him irritable. Well, more irritable than normal, anyway. And he'd only just about calmed down since his full-blown shouting fit with the miserable cow at the airport's lost baggage desk.

It must have been at least 40 degrees in the mid-afternoon heat. His skin prickled as the sun hit him. Sweat had already formed into a painful trickle running down his back and into the crack of his arse. He looked around at all the men in their shorts and t-shirts. His heavy jeans and Oxford weave shirt had been a bad idea.

Freddie looked up at the grand building they'd parked outside. Stone-coloured with intricate architectural design. Large pillars sat either side of a huge entrance, which led into an expansive foyer with a shiny marble floor. Two security guards stood to attention beneath a sign with gold lettering that said *Malaga Grand Hotel & Spa*. Next to it, another sign with five large gold stars.

It was a lot more impressive than Freddie had expected. When his agent had first told him the retreat was being held in Malaga, he'd assumed he'd be bunked up in some shabby, two-star flea pit, crawling with beer-swilling morons in Union Jack t-shirts. He never expected anything this fancy.

No, this would do very nicely indeed, thank you very much.

He recognised a few crime writers on the coach from various book events he'd been to recently. Patrick Marcombe, who wrote about a twee German private detective, was doing his best to smile as a little old lady eagerly questioned him. Patrick was probably the tallest man Freddie had ever met, with a thick Cornish accent, large, square-rimmed glasses and, for a man clearly in his late fifties, suspiciously jet-black hair.

Two rows back sat Austin James, a plump, jolly little man with rosy cheeks and a fluffy white beard that always made Freddie think of Santa Claus. He was the author of a series of novels that followed the adventures of an amateur sleuth who solved crime by night and worked as a florist during the day. He was crammed into his seat on the coach, sweating and stroking his beard, and pretending to be interested as an even fatter man in a Hawaiian shirt spelled out the plot of his own dreary book.

A third of the way down the bus sat Lisa Smythe, a smart, serious-looking woman in her forties with a stark brunette fringe, black, thick-rimmed glasses and a posh Surrey accent. She was wearing pink shorts and a bright, floral-patterned t-shirt. To look at her, you'd think she was a businesswoman or a teacher. You'd never guess she had a successful line in seriously disturbing, gruesome serial killer books. She was nodding along politely to a bald man with a wonky moustache, trying to resist him pushing a giant wedge of paper into her hands.

Christ, that was early. They'd only just arrived at the hotel, and over-eager writers were already foisting their crappy manuscripts on people.

The journey from the airport had, thankfully, taken only 20 minutes. Freddie quickly realised, when climbing onto the coach, that everyone else onboard was heading to the same hotel for the same reason. Wannabe authors on their way to the writer's retreat, chittering and chattering and full of enthusiasm.

Freddie could feel the excitement. Budding writers almost shaking at the thought of rubbing shoulders with their literary heroes. All looking to learn the tricks of the trade, keen to make their work better. And, of course, the ones who were sure this would be the week they got discovered. All they had to do was get the right person to read their second-rate, poorly-written novel, and they'd be signing a million-pound book deal before they caught the flight home.

Freddie remembered how it felt to be that young and naïve.

Thankfully, nobody had recognised him. So, he climbed into a seat, put on his sunglasses, and pretended to be asleep. And before he knew it, the coach was pulling up at the hotel.

A mechanical whistle hissed as the luggage door raised on the side of the coach. The driver grumbled as he fought his way through the waiting crowd and started hauling suitcases out randomly, throwing them to the ground behind him. People jostled either side, straining their necks to see whose bags were coming out. Everyone was desperate to grab theirs first and go running into the hotel to get booked in.

"Go, love, go," a white-haired man in socks and sandals commanded his wife, with all the passion of a fallen soldier instructing his comrades to leave him behind and save themselves. "Get inside and get in the queue. I'll grab the bags."

The rest were like animals, bumping this way and that, barely letting the driver lift the cases before snatching them from his hands and running into the building. They were so desperate to start relaxing that they didn't mind trampling over everyone else to get there first. Freddie sighed as he figured this was probably a sign of the week to come.

Freddie wanted to get checked in too. More than anything, he just wanted out of this damned heat. But he had no intention of getting involved in that bunfight. Besides, thanks to the useless idiots at the airline misplacing his luggage, it's not as if he had a bag to collect anyway.

There must be a bar in there somewhere, he thought, where he could sit and wait with a large, cold G&T.

"Freddie?" called a voice. "Freddie Winters?"

Freddie turned to see an eager man with a clipboard walking his way. He was dressed in knee-length khaki shorts and a light blue shirt. He looked to be mid-forties, thin and lithe, with short brown hair and a gaunt face. A badge pinned to his shirt bore the logo killerbookclub.com – the words cleverly made from a series of interconnected knives, each one dripping with blood. Beneath the logo was the name Dan.

"Freddie," said the man again, reaching forward and shaking his hand. "Great to meet you. So glad you could make it. Big fan. Loved your latest book. So clever." He spoke with a plummy accent. Over-excited, like a little boy at a funfair.

Freddie looked back at him, an eyebrow raised in bewilderment.

"Sorry," said the man, "I'm Dan Josham. Owner of Killer Book Club and the organiser of this literary get-together. I've spoken with your agent several times, but we've not yet had the pleasure."

"Ah, right," said Freddie. "You're the man I've got to thank for a week of free food and booze."

"That's right." Dan laughed a little too enthusiastically. "And a great deal of fun too, connecting with fans and writers, sharing your expertise with the next generation of authors." He laughed again.

Freddie didn't laugh back. The man was clearly some kind of literary superfan. Or he needed to get out more.

"Mmm… yeah, sounds good."

The smile suddenly dropped from the man's face, replaced with an embarrassed look. "I heard what happened with your suitcase. Can I just say, I am so, so sorry…"

"Well, it's pretty fucking annoying, but you weren't…"

"Out of the whole flight, and yours is the only one the airline loses," continued Dan.

"Yep, just my luck."

"It's so embarrassing. You must think poorly of us."

He was laying it on a bit thick.

"Listen, it's not your fault," said Freddie. "But obviously it does mean I'm a bit…"

"Don't worry," interrupted Dan. "We'll take care of it. What size are you? 36-long trouser and probably a size large for a shirt?" he said, looking him up and down like a tailor. "Size… 9 shoe?"

"Exactly right," said Freddie.

"Say no more. I'll have someone pick you up some clothes. All on us, of course. As you can see, we're a bit remote here. The next town is quite a way away. But there's plenty of stuff in the hotel shop. We'll have you feeling more comfortable in no time."

They both looked at the large sweat stains leaching out from Freddie's armpits.

"Speaking of which," said Freddie, "it's pretty hot out here. Any place to get a drink?"

"Of course, of course. Let's get you settled in. I'd get you checked in personally but, well, as you can imagine, lots to do today. Plenty more people arriving. Lots of authors to greet. Can you believe, we've taken over half the hotel?"

"Christ on a bike," said Freddie. "Half of this place?" He looked up at the grand building which reached right up into the dazzling blue sky. "How many people are attending this thing?"

"We've got a few hundred. Should be an exciting event. I've left a full itinerary in your room. There's a schedule of all the talks and events you're taking part in and a list of everything else that's going on. Now, sorry to greet and run but…" he raised an arm high in the air. Seconds later, a short man in matching clothes came running over. "This is Miguel. He'll take care of you. Let him know if there's anything you need. And I'll be buzzing around here for a while longer, if there's anything else."

Dan was like a cartoon character. Freddie watched as he rushed over to a taxi which had just pulled in behind the coach. He winced slightly as the door opened and out stepped a grizzled-looking man with a pot belly, salt-and-pepper hair and tomato-red face. He was waving his arms wildly, grumbling about something. He was followed by a skinny woman with a sleek, jet-black bob hairstyle. A real bag of bones, like a skeleton in a designer dress and heels. She reached into an expensive-looking handbag, pulled out a large, blocky e-cigarette machine and raised it to her mouth. She puffed hard, breathing out a giant plume of vapour, and the resulting look of satisfaction on her lips was practically orgasmic.

"Well, well," said Freddie under his breath. "Edward Cross and Marylin Sharpe. Was there ever a more devious pair of deceitful, malignant bastards? Didn't expect to see you here. Bit below your pay grade. Maybe book sales are suffering a little." He giggled to himself. "And with all those divorces to pay for, maybe the great Edward Cross needs the money as much as everyone else."

Freddie watched as Dan reached out his hand to Edward Cross, gushing with excitement. Then Freddie felt a tap on his shoulder as Miguel beckoned him to follow. They walked into the hotel, and Freddie took great satisfaction as Miguel led him past the long queue of people and straight to a waiting receptionist. He could feel them staring daggers as he picked up his room key along with a large glass of complimentary champagne.

The receptionist then clipped a gold plastic band onto his wrist, which bore the hotel's logo and the word Premier. It was his 'All Inclusive pass', he was told, which he'd need to show in restaurants and bars to get free food and drinks. Finally, he was handed over to a hotel bellboy – a skinny man in his twenties, with dark, tanned skin and a shaved head. His hotel uniform hung loose from his frame, making him look a little unkempt and scruffy. He got slightly flustered when he saw there was no suitcase to carry and ran to press the button on the lift.

Minutes later, Freddie was stood in one of the nicest hotel rooms he'd ever been in. Scratch that, it was one of the nicest *rooms* he'd ever been in. More than a room, really. It was more of a suite. At least he *thought* so. He'd never stayed in a suite before. Never even stood in one.

A queen-sized bed sat across from a 60-inch TV mounted on the opposite wall. It was at least twice as big as the aged piece of crap Freddie had at home. Beneath it was a long black desk, with a series of built-in cupboards. On top of the desk was a phone, a notepad and a hotel-branded pen (no cheap biro; it looked expensive, and Freddie made a mental note to steal it on departure), one of those fancy coffee machines that you put the little pods into, and a big box of the pods themselves.

The bathroom, too, was immense. Expensive marble lined the floor. There was a giant wet room area in one corner, with one of those big, square rainfall shower heads. On the other side of the room was a huge whirlpool bath. A large mirror sat above a marble counter lined with tiny bottles of shower gel, body cream, shampoo, conditioner and, of course, the obligatory shower cap, sewing kit, and shoe shiner. It was a huge, shiny beacon of luxury and opulence. Even the toilet looked like it cost more than Freddie's first car.

The bellboy gave an enthusiastic performance, dashing round the room, showing Freddie around the seating area which contained a sofa, armchair and coffee table. The little table was lined with several literary magazines and a big A4 folder with the macabre Killer Book Club logo and the words *Freddie Winters' Itinerary* emblazoned on it.

"So, you've got all your kit there," said the bellboy. Freddie was surprised when he spoke with a strong Irish accent. He'd naturally expected him to have a Spanish inflection, and it was somewhat jarring. "The air con control is on the wall, there. All easy to understand. Here's a map of the complex." He handed Freddie a little booklet, then started pointing out different parts. "You can see all your pools there – three of them in total. Five bars around the place. That's the health and wellness centre – go there for massages and that. Or if you want to use the gym."

Freddie winced and raised an eyebrow. The bellboy smirked, as Freddie could have sworn he stole a cheeky glance at his protruding beer belly.

"This is the main restaurant," the bellboy continued pointing. "That's where they serve breakfast, lunch and dinner. All-you-can-eat buffet. There are three other restaurants – an Italian, a Chinese and a Steakhouse. You can get snacks at the pool bar during the day. And, of course, everything's included free of charge."

Freddie could feel the smile growing across his face. Four restaurants? Five bars? All you can eat? Free of charge? Oh, this would do very nicely indeed.

"You've got your minibar down there," continued the bellboy. "That's all free as well. And they restock it every day, so fill your boots, eh?" He gave a small chuckle.

"Free minibar?" said Freddie. He felt like he needed to sit down.

"Yep, all free. Beers, wine, some of those tiny little spirits."

Freddie did need to sit down.

"All you can eat?" he blurted out, as he perched on the end of the bed. "Free booze? Free minibar? Luxury accommodation? And they're paying me to be here?"

The man smiled back at him. "Okay, so that's the room. You've got your phone there; just dial 1 for reception if you need anything. My name's Johnny. Ask for me and I'll come running."

"Good to know," said Freddie, still gazing at the magical free minibar.

The bellboy smiled again, made his way back up the long hall and stood by the doorway, hands clasped in front of him, beaming even more. "So… er… do you have everything you need?"

Freddie looked up at him. Oh, yeah, here we go. The old shakedown.

"Yes, I'm all good, thanks," said Freddie, smiling back. Spend a few minutes showing me to my room, and now I'm supposed to bloody tip you, eh? Fat chance, mate.

The cheeky bastard still stood there. "Really? Because it's no trouble," he said.

"No… can't think of anything," said Freddie. Why exactly was he supposed to give him extra money? For doing his job? The thing he was already being paid for? It's not as if he even had a bloody suitcase to carry.

"Right, okay… well…" said the bellboy.

Freddie revelled as the smile on Johnny's face sank, his Irish lilt wavering. He could practically hear him thinking: *Is this miserable bastard really not tipping me?*

"No, you've been great. But don't let me keep you. Must have lots to do, eh?"

"Yeah… okay," said the bellboy. "Well, have a nice stay." The indignation rang in his voice as he turned and marched away, leaving the door wide open.

Freddie would usually have carried on grumbling, but his attention was already away, as he dashed over and opened the minibar. It was one of the most beautiful things he'd ever seen. A selection of foreign beers. Tiny bottles of red and white wine. Some strange little tubes of nuts, sweets and fancy crisps. And, of course, the miniatures. Freddie grabbed a tiny bottle of gin, a little can of tonic, and found a glass in one of the cupboards. He grabbed an ice cube from the pot Johnny had collected from a machine in the hall as they walked to the room (hmmm, maybe he did deserve a tip?), then poured himself a drink.

He plonked himself onto the sofa and downed half the drink in one swig. The sense of relief was immense, and he spent a few minutes gazing out the large glass balcony door at the bright blue sea. Oh, this would do very nicely indeed.

He picked up the folder which bore his name and opened it. On the first page was a list of all the authors in attendance during the week. He scanned it, annoyed that he made it a full three-quarters of the way down the page before he found his own name. He recognised most of the writers. Some he liked, others he didn't. Then one name in particular jumped out at him.

"Christy Collins," he whispered to himself.

That could be awkward. He'd have to work hard to avoid bumping into her.

He quickly flipped to the next page. "Right then. Let's see what this bloody thing's all about."

******

Three hours later, after Freddie had enjoyed a few more drinks from the minibar, he showered and changed into some fresh clothes. He'd been delighted and then equally dismayed when Johnny the bellboy had appeared back at his door half an hour previously, holding an armful of hideous clothes and barely attempting to conceal a smug grin.

He came practically dancing into the room and proceeded to lay out on the bed a collection of the most eye-damagingly, bright, ghastly Hawaiian shirts Freddie had ever seen. They were so garish even Elvis Presley would have thought twice about wearing them and the island of Hawaii could probably sue them for slander.

Accompanying the shirts was a selection of gaudy t-shirts. There was a bright orange one which featured a map of Spain. A red one with the phrase Viva Espana emblazoned in bright yellow lettering. And several t-shirts featuring comedy slogans like, *FBI: Female Body Inspector*, *I'm here for the Vitamin Sea*, and *Keep Calm and Holiday*.

To go with the shirts, Johnny also presented a pair of navy deck shoes, a pair of lime green flip flops, two pairs of swimming trunks (shocking pink and bright orange) and several pairs of differently coloured shorts. Freddie grimaced when Johnny almost burst out laughing as he walked back towards the door. A little revenge for his lack of tip earlier? Well, if he didn't get one then, he certainly wasn't getting one after presenting this pile of crap.

Freddie hadn't expected much from the hotel shop. But he also hadn't expected to spend the week dressed up like Liberace's pool boy. Still, there was enough to get him through the week. And at least it was free.

Freddie's itinerary had instructed him to report to the main function room for the first event of the week – a miserable sounding thing called 'Welcome Drinks and Get to Know You Party'. It sounded awful. Freddie had no interest in getting to know anyone. But his agent had warned him that he needed to attend all the obligatory events to get paid for the week.

While he had no desire to mingle with the crowd of bookworms and amateur writing nerds, he figured at least some of them would be there to see him. So, he should make an effort. He owed it to his fans. And it might even help him sell a few more books. Besides, if any of them were young and pretty, he might even get lucky. He was in a holiday resort, after all. And once the booze got flowing, anything could happen.

So, he ditched his sweat-stained shirt and trawled through the pile of clothing, eventually opting for a puke-inducing pink Hawaiian shirt with pictures of flamingos, drifting pink clouds and large green palm trees. It was so bright that just wearing it made his eyes hurt and he felt at risk of a plane landing on him. He topped the ensemble off with a pair of sky-blue shorts, the navy deck shoes, a smattering of the complimentary aftershave in his bathroom and an embarrassed grimace.

He was missing his special 'author jacket' – a natty-looking navy sports coat with brown leather patches on the elbows. He bought it when *Death of a Mailman* first took off. He thought it made him look distinguished and literary. So, he'd worn it to all his interviews, signings and author events. It made him feel like he was now officially part of the crowd. But thanks to the cretins at Gatwick airport, who had somehow failed to load his – and only his – bag onto the plane, he'd probably never see it again. Instead, he was stood there in… God, it really didn't do to dwell upon it.

Freddie sighed as he left his room and made his way down to the party. He walked through the lobby, his shoes slapping on the shiny marble floor, and strolled to the main room. A sign above the door featured the Killer Book Club logo and the words 'Welcome Party'.

Miguel was standing at the entrance, greeting people and handing out laminated name badges on lanyards.

"Looking good, Mr Winters," he said, smiling. Freddie couldn't tell whether he was taking the piss, or just a bit simple.

Freddie took his lanyard. He'd usually have chucked it straight in the bin. Firstly, why on earth would any sane person want to walk around wearing a fucking lanyard? Secondly, he liked to think he was famous enough now that people might know who he was.

But being a famous author is not like being a famous actor or musician. While people might know your name, they rarely recognise your face. Why would they? The one good thing about his badge was that it featured the word AUTHOR in big bold type below his name. Not only would it help his fans to know who he was, it would also clarify that he was a real author, and not one of the course attendees.

Freddie hung the lanyard around his neck. He looked down at himself, shuddered and stepped through the large doorway.

The room was already buzzing. People mingling, chatting and swigging their drinks. The level of schmooze was already making him uncomfortable. He needed to get his alcohol level up even further.

"Freddie Winters, as I live and breathe."

Oh, for God's sake.

Freddie turned to see Nick Foster, a colleague of sorts, and someone he'd hoped to avoid. A meek little man with scruffy hair, a red face and an over-enthusiastic smile.

"Jesus, don't tell me they invited you to this bloody thing?" said Freddie.

"Ha ha, good old Freddie. Love that sense of humour."

He punched Freddie playfully on the arm. Freddie raised an eyebrow.

"Great to see you, mate. Had no idea you were gonna be here," said Nick. "Then again, they kept it all mysterious, didn't they? I didn't know who else was going to be here. So, who have you seen so far?"

"Um… I don't know," said Freddie. "I saw that devious, deceitful old windbag Edward Cross earlier. And a few other writers on the coach."

"It's exciting, isn't it? So many crime writers assembled at the same time. Let's hope nobody gets killed, eh?" Nick chuckled and slapped Freddie's shoulder. "Hey, when was the last time we saw each other? Cheltenham?"

"Er… I'm not sure."

"So, when did you get here? What flight were you on? What's your room like?"

The man was incessant. Freddie had never known anyone to ask so many questions in a row, without ever waiting to hear the answer – aside from the annoying kid on the plane.

Freddie had first encountered Nick Foster at a literary festival – he forgot which one – four years previously. Freddie hadn't actually been invited to appear, of course. He'd snuck in with a duffel bag full of his own novels, set up a stall at the back of someone else's tent, and managed to last a good four hours before the organisers caught him and asked him to leave.

During the day, Nick had approached Freddie claiming to be one of his biggest fans. He told him he'd read all his books, was a keen writer himself, and asked Freddie for advice on getting published. Flattered by the endless compliments – and because barely anybody else had approached him all day – Freddie relented and offered a few writing tips.

A year later, Nick self-published his first novel. Against all odds it sold a few copies. Then it sold a few more. And a few more. And then a lot more, until it became one of the biggest literary successes of the year. Before he knew it, Nick Foster was one of the most sought-after authors. He got an agent, who secured him a five-book deal, and he was now one of the most successful crime writers in the country. The jammy bloody git.

Ever since that, he considered himself one of Freddie's best friends. And he sought him out at every single event.

"That is quite the outfit, by the way," said Nick, winking and producing a quick comedy whistle. "No lightbulbs in your room or something?"

"Fucking airline lost my fucking suitcase," sighed Freddie. "Fucking Sleazyjet."

"Oh my God," said Nick, trying and failing to hold in a chuckle.

"The organisers got me some clothes from the hotel shop. Apparently, this was the best they had."

"Well, I think you look good," giggled Nick. "Very colourful. And nobody's gonna miss you in a crowd."

"Yeah, anyway… how are you?" said Freddie. "How's sales?"

He didn't care how his sales were. If anything, Freddie would rather not know, as they were bound to be better than his. But it was the done thing to ask.

"Pretty good, thanks. The latest book's doing well. And I've just finished the first draft of a new one. This whole thing came at a pretty good time. Nice opportunity to relax before I get stuck into the editing. And they haven't scrimped, have they? My room's got a free minibar."

"Yeah, me too. I mean, it's a bit weird, though, don't you think?"

"How so?"

"How many other writer's retreats are like this? It's usually some cabin in the woods in Lincolnshire or something. Or some university campus during half-term, and they put everyone up in the empty halls of residence. This is another world. Spain. Fancy hotel. Free booze. All-you-can-eat restaurants. It's… I dunno… it just feels a bit… off."

"Trust Freddie Winters to find something to complain about," laughed Nick. "That's your crime writer's mind going into overdrive. This place is awesome. And it's really clever. I was chatting to the organiser. He gets a good deal on the hotel because we're out of season and they want to fill as many rooms as possible. He's got over 250 people signed up. You know why? Exactly what you said. I went on a few of these before I turned pro. And you know the worst things about them? Cheap accommodation. Smelly student halls. Cold weather.

Rubbery sandwiches and weak cups of tea. If this sort of thing was available when I was doing them, I'd have snapped it right up. You get a week in the sun. You get to meet writers and learn tips. Plenty of time to chill out and write. And there's loads of free food and booze. All for about 200 quid more than you'd pay for the same week in Lincoln-bloody-shire."

"Yeah, take your point," said Freddie. "I don't know, though. There's still something…"

"Gentlemen," said a voice that made Freddie jump. He spun round to see Dan Josham, the event organiser, who apparently had the ability to appear from nowhere and scare the living shit out of you.

"Dan," said Nick, "we were just talking about the event. Such a clever idea, holding it out here in Spain."

"Yes, thanks. We got a great deal on the hotel," said Dan. "And people really seem to like it. Sold out in two weeks. I actually had to book more rooms so I could put on extra tickets."

"Well, I'm loving it so far," said Nick.

"I see we managed to get you sorted with some clothes," said Dan. "Apologies, the shop doesn't really stock anything apart from… well… holiday clothes."

"No, it's fine," said Freddie. "I've always wanted to look like a gay pirate. Just need the pink eye patch to finish things off."

Dan flashed an awkward fake smile. "Well, at least you're a bit more comfortable. I've had one of my guys contact the airline about your bag. No news yet, but we'll keep you posted. Anyway, you seem to be getting along well. That's what I love about these events. Bringing people together."

"Oh, Fred and I are old friends," said Nick.

"Great, great. Two fiendishly clever crime writers, checking out the scene, eh?" He held his hand up like he was scanning the room with a magnifying glass. "I wonder what crimes you could think up just in this room alone."

"Well, I think there could be some murders taking place if I don't find the bar soon," said Freddie. Then he forced a laugh to make sure everyone knew he was joking.

"Of course," said Dan. "Back of the room. You know, I think this week is going to be something special. Speaking of which, sorry to run, but it's time for my big entrance."

Dan walked off, and a minute later the chattering in the room was interrupted by the thud-thud-thud of someone tapping a microphone. The crowd turned towards the stage at the far end of the room where Dan was standing with a huge smile on his face.

"Ladies and gentlemen, welcome!" he said. "Is everyone having a good time?"

The crowd responded with a light smattering of applause.

"I just want to thank you all for signing up to the very first Killer Book Club Writers' Retreat. We've got plenty of sun, plenty of food, loads of booze… and some of your favourite crime writers all assembled in one place."

Another smattering of applause. This time it even included an over-enthusiastic whoop.

"We've got a packed line-up of talks, seminars, book signings and writing workshops for you. We want you to be inspired. And who knows, maybe while you're here, one of you will get the idea for next year's blockbuster crime novel."

A buzz of excitement rushed through the crowd.

"And if that all gets too much, you can always go and chill out by the pool with a cocktail."

Another over-excited whoop.

"Now, I do need to start off with just a little bit of housekeeping. There are lots of us here at the hotel, but please do remember we're not the only guests. I think we take up about half of the rooms. So, I do just ask that you're mindful of the other people staying here. They're not book nuts like us. But let's not hold that against them, eh?"

The crowd rippled with laughter.

"As I say, we've got a host of amazing authors lined up for you to meet and hear from. We've got panels where they'll be discussing everything from how they come up with ideas to how they translate them onto a page. We've got masterclasses where you'll learn the secrets of writing. And, of course, they'll be spilling the beans on how to get published."

The crowd rippled with enthusiasm.

"Just looking around the room, I can see some genuine literary legends. And some real movers and shakers. There's Max Graves, author of last year's big seller."

Max forced a smile and waved half-heartedly.

"There's Christy Collins, of course," said Dan, pointing her out. "She's written several quite steamy crime books now, haven't you Christy?"

Christy gave a much more enthusiastic wave, beaming around the room.

"Ooh, there's Malcolm Alexander," said Dan, pointing to a grey-haired, distinguished-looking man. "CEO of Darkhouse Publishing. He is literally a legend in the industry, and definitely a good man to slip your manuscript to."

Freddie laughed as Malcolm did his best to turn an angry grimace into a smile.

"Oh, and another industry legend," said Dan, pointing out into the crowd. "Agent extraordinaire, Marylin Sharpe. She's managed some of the biggest, best authors in the world, like the great Edward Cross."

Freddie grimaced, muttering, "Arseholes," under his breath.

"She's another great potential contact," said Dan. "She's helped to shape many careers."

The crowd got really excited now as the amateur authors drooled at the thought of getting her to sign them up.

"Anyway, you've heard plenty from me. Remember, myself and the other Killer Book Club staff are on hand to help with anything you need. So just come and say hello. The party will be going on in here until 11. And if you haven't eaten yet, head next door to the restaurant and tuck into the all-you-can-eat buffet. But make sure you come straight back here and mingle.

"Now, how about we bring out our guest of honour and keynote speaker, eh?"

This time the crowd really got excited, whooping and cheering and clapping.

"This man needs no introduction," said Dan, "but I thought I'd have a go anyway."

More sycophantic laughter from the crowd.

"He's been one of the world's favourite crime writers for over 20 years now, with 20 books published and over 30 million copies sold around the world. He really transformed his career and his writing style 10 years ago with *The Terrible Bones*, his first DI Tom Hickox novel, which went on to become a highly acclaimed, incredibly successful eight-book series of its own. And word is, the next one is coming out very soon indeed."

Ooohs and aaahs flitted around the room.

"I mean, seriously, what a man. What a legend. What a writer. I don't know how he comes up with all those amazing ideas. But if we're lucky, he might let us in on some of his secrets this week."

The crowd laughed again.

"Anyway, I'll stop wittering on and get him out. Please welcome… Edward Cross!"

The crowd went crazy this time as Edward climbed up onto the stage and made his way to the microphone.

"Christ on a bike," said Freddie, sneering.

"What?" said Nick. "Don't tell me you don't like Edward Cross? The man's a legend."

"The man's a bellend," said Freddie dismissively. "Look at him, the pompous prick."

"Oh, come off it," said Nick. "He's one of the best crime writers ever. I grew up reading his books. *The Terrible Bones* is, like, my favourite book of all time. It's what inspired me to become a writer myself. I'd love to be able to write a book that good."

"I didn't think it was that good."

"Oh, you're just jealous," said Nick dismissively.

"Think what you like," said Freddie. "Anyway, I've got better things to do than listen to that prick wittering on. Now, where's this bloody restaurant?"

CHAPTER 3

IT WAS INCREDIBLE. A vision. Like something out of a dream.

Long stainless-steel counters spread out in neat rows. Food piled high. Enormous bowls of salad. Plates of cold meats, cheeses and pots of various sauces. Large metallic trays containing a myriad of steaming foods. Chicken breasts in gravy. Chunks of meat in different coloured sauces. Freshly cooked steak. Fish. Lamb. Pork. Giant prawns.

Another counter held large pots of soups and stews. Big bowls of pasta, rice and vegetables. Another was adorned with pizza, burgers, hot dogs, chicken nuggets and chips.

Holy shit. Freddie had never seen so much food all in one place. He gulped as he took in the magnificence of it all.

In one corner was a station with at least 30 different types of bread, rolls and baguettes. In the other, a self-service drinks station, with soft drinks, three different beer pumps, and taps for both red and white wine. Along the back wall was a long counter, behind which stood four cooks, all frying, stirring, chopping and serving just about anything you could want.

And there, in the middle of the room, was the pièce de résistance: the dessert station. A big circular counter covered with cakes, sweets, chocolate fountains, little pots of mousse, fresh fruit. And in the middle, a chirpy woman in chef's whites making fresh pancakes to order.

Freddie's stomach growled – half with hunger and half with excitement. And best of all, it was all-you-can-eat. Did these people not know what they were letting themselves in for, allowing Freddie to even walk through the door?

Having spent most of his life as a struggling author, Freddie had grown used to long periods of financial instability. As such, he was also more than acquainted with empty kitchen cupboards, desolate fridges, and the reality of not always being able to afford three square meals a day. Such lean times had often extended for several weeks – sometimes even months – which contributed to his skinny, gaunt and somewhat haggard appearance. He'd always been slim as a child and as he grew he'd never really filled out. So, he'd ended up a tall, slender man. And during his periods of financially enforced nutritional abstinence, his thin frame grew thinner and his features became sharper and more pointed. To look at him, you'd think he existed on nothing but a handful of raisins. But when presented with an opportunity to fill his face with free food, he'd become adept at shovelling down inconceivable amounts in one sitting.

During such times of monetary deficiency, when invited to friends' houses for dinner, Freddie had been known to greedily scoff down seconds, thirds and sometimes even fourths. At first, his hosts were incredulous. After a while, people knew to buy in extra supplies to feed the great glutton. Indeed, on one occasion, a dinner party had extended into the wee hours, with people drinking by the fire. Despite having already had three helpings of the main course, two desserts and at least half the cheeseboard, Freddie had taken himself to the kitchen to prepare a midnight snack – plus a couple of sandwiches, which he slipped into his jacket pocket to take home. He subsequently got drunk, forgot what he'd done and, several weeks later, whilst wearing the coat for the first time in ages, was reminded of his mischievous behaviour when he slid his hand into the pockets, and his fingers into warm, rancid ham and coleslaw.

To Freddie Winters, the words 'all you can eat' were not so much an opportunity as a challenge.

He'd once been asked to leave an all-you-can-eat Indian buffet, having consumed 13 full plates of food. He quite reasonably asserted that the sign stated 'all you can eat', so he was within his rights to continue filling his plate until he'd eaten 'all he could'.

"Yes, but as much as a *human* can eat," replied the manager, "not a fucking elephant."

Freddie knew he was taking the piss. And in truth, he doubted he could consume even one more forkful without causing digestive injury. But it was the principle. And he was not one to give in easily. In the end, he agreed to leave only when the manager – through sheer exasperation – waived the bill for the whole meal. And when Freddie returned a week later to try the same trick, he found the menu had been rewritten to feature a raft of disclaimers preventing anyone from doing the same thing.

Freddie picked up a large white plate and set to work. A few minutes later, he'd assembled the strangest mix of food he'd ever seen – rice, chips, lasagne, three fish fingers, two sausages, a spoonful of chicken curry, onion rings, pizza, something that looked like sweet and sour chicken (though he wasn't entirely certain), a bit of fried steak, some beef stew and half a baguette. There was no cohesion between anything on his plate aside from gluttony.

Freddie poured himself a beer and found a table, his food piled so high it risked an avalanche with every single step. Three forkfuls in, he looked up to see a face looming down at him.

"Still the same old Freddie," she said. "You know, you don't have to pile half the restaurant all onto one plate."

"Saves going back and forth," replied Freddie, with a mouthful of what turned out not to be sweet and sour chicken after all.

"Seriously, though, what is that? Pizza, sausages, stew… is that a chicken nugget?"

"It's tasty, it's free and it's best enjoyed in silence," said Freddie, waving his hand to shoo the unwanted guest.

Christy Collins sat down opposite him.

"I'm surprised to see you here," sighed Freddie. "I thought this event was for real writers."

"Oh, very good," she laughed. "What's your excuse? Are you dying of cancer and the Make-A-Wish Foundation arranged for you to feel what it's like to be a real author for a day?"

Freddie couldn't help but smile. That was a pretty good one.

"Seriously, though, Christy, I saw your name on a programme. *You're* doing a masterclass? What are you teaching? How to marry a famous author, divorce him for half his money, throw together some crappy, tawdry, semi-pornographic novel with a ridiculous plot and a murderer easier to spot than Where's Wally at a Ku Klux Klan rally, then shag all your ex-husband's industry contacts until some idiot publishes it?"

"How did you guess the title?" said Christy, smiling. "I was going to go with *How to be a miserable, self-loathing, second-rate writer who pushes away everyone in your life because you can't cope with your own lack of success and, rather than actually do something positive, just bitch and moan and act like a dick, until even the people that love you can't stand to be around you.* But you're more of an expert in that field."

That was a bit close to the bone. Freddie fought the urge to fire back by shoving a large forkful of lasagne into his mouth. They stared at each other as he chewed.

"So, how have you been, Christy?"

"Oh, you know, busy spending my ex-husband's money. I was pleased to see your latest book do well. Was it all really true?"

"Most of it, yeah," said Freddie, "although I added a few dramatic twists here and there. You know, keep it pacy."

"Well, I loved it. Can't wait to read your next one."

"What do you want, Christy?"

"What?"

"What's with all the compliments? You haven't been this nice to me since… well, you know…"

"You really are the same old, rude, belligerent dickhead, aren't you? God knows what I ever saw in… You know what, I actually did just want to compliment you on your book," she said, standing. "I thought it was brilliant. And I was pleased to see you finally getting some recognition."

"Oh," said Freddie, his cheeks reddening and his words catching in his throat. "That's really… thank you. That means a lot. Look, ignore me. Please, sit down."

Christy humphed and plonked back down into her seat.

"Hey, it really is good to see you," said Freddie, with a mouthful of chicken nugget. "Must be a bit awkward, though? You and Edward. Being here together."

"Yes and no. I've bumped into him at a few of these things since the divorce. He rarely speaks to me. Gets that old harpy to interject or rush him off so he can avoid me. To be honest, it's usually a relief that he doesn't want to talk to me."

"Still a twat, then?"

"Massively. You know, I think he's less upset about the divorce and me 'taking half his money'," she made quote marks with her fingers, "than he is that I made a successful career out of writing afterwards. He was always so impressed with himself. Acted like he had some God-given gift. He couldn't believe I managed to get published, too. I think he was genuinely offended by it."

"Hmmm," said Freddie, "although the highly publicised divorce couldn't have hurt when it came to getting publishers interested. What were you? Wife number four?"

"I was number two," said Christy. "Rachel was before me. And there were two more after me. That miserable bitch Julianne. And then… Cindy, I think."

"No wonder he's here," said Freddie with a mischievous grin. "Obviously needs the cash. Hasn't hurt your career, though."

Freddie saw a resoluteness come over her. She'd clearly fought off this accusation before. "You use whatever advantages you have. Like turning the story of your best friend's attempted murder into a novel."

"Touché."

"And if people didn't like my books, if they really were that bad, do you think they'd sell more than two or three copies? You know, there's a lot worse…"

"Okay, okay," said Freddie, cutting her off before she went into a well-worn speech. "I'm only teasing."

"Yeah, well… I don't know why he gets to be the one who feels so upset. He was the one cheating with an endless stream of young, pretty assistants, fans and marketing girls."

Quite a bit of anger in that last one, Freddie noticed.

"And you were completely innocent?" he smirked.

"I only slept with one person before we split up. And it was purely for revenge."

"Is that all I was? Revenge?"

"Oh, sweetheart," said Christy, with a pretend sad face. She stood and placed a hand on Freddie's cheek. "Good to see you. Glad you're doing better. I'm sure we'll bump into each other again."

She winked and walked out of the restaurant.

Freddie smiled at a pleasant memory. Then he looked down at his mountain of food and set to it with his fork.

******

An hour later, Freddie was feeling bloated to the point of nausea. He'd surprised himself by only having one plate of main course. He'd made up for that, however, with two trips to the dessert table, filling up on seven pancakes, three bits of cake, two pastries, five scoops of ice-cream, and a small bowl of marshmallows slathered in chocolate from the chocolate fountain. He was slightly annoyed that he'd barely scratched the surface of what the food hall had on offer. But he was equally conscious that if he ate another bite, he'd be in serious distress. He must be losing his touch.

At least he had the rest of the week to take full advantage.

He left the restaurant and headed back to the party. People stood chatting, laughing and drinking. Bright disco lights swept around the room in multi-coloured beams. Music pumped loudly – some Europop monstrosity, but people were enjoying it. Not a single person was dancing, though. This crowd was all business – either authors entertaining fans or would-be authors looking to pick up contacts. Freddie also spotted a few lurkers. Over-eager writers who went around the room, circling other people's conversations, listening in to gauge which writer, agent or industry figure could be most useful in getting their work published. When they found the right target, they'd swoop in and hijack the discussion with their own boring story. Freddie laughed as he watched several try and fail to interject themselves into other people's chit-chat.

Freddie recognised a few people now: authors he'd met at various industry events; the odd agent who had rejected him; a handful of industry bigwigs – presumably there for the free holiday, rather than expecting to find their next big signing. Pretty much everyone in the room was someone he wanted to avoid. Unfortunately, wearing a bright pink shirt – which somehow glowed even brighter under the disco lights – made it hard to remain incognito.

Freddie made it to the bar with only a handful of people pointing and laughing. He ordered a pint of lager and two gin and tonics, then spotted a table in the corner of the room where he could hide. As he walked through the room, he noticed several people glance at his name badge, then up to his face, trying to gauge whether they recognised him. A couple clearly knew the name but didn't know why. Others drew complete blanks.

Freddie shoulder-bumped with one man, accidentally splashing lager onto his wrist as they did the awkward 'sorry not sorry, look where you're going next time' dance. The man had greying hair, a chinful of designer stubble and a tired, hangdog expression. Freddie didn't think he was an author. Certainly not a famous one. And he wore expensive beige linen trousers and a Fred Perry t-shirt, so he wasn't a poor amateur writer. There was something familiar about him, though. Freddie was so sure he'd seen him somewhere before; he just couldn't place it. Damn, that was going to bug him. Like an itch in the centre of your brain that you can't reach to scratch.

Moving through the crowd, a lurker stopped spying on another conversation and turned to assess Freddie. A thin man with a mop of dark, curly hair and a cravat. The prick was actually wearing a cravat. To Freddie's mind, that made him an uber-lurker – someone so deluded they'd started to dress like the famous author they knew they were destined to become. These people were always the worst writers of the bunch.

Cravat Man squinted at Freddie's name badge, smirked at his shirt and, apparently judging him as not worthy of his time, he rolled his eyes and went back to infiltrating a conversation between Austin James and Bill Pascale.

Bill was a great author who wrote a series of books about a former detective turned Michelin-starred chef who solved mostly food-related murders. A short, stocky man with white hair and a bushy white moustache, Bill was the best-dressed of Freddie's acquaintances – always very neatly pressed, dressed and presented. He had a calm manner, a quiet speaking voice and he always had an interesting story to tell. He was also a rarity in that he was someone with whom Freddie actually enjoyed talking.

Freddie made it to the table, pulled out his notepad and pen, and downed one of the G&Ts in a single gulp. Then he sat back to see if he could find some inspiration for the book he should have already finished writing.

*****

On the other side of the room, Marylin Sharpe was watching Edward Cross nursing a Scotch and doing her best to ignore his overacting as he contorted his face into a series of dissatisfied grimaces.

"Eurgh, what is this cheap muck?" said Edward. "Tastes like burnt oranges and mud. God, what I wouldn't do for a decent Macallan. Even a Glenfiddich. This hotel might look classy but, without any decent whisky behind the bar, they should have their five-star rating taken away. If it really is five stars. The Europeans do things differently, don't they? I read that apparently five stars in Spain is really the equivalent of three in England."

For the love of God. It was late, and she'd already had enough of his whining.

This was going to be a long week. Perhaps she could fake an emergency back home? A good excuse that meant she'd have to leave him here and fly back early. That'd show him. See how long he'd last having to do things for himself.

"I still can't believe you didn't tell me *she* was going to be here," whined Edward.

"Oh darling, are we still talking about this? I've told you; the organisers never gave me a full line up. I was as shocked as you," she lied.

Marylin had, of course, known that Edward's ex-wife was going to be there. And she knew he'd be pissed off about it. But with a new book soon to be released, the potential social media coverage was too good to turn down. Edward Cross and Christy Collins both appearing at the same literary event, after the acrimonious divorce and all the muckraking in the tabloids, was sure to have tongues wagging and tweets trending. You just couldn't buy that kind of publicity.

"You'll hardly see her," continued Marylin. "You're not on any of the same panels. And you can avoid her at parties." Her brain started racing with all the possible ways she could engineer the exact opposite and make sure plenty of people with camera phones were there to capture it.

"This is hardly a premier event, though," Edward grumbled. "Have you seen who else is on the bill?"

"There are loads of great authors. Some really big names."

"Like Max Graves? Ridiculous bloody name. How did that little fucker ever get published? Decent editor, I'll grant you. Did a good job on my books. But he was never a writer."

"Tell that to the public, darling. Have you seen his sales?"

"Have you read it though? I don't care how many people buy it, it's a pile of crap. Totally derivative. Ripped off the plot from that… oh, what's it called? And I swear there's some of my stuff in there. Maybe we should get a lawyer to look into it?"

"We're not hiring a lawyer."

"That's what you call a big name, though, is it? I haven't heard of half these people. Even James Patterson couldn't be bothered, and he'd turn up to a letter opening if he thought he'd sell a few more books. I swear I even saw that fucking leech Freddie Winters skulking about the place."

Marylin pressed her e-cigarette to her lips and took a huge drag. She sighed and rolled her eyes as she blew out a huge plume of candyfloss-flavoured vapour.

"This is a good event," she said, adopting the strict headmistress tone she used to keep her authors in line. "Look at the venue. Five-star hotel. Luxurious setting. And trust me, you wouldn't want Patterson here. Remember the last time you two were at the same event? Like a couple of bickering schoolchildren. Honestly."

Edward humphed and twisted his face as he took another sip of whisky.

"The organisers have lined up a decent selection of crime writers. Anyone who's had a successful book in the last few years is here. Even Winters had one of the biggest crime novels last year. Trust me, this is the place to be. And it's bloody sunny, for God's sake. Worst comes to worst, you can just sit by the pool and drink cocktails. So, cheer up, will you?"

"S'pose so," he sulked. "You have to admit, though, there's something a bit weird about the whole thing."

"How so?"

"I dunno. It's just... I've never heard of this event before, have you? Killer Book Club? New company, is it?"

"Relatively new, I think," sighed Marylin.

"Well, where do they get the money to host such a lavish event? These things are usually held in a fucking Portaloo in Swansea or somewhere. This is a fair bit better than that. Even if you can't get a decent whisky. It's just a bit... weird."

"I don't know. Why question it? New events like this pop up all the time. This is just a bit nicer than most."

"But how do they afford it?"

"Internet, darling. It's a web company. They've been going for a few years now. It's all about social media. YouTube. Instagram. TikTok. They post online reviews of books, little videos on how to become an author, all that kind of stuff. Big web following. Make most of their money from advertising, I should think. And all the sad sacks will have paid a few quid for their spots here."

"Well, I don't care what you say," said Edward. "I've got a creepy feeling. Something feels a bit... off."

"You bloody crime writers. So suspicious. Always looking for a mystery that doesn't exist. Seriously, darling, take a day off, will you?"

Edward slumped back into his chair. He watched as the crowd bristled and turned towards raised voices on the other side of the room.

******

"How the fuck did a no-talent loser like you get an invite to this?" slurred Freddie. He was swaying from side to side, beer slopping out of his pint glass as he pointed it in the man's direction.

"Good to see you too, Freddie," said Max Graves, wiping beer from his arm.

Freddie's first pint had gone down too easily. So had his second and third. And the two accompanying gin and tonics. So, he was feeling somewhat worse for wear when he stumbled to the bar and bumped into another of the week's literary stars.

"Max Graves? Seriously? What kind of name is that? I mean, it's a bit on the nose for a crime writer, isn't it? How many seconds did it take your publicity team to think that one up?"

"I think it's a good name, actually," said Max. "And it looks great in shop windows. Or blown up really big on posters. Not that you'd know about that."

"At least it's better than your real name, Dick Smithers. Can't see that shifting too many copies."

"It's Richard. Nobody calls me Dick."

"Yeah, that's what you think," laughed Freddie.

A few people on either side giggled along. Their heated exchange was gathering interest as people lurked nearby to listen in.

"Well, everyone calls me Max now. And what does it matter if I use a pen name? Lots of people do it. Even Lee Child isn't really called Lee Child."

"Doesn't surprise me, actually," laughed Freddie. "Everything else about your writing is either fake or stolen. Why not have a fake name as well?"

"What's that supposed to…"

"You could have gone with something that really summed you up, though. Like, I dunno… Mark Obvious-Plot-Twist. Andrew Shitwriter. Or Daniel Plagiarising-Bastard."

"What are you suggesting?" said Max.

"You know exactly what I'm saying," said Freddie. "Your so-called blockbuster novel? It was about as original as gifts at Christmas. Bland writing. Paper-thin characters. Just about every obvious, over-used, predictable crime-writing trope you could wedge in there. And there were several bits that were just a little too close to things that have featured in my books."

"Oh my God," laughed Max. "The delusion. The arrogance. You really think I'd steal from you? Christ, if I was going to steal anything – which I did not and would not – I certainly wouldn't go trawling through your second-rate crap for ideas."

More people gathered around. The hustle and bustle of the other conversations died as everyone listened in.

"Hey, I know what I know," said Freddie. "And so does everyone else. You're a fraud. A pathetic loser who dreamed of becoming a writer, but you just didn't have what it takes. So instead you become an editor, so you can act all high and mighty and reject other people's work and…"

"Christ," laughed Max. "That's what this is about. You're still upset because I turned down one of your books, what… 11 years ago? Get over it."

"Yeah, yeah, whatever," said Freddie, with a dismissive wave. "That book was too good for you anyway." He took a long swig from his beer, then squinted, trying to get back onto his train of thought. "Yeah… so… you become an editor instead. And then, one day, somehow you've managed to 'write your own book'." He curled his fingers into sarcastic air quotes. "Wow. And then you cash in favours with your industry cronies and, what a surprise, the book gets published. Talk about bloody nepotism."

Someone in the crowd sucked in a shocked breath.

"Of course they published it," said Max. "It's a good book."

"Good book? More like a series of good books stitched together. The central detective's a rip-off of Jack Reacher. The main plot is basically Rear Window. One of the murders is identical to one in a James Patterson book. I mean, come on. Even stealing from Patterson? There are so many other writers you could plagiarise. And the plot twist? Christ, you can see that coming from page 10."

The crowd was bustling now. Freddie could feel the excitement surging through them. Like a gang in a school playground, ready to chant: 'FIGHT! FIGHT! FIGHT!'

Max's face was flushed red, his eyes tightening and his jaw clenching. He was clearly doing his best to remain calm, but the way he pushed his shoulders back betrayed the anger building.

"You're a sad, pathetic, jealous little man, Freddie," he said calmly. "I feel sorry for you."

"What did you do, exactly?" said Freddie, taking another long gulp of beer. He was very woozy now, his words slurring together. "Did you literally just take all the best bits of about 10 other books and stitch them together? Cos that's what it fucking reads like."

A strange look flashed briefly in Max's eye. Almost imperceptible. But Freddie saw it. And Max knew Freddie had seen it.

"You know what," said Max, "I don't fucking need this. You're just a hack, Freddie. Everyone knows it. You might have had one success but so what? You're a one-trick pony. So enjoy this week. Enjoy feeling like a *real* writer. Because this time next year, nobody will even remember your name."

"I'm a hack? You might have everyone else fooled. People might have bought your crummy book. But they'll soon figure out what you've done. There's nothing clever or talented about stealing ideas. Actually, do you know what? I can't wait until your little talk tomorrow. What's it about again? *How to plot a successful crime novel?* That's a bloody laugh."

Max gripped his fists tightly by his side. His jaw clenched and his shoulders raised. "You come anywhere near my talk," he shouted, "and I'll... I'll..."

"You'll what?" said Freddie, jabbing a finger hard into Max's chest.

Max's hand darted up, gripped Freddie tightly around the throat and squeezed. Freddie spluttered as he was pushed back, his feet scrabbling around on the floor, trying to get a grip.

"I'll fucking end you," shouted Max, his eyes wide with rage. "I will fucking..." Then he stopped, suddenly aware of the stunned faces gawping at him from all directions. He released his grip on Freddie's throat, sending him tumbling to the ground.

Freddie landed with a thump. He rubbed his throat, looking up at Max, coughing and trying to compose himself.

"Stay away from my talk. And stay away from me, you sad, pathetic prick," said Max. Then he pushed back his shoulders, took a deep breath, and walked through the crowd and out of the room.

Freddie climbed up from the floor, fighting off the eager hands trying to help him. His head was woozy now. The room spinning wildly. He stumbled as he stood. People stared, half of them embarrassed, the other half delighting in what was probably the most drama they'd seen in years.

"What are you all looking at?" Freddie shouted. "Never seen two authors have a heated literary discussion before?"

He thought about going to the bar and ordering another handful of drinks. But fuck that. He was done with these people. At least for tonight. And there was still plenty of booze in his minibar. So, he straightened himself up, burped loudly and staggered out of the room.

CHAPTER 4

TUESDAY

FREDDIE TWISTED HIS head on the pillow and looked out into the strange room. Definitely not his flat. Far too spacious and nicely decorated. And warm. His flat was never this cosy. That shithole somehow managed to retain a horrible icy chill even during the peak of the British summer. Which was not exactly saying much, but still.

Where the hell was he?

He lifted his head. Tried to sit up, but a skull-cracking pain shot right through his brain. After several deep breaths, he forced himself upright and squinted at his surroundings. Anxiety surged through him. That horrible feeling of not knowing where he was, or how he got there.

It wasn't the first time Freddie had experienced this feeling. He'd once woken up, after three days of non-stop drinking, to find himself in a caravan in Dorset, dressed in lederhosen, with half his head shaved and his pockets full of Chinese fortune cookies – none of which he'd ever been able to account for.

Sun poured in through the balcony windows. A rumble of waves crashing. The faint sound of people chattering in the distance. Yeah, definitely not his flat. He ran a hand through his messy hair, his stomach turning at the smell of his own rank breath. Exactly how much had he drunk last night?

As he looked around the room, memories started appearing like half-drawn pictures. He remembered being on a plane. Arguing with a shrill woman. Something to do with a suitcase. He remembered being hot, sweaty. The dry, acrid air inside a coach.

A mess of pink fabric on the floor caught his attention, and the image of a smirking Irishman holding an armful of hideous clothing flashed into his mind. He smiled as he caught sight of the minibar. Then he grimaced as the thought of booze brought on a wave of nausea.

The pictures in his head started colouring in until he remembered exactly where he was and why. Then something else popped into his head, like a thousand camera flashes going off at once. The feeling of a hand around his throat. Angry shouting. Shocked faces.

"Christ, good going Freddie," he sighed, "not even been here one full day and you've already had a row."

He should probably seek Max out. Apologise. Blame it on the booze. Show contrition and hope for no hard feelings. He almost laughed as he thought of saying sorry. No, much easier to ignore the situation, pretend it never happened and avoid Max for the rest of the week.

Freddie climbed out of bed and stumbled to the bathroom. No obvious signs of destruction, vandalism or drunken tomfoolery, which was good. No random strangers passed out anywhere in the room, which was even better. And best of all, no unexpected sleeping partners in the bed. Not that Freddie was averse to having one-night stands. But it always seemed a shame to have been so drunk he couldn't remember the sex part.

It appeared that he'd simply come in drunk, climbed into bed and passed out. Which was probably for the best. But also disappointing.

"Must be losing my touch," he said to himself.

The shower worked wonders in reviving him, but his brain was still thudding with pain. He considered going to the buffet for a hefty plateful of fried food, but his stomach was still too volatile to eat. First, he needed coffee.

He selected some khaki shorts from his pile of temporary clothing and paired them with a horrendous orange and blue Hawaiian shirt. Then he sat down in the lounge area of his ridiculously large hotel room and consulted the hefty folder left for him by the event's organisers. Flicking through the pages, he was happy to discover that he didn't need to be anywhere until 2pm, when he was due to sit on a panel discussion entitled: *How to plan the perfect literary murder – and get away with it*. Christ, who thought up these ridiculous names?

Freddie grimaced at his watch. It was still only 9.17am. Far too bloody early. Still, he was up now. And he really needed coffee. A cursory glance at the machine on the side and he instantly gave up. Far too many buttons. He wasn't playing the bloody Krypton Factor just for a measly cup of coffee.

Roughly 10 minutes later, after navigating several long hallways, he found his way outside into the sunshine, looking down at the largest of the three swimming pools. The thing was huge, laid out in a figure of eight, with a swim-up bar plonked right in the middle. A small bridge stretched from the edge of the pool to the bar, which you could both walk over and swim under.

Freddie made his way through the higgledy-piggledy tessellation of sunbeds, noticing they all had towels on. Every single one. For fuck's sake. It wasn't even 9.30am and every single sunbed had been claimed. Not only that, hardly anybody was using the bloody things. The smug gits had come down at the crack of dawn, laid out their towels like triumphant explorers planting a flag to claim new land, then fucked off back to bed to sleep off the booze. Or they'd sloped off to the buffet to stuff their fat faces.

Freddie humphed as he looked at the sea of sunbeds. Then he did a double take as he noticed one figure sprawled out asleep. It was Max Graves, still wearing the same clothes from the previous evening. He must have been there all night. Probably wandered down after the party and passed out.

Perhaps he should go over? Apologise. Nip things in the bud. Be the bigger man.

Unfortunately, Freddie was never comfortable being the bigger man. It was far easier and – let's be honest – usually a lot more fun to be the small, mean, petty-minded man.

Fuck Max, he thought. Let him come and apologise to me.

Freddie was also never one to let propriety stand in the way of getting what he wanted. So, he worked his way to the edge of the pool and found a little cluster of four sunbeds, neatly arranged under a large umbrella. Two of the beds were draped in standard hotel-issue towels. The third was covered with a red monstrosity, emblazoned with the logo of some football team. The fourth had a slightly smaller towel which featured the image of a large, pink cartoon pig. Freddie bent down, swooped them all up and flung them into the pool.

He heard a few audible gasps from the handful of people actually using their sunbeds. He gazed over at the worker in the pool bar, who was staring back open-mouthed.

"Uno café, por favor?" shouted Freddie, raising his hand with a triumphant thumbs-up. Then he flopped down onto one of the sunbeds, lay back and closed his eyes.

The barman appeared minutes later, a wry smile pinning back one side of his mouth, as he delivered a cup of coffee. Freddie sipped it, feeling the synapses in his brain spark back to life with every delicious mouthful. He breathed deeply, enjoying the warmth of the air. He listened to the rhythmic sound of waves crashing gently on a nearby shore. And as his headache started to ease, he felt something he hadn't experienced in some time. He was starting to relax.

He picked up the notepad and pen he'd bought specially for this trip. He wrote the words NEW IDEA at the top of a page in large, capital letters. He underlined it, then underlined it again. He pressed the tip of the pen to his lip as he looked up at the dazzling blue sky and breathed deeply. Then he closed his eyes – just for a second – as he searched his brain for a brilliant idea.

******

"You know, I don't think I slept more than a couple of hours last night," grumbled Edward Cross. He sneered at the plate of food in front of him. "And what's with this stuff? They try and pretend it's bacon, but it's not. I mean, what is it? Ham? It's all stringy and they've cooked it for far too long. And don't even get me started on these eggs. I said a runny yolk. Does that look runny to you?"

Marylin sighed as she listened. Christ, it wasn't even 10 o'clock and he was already going off on one. She had a sudden urge to grab the fork out of his hand and jab it into his eyeball. Give him something worth complaining about.

Just think of the money, she thought, repeating her well-worn mantra. Just think of the money.

"Well, I wouldn't know, darling. I never eat breakfast. Slows me right down in the morning. At least the coffee's halfway decent. That's all I need." She took a sip and widened her eyes as if to prove a point. "But why no sleep? Something wrong with your room? Do you want me to go and shout at someone?"

"No. The room's fine. I just… oh, I don't know. Too many familiar faces here, perhaps. Too many people from the past."

"Oh, I knew she'd upset you. I promise, I had no idea Christy was going to be here," lied Marylin. "You know I'd never have agreed to you being here together."

"Any of the other wives," sighed Edward. "Julianne. Cindy. Christ, even Rachel would have been better." He shuddered when he thought of them. "I mean I wouldn't want to see them, but any of them would have been better than her."

"Yes, darling, but none of the others went on to have successful publishing careers," said Marylin, "so they'd hardly be likely to make the guest list."

"Yeah, well, it's not just her," said Edward, dropping his fork onto the plate. "Too many people from… you know. Like the worst bloody reunion ever. People that were there when…"

"Let's not start down that road, darling," said Marylin, cutting him off. "We don't talk about those days. It only ever gets you upset. No point reliving the past, eh?"

"Yes, but it's all a bit spooky. I mean…"

"Seriously, darling, what part of let's never speak about this again do you not understand? We've all got far too much to lose, just because you're feeling sentimental. And I for one don't intend to…"

"Yeah, I get it, okay. I'm just saying, there's something weird about all this. It's giving me the creeps."

"I promise you, darling, everything is fine. There's nothing weird going on. You'll feel much better once you do one of your talks. Nothing cheers you up like talking about yourself, does it?"

She winked and flashed a mischievous smile.

Edward snorted.

"Speaking of which," said Marylin, opening a binder with the Killer Book Club logo on the front, "looks like you're on stage at 12pm. Plenty of time to finish your breakfast then freshen up a bit. Then you've got nothing else for the rest of the day. So you can relax by the pool and de-stress a bit, eh?"

"S'pose," said Edward, pushing his plate away. "Hey, maybe they've got some pastries, or something?" A childish smile flashed across his face as he got up and went in search of them.

******

"What the fuck is going on here?"

Freddie was jolted awake by an angry man with a shaved head and a Union Jack tattoo on his bicep who was holding an armful of soaking towels. He was flanked either side by a furious, pinch-faced woman with bleached blonde hair, a teenage boy and a distraught little girl in a swimming costume with a cartoon pig on the stomach. Clearly some of the hotel's 'other' guests, and not book fans looking for an autograph.

"I'm sorry, can I help you with something?" said Freddie innocently.

"These are our sunbeds. You're on our fucking sunbeds."

"Really?" said Freddie, looking around, pretending to be confused. "I don't think so."

"Yes, they are. We had our towels on them."

"Oh, well, there were no towels on them when I sat down."

"Yes, there were. We left our towels to reserve them, then we went for some breakfast."

"Oh nice. I haven't been yet. How was it?"

"Yeah, it was all right," said the man. "Decent spread. Nice eggs. But they only had that weird Spanish bacon. And you can never get a decent sausage in these…"

He stopped mid-sentence, his wife poking him in the ribs to make him aware he was drifting off topic.

"Anyway, that's not the point," he continued. "You're on our bloody sunbeds."

"No, I'm not."

"Yes, you are," he said.

"No, I'm really not. I'm not on *your* sunbeds. I mean, do you own them?"

"What? No, course not."

"Have you paid money to rent them for the day?"

"No."

"Then how can they be *your* sunbeds?" Freddie smiled, starting to enjoy himself.

"Cos we reserved them. With our towels."

"Oh really? Despite that?" Freddie pointed to a sign at the edge of the pool. It featured a diagram of a sunbed with a towel on and a large red cross stamped over the top. Text below the image read: *It is not allowed to reserve sunbeds. Any towels left on sunbeds for more than 30 minutes will be removed by staff.* The same text appeared in Spanish, French and German. At least, Freddie assumed it was the same text.

"What? Well, yeah, but that…" said the man. "But I mean… everyone does it."

The man's face was growing dangerously red. The woman by his side grimaced like she'd just swallowed a cactus. The little girl was sobbing, her shoulders bouncing gently up and down.

Freddie looked around the pool to see sunbathers gawping back, like they'd just tuned into their favourite soap opera. The waiter who'd brought Freddie his coffee was behind the bar again, trying not to laugh.

"I don't know what to tell you," said Freddie. "The sign says you're not allowed to reserve the sunbeds. Maybe the staff removed them."

"Bollocks. They only removed ours. What about all the others?"

Freddie shrugged in response.

"He did it," said a voice to Freddie's left. He turned to see an old lady, completely topless, with a short mat of messy, grey hair. Freddie winced as he caught sight of her leathery brown, naked breasts, sagging like two fried eggs sliding off a plate. A cigarette dangled from the corner of her mouth and a copy of The Sun newspaper rested in her lap. "I saw him. He threw your towels in the pool."

"Who asked you?" said Freddie.

"Is that right?" said the angry man, dropping the towels onto the ground with a slop and balling up his fists.

"Listen," said Freddie, "let's not get carried away. I'm sure there's a perfectly reasonable explanation. And…" he feigned looking at his watch, "ooh… I'm late for an appointment. I'm doing a talk. As part of the literary retreat. So, perhaps it's time I made my own retreat." He coughed out a fake laugh.

"Do what?" said the man, grimacing like a confused ape trying to work a microwave.

"Why don't you and your lovely family take these four sunbeds?" said Freddie, using his posh author voice and laying on the fake charm. He always enjoyed winding people up. But when it looked like violent confrontation might ensue, he found it best to placate people and make for a rapid exit. Some would call it cowardice. And Freddie had no problem with that – especially if it meant he *didn't* get punched in the face. "I'll see if I can get someone to bring you some dry towels, eh? And perhaps a round of drinks, too? You look like a Stella man to me."

"Yeah, Stella's good," said the man, looking even more bamboozled.

"No way," said the pinched-faced woman. She crossed her arms tightly and raised her eyebrows so high they practically joined with her hairline. "You don't think you're getting away with that, do you?"

Freddie paused. Shit. His charm skills must be rustier than he thought.

"You're not starting on the Stella," she said. "You've only just had breakfast. At least wait until 11 o'clock."

"Fuck's sake," said the man, deflating as he turned to her. "We're on holiday. You can drink whenever you want."

"You're supposed to be spending time with your family, not just getting lashed all day."

"But that's…"

Freddie took this as a good opportunity to withdraw. As the couple descended into a full-blown row, he quietly sneaked away, making sure to spill the cold remnants of his coffee cup all over the old lady's newspaper as he passed.

She squealed and grunted, nearly choking on half a Dunhill, as Freddie whispered, "Serves you right, you nosey old bat."

He scampered away before anyone could make chase, quickly traversing the tightly packed sunbeds. He turned this way and that, not sure which direction he was going, and before he knew it, he was practically tripping over Max Graves, still prostrate on his sunbed.

Fuck it, thought Freddie. There was no avoiding him now. Best just get it over with.

"Hey, Max," he said, glaring down at the motionless figure.

Max did not respond.

Freddie looked closer. They were the same clothes as the previous evening. A glass on the table next to him contained the dregs of what appeared to be whisky. Max had sunglasses covering his eyes and a copy of *The Terrible Bones* by Edward Cross opened across his chest.

Weird, thought Freddie. Why would he be reading that?

"Listen," said Freddie. "About last night. Look… I was drunk… and I probably said a few things I shouldn't have. And… well, I was probably a bit out of order…"

Max didn't move or react in any way. How bloody rude. The least he could do was take off his sunglasses and look Freddie in the eye.

"Anyway, we're both here for a week… so why don't we just shake hands and…" Freddie reached out his hand.

Still Max didn't move. The rude twat. Fine, well, two can play it that way.

"Look, I'm trying to be the bigger man. But if you can't meet me halfway... " said Freddie. He leaned forward and jabbed an angry finger into Max's shoulder.

Max didn't move or react at all. He just lay there motionless as the book slipped off his chest and thumped down onto the ground.

Christ, he's totally out for the count, thought Freddie. Exactly how much had he drunk? Freddie had been legless in his time, but he couldn't remember ever being so drunk he was still totally catatonic the next morning. What a lightweight.

Freddie tapped Max on the shoulder again. "Oi, sleeping beauty."

Nothing. Not even a twitch.

Freddie sighed loudly and touched Max's face. Christ, he was freezing cold.

"Max? Hey, Max?" said Freddie. Still nothing.

Freddie grabbed one of Max's hands. It was freezing cold, too. He placed a finger on the wrist and felt for a pulse. Nothing.

"Max? Max, are you okay?" Freddie placed a finger on Max's throat. Still no pulse. What the fuck?

Freddie took a step back and practically tripped over Dan, the event organiser, who had sneaked up behind him.

"Freddie?" he said. "Good morning. How's everything so far? I trust you're settling in okay. Did you sleep well?"

"What? Er... I, er... what?" said Freddie.

"Oh, goodness, I take it you enjoyed the party last night. I've seen a few sore heads around the place this morning."

"What, eh? I..."

"Anyway, I'm just doing my organiser bit. Checking everyone knows where to be and when." He opened the folder he was carrying and scanned through a list. "You're not down for anything until this afternoon. So, you can just relax and take it easy. As for Mr Graves..." he said, looking down at Max and again running his finger down the list, "I believe you're due on stage in just under an hour."

"Yeah, I'm not sure he's gonna make that," said Freddie.

"Oh really?" said Dan. "Is there a problem?"

"I'd say so," said Freddie. "I think he's dead."

CHAPTER 5

"WHAT DO YOU mean, he's dead?" said Dan, his eyes widening as the colour drained from his face.

"Well, I'm no expert, but he hasn't moved in the last few minutes, despite me poking him. He's stone cold to the touch. And he doesn't appear to be breathing," replied Freddie. "So, you know… probably dead."

"Christ," said Dan. "Fuck. Fuck, that's not good. Max?" he said, bending down and looking closely at the man's face. "Max, are you dead?"

"Are you expecting him to answer that?" sneered Freddie.

Several seconds later, following both Freddie and Dan poking Max repeatedly and failing to elicit any response, Dan went running off in a panic. He returned with the hotel manager and the resort doctor, who examined Max with a slightly more scientific approach and reported that he was, in fact, deceased.

"Fuck," said Freddie.

"Fuck," said Dan.

The hotel manager lifted a walkie talkie from his belt and rattled off something in Spanish. There then followed a mad flurry of activity as hotel staff appeared from all sides, closed the pool bar and shooed disgruntled sunbathers away to the other swimming pools. Their angry outbursts were quickly soothed, however, when three waiters appeared with large trays of free sangria.

Large screens were quickly erected around Max's sunbed. And within just five minutes, the whole pool area had been closed, evacuated and roped off.

It was so well-orchestrated, Freddie had to wonder whether it was a drill the hotel staff performed regularly in case of such an eventuality. Or maybe they just had a lot of people die by the pool.

"The police are on their way," the hotel manager said to Dan. "I'll send a security officer to guard the area until they arrive. I'm sure they'll have questions for you, so please stay close by." Then he spun around and strode off back to the main hotel building.

"Blimey, he's a bit cool, isn't he?" said Freddie.

"I… God… I mean, I just… God…" said Dan.

"Here, do us a favour and keep guard," said Freddie. Then he shifted one of the large screens and sneaked inside.

Max was slumped back on the sunbed. Freddie bent down for a closer look. He leaned forward and slid Max's sunglasses slightly down his nose, revealing his partially open and heavily bloodshot eyes. His lips were dry and cracked, with small deposits of dried, white spittle in the corners of his mouth. His skin was pale and clammy, with a greyish hue. He was quite clearly dead.

"What are you doing?" said a panicked Dan from behind the barrier.

"I'm investigating," Freddie called back in a loud whisper.

"Erm… should you be… doing that?"

"Just shut up and keep a lookout," said Freddie. "And let me know if anyone comes."

Freddie bent down and took a closer look at Max's face. "No obvious signs of bruising or trauma," Freddie whispered to himself, as if talking into a Dictaphone like a medical examiner on a TV crime drama. He scanned the length of Max's body. "Nothing suspicious that I can see."

With no medical or police training, Freddie had no idea what he was looking for. And he didn't know what would or wouldn't be considered suspicious. But he was enjoying the make-believe.

Freddie stepped around the sunbed and knelt, so his nose was just inches from Max's glass. He took a long sniff.

"Hmmm… definitely whisky," he whispered to himself. "Could there be traces of something else? Fuck knows, to be honest."

Freddie picked up the book that had been open on Max's chest. "Now, why would you be reading this?" he said. "Didn't you edit it? Why on earth would you want to read it again? It's not even that bloody good."

He opened the book and flicked through the pages.

"Interesting," he said, stopping as he noticed the single word *thief* had been circled on a page in red pen. He carried on flicking, finding more words circled: *liar, cheat, criminal, scandal, betrayal* and many others. Freddie also found that several fragments of sentences had been highlighted: '…know what you did…'; '…won't get away with it…'; '…caught out…'; '…what you deserve…'; '…coming for you…'; '…face your punishment'. Then, as he neared the back of the book, the markings took on a more sinister tone, with words like *die*, *kill*, *punish* and *murder* all scrawled across whole pages in red pen.

Freddie grabbed his phone from his pocket and took pictures of the random scrawls. What the hell did it mean? Had Max done this? Was it some kind of protest against the book's author? Was there something between him and Edward, some unresolved grievance? Come to think of it, hadn't Freddie heard they'd parted company on less than amicable terms?

"Ahem! Ahe-he-hem!"

Freddie heard Dan's less-than-subtle signal just in time. He used the bottom of his shirt to wipe the book's cover – just in case he'd left any fingerprints – then placed it roughly back in its original position. He pulled the barrier aside and snuck out just before the security guard arrived.

The two men smiled at the guard, then quickly walked away.

"Well?" said Dan, as they got far enough away to talk unheard. "What did you find?"

"Oh, he's definitely dead," said Freddie.

"Yes, I know that," said Dan, his voice high and strained. "What else? Were there any signs of… foul play?"

"How should I know? I'm not a doctor. Or a detective."

"Then why did you sneak in to investigate?"

"Dunno, really. Curious mind, I suppose."

Freddie had no intention of revealing any of the details he'd uncovered. Not until he'd had time to think about them. This sort of thing, he'd learned from experience, was best kept a secret for as long as possible.

"Anyway, can you believe it's already 10.30?" said Freddie, looking at his watch. "I don't know about you, but I'm absolutely starving. I think I'll go and see if there's any breakfast left."

"Breakfast?" said Dan. "How can you eat at a time like this? A man's dead."

"Yeah, well, he's not gonna get any less dead just because I have a bit of scrambled egg, is he? Look, you go and process all this, or whatever it is you need to do. I daresay you'll have a few events to reschedule now, eh?"

"Oh God, Max's talk. Oh fuck. Yes, I'd better…" Dan went running into the hotel building, flicking through his binder as he went.

Ten minutes later, Freddie was in the restaurant, looking down at a plate piled high with scrambled eggs, mini hotdog sausages, beans, mushrooms, fried potatoes, something resembling bacon (but definitely not actual bacon), chunks of melon and strawberries, four pancakes, three croissants and a chocolate doughnut. It was one of the more unusual breakfast combinations he'd had. But probably not the weirdest.

His stomach churned and gurgled with another small wave of nausea. It could have been down to hunger. It could have been the continued after-effects of the previous night's booze. Or it could have been caused by discovering a sunbathing corpse. Whichever it was, food was likely the best cure, so he started wolfing it down in large forkfuls. He managed just a few mouthfuls of egg and sausage before he heard a small voice to his left.

"Hello," it said.

Freddie looked down to see a small boy standing next to him. It took him a second to realise it was the same annoying boy from the plane, who'd spent most of the flight asking him monotonous questions.

"Oh," said Freddie. "What do you want?"

"What are you eating?" said the boy.

"What's it to you?"

"Are you having breakfast? I've already had my breakfast. I had a bowl of cornflakes, and then I had some toast with jam. What are you having?"

"I should have known you'd end up staying at this hotel," said Freddie. "Just my bloody luck."

A look of quiet outrage flashed across the boy's face. "Ummm, you said another swear."

"What? Shit, sorry. Oh, f- sorry about that one too."

"You're not supposed to say swears. My mum says so."

"Well, she's probably not wrong. Speaking of which, where is your mum, and why is she not doing a better job of stopping you from bothering people?"

"She's asleep. On the big bed by the swimming pool. I came to get a drink from the fizzy drink machine." He pointed over to the self-serve Coca-Cola dispenser on the other side of the room.

"So, then why are you stood here talking to me?"

"I can't reach the glasses."

"And what do you want me to do about it?" grumbled Freddie.

"Can you please get me a drink?"

"Hasn't anyone ever told you not to talk to strangers?"

"You're not a stranger. Your name is Freddie Windows. We met on the plane."

"It's Winters," sighed Freddie. "And fair point. But can't you ask one of the staff?"

The boy looked down at his feet, his bottom lip quivering. Christ, why did this always happen to Freddie? He'd spent years cultivating the perfect rude, cantankerous demeanour to ward off annoying chit-chatters, bothersome shop assistants and the loathsome people who ask if they can share your table in coffee shops. And for the most part, it was very effective. A simple sneer, or a roll of the eyes was enough to send them packing. But for some inexplicable reason, it seemed to make him an even greater target for inquisitive children and pestering dogs. They just seemed to love him, despite his complete disregard for them.

"Fine," said Freddie, dropping his knife and fork onto his plate. "What do you want?"

"Lemon Fanta," said the boy.

"Wait there." Freddie marched off, huffing under his breath and returned a minute later with three glasses of fizzy lemon drink, the bubbles bursting out the tops of the glasses and spattering his wrists. "There, that should keep you out of my hair for a bit. And it'll keep your mum busy once you've necked all that sugar."

The boy lifted one glass, put it to his lips and downed the entire contents. Then he looked up, opened his mouth and threw out a belch so loud the whole restaurant turned to see. Freddie couldn't help but smile.

"Now," said Freddie, "bugger off and leave me in peace. And before you say anything, yes, that was a swear. But it was only a little one, so I don't care."

The boy grabbed his remaining drinks and walked away, careful not to spill anything. Freddie picked up his fork and was just about to spear a sausage when he heard another voice behind him.

"Freddie," said Dan, hushed but urgent. He was jumpy. Panicked. Looking around as if he expected an army of police to appear at any moment. "Can I have a word?"

Freddie sighed and placed his fork down. "Yeah, sure, why not? It's not like I'm trying to eat, or anything."

"Well, it's about… the… er… the… you know what."

"Sorry, you're going to have to be a bit more specific," said Freddie, pinching his lips into a confused frown.

"It's about… the…" More furtive glances around the restaurant. "About the… body." He silently mouthed the last word.

"Oh, the dead author by the pool," said Freddie, loudly and with an evil smirk.

"Shhh… keep your voice down," implored Dan.

"Oh, sorry," said Freddie, suddenly whispering. "Say no more. What can I do you for?"

"I've gathered all the authors together. Would you mind joining us?"

"But I've just sat down."

"It won't take long."

"But my breakfast…"

"Please. It's important."

"Fine." Freddie stood, picked up his plate and followed the man to the large hall where the party was held the previous night. The room was now set up for a talk, chairs arranged in long, neat rows. The other authors were already assembled, looking confused, annoyed and curious.

Dan climbed up onto the stage and, with his face pale and bottom lip quivering, he went on to detail that morning's events. He explained how the police were now on scene and would be investigating to find out what had happened. And he told the audience that, while an obviously tragic thing had happened, they were planning on continuing with the event as planned – with a few obvious adjustments to the line-up.

"Don't you think we should cancel the event?" said a voice at the front of the crowd. "As a mark of respect?"

A small ripple of approving voices followed.

"Well, now, let's not be hasty," said Dan, squirming slightly. "We're already here. A lot of money has been spent. To cancel the event now would mean giving our customers full refunds. And that's something

54

that would leave us in a big deficit. Which would mean funds would, of course, need to be reallocated… meaning other pots would be lacking even more… and…"

"What does all that mean?" said a confused voice in the middle of the room.

"It means," said Freddie, with a mouthful of pancake and potato, "that the organisers would go bust and none of us would get our appearance fees. We'd probably have to pay for our accommodation ourselves as well."

"Is that true?" said a voice at the front of the room.

Dan, squirming more than a bucketful of eels, shrugged softly and said, "Pretty much, yeah."

Another ripple shot through the crowd, much louder now and deeper in tone, as the authors voiced their disapproval.

"So, what can we do to help?" said one voice.

"Are my talks all going ahead as planned?" said another.

"Will there be any opportunities to do extra talks?" said another.

Typical bloody authors, thought Freddie. More than happy to get out of an obligation. But mention they won't get paid and they'll back-track faster than a Tory politician caught fiddling their expenses.

"All events will be going ahead as planned," said Dan, relieved to get the crowd back onside, "although some panels will obviously fall short. You know… what with Max… So, if you want to join any extra panels, please see me after this. And in the meantime, if we could try and keep the news to ourselves, that would be ideal. We'll obviously issue a statement in due course, but we'd rather not spook any of the guests."

"Why?" said a voice at the back of the room. Freddie turned to see it was coming from Colin McMaster, a grizzled former police detective who now wrote gruesome serial killer books with some of the most hideous murders Freddie had ever read. "Do the police suspect foul play?"

On stage, Dan let out a small, anxious laugh. "Why would you think that?"

"You're talking to a room full of crime writers," said Colin. "Of course I'm gonna think that. I've already thought of at least five different reasons he might have been killed. And three ways the killer might have done it."

"Well, now, I think it's too early to be thinking like that," said Dan. "The police have only just arrived. I'm sure it's just a very sad, tragic thing that's happened."

"Hmmm," said Colin loudly, eliciting several similar responses from people in the crowd.

Hmmm, thought Freddie, thinking about the book Max had been holding, with all the circled words and crazed scribblings.

"Anyway," said Dan, "that's everything for now. If you could all just carry on as normal for the time being, attend the events you're booked in for and enjoy the rest of your stay. I'll let you know any updates as soon as I have them."

The crowd of writers filed out of the room, chatting and comparing theories as they went. Freddie knew it wouldn't take long. As Colin said, it was a room full of crime writers – the most suspicious people you can ever meet. Tell a crime novelist someone's pinched your yoghurt from the office fridge and within minutes they'll have concocted a web of conspiracy that tracks all the way back to Buckingham Palace, with a trail of dead bodies longer than the queues at Disneyland. Freddie was sure they'd all be desperate to crack the case – although he was still the only one to have seen the biggest clue. Not that he had any idea what it meant.

He waited until everyone had gone, placed his half-eaten plate of food on the chair next to him and shuffled out of the room. He didn't make it further than the door, however, before he was stopped by a woman in a white power suit. She had long, dark hair tied back into a ponytail, with olive skin and bright red lipstick. She looked to be in her mid-40s, with a slim body that had aged well. She was flanked on either side by two Spanish police officers, in black short-sleeved shirts and peaked caps. Black pistols, fixed tightly into holsters, sat menacingly on their hips.

"Mr Freddie Winters," she said, smiling. Her Spanish accent was distinctive, but she clearly spoke very good English. "I'm Inspector Sofia Perez. I think we need to talk."

CHAPTER 6

FREDDIE WAS LED behind the reception desk, down a narrow corridor and into a small, claustrophobic office. He watched as Inspector Perez sat behind a small desk, then he sat down in a chair opposite. The door remained open, with the two black-clad police officers standing guard outside.

"So, you are Mr Freddie Winters," said the Inspector, "from London."

"That's correct," said Freddie, feeling that awkward surge of guilt people can't help but feel when confronted by law enforcement.

"And you're a writer? Here for the writing festival?"

"I'm not sure I'd call it a festival exactly," chuckled Freddie. "More of a village fête, if anything."

The detective stared back stony-faced, not understanding the reference and clearly not in the mood for jollity.

"I understand you were the one who found the body," said Perez.

"I suppose so. Not sure I really *found* him. There were plenty of other people by the pool at the time. I'm just the one who poked him and realised he wasn't breathing."

"And what were you doing by the pool?"

"Just relaxing. Doing a bit of writing, that sort of thing."

"Hmmm," said the Inspector, a wry smile creeping into the corner of her mouth, "not throwing people's towels in the pool and then arguing with a family from England?"

Freddie smiled blankly. What the fuck? How the hell did she know that?

"Don't worry, Mr Winters," she said, smiling even wider. "I'm not from the towel police. I don't work for the sunbed taskforce. And, if you ask me, I hate it when people put their towels on sunbeds and don't even use them. So rude."

"Exactly," said Freddie. "You know, I have to say, you speak very good English."

"Thank you. I spent three years living in London, working on secondment with Scotland Yard. There's nothing like living in a country to help you pick up the lingo," she smiled, winking as she said the last word.

"You speak it very well," said Freddie, laying on the charm.

"Do you often argue with people?" she said, suddenly straightening again. "You were arguing with Mr Graves last night, too, weren't you? And then this morning he turns up dead. How do you explain that?"

So that's your tactic, thought Freddie. Get me on side, make me think we're having a friendly chat, then start throwing accusations around?

"Max and I did have a few heated words," said Freddie.

"More than heated, I think. I believe at one point he had you by the throat, making threats against you. Don't worry, we have it all recorded by the security cameras." She pointed to a large wall of monitors on the other side of the room. Eight screens all subdivided into eight smaller images, depicting different scenes from around the hotel, conference areas, pools and restaurants.

"I'm sorry," said Freddie, "but I think I must have missed something. Is there something suspicious about Max's death? I mean, why else would you be asking about arguments?"

"Just trying to establish a few facts," smiled the Inspector. "For instance, since checking into the hotel, you've upset quite a few people and ended up in at least two arguments. Are you quick to anger, Mr Winters?"

"Perpetually pissed off and grumpy," replied Freddie. "So, angry, yes, but not violent. And certainly not a killer, if that's what you're getting at."

"Killer?" said Perez, her face a picture of confused innocence. "Who said anything about a killer?"

"Please, Inspector, you clearly know about me. And you know I write stuff like this for a living. So, why don't we dispense with the whole cat-and-mouse thing where you try and trick me into saying something I shouldn't? Are you saying there was something suspicious about Max's death?"

"I don't know yet. We're still examining the scene. And we're waiting to find out the cause of death, but something feels a bit… strange."

"Strange? How so?"

"He was a relatively young man, late-thirties. Seems unlikely he'd just die by the pool. A heart attack is possible, but not likely, I think. And there was… an item."

"An item?"

"Found with the body. Forgive me, I can't reveal the details."

The book, thought Freddie. She'd obviously seen the contents, hence her suspicions.

"So, tell me, what were you and Mr Graves arguing about last night?"

"It was nothing. He'd had a little too much to drink. I'd had a lot too much to drink. I made a small comment about how he's a talentless hack who basically plagiarised his whole novel…"

"Plagiarised?" said Perez, wrapping her tongue around the word.

"Stole. Copied off the other boys. Pinched the story for his book from lots of other books."

"I see. So, you were upset about this?"

"Not especially. Like I say, I was just drunk and sounding off."

"And Mr Graves took exception to you saying this?"

"He certainly didn't like it. Things got a bit heated. We had a bit of a tussle." Freddie mimed fists moving and a hand around his throat. "But that was it. Quickly fizzled out, and I left the party."

"Right," said Perez. "And where did you go? Can you account for your whereabouts?"

"Like I say, I was pretty drunk. I headed back to my room and woke up this morning with a terrible hangover. But like you say, there are plenty of cameras," Freddie pointed at the large wall of screens. "So, I'm sure you can see exactly where I went."

"Yes, we'll look into that," she said. "And tell me, what do you know about Edward Cross?"

"You mean the book?"

Perez looked back in surprise.

"I take it that's your 'item'," said Freddie. "I noticed it when I first found Max. It fell onto the floor and when I picked it up, I couldn't help but notice all these strange scribblings inside. Pretty weird stuff."

"Oh, really?" said the Inspector, lifting the book, now carefully concealed in a large plastic evidence bag.

"Yeah, I mean obviously I wasn't snooping. It fell, I picked it up and was going to hand it back to Max. I couldn't help but glance inside. That was before I knew he was dead, of course."

"Of course."

"So, that's why you're asking about Edward?"

"What was their relationship like?" said Perez.

"I don't know either of them that well," lied Freddie. There was no sense in showing his hand too early. "Only in passing really. I know Max used to be Edward's editor. In fact, I remember thinking it was strange he'd be reading *The Terrible Bones* because he edited it. Why would he want to read it again? Then I saw all those manic scribblings. Do you think he did them?"

"At the moment, we don't know. But we can't rule anything out. So, apart from working together, what were they like?"

"Again, I can't really say. You'd have to ask Edward. I did hear they had a bit of a disagreement a few years back. Max quit as Edward's editor so he could try his hand at being a writer. Rumour has it Edward didn't take too kindly to it, and they parted on less than amicable terms. Is Edward a suspect?"

"At the moment, we don't even know if a crime has been committed," said Perez. "So we have no suspects. But we will keep a close eye on everybody." She looked Freddie straight in the eye, a long pause lingering between them.

"Right, well, it doesn't sound like you need me anymore. And I'm due to speak in a panel discussion soon. So, if you don't mind…"

"Oh really?" said Perez. "What is this discussion about?"

"Well, funny you should ask," laughed Freddie. "It's about how to plan the perfect murder and get away with it. Purely fictional, of course. And completely hypothetical."

"Interesting. Perhaps I'll come and listen. Maybe I can learn something about solving murders?" she laughed, but only with her mouth. Her eyes stayed straight and focused on his.

"So, I'm free to go?"

"For now, Mr Winters. But don't go too far. I'm sure we'll be speaking again."

******

The air in the room was thick and warm, dragging Freddie's eyelids downwards as he fought to stay awake. He was on stage in the main auditorium, looking out on around 100 eager crime writers, all keen to learn how to plot literary murders. He was joined on stage by three

60

other novelists – Kevin Wollenstone, Helen Brennan and Michaela Kemp. They were each detailing their preferred methods for murder – in a purely literary sense. Helen, a very smiley lady with long, curly brown hair and freckles had just described a torturous death from her last book, in which the killer removed body parts with a pair of garden shears. It seemed highly out of character. Freddie always thought Helen seemed more at home knitting and stroking cats than she did imagining brutal murders, but there was something about the way she smiled as she described her killings that made Freddie wonder whether she'd ever put her techniques into real-world practice. The sound of scribbling floated around the room as the audience eagerly jotted down notes.

The conversation had started well. The first 45 minutes had been lively, with some decent questions, fun anecdotes and interesting bits of advice. All until the microphone was passed to Kevin.

Kevin was short, podgy and had no neck – somehow his head seemed inexplicably attached to his shoulders with nothing in between. He had a bald head with short tufts of ginger hair which clung onto the sides of his skull for dear life. And he always wore his trousers high up on his waist, his belt circling the middle of his body and making his plump belly look even bigger and rounder. The resulting effect made him look exactly like a Weeble. He was also the most tedious man Freddie had ever met. Honestly, the man was so dull, Freddie was waiting for the police to drag him away for attempting mass murder through boring people to death. His slow, deep, monotone voice droned on and on, without ever seeming to stop.

Freddie had lost track of what he was talking about. He vaguely remembered a question about choosing murder weapons and Kevin had spent the last 27 ½ minutes talking about different types of antique swords; what kinds of metal they were; how sharp they were; what effects they'd have on different body parts.

Christ, what Freddie wouldn't have given to have an antique sword in his hand right there and then.

Freddie looked out at the audience. What had been a lively, excited crowd had now descended into a roomful of drooling snoozers. In fact, Freddie was sure he could hear at least three different people snoring. It was like an old people's home after dinner.

Michaela Kemp – a decent novelist who wrote gritty gangland crime fiction – was supposed to be moderating the discussion. Michaela was one of the funniest people Freddie had ever met. Witty and always with a quick, cutting comment, she had long blonde hair, a petite frame and she was toned, as if she did yoga three times a week. She had kind eyes, a pretty smile and she was always lively and enthusiastic. However, after trying to cut Kevin off several times, and failing to wrestle the mic out of his hand, she was sitting slumped back in her chair, the life drained from her face and a glassy look in her eyes.

That was it. Freddie couldn't take it any longer. He sat bolt upright in his chair and started smashing his hands together, cutting Kevin off with a loud clap that jolted the audience awake. "Great stuff there, Kevin," said Freddie loudly. "Really interesting advice." He marched the four steps over to Kevin and grabbed the microphone.

Kevin wasn't giving it up, though. So, Freddie reached forward with his other hand and pinched the skin of Kevin's wrist, stepping down hard onto his ankle at the same time. Kevin squealed with pain, released his grip, and Freddie could swear he heard the audience sigh with relief as he yanked the mic away and walked back to the other end of the stage.

"So, what I guess Kevin's trying to say – in not so few words – is pick a weapon that feels right for the character. Do your research and get all the little details right. Now, does anybody else have a question?"

The rest of the talk picked up pace, with questions flying in and being answered. Freddie took over the job of moderating. This was partly because Michaela was still shellshocked, partly because it gave him the chance to wax lyrical himself, but mostly to keep Kevin away from the microphone – something everyone apart from Kevin was pleased about.

Half an hour later, Freddie was sitting behind a table at the back of the room, a neat little stack of his latest novel piled up. A modest queue stood in line to speak with him. It was by no means the biggest queue, but certainly not as short as Kevin's, which consisted of a regretful-looking woman who'd been trying to release her hand from his grip for at least four minutes.

People came and went. Freddie did his best small talk and signed their books, writing asinine personalised messages as he held a rictus grin on his aching jaw. He'd just finished with a little old lady who'd felt the need to tell him his latest book was better than any of his previous ones – which were all obvious, poorly written and full of bad language. In fact, she'd only read his latest because her book club forced her to, and nobody could have been more surprised than her when she'd enjoyed it. Freddie fought the urge to reach forwards and rip the curly white hairs from her chin. He even managed to restrain himself from writing something vulgar in her book. He'd promised his agent he'd save up all that bad behaviour until the last day – although his agent had insisted he should behave like a grown-up and not do anything like that at all. The poor, naïve creature. It was like she didn't know him at all.

Freddie was just starting to plot some of the ways he could enact his revenge on the horrible old bag, when he looked up and saw something that made him squeal almost as loudly as Kevin had on stage. Smiling down at him was a woman with dark hair, a maniacal smile and a t-shirt emblazoned with a large picture of a cat.

"Caroline? What the hell are you doing here?"

"Hey, babe, great to see you. You're looking really well," she said.

"Seriously, what the hell are you doing here?"

"I came to see you, silly. Aren't you happy to see me?

"Shouldn't you be parked outside Dylan's house with a high-powered lens?"

To say Freddie was surprised to see Caroline was more than an understatement. He'd first met her a year and a half previously, when she'd infiltrated his life to get closer to his good friend Dylan, whom she was stalking. The same Dylan whose murder Freddie had managed to thwart, leading to Freddie being propelled into the public eye and gifted the plot for his most successful novel ever.

Caroline had wormed her way into Freddie's life, unceremoniously sleeping with him just to get a peek inside Dylan's flat, where Freddie was living at the time. Freddie had soon realised there was something quite unstable about the woman – for starters, she never wore anything that didn't feature a picture of a cat. At one point, he even suspected her of being involved in the attempt on Dylan's life. But he soon realised she was just a harmless, lonely woman who was obsessed with his friend.

Obviously, Freddie slept with her a few more times, even after he became aware of her true intentions. She was attractive, with a decent figure, and more than a little enthusiastic in bed. She was just a bit deluded. Finally, everything came to a head when Freddie revealed that he knew what she was up to. They'd argued and he hadn't seen her since.

"You know it's not like that," said Caroline. "I was never a… stalker." She had to force the last word out, like it tasted bitter in her mouth. "No matter what the police say. I was just a fan of Dylan's writing. Besides, I'm over that now. I don't really follow Dylan's career anymore. I didn't even go to his last book signing."

"Yeah, because of the restraining order, you loony."

"No, actually. And I'm not…" She paused to take in a deep breath. "I didn't really like his last book. Not up to his usual standard. Plus, he's gone back to his ex-wife now, so…"

"Great," said Freddie. "You've moved on. You're not stalking Dylan anymore. What the hell are you doing here?"

"Like I said, silly." She curled her hair around her finger and smiled, "I'm here to see you. I've missed you. I thought we could pick up where we left off."

"Are you out of your tiny mind? Actually, don't answer that. What makes you think I'd have any interest in that?"

To be fair, she was looking very well. Her brunette hair was slightly longer than he remembered it, curling just above her shoulders. Her big, brown eyes sparkled as she smiled. And despite featuring a ridiculous picture of a cat, her tight, white t-shirt clung very sexily to her slim body, making her breasts look even bigger than he remembered. Judging by her toned legs and pert bum, she'd also clearly been going to the gym.

Caroline was an attractive woman – she always had been – hence why he'd slept with her in the first place. And he could definitely be tempted again, were it not for the knowledge of all the crazy that went with the package.

"We were good together, weren't we? We had some fun times?" she said.

"You tricked me into thinking you liked me so you could sneak into Dylan's flat and snoop around."

"Well, yeah, but apart from that."

"And why now exactly? I haven't heard from you in over a year."

"Yeah, but I've seen you. I've been following your career, you clever boy. Your latest book was brilliant. So well written. I saw all your TV appearances and read all your interviews. I've never been out with a celebrity before."

"So, what? Now I'm a little bit famous, you fancy me? Are you completely mental?"

"You know I don't like that word, Freddie," she said, her tone turning angry just for a second. Then she smiled again. "I don't care what you say, we had something special. And I'm not giving up on that."

"There was nothing between us, aside from a couple of dodgy bunk-ups."

"I'm going to win you back, Freddie Winters. Just you wait and see."

"Sorry, love, but you're really not."

"I can't wait for your next talk," she said, lifting a guide to the week's events. "And maybe we'll see each other in the bar later. Or by the pool. Or at dinner."

She giggled, blew him a kiss and walked out of the auditorium.

Christ on a bike, as if he didn't have enough to deal with already, Dylan's former stalker was apparently now stalking him instead. And it was only day one of the retreat. How much stranger could this week get?

Freddie looked up to see five more people lined up at his desk, but his eyes were quickly drawn to someone on the other side of the room. He was wearing shorts, flip-flops and a hooded sweatshirt with the hood pulled right up over his head, almost completely concealing his face.

Weird, thought Freddie, it was baking in there, despite the air conditioning. And at least 30 degrees out in the sun. The guy must be sweltering in that jumper.

The man shifted this way and that, not seeming to know where he wanted to go. He looked at Freddie and as the two locked eyes, he immediately looked away. He stumbled backwards, almost tripping over his flip-flops. Then he marched off quickly, practically running out of the room.

"You Freddie Winters, then?" said a man looking down at him. He was in his forties, with salt-and-pepper hair and wearing a sky-blue polo shirt. He handed Freddie a copy of *Death of a Mailman* to be signed. Another cheap fucker bringing their own copy, rather than purchasing one of the heavily marked-up copies on Freddie's table.

"Can I just say, I absolutely loved this book," said the man.

"Thank you. I'm so pleased," said Freddie, opening the copy and readying his pen.

"Oh, please make it out to Norman. In fact, I'm a novelist myself," said Norman. "Not published yet but working hard. I'd love to get your feedback on some of my plot ideas. Maybe we could meet in the bar for a drink tonight?"

Oh, for fuck's sake.

******

Moisture beaded on the glass in Freddie's hand. The snap and pop of the fizzy tonic was just audible over the rhythmic whooshing of the waves outside his window. The hubbub from the nearby pool had ceased as the sun started to set and people retreated to their rooms to get ready for the evening. Freddie had taken the opportunity to pour himself a large G&T from his minibar. The cold liquid was doing its job of refreshing his throat and soothing the last remnants of his hangover.

It had been a successful day – aside from discovering a dead body by the pool, finding himself a suspect in the man's death, and seeing his crazy former lover turn up out of the blue. But his first talk had gone well. He'd sold a few copies of his book at the signing. He'd even managed to fit in a bit of rest time by the pool. Overall, it was lining up to be a decent trip.

He sighed as he checked his itinerary. He was due to teach a writing masterclass the next day at 11am. He had nothing prepared. No fancy PowerPoint presentation. No inspirational quotes. No handouts or worksheets. No thought at all. But the class was about how to write a book, and he'd spent his whole life doing that, so he figured he could wing it.

He'd also been sent the first 5,000 words of his class's current writing projects, which he was supposed to have read and marked with feedback. Naturally, he hadn't bothered to do that either. He could have spent a couple of hours skimming them that evening. But there were 20 people in the class and there was no way he was reading that much drivel. He was on holiday (of sorts, anyway). He had no intention of working, especially with all that free food and booze to enjoy. And there were bound to be a few singletons, hanging out at the bar, looking for a holiday romance. It would be rude not to oblige them.

Another look at the itinerary showed some dreary-sounding event called 'The Poolside Readathon'. Everyone was to gather by the main pool (which had now reopened following the discreet removal of Max Graves' corpse) and budding writers would be encouraged to read their work aloud. A panel of expert judges would then provide a bit of feedback, and one writer would be judged the most promising. It sounded horrendous. The last thing Freddie needed was to sit and listen to the poorly formed ramblings of a load of second-rate amateur novelists. He decided to give that one a miss.

He took another large swig of his drink, sat back on the sofa and closed his eyes. Then he heard a knock at the door. Bollocks.

He opened the door to find a manic-looking Dan, shuffling about impatiently.

"I've just heard from the police," he said, barging past Freddie into the room.

"No, please, do come in," said Freddie, following behind. "Can I get you a drink?"

"What? Erm… no. Thank you. Listen, I just had a call from Inspector Perez."

"What did she say?"

Dan looked around the room, as if checking he wasn't being overheard. "She said it was murder."

"Fuck. Really?"

"Poison. Apparently, they found traces of something called ethylene glycol in his blood and in the glass of whisky by his side."

"Ethylene glycol? Isn't that…?"

"Antifreeze, apparently. They said he wouldn't have noticed the taste, especially if he was already drunk. Oh, it's so horrible."

"Christ. So, they're certain? Somebody killed him? Do they have any suspects?"

"Not that they've told me. Perez wants to speak with me again tomorrow. And I guess they'll be carrying out a more thorough investigation. They'll probably want to talk to you as well."

"Christ. Max murdered. Who would want him dead? I know he was a dick, but murder?"

"I can't believe it. To think the killer might still be in the hotel…"

"And the plan for the rest of the event?"

"We'll just have to keep going. If we don't want to go bankrupt."

"Well, good luck with that. You won't be able to keep things secret for long."

"Maybe not. But maybe just long enough. Speaking of which…"

Oh, here it comes, thought Freddie.

"Tonight's readathon…" said Dan hesitantly. "Max was due to be one of the judges… and I was hoping you might…"

"No way," said Freddie. "I've got a quiet evening planned with my good friends Gin and Tonic."

"Please, Mr Winters. I wouldn't ask unless I was desperate. It's going to look odd enough that we're a judge short, let alone having people wonder why. If we can slip you onto the panel, people might not even notice. It should be enough to buy us some time."

Freddie grumbled to himself and downed the last of his drink. "Fuck's sake. Fine. But there'd better be plenty of booze. And I'm not sugar-coating anything. If I think someone's work is shit, that's exactly what I'm going to say."

CHAPTER 7

THE READATHON WAS every bit as bad as Freddie had imagined. For nearly two hours, he was subjected to nervous, jittery, quiet-voiced people standing up and reading from their unsurprisingly yet-to-be-published work. In fairness, there were a few rough diamonds. Some had an interesting writing style or a quirky turn of phrase. Others had the basis of an interesting plot. And one aspiring writer did present some intricately crafted prose, although it lacked any sense that there was a story buried anywhere in there.

Other than that, everything was shit. Worse than shit. Absolute, complete and utter garbage. There were poorly formed paragraphs. Sentences that went on for a week. Dialogue worse than a daytime BBC soap opera. There were characters that changed names several times within one page. Samples that slipped back and forth between the past and present tense so many times Freddie wondered if the writers were trying out a new way of writing about time travel. Quite how he was supposed to give constructive feedback was beyond him. The kindest thing would be to take these abominations out the back and shoot them. And then shoot the writers, too, if they ever went within 10 feet of a laptop again.

There was one saving grace, however. Freddie took great joy in realising that the most serious, confident, arrogant wannabes were also the very worst. Each time one of these buffoons stepped up to the microphone, chest bursting with hubris, Freddie practically rubbed his hands with glee. So impressed were they with their own efforts, they thought they just had to utter the first sentence of their masterpiece and the panel would be tripping over themselves to offer the biggest book deal of the decade. And each time one of them opened their mouths, Freddie was delighted to find the works getting worse and worse. And he didn't hold back from telling them. But it did no good. Because the other quality they all shared was a certain, unmistakable glint in the eye. The one that said: 'You clearly don't understand the work'. Well, more fool them.

Freddie was joined on the panel by crime-writer Bill Pascale; Freddie's panel-mate from earlier, Michaela Kemp; Jenny McHale, a junior agent who'd signed some seriously big deals that year and had a lot of industry buzz about her; and Malcom Alexander, publisher and CEO of Darkhouse Publishing – one of the biggest crime fiction publishers and, coincidentally, home to both Edward Cross and Max Graves. It was a decent line up, so no wonder people were keen to read their work. It really was a great opportunity for new talent to be discovered. Shame there was nothing worth discovering.

"Right, well, I suppose we'd better sift through this lot and pick the best," sighed Malcolm, as the last of the speakers wrapped up and the judges huddled together.

"More a case of trying to determine the least bad," laughed Freddie.

"Oh, I don't know," said Bill. "A couple of them showed promise, I thought."

"Bet they don't have you quaking in your boots that they're gonna steal your sales, though," said Michaela. Freddie was pleased to see she'd recovered from her draining experience as host and was back to her usual acerbic self.

"What do you think, Jenny?" said Malcolm.

"There were a few that wrote with confidence and pace," she said. "But there wasn't anything that made me fall in love with the story."

After 10 minutes of going back and forth on the 17 writers that had presented their work, the panel came to a decision and the winner of the evening was announced. Sadly, the 10-centimetre-high plastic trophy they were presented didn't meet the expectation of the six-figure book deal they thought they were getting. But again, Freddie delighted in the disdain etched on the faces of all the over-confident writers who couldn't believe they hadn't won.

"Well, thank Christ that's over," said Malcolm as the crowd dissipated. "Anyone fancy a drink?"

"Damn right," said Freddie.

"Not for me," answered Bill. "Got an early talk tomorrow and still need to go over my notes. You know what they say, fail to prepare and you prepare to fail." He gave a jolly little chuckle, which irritated Freddie. Not because he disagreed with Bill. Quite the opposite. He was angry with himself for doing exactly what Bill said – preparing to fail for his own class the next day. But he figured that feeling would quickly wear off with a pint or two.

"I'm out too," said Jenny. "Got a stack of contracts to go over."

"Well, I'm in," said Michaela. "I need at least three glasses of wine to get over that."

"Great," said Freddie, spotting a selection of lurkers shuffling slowly towards them. "Although perhaps we should go somewhere a little more private. Otherwise, we're in danger of having what's left of our ears chewed off."

"They've allocated the little piano bar upstairs just for authors and industry types," said Michaela. "How about there?"

The three of them stood up from the judging desk, careful not to look any of the lurkers directly in the eye.

"Go!" shouted Freddie, and they all dashed off, running through the stacked-up sunbeds, round the edge of the pool and into the main hotel building.

"Nice choice," said Freddie, as they sat down at a table in the corner of the piano bar. The place was packed with the leading lights of British crime fiction – plus a few second-raters to bump up the numbers. But there wasn't a lurker or amateur novelist in sight. A real chance to relax, thought Freddie, without someone shoving a poorly written sample in your face.

"Well done on your latest book, Fred," said Malcolm. "Got some decent sales. I think we might even have put in a bid, before you settled on that other mob."

"Hey, you've got to follow the money," said Freddie. "Speaking of which, I'm surprised to see you at this kind of event. Shouldn't you be off on a fancy yacht somewhere, sailing round the Caribbean?"

"That's next month. No, I thought this might be a jolly little trip away. Chance to get in touch with the cream of the industry. Rub shoulders and see if any of you clever authors have new books I can poach away from the competition. Plus, who's gonna say no to a free week in the sun? Don't pretend that's not why you're both here."

"Don't know what you mean," said Michaela, smiling as she swigged from a large glass of red wine.

"So, who's working on something new?" said Malcolm.

"I've got one coming out next month," said Michaela. "Just doing a third draft on the next one, and I'm plotting out a new book now. Busy, busy."

"Christ," said Freddie, "do you wanna slow down a bit? You'll make the rest of us look bad. I'm already late delivering my next book."

"And how's it going?" said Malcolm.

"Oh, you know. Slow and steady," said Freddie, thinking back to the page in his notebook which featured nothing but the words 'New idea'. "Just got to get the first draft finished, you know?"

Freddie wouldn't usually sit drinking with the likes of Malcolm Alexander. They didn't exactly mix in the same circles. With his neatly coiffured, salt-and-pepper quiff, you could tell Malcolm was rich just by looking at him. He had that sort of tangerine-coloured skin you can only achieve by spending half the year in St Tropez or lazing on your yacht docked off the coast of Monaco. He always wore ridiculously expensive suits and Freddie was sure the man didn't own a pair of socks that cost less than a hundred quid. But more than that, he had that certain arrogance – a glint in the eye and smirk in his smile – that just seemed to suggest he was loaded.

Freddie didn't particularly dislike Malcolm. No more than any other pompous bigwig who'd failed to publish any of Freddie's books. In fact, of all the publishers Freddie knew, Malcolm was probably the least likely to annoy him. Arrogant, rude and pompous, Freddie wouldn't have trusted Malcolm to hold a handful of mud without expecting to come back to half as much as he'd left him with. But at least he didn't try and hide it. Malcolm was a deceitful, repellent prick, but he didn't pretend to be anything else.

He'd been like that throughout his whole career – stabbing writers in the back; swooping in and stealing deals from other publishers; blacklisting agents that refused to give him kickbacks; signing up-and-coming writers onto three- or four-book deals with miniscule advances and pathetic royalties, so that he literally owned the first five years of their careers. Rumour had it, he even bought himself a ludicrously expensive silver Montblanc pen, which he used to sign his biggest, most outrageous deals. If anyone could write a book called 'How to be an arsehole in publishing', Malcolm was top of the list.

However, judging by his CEO status, his mansion in the Surrey hills and his Bentley – which probably cost three times more than the tiny flat Freddie lived in – it was clearly working for him. And nobody could have been more surprised than Freddie when he found himself enjoying the man's company over a pint.

The three of them sat for a few hours, drinking and talking about books, upcoming projects, and the state of the publishing industry. When Freddie announced they should order cocktails, Michaela decided enough was enough and headed off to bed. Malcolm followed suit one Sex on the Beach later, leaving Freddie alone and very much the worse for wear.

Deciding he needed something to help him sober up, Freddie swayed out of the room and went in search of the snack bar he'd heard people talking about.

******

Marylin Sharpe was sitting on the far side of the bar, gazing at her smart phone, half-listening to Edward grumbling again as he sipped his whisky.

"God, that saccharine soft jazz piano is like worms burrowing into my ears. Honestly, how did I ever let you talk me into coming here?

"And have you seen how many authors there are here? I swear I know most of them. A few new faces I don't know. Of course, they'll know exactly who I am. You can see them, glancing over, trying not to be too obvious. No doubt working up the courage to come and talk to me. Sweet, really. Honestly, look at that guy there. He looks like he's rehearsing what he's going to ask me."

Marylin looked up to where Edward was pointing, to see a man clearly having a conversation with a friend, and in no way rehearsing an opening line. She went back to her phone.

"You have to hand it to the organisers, though," continued Edward. "They've done a decent job with the line-up. Few big-name stars. Few lesser-knowns. Couple of whippersnappers who probably think they're going to be the 'next big thing'. I swear the whole of the Amazon UK top 20 in Crime Fiction are here just hanging out at the bar and chatting. How much must it be costing in appearance fees alone? Not everyone will be getting as much as me, of course. But it must be costing them a pretty penny. Actually, how much am I getting paid?"

Marylin pretended not to hear the question. She went to look up at Edward, then something on her phone caught her attention.

"My God," she said, sucking hard on her vape and blowing out a great plume of butterscotch-scented vapour, "you'll never guess what I've just seen."

"Big sale on huge, bright, ridiculously overpriced handbags?"

"Ha ha. Very droll," she said, placing her favourite red Prada bag carefully on the seat next to her. "No, I've just received a message with some very serious news. Max Graves has died."

"What?" said Edward. "Max is dead? But he's here."

"I know. Found dead by the pool, apparently. But that's not…"

"Jesus," said Edward, cutting her off. "I can't believe it. I was only talking to him yesterday."

"I know, darling, it's tragic. He was so young. And so talented. Such a waste. But…"

"Well, not that talented," said Edward, screwing his mouth up like a disgruntled child who'd just dropped their ice cream.

"No, not compared with you, darling," said Marylin, sycophancy dripping from her tongue. Christ, what a baby. Honestly, you couldn't say anything nice about anyone else without him taking it as an insult that the compliment wasn't directed at him. She gulped a big mouthful of wine.

"His book was fine," sulked Edward, "but not that great. I honestly don't see why everyone was so enamoured by it. He was a better editor than a writer and, even then, he used to wind me up with some of his suggestions."

"Of course, of course," said Marylin. "I just mean it's a shame. He obviously learned a great deal from working with you, seeing how you constructed plots, created characters, wrote such wonderful prose. It's no wonder his book did so well. Look who his mentor was."

"Yes, well… I suppose you're right, actually," said Edward, taking another sip. "You could tell he'd picked up a lot from me. And it's a shame the world will be deprived of what else he might have done. You know, with the right guidance."

"Anyway," said Marylin, "if you'd let me finish, it turns out there's a lot more to the story." She raised up, looking around furtively to check nobody was listening in, then leaned in closer to Edward. "Murder," she whispered.

"What?"

"Murder."

"Don't be daft."

"No, I'm serious. Someone killed him. Poison. The police are investigating."

"Ridiculous," laughed Edward. "Who'd want to kill Max?"

"More people than you'd think," she scoffed, again scanning the bar.

"Seriously? Well, how do you know?"

"Come on, darling. You know I have my ways. Nothing gets past me."

It was true, Marylin had spies dotted all over, relaying information back to her. Nothing happened in the publishing world – a contract being signed, an editor moving companies, an agent taking on a client, an awards shortlist being decided – without Marylin Sharpe finding out within the hour. And now, apparently, she also had the ability to find out about ongoing police investigations – in foreign countries.

"Jesus. Really? Murder?"

"Hand to God," said Marylin, actually raising her hand.

"But when? Who? Why?"

"There he goes," said Marylin, "the crime writer's brain takes over. They don't know what happened, only that they found poison in his drink. It happened after the party last night. Max obviously drank the poison, went down to the pool, fell asleep and then never woke up again."

"Poor Max," said Edward. "True, we didn't part on the best terms. But I'd never wish him dead."

"That's not the worst part," said Marylin, again checking her surroundings. "He was found with a copy of your book."

"My book? What?"

"Apparently, he was holding a copy of *The Terrible Bones* when they found his body. And get this. He'd gone through it with a pen, scribbling all over the pages."

"Scribbling? Scribbling what?"

"Don't know, darling. That's all my source could find out."

"You don't think it could have anything to do with…" said Edward, reaching forward and taking a large swig of the smoky, bitter whisky.

"Hush, darling," said Marylin, her eyes widening and mouth puckering into a hard circle. "You know we don't talk about that."

"Yes, but I mean…"

"No."

"I know, I know, but you have to admit… It's a real coincidence… And Max was one of the only people who…"

"How is this *not* talking about it?"

"Yes, but…"

"Darling, what's happened here is a tragedy. But there's no point speculating about… anything. You have nothing to worry about. Trust me on that."

"Okay," said Edward, sitting back into his chair, "you're right."

"Probably worth being prepared for a visit from the police, though," said Marylin. "It's a safe bet they'll want to speak with you at some point, so we need to get our strategy right."

"Strategy? What strategy? The police can't think I had anything to do with…"

"No, darling. Our social media strategy. It won't be long before the press gets hold of the story. *Murdered author found clutching book by Edward Cross.* We need to get out ahead of it. Tweet about how sad you are and how much you respected Max. Something like that. I'll get the press team working on it."

******

The hideous pattern of the hotel carpet was swaying, swirling and melting as Malcolm Alexander edged his way carefully along the narrow corridor. Door after door lay out in front of him in a seemingly never-ending line. Christ, whose idea had it been to start drinking cocktails? The tang of rum and fruit juice tasted stale and sickly in the back of his throat. He really needed to eat something. Maybe there'd be some food in his minibar. Crisps would be good.

He finally found the door with the same number as the little card in his hand. He swiped it against the door handle and, after several attempts, it lit up with two tiny, green lights and a mechanical click. He pressed down hard on the handle, the door flying inwards, and he only just managed to stay upright as he stumbled into the room. He straightened up, holding the wall to keep his balance.

As he clambered into the bedroom, he suddenly became aware of a figure in front of him. Waiting for him.

"What the fuck?" said Malcolm, squinting to focus on the stranger's face. "Oh… it's you. How the hell did you get in here?"

The stranger made no reply.

"Well, look, I'm sorry but I'm not really… you know… Truth is, I'm a little bit drunk," he giggled, raised a hand to lips and made a shushing sound. "So, whatever it is, it'll have to wait until morning."

Still, the dark figure made no sound.

"Did you hear me? I said I need to go to bed. So piss off, will you?"

The next thing Malcolm saw was the flash of silver in the stranger's hand. The figure lurched towards him, hand high in the air, the silver thing twinkling in the moonlight. Then the silver thing was in his neck. Pain exploded in Malcolm's throat. He stumbled backwards. He tried to scream but no sound came from his open mouth.

The stranger yanked their hand back, taking the silver object with it. The pain throbbed even harder. Something warm and sticky bursting out of Malcolm's throat. Splattering his chest and arm. His neck throbbing. Liquid oozing and pulsing and coursing down his skin like lava.

The stranger jabbed at him again. Once, twice, three times. Each thrust puncturing Malcolm's throat in a different place. More pain. More thick, warm liquid. Hard to breathe now. Hard to stay upright. Again, Malcolm tried to scream, but not even air could escape his mouth.

Then he was on his knees, tumbling down as the killer continued thrusting, jabbing and stabbing him in the neck, chest and face. He collapsed onto his back. The world narrowing as he looked up at the figure stood above him. He tried to mouth one word: 'Why?' But his mouth was now filling up with hot, thick blood. He coughed, spluttering loudly as all the energy drained from his body. There was no pain now, only a strange sense of calm.

He looked up at the killer again. They said something but Malcolm couldn't hear it. The killer took one last swipe, the silver object creating a strangely beautiful arc in the air before being stabbed hard into Malcolm's left eye. Then the world turned to black.

CHAPTER 8

WEDNESDAY

IT WAS ANOTHER strange mix of breakfast food. Mini hotdog sausages, stringy Spanish bacon and two fried eggs were joined on the plate by slices of pale cheese, chunks of pineapple and a few prunes. Freddie had also piled on three sugar-glazed pastries, a chocolate doughnut, a freshly cooked waffle and two deep-fried churros. He'd then drizzled the plate in maple syrup and adorned it with a large scoop of strawberry ice cream. Quite why they were serving ice cream at breakfast he couldn't say, but he also couldn't resist lumping it onto his plate. He was starting to regret that decision, however, as the fillings in his teeth throbbed each time he washed it down with a mouthful of hot coffee.

The room was noisy. About a hundred people chittering and chattering, chewing and slurping. Waiters buzzed around, refilling coffee pots, clearing tables and scraping food into bins. People stomped and shuffled, clattering plates, bumping into each other and grumbling that someone else had just taken the last whatever it was they wanted. The cacophony of noise whirled around the room, stinging Freddie's ears as a wave of hangover washed over him.

Thankfully, the food was helping. The greasy, stodgy elements were settling his queasy stomach as the sugary treats boosted his blood sugar levels. He'd woken once again with a throbbing head and made his way down to the breakfast room to jumpstart the healing process. He'd also been disappointed to have woken up alone again. Maybe he was losing his touch. Or maybe he'd never really had it in the first place. Come on Fred, he berated himself, you're on holiday for God's sake. Get out there and get your end away.

His mind drifted briefly to his estranged wife, Nina, and a scene of them eating breakfast in a little French café. They'd gone to Paris on holiday. One of the few he'd ever been able to afford to take her on. They drank strong coffee and ate warm croissants. They laughed and joked and spoke bad French, then walked hand in hand along the river, lost in each other.

God, he'd loved her. She was so funny and smart, and one of the few people who he felt ever really understood him. And things had been good between them, for a while at least. Until he did what he did with every good thing in his life and pushed her away through his own self-obsession and feelings of inadequacy. She hadn't deserved that. And he'd never since met a woman who came anywhere close to her. Probably never would.

He pushed a forkful of sausage, pineapple and doughnut into his mouth, as he pushed the memory out of his head and worked hard to keep his eyes open and his head upright. Having checked his Killer Book Club itinerary before leaving the room, his heart had sunk to learn he had just over an hour before he was due to start teaching his masterclass. That meant two hours stuck in a hot room with a pounding head trying to teach a room full of wannabes how to write a book. He'd usually have tried to come up with some elaborate excuse as to why he couldn't make it, but he was too tired and hungover to bother. Christ, what was happening to him? It seemed easier to teach a class than to think up a way of getting out of it.

The class was going to be awful. He hadn't prepared a single thought or sentence. He had no idea what he was going to tell them. Still, he was pretty good at bluffing his way through this sort of crap. And all he had to do was make it through a few hours, then he could sit by the pool, drink cocktails and work on his new, most important mission of getting a bit of holiday sex.

There was also the mystery of Max's death. Now that it had been ruled murder, the investigation would step up a gear. No doubt that police inspector would be back to talk to him.

"Morning, Freddie."

Freddie looked up to see Nick Foster holding a plate of food and a cup of coffee. "Don't mind me joining you?" he said, not registering the 'fuck off' look Freddie was attempting to convey.

He really must be losing his touch.

"Why would I?" smiled Freddie through gritted teeth.

Nick smiled and sat down.

"That's quite the combination you've got there," he said, pointing to Freddie's plate.

"Well, it's important to eat a balanced meal with all the food groups," Freddie smiled.

"Have you heard about Max Graves?" said Nick in a conspiratorial whisper. "Murder, apparently. Poison. Everyone's talking about it."

"Yes, I had heard," said Freddie, another shockwave of hangover rattling through him and making him shudder.

"God, it makes me feel really uneasy," said Nick, looking around the room. "To think somebody actually killed Max. I mean, they might still be in the hotel. They could even be in this room right now, eating sausages, drinking coffee and planning their next attack."

Freddie scanned the room, squinting at people's faces, trying to read their lips. Nobody looked like a murderer. But then, what does a murderer look like? Freddie had only ever encountered one actual murderer in his life, but that guy had been a complete moron, and had technically only killed someone by accident – the wrong person at that.

Freddie had created plenty of killers for his books, but they were fictional – based on ideas in his head, details he picked up in newspapers and hours of research online. And, of course, years spent shadowing and working with real police detectives. Plus, he had to admit, at least a pinch of crime thriller cliché thrown in for good measure. But what does a real murderer look like? Years of writing about it told him it could have been literally anyone.

"Any thoughts, then?" said Nick, talking through a mouthful of sausage and egg.

"Thoughts?"

"Yeah, you know. Who did it? How did they do it? And why?"

"No. No thoughts," said Freddie.

"Oh, come on. I know that crime writer's brain will already be racing. Mine has. You must have been thinking about it."

"Really, so what are your theories?"

"Nothing conclusive yet. Still trying to piece the plot together."

Christ, the man was seeing it as the plot of a crime novel. Did he really think he could solve it, just like that?

Leave it to the professionals, thought Freddie. The police. And the writers who've actually thwarted real-life criminals, not just dreamt them up on the page.

"So, why would anyone want to kill Max?" said Nick.

"Well, he was a bit of a bellend," said Freddie. "But is that reason enough to poison someone?"

"If it is, you've probably got a pretty long list of assassins after you," laughed Nick. He quickly focused his attention on his breakfast when he saw that Freddie wasn't laughing along.

"He was a book editor," said Freddie. "Or, at least, he had been in the past."

He figured he might as well humour the man. And bouncing ideas off him might help Freddie piece the puzzle together in his own mind.

"Right," said Nick, not quite understanding.

Freddie humphed. "There'll be a long list of people whose books he rejected over the years. Writers who couldn't believe he refused to sign them up. Disgruntled would-be novelists who might just be looking for revenge."

"Hmmm," said Nick. "But is that reason enough to kill someone?"

"People have killed over far less. Besides, we both know how crushing that rejection can be. Obviously, we both got over it. But some of these other budding writers? They might not take it quite so well."

"But wouldn't that list include you?" said Nick.

"What's that?" said Freddie, pretending not to understand.

"You're in that list of rejected writers. The other night, when you were arguing with Max, he said how he'd rejected one of your books."

"Yeah, so?"

"Well, maybe *you* fancied a little revenge? Maybe *you're* the killer?" He slapped the table and shoved another mouthful of sausage into his giggling mouth.

"Yeah, all right. I did send him a manuscript, which he stupidly rejected. And I might have been a little peeved at the time. Angry enough to slash his car tyres, kidnap his cat and put it on a train to Wales, then break into his office and fill his desk drawers with butterscotch flavour Angel Delight. Possibly. But you can't prove anything. Anyway, that's just standard revenge stuff. I didn't hold a grudge for 11 years until I could enact my murderous revenge. Honestly, I don't have the patience to see something like that through. I'd have given up within a week."

"Hmmm," said Nick, pretending to curl the edge of an imaginary moustache.

"Besides, you can't tell me you never sent him a book over the years. You sent them to everyone else."

"Hey, don't turn your magnifying glass on me," said Nick. "Yeah, I probably did send him a manuscript. In fact, I'm sure I did. I was eager in the early days, emailing agents, editors, publishers, you name it. Probably got about a two-percent response rate out of hundreds of submissions. If I was getting revenge on everyone who snubbed me, there'd be a huge pile of bodies in my wake."

"Max could be the first victim in your murderous rampage," smiled Freddie, pushing a forkful of bacon, donut and melon into his mouth.

"I always say the best revenge is living well. I reckon taking control of my own career, successfully self-publishing three books, getting the attention of an agent who got me a sweet deal with a big publisher and selling over a million copies is revenge enough for me."

"Or is it just an elaborate cover story to divert attention when you do start your killing spree?" laughed Freddie. "And no need to rub it in with the sales figures, you dick."

"Sounds like someone's jealous. But jealous enough to kill?"

The two men laughed.

Nick could be all right, when he wasn't being annoying.

"So, I know I can rule myself out," said Freddie. "And I can probably rule you out, too. But look around you. This place is teaming with sad-sack wannabe novelists, all chasing that same dream. And you can bet they've all got a list of rejections even longer than their dreadful manuscripts. Any one of them could be the killer. Fuck, maybe I should be a bit nicer when I'm giving them feedback."

"Maybe you should."

There was also the book to consider. But Freddie wasn't sharing that clue with Nick. Why the hell was Max clutching a copy of *The Terrible Bones*? And what the hell was all that stuff he'd scribbled inside it?

"Poison. That's a premeditated thing," said Nick. "It's not as if you have an argument, lose your temper, then poison someone."

"True," said Freddie. "If he'd been battered to death, or strangled, or thrown off a balcony, that could be spur of the moment. But you're right, poison takes a bit of planning. I mean, did the killer bring it with them? How did they get it into Max's drink? And how could they be sure he'd even drink it?"

"I heard it was antifreeze," said Nick. "I mean, you could syphon that out of any car in the car park. But getting it into the drink and making sure he'd drink it? Definitely premeditated. The question is, will it stop there?"

"What do you mean?"

"Are there any more victims to come?"

"What makes you think there'll be more?"

"Hey, it's your theory. Disgruntled writer taking revenge on those who rejected them? They could have a beef with a lot more people here."

"Good point," said Freddie, glugging down the rest of his coffee and standing up. "Unfortunately, our investigations will have to pause for now. I'm teaching a writing masterclass in 15 minutes and I haven't even showered yet."

"Good luck," said Nick. "And hey, watch your back."

CHAPTER 9

"WELL, IF YOU'RE not going to listen to me," said Freddie, two thick trails of crimson running from his nostrils as he held Cravat Man in a headlock, "how am I supposed to teach you how to write a bloody book?"

The class was not going well.

Things had started out better than Freddie expected. He'd walked into a room full of the standard writing students. There were a few lurkers he'd seen over the last few days. He saw the strangely familiar guy he'd spotted on the first night – he still didn't know how he recognised him. The weirdo in the hooded jumper was sitting on the back row, trying to blend into the background. And, of course, front and centre sat the dickhead with the cravat.

The audience sat with their notepads and pens poised – eager, attentive students, all convinced Freddie was going to impart the secrets of not only writing a novel, but also how to get it published and, most importantly, how to earn money from it. He could see it sparkling in their eyes. The dream of leaving their dull, uninspiring jobs behind them. The belief that they had something special within them and were destined to become an overnight success. And Freddie held the key to unlocking it. After all, he was a success. He'd spent last summer at the top of the bestseller lists.

What they failed to realise was that Freddie had no idea how to help them unlock their talent. In fact, as he looked out at the starry-eyed morons, he doubted they had more than a thimbleful of talent between them. If the previous night's dreadful readings were anything to go by, they'd have been better off spending the fee they'd paid to be here on something more useful, like a chocolate teapot.

Freddie didn't have the answers to being successful. Yes, he knew how to write books – and pretty good ones, too, if he said so himself. But how to get agents, editors and publishers interested in them? That was getting harder by the day.

And the holy grail of getting enough people to buy your books so you could live off the royalties? That was anybody's guess. Freddie's recent success had been pure fluke. Not to say that it wasn't a good book. He just had no idea when writing it that it would be a success. There was no special sauce that he poured into the first, second or even final draft. The real-life angle of it helped garner interest. And Freddie whoring himself out for TV, radio and newspaper interviews must have helped. But why people had bought his novel, he couldn't say. He wished he did have the secret – he would have been using for the last 20 years.

Which was another thing. Overnight success? Freddie's own personal overnight success had taken him more than 20 years of living in squalor, earning a pittance, fighting hard to get every book published and setting up his own book signings (much to the annoyance of the bookshop owners who had not granted him permission to clear their featured book tables and set up at the back of their store). And his success was running out faster than he'd like. If he didn't stop pissing about with nonsense like this class and write another book, he might find he'd already lost it for good.

Freddie had none of the skills required to teach these people what they wanted to learn. More importantly, he had no desire to teach them. Which was why he hadn't prepared for this class. And why it had descended into anarchy just after the halfway mark. As soon as he saw Cravat Man in the audience, he should have known there was going to be trouble.

He'd started by going around the room, asking people to give their elevator pitch – a short sentence which explained very quickly the unique selling point of their book. He'd then asked the audience to vote on each other's pitches. The idea was to illustrate how hard the publishing industry was, how they needed to sell their book with just a few words, and how they'd need a thick skin to handle rejection.

It was also a great way of getting the class to take care of the first 10 minutes of the session, as he pretended to listen and tried to figure out what else to tell them.

From the way they spoke, Freddie could tell the ones that were keen to learn, and those that were here to be discovered. Sweet but deluded. Some over-confident and closed to feedback. They'd already written a bestseller, thank you very much, and they didn't need help improving it. They just needed to get in front of the right agent, publisher or editor and the bidding war would start. Or failing that, get a fellow writer to fall in love with it and insist their own publisher take it on.

Well, good luck if they thought Freddie was going to be that man.

As Freddie scanned the crowd and noticed the pretty, blonde, twentysomething girl in the front row with the skimpy vest top and sexy glasses pushed halfway down her nose, he decided he shouldn't be too hasty in judging them. After all, it was possible at least one of them had something to work with. And if a little extra tuition – over a late dinner and a handful of cocktails – could help them craft it, who was he to deny them access to his years of experience?

"This class is designed to teach you how to write a successful crime novel with an intriguing plot, interesting characters and engaging, edge-of-your-seat prose," said Freddie. "Listen to the lessons I teach you over the next two hours, and you'll have the keys to writing a book that tells a great story. Something people will want to read. And most importantly, something they'll want to buy."

A hum of excitement buzzed around the room as people eagerly scribbled in their notepads. The pretty blonde smiled at Freddie and he gave her a little wink.

Freddie then set about 'teaching' his class.

He told them about plot and narrative, and how to plan the structure of their stories. He explained the importance of character development, and how the main character needs to go on some kind of journey. He explained how as a writer, you need to torture your characters, putting a series of obstacles in their way – like making them teach a writing class to a bunch of twats when he could be sitting by the pool with a cocktail and a burger, working on his own book. He made sure to just think that last part, and not actually say it.

He got lost for five minutes, delivering an angry rant about online book reviews and how the people who leave bad ones "wouldn't be that bloody brave if they saw him in the street". He saw the horror on his students' faces, and quickly lightened the mood with a humorous anecdote about the time he saw James Patterson at a literary festival and slipped a couple of sleeping pills into his drink half an hour before he was due to go on stage and give a speech.

Freddie continued blabbering for a good hour, covering some key points, going off on a few wild, rambling digressions, but generally keeping it together. When he ran out of steam, he invited the pretty blonde to read the first couple of pages of her manuscript, so he could give live feedback.

Her writing was awful, of course. But Freddie held back on the vitriol, offering some genuinely useful thoughts on how she might try and polish the giant turd she was holding (although, again, he remembered not to actually say that final part).

It wasn't long, however, before some people in the crowd got restless. They wanted to be the centre of attention, receiving one-on-one tutorials and impressing the rest of the room with their literary genius. It finally came to a head when the twat in the cravat stood up and said, "I'm sorry, but I don't think you know what you're talking about. You clearly haven't prepared for this. And you barely seem bothered to be here in the first place – aside from perving over young women."

"Perving?" said Freddie. "If you mean…"

"You've barely given anyone else a chance to speak in the last hour. You're just trying to get into her knickers."

The blonde opened her mouth to speak, but Freddie raised a hand to stop her. He took a deep breath and sighed loudly, shaking his head as patronisingly as he could.

"Now, this, ladies and gentlemen," said Freddie, "is what I like to call a teachable moment."

Bullshit, of course. It was something he once saw someone say in a dreadful American TV movie and he figured it sounded like the sort of thing someone teaching a class might say.

"There are basically two types of writers: those who are curious, dedicated and keen to learn." He stood up from his chair and started pacing in front of the crowd. "After all, as writers, aren't we really observers? Aren't we always learning? Finding new ways to tell our stories and paint the world as we see it?"

It was getting really wanky now and he could barely keep the smile from his face.

"Aren't we always striving to find inner truth and pour the beauty within our hearts out onto the page?"

That was it. He had to turn and face the other way, biting his tongue to stop himself laughing. He turned back to see people looking up in awe, scribbling this guff into their notepads.

"But there's the other kind of writer," said Freddie, turning the corners of his mouth down. "Those who think they already know everything." He shook his head for emphasis. "They believe they've already written the perfect novel. Not a word could be improved. No amount of help, advice or constructive criticism could benefit them. They're lost in the delusion of their own genius. And that's why – the very saddest thing of all – they'll never realise just how bad their work really is. Now, take my fourth novel…"

"Fucking bollocks," interrupted Cravat Man. "So you're saying my book is no good, are you? How could you possibly know? You haven't read it."

"You're right," said Freddie. "I haven't read it. But once again, you fail to understand what I'm saying. It's not all about the words on the page. It's about attitude. It's about listening. It's about the ability to look at ourselves and our work under the microscope and examine what we are."

People continued furiously scribbling notes.

"Without that ability to learn, how can anyone really expect to write?" He was going overboard now. His voice had slowed, elongating words so he sounded like some mystical guru giving a lecture on inner peace. "Another teachable moment, and possibly the hardest one you'll ever hear. Some people – no matter how hard they try – just don't have what it takes to be a writer. And I'm afraid our friend in the cravat is one of them."

Very slowly, very calmly, Cravat Man placed his notepad and pen on his chair. Without saying a word, he shuffled past the other people in his row and walked to the front of the room. He stood face-to-face with Freddie, looked him in the eyes for a few seconds, and then punched him square in the nose.

Freddie lurched backwards, pain exploding in his face, tears streaming from his eyes. He stumbled, just managing to stay upright, coughing and spluttering as hot blood poured from his nose.

"You fucking prick," he said.

Then he lurched forwards, lunging at Cravat Man.

He threw out a fist, attempting to connect with the man's chin, but the tears in his eyes and his wobbly legs had thrown his depth perception way off. Instead, he ended up connecting with Cravat Man's ear, which elicited a wild, high-pitched scream. Connecting with the side of a skull, rather than a fragile chin, also hurt Freddie's hand more than expected, and he screamed even louder than the man he'd punched.

Cravat Man fell forwards, arms flailing as he grabbed Freddie in a loose bear hug. Freddie retaliated, twisting this way and that as the two men struggled against each other, like two drunk seals doing the tango. They slithered and writhed, bumped and twisted, until Freddie somehow managed to wrap his arms around Cravat Man's neck. He straightened up, just about managing to stand. He pulled and tightened his grip until his opponent went limp in surrender.

Ten seconds later, the doors to the conference room opened and in walked a very panicked-looking Dan. He was followed very quickly afterwards by Inspector Perez and the hotel manager. The Inspector's black-clad pet police officers had multiplied and eight of them filed into the room, fanning out to surround the group.

Freddie released his grip on Cravat Man's neck and the two straightened up like naughty schoolboys caught out by their teacher.

"Ladies and gentlemen," said the hotel manager, "I'm afraid today's class will be finishing early."

He was a short, balding man with a bulbous stomach and a thick, bushy moustache. He, too, spoke very good English, but he spoke with a slow, determined voice to make certain he could be understood. His face remained straight and calm, like this was nothing out of the ordinary. Like he was clearing the building as part of a fire drill he'd done a thousand times before. But something in his eyes suggested just a hint of fear.

"I'm going to have to ask you all to return to your rooms and remain there for the time being. The pools, restaurants, spa and all communal areas are currently closed, and the hotel has been placed under lockdown."

The crowd erupted into panic, bustling and grumbling.

"What the fuck?" said a man in a t-shirt slightly redder than his sunburned face. "What do you mean, lockdown?"

"What's happened?" said a scared, elderly woman. "Has there been a terrorist attack?"

"Does this mean we won't be getting our book samples reviewed?" said a man with a Hawaiian shirt and an obvious comb-over.

"I'm sorry," said the manager. "We've had an... incident at the hotel and the police have asked us to lock the place down. Nobody is allowed in or out, and we're asking all our guests to remain in their rooms." He gave a weak smile. "We'll give you more information when we can. But in the meantime, please head back to your rooms and wait there."

The crowd humphed and cursed.

"What the hell's going on?" said Freddie, looking at Perez. She remained quiet, staring at the group, assessing each one of them in turn.

Freddie looked to Dan. His face was pale. His eyes watery. His voice wobbled as he spoke, and he sounded like he might burst into tears at any second. "It's, er, it's... happened again."

CHAPTER 10

"YOU SEEM TO make people angry, don't you, Mr Winters?"

Freddie was sitting in the Hotel Manager's office, Perez looking down at him as two uniformed officers stood guard at the door. Dan was sitting on the other side of the room, in front of the large bank of security monitors, hyperventilating with his head in his hands. The atmosphere in the room was tense. The Inspector seemed worried. The other officers were even more stony-faced than before.

"Why would you say that?" asked Freddie.

"The first time we met, you'd recently had an argument with Max Powers. Now you have a broken nose and two black eyes. And when we entered the room you were holding that other man in a headlock."

"That was just a heated literary debate," said Freddie, forcing a fake laugh.

Something was up. Something bad. And he didn't want to be in the firing line for it.

"Really?" said Perez. "What were you debating?"

"Well, he thought he was a good writer. I was of the opinion that he was shit. We went back and forth with our arguments until he punched me in the face. We had a minor literary tussle, and that's when you came in. Why was that, exactly? And why is the hotel under lockdown?"

The edges of Perez's mouth curled up slightly for just a second. Somewhere in the background Dan whimpered like a forlorn toddler who'd lost his favourite stuffed toy.

"Where were you last night between the hours of 11pm and 3am?" said Perez, pulling out a small notepad and pen.

"Christ knows," laughed Freddie, "I was pissed as a fart."

Perez didn't laugh along. She seemed to get even more irritated and stony-faced.

"I mean to say," said Freddie, sensing the tone in the room, "I did the Readathon thing down by the pool. That lasted until about 9pm. Then I went to the bar with Malcolm and Michaela."

"Malcolm and Michaela?" asked Perez.

"Erm… Malcolm Alexander and Michaela Kemp," said Freddie.

"And who are they?" said Perez, scribbling in her notepad.

It was obvious she already knew who they were, but he played along anyway. "Two of the other judges from the Readathon. Michaela is a fellow novelist. And Malcolm is a publisher. Bit of a shit, but surprisingly all right to have a drink with."

"Go on."

"We sat and drank for a few hours. Michaela left first. Then Malcolm headed off and I went in search of the snack bar. All a bit foggy after that, to be honest. I seem to remember getting a hotdog and a bit of chocolate cake. Then I headed back to my room. Woke up still fully clothed at about nine-ish this morning."

"And can anybody confirm this?"

"Yes. Michaela and Malcolm can."

"And what about after you left the bar?"

"I don't know. I went to the snack bar on my own. I don't remember if I bumped into anyone. Then I went to my room alone. Seriously, what is this about? Dan, you said it's happened again. What did you mean?"

Dan didn't speak. He just sat there, looking at the floor.

"And who else was in the bar?" asked Perez.

"I don't know, I didn't take a bloody register," said Freddie. "It was the bar specially reserved for writers and industry people. There were a few I recognised and quite a lot I don't know. I'm sorry, but will somebody please tell me what the hell's going on?"

Perez walked around to the other side of the desk, sat down and placed her notepad and pen in front of her. She looked at Freddie for a few seconds, silently squaring him up.

Then she said, "Malcom Alexander was murdered in his hotel room last night. And you were one of the last people to see him alive."

"Fuck," said Freddie.

"Yes," said Perez.

"Oh God, oh God, oh God," whimpered Dan at the back of the room.

"You seem to be making a bit of a habit out of this, Mr Winters," said Perez. "Two people have been murdered in this hotel in the last two days, and you're right there at the centre of things. Can you explain that?"

"I… erm… I… but… I… oh, fuck!"

"Yes," said Perez.

"The cameras," said Freddie, pointing out the bank of monitors on the other side of the room. "You can check the cameras. They're all round the hotel. You'll see me going back to my room alone."

"Yes, I seem to remember you having the same idea the last time we spoke," said Perez.

"There you go, then," said Freddie, sitting back and crossing his arms with a smug grin.

"I did actually think to do that myself. You know, being a police detective. But somebody disabled the cameras."

"You… er… what?"

"The cameras show you all entering the bar. They also show you leaving the bar alone at around 10pm. Then, mysteriously, the cameras were disabled. They were all still on, but nothing was recorded. So we don't know where you were, and your story isn't adding up."

"Hang on, around 10?" said Freddie, thinking. "Yeah, okay, I did leave the bar briefly. But I went straight back and carried on drinking. I was gone for, like… five minutes. I certainly wasn't running around disabling security cameras. I wouldn't even know how."

"Well, that's not true, is it, Mr Winters?"

"What?"

"You were in this room yesterday. You had plenty of time to get a good view of the monitors. Plenty of time to see what areas of the hotel are covered and which aren't. Plenty of time to see what kind of recording equipment they use."

"What are you saying?" said Freddie, his mouth turning dryer than a week-old pitta bread.

"I've been doing some reading since we met yesterday. A bit of research into you. You're a crime novelist, aren't you? Not a very good one…"

"Hey!" interrupted Freddie instinctively.

"As I was saying, not a very good one, but you do spend your days thinking of ways to kill people. And more importantly, how to get away with it."

"Inspector Perez, that describes about half the people in this hotel," argued Freddie.

"Yes, but not all the other writers have been so close to the two victims."

"You don't know that. They could have been."

Perez shrugged. "Maybe. But you're the only one lying to me."

"Lying? About what?"

"You said you don't know how to disable the cameras. That's not true is it? In your book, *Death on Floor 29*, the murderer's plan for killing their boss revolves around making sure they're alone in a specific room at a specific time. The killer then sneaks around the building, using a series of disguises and camera dark spots, disables the security cameras, then heads back and throws their boss down an elevator shaft. All without being seen. So you do know about disabling cameras and sneaking about buildings unseen, don't you?"

"You've read one of my books?" said Freddie, smiling. "Well, it's always nice to meet a fan."

"Skim-read," said Perez. "When we met yesterday, I knew there was something suspicious about you, so I had my team track down copies of your books. Not easy. Most of them are out of print."

"All right, no need to rub it in," said Freddie.

"We skimmed through them, looking for anybody killed by poison."

"I could have saved you the trouble. I've never done a poisoning. Although I might now, having seen how effective it is."

Perez raised her eyebrows.

Freddie coughed and winced and stared at the floor.

"But you do know how to disable security cameras. You go into detail about how the killer researched security systems, learned how to hack them, and how to stop them recording. That's all research you must have done yourself."

Freddie sat silently, weighing up his options.

Finally, he said, "All right, yes. You're right. It looks like a simple system from here. You've got eight monitors, all subdivided into eight images. The images are static, they're not flipping from one shot to the next. That means you've got 64 cameras around the building and what you see is what's being filmed. The main hotel areas, obviously. The pools, restaurants, parts of some of the bars. Some of the larger corridors, but not all of them. It's easy to see what areas are being covered, and with a bit of planning you could figure out which bits aren't. So it wouldn't be hard to make it around the hotel without being spotted. As in my book, you might need a disguise or two to make it past a couple of cameras, but that's easily done.

"The recording equipment itself looks basic. Just a simple plug-and-play device with all the main controls on the actual unit. Maybe five or six years old, at a guess. It probably has a small hard drive built in, but I can also see that it's plugged into the computer tower under the desk, so they'll have all the footage backed up to that. No surprise, with all that footage. Although, with such a lacklustre system, they might not even be recording all 64 cameras.

"Done right, you could probably password protect it to prevent access. But it's not locked away, so they've probably been a bit lax in that area too. Best guess, if you wanted to disable the cameras, you'd sneak in here when it's quiet or empty, press the button on the front of the unit to stop it recording, then sneak back later to turn it on again. The cameras would all stay active, but they wouldn't be recording, so it would appear as normal, unless someone was really looking. And judging by the Post-it note next to the record button that says 'No presionar', I'm guessing nobody would expect it to have been turned off. So it could go unnoticed for some time."

Freddie sat back, crossed his arms, and grinned just a little too smugly.

"So, you admit you were lying?"

"Eh? What…" said Freddie, a cold shiver of regret coursing down his spine. "I… er…"

"Why lie about it?"

"Look, just because I've done a bit of research, doesn't make me a killer. Yes, I wrote a book with a plot that features disabling security cameras. And yes, I did some research into how you would do it. Over the years I've planned and carried out dozens of literary murders. I'm careful. I'm clever. I'm intricate. And I'm damned good at it. If I wanted to be a murderer, I'd be damned good at that, too. But just because I could kill someone, doesn't mean I actually did. So, of course I lied about it because I'm not stupid. I know how it looks."

"And why should I believe you now?"

Freddie sighed. He looked at the bank of monitors. Then it hit him. "Check the footage," he said.

"What?" said Perez.

"You know what time the cameras stopped recording. So just check the footage for a few minutes before that and see who walked into this office."

Perez sighed and shook her head. "There you go again, Mr Winters. Don't you think I already did that? Of course, we checked the footage. But there isn't any. Not only did someone stop the cameras from recording; they also went onto the computer and deleted everything from the previous week. It was there yesterday when we checked it. But today it's gone. So, we don't know when the cameras were disabled, but we know it was some time in the last 24 hours. And, as you've just told us, that's something else you'd know how to do."

Shit! Of course, she'd have checked it. And, of course, the killer would have deleted the footage to cover their tracks. Freddie was making himself look like a right tit. And a guilty one at that.

"Sorry. I just thought it was…"

"Where did you go?" said Perez, cutting him off.

"Sorry?"

"You said you left the bar briefly and returned. Where did you go?"

"I'd… er… I'd rather not say…"

"Really? Well, I'd rather you do say," said Perez. She flashed a look at her two pet police officers at the door, who straightened, placing their hands noisily on their holstered guns.

Freddie knew it was all for show. They weren't actually going to shoot him. But judging by the tiny amount of wee that leaked out into his shorts, it still had the desired effect of intimidating him.

"It really doesn't matter where I went…" he said.

"Mr Winters, this is a double murder investigation. So far, I've kept things civil. But if you don't tell me what I want to know, or if I suspect you're keeping things from me, we can go back to the police station and I can be less… civil."

"It really doesn't matter where I went."

"Tell me."

"Honestly," said Freddie. "It's completely immaterial…"

"Mr Winters," shouted Perez, banging her fist onto the desk.

"I was washing my balls," said Freddie.

He sighed loudly and stared at the floor.

"I'm sorry… what did you say?"

"I was washing my balls," he repeated, sounding even more embarrassed. "I was in the bar, and I was hitting it off pretty well with

Michaela. I thought my luck might be in. But I'd also worked up quite a sweat during the day. And no woman wants to be presented with a whiffy crotch, no matter how drunk they are. So, I nipped back to my room to give the old tackle a quick wash, then I went straight back to the bar."

Perez sat open-mouthed for a few seconds, her eyebrows so high they were in danger of pinging right off her head.

"And I don't suppose anyone can verify this?" she said, rubbing her eyes with her fingers.

"Yes, of course, just ask my butler. He was doing the scrubbing," said Freddie, unable to contain his natural snarkiness.

"You're not really helping yourself, Mr Winters. You were one of the last people to see the two victims alive. You have no alibi for the time of death of either of the victims. You've admitted you know how to disable security cameras. And you left Mr Alexander for long enough that you could stop the cameras recording, leaving you able to sneak around the hotel unseen. And worst of all, Mr Winters, you lied to me. Tell me, as a crime novelist, how would you say things are looking for you right now?"

Freddie sighed heavily. "Not good. But you're forgetting one key ingredient. Motive. Why would I want to kill Malcolm Alexander?"

"That's what I'm trying to figure out," said Perez.

"I get how things might look suspicious with Max. I didn't particularly like him. And it looks bad that we argued – quite publicly – then the next day he turns up dead. But I swear I didn't kill him. I might have thought the guy was a dick, but I wouldn't want him dead.

"And Malcolm? Last night was the first time I ever really met him. The guy was an arsehole, but we got on. Kindred spirits, I guess. He was a laugh. We spent a pleasant evening getting pissed and talking about books. And that's it. I had no reason to want him dead. And no plan to sneak around the hotel unseen and… and… and then I have no fucking idea. I don't even know how, when or where he was killed. I mean, are you sure it was murder?"

Perez stiffened like a cat with its hackles up. "I can assure you, Mr Winters, I know a murder scene when I see one. I haven't figured out why you would want to kill Mr Alexander. But I'm watching you. Killers always slip up and, when you do, I'll be there to catch you. In the meantime, the hotel is under lockdown. Don't try to leave. My officers will escort you back to your room. You can also give them the clothes you were wearing last night. I assume you still have them?"

"My clothes? Yes, but…"

Perez stood up from the desk and made to leave as one of the black-clad officers turned and walked towards Freddie.

"How did he die?" said Freddie.

Perez stopped, gesturing for the officer to wait.

"How was he killed?" continued Freddie. "Was it poison as well? Did the killer leave anything in the room, like the book from before?"

Perez froze. Something in her eyes.

"There was something, wasn't there? The killer left something at the scene. What was it? Another book? A pen?"

"Why would you say pen?" said Perez, her eyebrow arching.

"I don't know. Next obvious thing that occurred to me. Book, pen, phone, candlestick…"

"Candlestick?"

"Have you never played Cluedo?"

A curious smile sneaked onto her lips.

"Talk to me, Inspector Perez. You said it yourself; I spend my days planning how to kill people and get away with it. I might be able to help. I had a friend back in England. A detective who I spent a lot of time with, helping him with his cases to pick up inspiration for my books. His name is DI Richard…"

"Stone," said Perez, cutting him off. "Oh, I know all about you and DI Stone."

"Really?" said Freddie, taken aback.

"I told you: I've been doing my research. I called Scotland Yard and spoke with Inspector Stone. He had a lot to say about you."

"Really?" said Freddie, a nervous laugh escaping his lips. "All good, I hope."

"He told me you were the…" She picked up her notebook, flicked through the pages and read from it. "…most devious, untrustworthy, skitchy? Sketchy? I'm sorry, I don't know this word, but I'm guessing it's bad. Unreliable, annoying, cowardly, backstabbing, shitty excuse for a human being he's ever met."

"Hmmm, could be worse," smiled Freddie.

"He told me not to trust you, not to listen to you and, if I get the chance, to lock you up for as long as possible. Not exactly a fan."

"Well, we had kind of a… disagreement…"

"Yes, you seem to have lots of those, don't you? Alejandro, please take Mr Winters back to his room."

The black-clad officer grabbed Freddie roughly by the arm and pulled him up out of the chair. He dragged him across the room towards the door.

"Oh, and Mr Winters…" said Perez.

Alejandro ceased his dragging. Freddie looked back at the Inspector.

"Just so you know," she said, "Mr Alexander was stabbed to death. With a pen."

"Oh fuck," said Freddie.

*****

This was not good. Why did he have to say pen? Why didn't he just keep his big mouth shut? And what was all that about the security cameras, showing off and trying to make himself look smart?

Seriously, what a dick.

Freddie walked into his hotel room and slammed the door in the face of the police officer who'd escorted him there. He opened his minibar and punched the air in celebration. Despite all the murders, chaos and hotel lockdown, the maid had still been in to make up the bed, clean the bathroom and re-stock his minibar. He really must remember to leave her a tip.

He poured himself a gin and tonic and sat down on the sofa, gazing out the window at the abandoned swimming pool and the eerie scenes of the empty hotel.

This was not good. Somehow, he'd landed himself as the main suspect for a double murder. Assuming it was a double murder. Maybe the two killings weren't linked. Could it have been two separate killers, bumping off their intended victims without any knowledge of each other? A bit far-fetched, he thought. Although, it could make for an interesting plot twist. He made a mental note to explore that further for a book. For now, it made more sense to assume it was one killer on a spree. But what was next? Had the killer completed their roster of victims, or were there more to come? And was Freddie's name on that list?

Why would somebody want to kill both Max and Malcolm? There was no obvious connection between the two. He pulled out his phone, logged into the hotel free Wi-Fi and started Googling.

Freddie already knew Max had worked for Malcolm's company, Darkhouse Publishing, as an editor. He'd worked on several of Edward Cross's books, including the one he'd been found dead with. Freddie hadn't realised, however, that Malcolm had also published Max's book. He found a news story on The Bookseller website with the headline: *Darkhouse signs former editor in million-pound deal.* The story told how Malcolm had secured the rights to Max's first book for a huge advance – much more than a debut author would usually get, especially without a bidding war between rival publishers.

It also seemed out of character for Malcolm. The man was renowned for screwing over authors with measly advances. The book was crap as well. Certainly not original or likely to be a sure-fire hit. So, why the big payday for Max? Something didn't add up.

Freddie found an article on the Guardian website – a sycophantic interview with Max, which heralded his meteoric rise from editor to author. There were quotes from Max, saying how Darkhouse had supported his move and how privileged he felt to be published by them. There were quotes from Malcolm, extolling Max's literary genius, and patting himself on the back for discovering Max's talents. The whole thing was so saccharine, Freddie thought he might throw up in his mouth.

A bit more Googling and Freddie didn't come across anything revelatory about the two men or their relationship. Nothing dark or duplicitous. And nothing that marked them down as potential murder victims. So, what the hell was going on? Who would want to kill these two men, and why?

More importantly, how was Freddie going to get Inspector Perez to stop suspecting him?

There was only one thing for it. He'd have to solve this case himself. But to do that, he'd have to see what he was working with. He had to get a look at the crime scene and see how Malcolm had been killed. He needed to inspect the murder weapon. He had to sweep Malcolm's hotel room for clues and see if the killer had left anything.

There was just one problem. How the fuck was he going to do any of that?

CHAPTER 11

FREDDIE SPENT THE next hour in his hotel room, ruminating, Googling and making notes. But there was only so much he could do there. Without having a look at the crime scene, there was no way to know what really happened. Plus, the closer he stayed to his rapidly depleting minibar, the more prone he was to becoming drunk and sleepy, and losing focus entirely. He had to get out of his room and start properly investigating.

He grabbed his trusty notepad and pen, then fished something out of his trousers hanging in the wardrobe. Thank God he'd thought to carry it in his pocket, rather than in his suitcase. Fearing Perez might have left her goon stationed outside, he very slowly, very gingerly opened the door and peered outside.

The hallway was empty. Eerily quiet apart from the noise of TVs in bedrooms and the distant grumbling of holidaymakers peeved at being confined to their rooms. Freddie cautiously stepped out into the corridor, careful to make as little noise as possible. He'd need to be quick. He wasn't sure how long he'd be able to move around the hotel unnoticed. Perez was clearly aware of the security cameras, which would be filming him right now. And the place was crawling with police.

He had to get to Malcolm's room. Trouble is, he had no idea which room it was.

Freddie hustled down the corridor, moving as quickly and quietly as he could. He made it outside, dashed across the courtyard and past the main swimming pool, traversing through the mess of sunbeds. He sneaked in through the main doors, hugging the wall as he moved, and managing to avoid the attention of the two police officers stationed there. Then he dashed across the large hall.

The reception desk was abandoned. All the staff were conveniently congregating in the large conference room. The manager was up on stage, talking very quickly. Freddie didn't speak much Spanish, but he could understand the odd word. It sounded like he was debriefing the staff on the events of the past few days and informing them that the hotel was locked down. From the huge sigh that erupted from the crowd, Freddie assumed the manager had just announced that all leave was cancelled, and personnel were required to remain on site. And when he heard an even bigger, more disgruntled sigh, he knew they'd just been told there was still a hotel full of pissed-off guests to look after.

Freddie tiptoed across the hallway and sneaked behind the reception desk. He wiggled a mouse to make the computer screen come to life, then sighed when it revealed he'd need a password to get in. Shit! He sighed, ran his hands through his hair and thought.

Several years ago, while researching his novel *Half Past Dead*, Freddie had spent time with a few nefarious characters who, in exchange for Freddie buying lots of rounds of drinks, had revealed the devious methods they used for relieving unsuspecting people of their money. He'd learned about fake email scams, phone scams, identity theft, credit card fraud, and creating and planting computer viruses that let you steal people's personal details.

One particularly devious chap – affectionately dubbed Wanker Pete by the others on account of how ruthless he was – tutored Freddie in the various ways to work out someone's online passwords.

"People are idiots," he'd said. "The amount of people whose password is actually 'password', you wouldn't believe. Or they worry they're gonna forget 'em so they pick fings that are deeply ingrained in their memories. But they fink they're fings only they know. So, they fink they're safe. Trouble is; dodgy bastards like me can figure that shit out in seconds. You ever do one of those stupid online fings, where you find out your pornstar name or your rapper name by adding your first pet's name to your mother's maiden name, or the first street you lived on, or the name of your school or summink stupid like that? I guarantee you; someone somewhere is looking at those names and rubbing their hands. Cos that's the shit people use for passwords. Once you've got that info, you're in. Either people are so dumb they just use the words as they are. Or you go through and change an I to a 1 or and E to a 3. It's much easier than you'd fink."

Freddie looked around the desk, tapping his chin for inspiration. He had no idea whose computer it was, or any personal details about them. Plus, whoever used this computer was most likely Spanish, so the language barrier added another level of complexity.

Then Freddie remembered something else Wanker Pete had told him. "Not only do people pick the easiest passwords possible, nine times out of ten, they've written it down somewhere. And they leave it right next to the computer."

Freddie started picking up random objects on the desk and inspecting them. He ran his hands along the underside of the desk and across the back of the computer monitor. He sifted through a stack of papers next to the machine, then lifted the computer keyboard and flipped it over. Bingo. There it was. A Post-it note with all the login details he needed. Good old Wanker Pete.

Freddie logged into the computer and opened a database with all the hotel room numbers and corresponding guests' names. He scanned down until he found Malcolm's room, then put the computer back to sleep.

He made his way quickly through the hotel, carefully avoiding policemen, until he came to the right corridor. A policeman was standing guard outside a door. Malcolm's room.

All right, Freddie, he thought to himself, be big and bold. Be confident. And hope that copper isn't one of the ones you've already met.

Freddie marched along the hall with purpose. He approached the policeman and looked him square in the eyes. He pulled something from his pocket and showed it to the officer.

"Detective Inspector Richard Stone," said Freddie. "I'm here to consult with Inspector Perez. I'll need to get into that room and inspect the scene."

The man looked at the fake police warrant card in Freddie's hand. Another thing Wanker Pete had been particularly useful in helping Freddie acquire was a collection of fake documents – the warrant card being one of them.

Back in the day, Freddie had enjoyed a fruitful relationship with the real DI Richard Stone. He'd shadowed him for research and to help him get all the little details about police work right. It had helped Freddie's writing no end. He and Richard quickly became friends, spending hours at crime scenes, drinking tea at the station or downing pints together at the pub – always talking about Richard's job and how he went about solving crimes. Freddie even ended up consulting on a few cases, helping Richard work through clues, determine motives and catch the bad guys.

Unfortunately, Freddie decided to use DI Stone as inspiration for the main character in his next book – albeit a heavily twisted, corrupt and morally bankrupt version of the man. Where the real Richard was a jovial family man who loved his wife, loved his kids, never questioned authority and always did everything by the book, his literary counterpart was quite the opposite. He was a real dick. A grizzled, functioning alcoholic who hated his bosses, lived and worked by his own code of conduct, cheated on his wife and had a loose interpretation of the law – more than happy to break it when it served his purpose.

The real mistake Freddie made was using Richard's actual name, changing it only slightly to Dick Stone. Richard's wife and colleagues found it hard to separate fact from fiction. Where there's smoke, there's fire. Before he knew it, Richard was being interrogated by his superiors, who feared the fictional character's wrongdoings were based in truth. Richard's wife also suspected that Freddie's hard-drinking, gambling, womanising character couldn't have been completely made up, and started suspecting her husband of having done similar horrible things to those in Freddie's book. And then she left him.

Naturally, Freddie was devastated when he saw the fallout of his literary creation. Try as he might to plead with Richard's wife, and explain it was all fictional, he couldn't make her believe it. Why had he used Richard's real name? How could he have been so short-sighted? He'd have done anything to go back and change it, but the damage was done. Nothing Freddie said or did could change it.

Having inadvertently ended the poor man's marriage, and nearly derailed his entire career, Freddie's relationship with Richard soured instantly. Richard refused to speak with him, let alone consult on any future cases. And Freddie knew Richard could easily have had him arrested and imprisoned on some trumped-up charge for revenge – the irony being that it was only because he was such a good, honest detective that he didn't. The worst of it wasn't that Freddie had lost his police consultant – he'd really grown to like Richard and ended up losing the best friend he'd made in years.

No longer able to accompany Richard to crime scenes for inspiration, Freddie instead came up with the very effective ruse of turning up *as* him. He paid Wanker Pete five hundred quid for a fake warrant card with Richard's name on, and he suddenly had instant access to any crime scene, court or police station he wanted to visit. It also came in handy for getting out of speeding tickets, shooing away busybodies in coffee shops that wanted to share his table, getting the odd free drink or meal in pubs and restaurants, and intimidating people he just didn't like the look of. Best five hundred quid he ever spent.

The police officer gazed at the warrant card, inspecting the blue bar at the top which held the small crest and the words Metropolitan Police. He read the words Detective Inspector and the name Richard Stone. Then he looked Freddie up and down, taking in the bright blue shorts he was wearing, and the yellow Hawaiian shirt dotted with little pictures of blue sharks. He raised a quizzical eyebrow.

"Yes, I know," sighed Freddie. "I'm not even on duty. I'm on holiday down the road with the wife and kids. Perez called me. We go way back. Worked together a few years ago when she was seconded to Scotland Yard."

He had no idea how well this man knew the inspector, but it never hurt to drop the odd extra detail to make a lie more realistic.

"Anyway, apparently a couple of Brits have been killed here. She asked if I'd pop over and take a look. So, if you don't mind..." He pointed at the door.

The police officer looked him up and down again. He stared at the warrant card for a few more seconds. Then he nodded and stood aside. Freddie took a long, deep breath, prayed that Perez wasn't inside the room, then pushed the door open and walked in.

"Hello?" said Freddie, cautiously. "Anybody here? I'm Detective Inspector Richard…"

No reply. Freddie sighed with relief. But he didn't have much time. Perez or a forensics team could be there any second. He stepped into the room and closed the door behind him.

The first thing that hit him was the smell. A dank, pungent, sickly sweet aroma that invaded his nostrils and made him cough. Freddie moved along the corridor, into the main bedroom, the stench of rotting meat and the metallic tang of iron from the drying blood growing stronger as he walked. The body was right there in front of him. Malcolm Alexander twisted and prostrate. Covered in blood and very obviously dead.

It was a horrific scene, like something out of a horror film. Swathes of crimson surrounding the body, leaking out and pooling in large puddles on the tiled floor. Blood spatter was sprayed up the walls, speckling the bed sheets and arcing up over the ceiling in a series of random curved lines.

And what the fuck? This room was easily twice the size of Freddie's room. Cheeky bastards. I mean, that really took the piss. Freddie was supposed to be one of the stars of this week. And he got stuffed up in some tiny room, while Malcolm got the extra special treatment? Unbelievable.

Freddie stepped nearer to the body. He peered in closer. Shuddered slightly as he looked at the man's face. Freddie had seen dead bodies before. He'd been to lots of crime scenes and witnessed things far more horrific than this. But it had never been somebody he knew. Someone he'd been chatting and drinking and laughing with less than 24 hours previously.

Malcolm was slumped at the end of the bed. His body was bent into a strange shape where he'd hit the ground. His mouth was contorted into a wide, surprised, soundless scream, a small pool of blood congealing in the back of his throat. His face, hair and clothes were drenched with thick, sticky blood, which was turning dark brown as it dried. His shirt was ripped in several places. The skin on his neck, face and chest was peppered with tiny, blood-soaked puncture marks. And there was a silver pen sticking right out of his left eye.

The sun shining in through the large patio doors made the pen glint and wink. Was that the special deal-signing pen Freddie had heard about?

Freddie scanned the room. Nothing odd or out of place. Nothing strange or unexpected. The bed was still fully made, albeit drenched in blood, which meant Malcolm hadn't made it to bed. The cushions on the sofa looked plump, suggesting they hadn't been moved or sat on. Chairs were still neatly tucked in under the table, as was the chair in front of the desk opposite the bed. No glasses on the table. No empty miniature bottles or beer cans. Aside from the corpse and the litres of spilled blood, there was nothing to suggest the room had been touched since the maid last cleaned it.

Freddie spotted a small wastepaper bin pushed right in under the desk. The maid could easily have missed it there. He pulled it out and peered inside. Two used condom wrappers. Who had he been entertaining? There was a receipt from the hotel shop for a large bottle of water, a bottle of sun cream and a Magnum ice lolly. There was also a crumpled piece of paper, which he picked up and unscrewed. It bore the name and logo of the hotel and matched the complimentary pad on the side. A handwritten note read: *Tuesday 11.30. Meeting with RF. New book? Opportunity?*

Interesting.

Freddie placed the note back and fished out a tiny glass bottle. The label read: *Vape Flave, Butterscotch Flavour.* Weird. Malcolm wasn't a smoker. Or a vaper. The whole night they'd been together – at the Readathon event, then in the bar afterwards – Freddie hadn't once seen him pop out for a vape. So, whose was it?

Freddie was sure he'd seen that old hag Marylin Sharpe sucking on a big vape machine. But then Helen Brennan was also a vaper, as was Patrick Marcombe and Michaela Kemp. At least a quarter of the other authors and attendees at the event had been puffing away on the things. You couldn't walk 10 metres through the hotel complex without being bombarded with the whiff of candyfloss, strawberry, watermelon or cappuccino vape clouds. Didn't anyone smoke good old-fashioned cigarettes anymore?

The used condom wrappers in the bin must have been from the previous evening. The room was too untouched for him to have done anything in there last night other than get murdered.

Malcolm must have left the bar, come back to his room and been killed almost straight away. Had the killer been waiting in the room? If so, how did they get in? The balcony doors were locked, so they hadn't come in that way. But then, if the killer had been smart enough to disable the cameras, could they also have programmed a replica key card for Malcolm's room?

Maybe the killer had followed Malcom back to his room, sneaked up behind him and forced their way through the door as he opened it? Or was it someone Malcolm had known? Someone he'd invited back to his room?

Freddie dashed around, conscious he could be interrupted at any minute. There was nothing in the bathroom. Nothing strange or suspicious on the balcony, in the hallway, in the large wardrobe, the back of the cupboards or on the long dressing table.

And then Freddie found it. Hidden in the bedside drawer was a paperback copy of *The Terrible Bones* by Edward Cross.

Freddie exhaled loudly as he saw it. His hand shook as he reached forward and picked it up. It was brand new, the cover still taught and shiny, the pages crisp with that unmistakable new book smell. The cover was different to the one he'd found next to Max's body. That one was from the original print run, whereas this one was from a more recent reissue.

Freddie opened the cover and flicked through the pages. And there it was. The same words circled and highlighted: *liar*, *cheat*, *thief* and so on. The same manic writing, growing bigger, wilder and more aggressive as he kept on flicking through.

Freddie carefully placed the book back in the drawer. Then, remembering something he'd seen in a film, he picked it up again and wiped it all over with the hem of his shirt. He dropped it back into the drawer, then looked around the room. Shit. Had he touched anything else? Only the doorknob. And various drawers and cupboards. And the bin. And the contents of the bin. Bollocks. The last thing he needed was the police finding his fingerprints in the room. It already looked bad enough for him without that.

Freddie scanned the room again. He heard noises outside in the hallway. He had to get out of there. He dashed over to the bin, grabbed a handful of tissues from the box on the side, and wiped the bin all over. He did the same to the tiny bottle, the condom wrappers and the bits of paper, then ran around wiping anything else he'd touched. He tiptoed to the door and wiped the handle.

The noises in the hallway grew louder. Footsteps and voices. Shit. He had to get out of there. He pulled open the door, wiping the outside handle with the tissues as he nodded at the guard outside.

About 20 feet away, at the other end of the corridor, he saw a man and a woman, both wearing bright, white, full-body plastic suits. They were each carrying a large, black holdall emblazoned with the word POLICIA. As they met his gaze, they both looked confused and started walking quicker towards him.

"Thanks. All done now," said Freddie to the police officer. "Tell Perez I'll call her later. Oh good, looks like the forensics team are finally here."

He patted the officer on the shoulder and walked off down the corridor, away from the forensics team, who were now calling out to him. Pretending not to hear, he made it to the end of the hallway and pushed through a glass door out into the sun. He glanced around, making sure the coast was clear, then he sprinted across the courtyard, past the entrance to a crazy golf course, down a narrow alleyway and round to the front of the hotel. He stopped to catch his breath, then casually walked in through the main entrance to the hotel reception.

The place was buzzing with activity now, the staff having been released from their meeting, as maids, waiters, chefs and reception staff dashed this way and that. Freddie took the opportunity to mingle and hide in the crowd (as best as he could, considering his Day-Glo outfit) and made his way through the lobby, out the door, across the pool area and back to his room without being seen. He opened the minibar, pulled out a can of San Miguel and downed the whole thing in one go.

CHAPTER 12

"LADIES AND GENTLEMEN, thank you for your patience," said the hotel manager, looking down from the stage at the assembled guests. Perez stood behind him, stony-faced and serious, and flanked on either side by her police officers. Freddie looked around to see others positioned around the room, glaring into the crowd and guarding the doors.

They were in the main conference room, having been collected from their rooms and corralled there by a team of frantic hotel staff. Roughly 500 people – more than half of whom were there for the writing event – jostled and grumbled, waiting for the man to get to the point.

"As you know, there was an incident yesterday at the hotel," said the hotel manager, his voice wobbling as he spoke. "Unfortunately, one of our guests was found… deceased."

Yeah, and the rest, thought Freddie.

"Well, I'm sorry to say," said the hotel manager, "that another guest was found dead this morning…" – sharp intakes of breath from the crowd; confused squeaks; rustling and bustling – "… and the police are treating the deaths as suspicious."

That really set the crowd off. Panic rising. Shocked squeals and murmurs echoing around the room.

Perez stepped forward, placed a hand on the manager's shoulder and pushed him slightly to the side. She raised a hand to the crowd, calling them to quiet order. "We believe these two men were murdered," she said. "Mr Max Graves was found dead yesterday by the pool area. He would appear to have been poisoned. This morning, Mr Malcolm Alexander was found dead in his hotel room. He was stabbed to death."

Again, Perez paused as the hubbub reverberated through the crowd.

"We're investigating these cases with urgency. It's possible the killer is still here in the hotel. They could be in this room."

That was it. The crowd went manic, chattering and screeching. Freddie looked around, watching people eyeing each other suspiciously. What the hell was Perez doing? Was she trying to start a panic?

"Please, ladies and gentlemen," she shouted, trying to calm the crowd. It was no good, they were like manic kittens, screeching and bouncing off each other. Perez signalled to the police officers around the room, who all pulled batons from their belts and, like the scariest Morris dancers that ever lived, banged them simultaneously off the wall. The noise was deafening and silenced the crown instantly.

"Ladies and gentlemen," continued Perez, "as I say, we're investigating these incidents with the highest priority. Unfortunately, that means we must keep the hotel locked down. Nobody can enter or leave. The staff here will talk with you about rearranging your flights home. We appreciate your help earlier by remaining in your rooms. We won't be asking you to do that any longer. You can move about the hotel. The pool areas will be reopened. Food and drink will be served as normal."

Freddie was impressed. Perez spoke like a seasoned professional. Firm and understanding. No nonsense, but with just enough compassion. Like a battle-hardened politician delivering tough but necessary news.

"My officers will be coming around to interview everyone. This will not take long, and we appreciate your assistance. Otherwise, enjoy the rest of your time here, and we'll try not to bother you too much."

The crowd looked on. Silent and confused. Then all hell broke loose.

"What do you mean we can't leave?" shouted an angry, bald man with a sunburnt face. "I've got to get back to work."

"There's a killer in the hotel?" shrieked a blonde woman in a blue summer dress.

"What time are they reopening the buffet?" screamed a fat man in a t-shirt two sizes too tight for his rotund frame.

Perez smiled down at the manic crowd as the questions came thick and fast. Then she turned, walked to the back of the room and disappeared through a door. Freddie raced after her.

"Inspector!" he called out, catching up to her in the hallway.

"Mr Winters, what a surprise."

"How's the investigation going?"

"Early days," she said. "But things are moving along. We already have one suspect. An annoying man who always seems to be there right before the murder takes place. An interfering type, who can't stay out of trouble, and always seems to just be there, wherever I go…" She paused for effect. "And who thinks it's a good idea to sneak into an active crime scene and go poking around."

Freddie felt his face flush crimson. "Oh, you know about that?"

"I know about everything, Mr Winters," smiled Perez.

"Right," said Freddie.

"I could arrest you just for that," she said.

"Then why haven't you?"

"I don't know," she smiled. "Call me crazy, but I kind of want to see what you'll do next."

"So, what was all that about?" said Freddie. "Telling the guests about the murder. Getting them all hyped up and scared."

"I want them scared, Mr Winters. There's a killer on the loose. I want them to be… how do you say… on their guard. And I also want to see who *isn't* scared. The only person who wouldn't be scared about a killer on the loose is the killer themselves, wouldn't you say? And you don't look particularly scared."

Freddie smiled nervously. "But is it really a good idea to let people roam around the hotel?"

"People need to eat. They want to feel free. The last thing I need is hundreds of caged animals, all locked in their rooms, looking out at the sunny weather and sparkling blue pools. We'd have a mutiny within minutes. I need my officers investigating, not just controlling angry tourists."

Freddie shrugged.

"Besides, if the killer is here, I won't catch them if they're locked in a room. Better to let them think they're getting away with it. That's when people slip up."

"Risky," said Freddie. "So, what can I do to help?"

"Help? With what?"

"With the investigation. I can be a real asset for you. I know these people. I assume you've found the other book. What did you make of it? Pretty weird, right? The same book, but a different imprint. First, they leave one with Max, the book's editor. Then they leave one with

Malcolm, the book's publisher. That's significant, right? And what's with all the crazy scribbling?"

"Mr Winters…" said Perez.

"What do you think? Disgruntled ex-employee from Malcolm's company? Maybe a writer he shafted in the past?"

"Mr Winters…" said Perez again, louder.

"Have you spoken to Edward? He must be a suspect, right? I mean, it was his book."

"Mr Winters!" shouted Perez. Freddie slammed his mouth shut in surprise. "Stop trying to help. Stop questioning how I do things. Stop deluding yourself that you're a real detective. And stay the hell away from my crime scenes."

******

"First Max and now Malcolm. I can't believe it."

Edward Cross was sitting in the private jacuzzi on the balcony of his 15th floor hotel suite, the water bubbling and frothing as a strong jet pulsed against his lower back.

"I know, darling," said Marylin, her head barely visible above the waterline. She'd squeezed her bony, leathery frame into a bright red one-piece swimming costume and the majority of her was hidden beneath the surface of the water. "Malcolm was such a… I mean he was so… okay, let's be honest," she said, sighing, "he was a complete bastard. But I've known him for years. It's such a shock. And I was just lining him up for a big advance on your next book, too."

"What does this mean, though? Will Darkhouse still publish the current book? I mean, you know," said Edward, adopting a sombre tone and looking around to check nobody was listening, "I'm devastated about what's happened. And obviously a book is not as important as a man's life. But life goes on. And it's not me I'm worried about. It's the fans. They'll be wondering about the new book…"

"Of course, darling. Terrible thing that's happened. Terrible. But we must remember the fans. I'll talk to the people at Darkhouse when the dust has settled, of course."

"Of course," said Edward.

Marylin took a long drag on her e-cigarette and blew out a huge white plume. Caramel? she wondered. Or maybe Cappuccino? She couldn't remember which flavour she'd loaded into it last.

"Strange coincidence, though, don't you think?" said Edward.

"How's that?" said Marylin.

"Coincidence," repeated Edward. "Max and Malcolm, both being…"

Marylin's eye darted around. She pursed her lips tightly and her hand shot up to nervously scratch her neck.

"You know something, don't you?"

"What?"

"Come on, Marylin, I know you. You're keeping something from me. What is it?"

"Oh, it's nothing, darling. Not really."

"Come on, out with it."

"Well, it's just… look, promise not to worry."

"I make no such promise," said Edward, sternly.

"Okay, well… it turns out something was left at the scene of both murders. It was a copy of one of your books." She shivered slightly as she said it.

"My book? They found copies of my book at the murder scenes?"

"Yes, darling." She took another long drag from her e-cigarette.

"Well, that's… I mean, it could be… but it doesn't mean…" said Edward, his eyes widening. "Well… what *does* it mean?"

"I don't know," she said, "nothing probably."

"No. Lots of people have my books. It could be…"

"Exactly."

"Max edited my books," said Edward. "Malcolm published them. It's perfectly possible they'd have copies."

"Yes, darling… There is one thing, though."

She told him about the markings. The circled words. The manic messages scrawled over the pages. The books being placed directly in the crime scene for the police to find.

"Fuck," said Edward. "How do you know this?"

"I have my spies, darling. Nothing gets past me."

"Right. Yes. But… hang on." A terrified look swept over Edward's face. A horrible realisation. "Which book?"

"*The Terrible Bones*," said Marylin.

"Fuck," said Edward. "But that's…"

"Yes, I know," said Marylin.

"You don't think… I mean, it couldn't have anything to do with… Nobody else knew, did they? You told me it had all been taken care of."

"It was, darling. Everything was handled. It's just a coincidence. Or someone playing silly games."

"Yes, but who? And why?"

"I have no idea, darling."

"It doesn't mean…" said Edward, standing up in the whirlpool and looking around suspiciously. "You don't think I could be next, do you?"

"What?"

"Someone's killing people close to me. And leaving my books behind as a calling card. What if I'm next on the list?"

"Hmmm… I suppose it's possible," said Marylin. Then, noticing Edward's bottom lip start quivering, she quickly said, "But there's nothing to worry about, darling. I always take care of you. I won't let anything happen. I'll make a few phone calls, find out a bit more information. You'll be fine."

"Yes, okay," said Edward.

"To be honest, I was more concerned that someone was bumping people off and trying to pin the murders on you," she laughed.

She stopped when she realised Edward wasn't laughing along.

"Now, honestly darling," said Marylin, "either sit down or go and put on some trunks, will you? You're leaving literally nothing to the imagination."

******

The restaurant hummed with activity. People jostled this way and that, carrying plates piled high with food and glasses spilling over with booze. Kids queued at the ice cream station, waiting to infect the scooper with their grubby, sticky, germ-ridden little hands. A fat man in a flowing pink shirt and yellow shorts hummed and smiled as he piled an inconceivable number of chips onto his plate. A grey-haired woman tutted as she had to wait more than five seconds to get to the coffee machine. A wiry man, who'd ignored the restaurant's dress code and was strutting around in horribly revealing Speedos, looked around sheepishly before surreptitiously abandoning the full plate of food he'd assembled, having seen something else he'd rather have instead.

Less than 30 minutes after the inspector's announcement, the hotel was back to normal. People smiled and joked. They drank and ate. Aside from the odd suspicious glance, there was nothing to suggest these people had been told they were in the presence of a possible serial killer.

That's the good old British fighting spirit, thought Freddie, as he speared a sausage with his fork. Never let the imminent threat of death spoil a good buffet.

He glanced at the assortment of chicken curry, chips, lasagne, sausages, tuna pasta bake and salad on his plate, and sighed heavily. What would normally give him so much joy was barely able to raise his spirits.

Fucking Inspector Perez. Who did she think she was? He could hear her voice, spinning around his head: "Stop thinking you're a real detective. Stop trying to help."

What the hell did she know? This wasn't Freddie's first rodeo. He'd worked on loads of cases like this. Okay, most of them were fictional. And, yes, he always knew who the killer was because he'd invented the story, the characters and all the plot twists. But he knew how murderers thought. How they acted. Why they did things. His knowledge of crime writing could be useful to her. Not to mention the real-life murder plot he'd managed to thwart. And she'd just dismissed him like some annoying child.

There was also the concerning fact that she thought he was involved in the murders. Why did he have to go shouting his mouth off about security cameras, trying to look clever?

Well, he'd show her. He was going to solve this case, catch the killer, clear his name, and make Perez look like a right dick.

"Hi, Freddie."

Christy Collins sat down across from him, a large glass of red wine in her hand.

"Christy. How are you doing?"

"Little shaken up, to be honest. I still can't believe it. Poor Max. And now Malcolm. What the hell's going on?"

"God knows," said Freddie. "Somehow I seem to be the prime suspect."

"What? Why?"

"Wrong place, wrong time. I was the one who found Max's body and well… you probably saw the little tête-à-tête we had. Doesn't look good for me. And I was apparently the last person to see Malcom alive. Well, aside from the actual killer, but try telling that stupid detective. You know, she's a real…"

"So, you've spoken with the detective?" said Christy, cutting him off.

"Yeah, why?"

"Oh, no reason. I just wondered if they had any theories. Who might be doing it and why?" She gave an over-enthusiastic smile, but there was something else in her eyes. "I mean, how often do we get access to real-life crimes like this? Dream research, isn't it?"

She flashed Freddie a flirty smile and stole one of his chips. She went to eat it, then looked closer, turned her nose up and dropped it back onto his plate.

Freddie raised an eyebrow. "What are you after, Christy?"

"What makes you think I'm after something?"

"Because you're always after something. And if you're sat here with me, pretending to flirt, then you really must be after something."

She flashed a wounded, how-dare-you look.

"I was chatting with Helen Brennan earlier. She's full of theories."

"Brennan?"

"You know, she writes about the private detective with amnesia. He has no idea who he is, or where he came from, but every murder he solves unlocks another clue to his own past. Pretty good writer. Neat concept for a series."

"Oh yeah, I've read a couple of her books. So, what does she think?"

"Oh, the usual. Deranged madman hanging out in holiday resorts bumping off tourists. She reckons the literary thing is a red herring. Nothing to do with the motive, just a bunch of writers in the wrong place at the wrong time, getting picked off by a loony."

"That could work," shrugged Freddie, taking another large swig of beer. "Interesting twist. What do you think?"

"Too much coincidence. And too much set up for it to have nothing to do with the plot. That's the sort of rug-pulling crap that really pisses readers off."

"You know this isn't a book, right? Two people have actually been murdered. Besides, what do you know about complicated plots? The most complicated thing in your books is which kind of dildo they use to beat people to death."

"Get stuffed," said Christy, glaring hard at him. Then, failing to hold back a smile, she said, "Honestly, you write one book where the killer uses sex toys as murder weapons and you never live it down."

"I'll never look at a nipple clamp the same way again," said Freddie.

The two laughed, lost for a second in a memory of a happier time.

Then Christy straightened, as if suddenly remembering why she was scared.

"So, come on, what's your theory? I know you have one."

"Too early to tell," said Freddie.

"Bollocks. You've been talking to the lead investigator. She probably thought she was interrogating you, but you would have been sizing her up as well, figuring out what she knows and what she thinks."

"Honestly," said Freddie, "I really don't know yet."

He wasn't sharing any theories until he'd had time to do more digging. Besides, he had no idea who the killer might be. He had to treat everyone with the same level of suspicion. "I can tell you this, though. I'm pretty sure the victims knew the killer."

"Really? Why?" said Christy, her eyes widening.

Hmmm, thought Freddie, she knew more than she was letting on. But what?

"Stands to reason," said Freddie. "Max was poisoned. The killer had to get close enough to put the stuff in his drink."

"Maybe," countered Christy. "But it's a busy hotel. Crowded party. Easy to leave your drink unattended, or even just let your guard down for a second. It could have been a waiter, a bartender… or anyone in the room, if they were sneaky enough."

"Yes," said Freddie, "if they just wanted to poison him and leave it at that. But there was more. They wanted his body to be found by the pool. It was all very deliberate. Very calculated. They'd had to lure him to that spot. And then leave the clue."

"Clue? What clue?"

"Wouldn't you like to know."

"You bloody sneak," said Christy, kicking him under the table. "I knew you knew something. Come on, spill it."

"I may just happen to know about a significant clue that was left at the scene of both murders." He shoved a large forkful of lasagne into his mouth. He then chewed slowly, waving his hand in the universal symbol for 'sorry, I can't talk, I've got a mouthful of food'.

Christy sighed loudly. "Do you *want* me to kick you again?"

"All right, all right," said Freddie, flinching under the table and swallowing. "Get this. The killer left a copy of the same book at the scene of both murders. *The Terrible Bones* by..."

"Edward," she said, cutting him off.

"Exactly. But that's not the weirdest thing. Both books had been scribbled in. Words circled. Mad ramblings scrawled on the pages."

Christy's eyes widened. Her face turned pale. She took a large swig of red wine, coughing as she gulped down too much.

"Words?" she said. "What words?"

"Weird stuff," said Freddie. "Liar. Cheat. Thief. Stuff like that. Both books were the same. Although they were different prints. Not sure if that's significant. Why?"

"Oh, erm... I don't know," said Christy, forcing a smile. "Just... you know... it's intriguing, isn't it?"

"Why do I get the feeling you're the one who knows something now?"

"Know? I don't know anything. Why would I?"

"Because you were married to the author of the book that was left behind? And you were married to him at the time he wrote and published it? And because you must have known Max when he was Edward's editor. Oh yeah, and because your first three books were published by Darkhouse Publishing, which Malcolm just happened to be CEO of."

"That's all circumstantial," said Christy, her voice wavering. "Doesn't mean anything."

"Maybe not. But didn't you and Malcolm have a little... you know?"

"What does that have to do with anything?"

"Tell me, was he before me or after me? Or were there a few others in between? It was hard to keep up in those days."

"You can be a real prick, you know?"

"Yeah, I hear that a lot."

"Yes, I slept with Malcolm," she said, her words sharp and angry. "I made a lot of very bad mistakes back then." She raised her eyebrows and looked directly at him.

"Careful," said Freddie, "you might just hurt my feelings."

"You don't have any feelings. Anyway, what the fuck has that got to do with anything?"

"More clues," said Freddie, smiling as he shoved a large bite of sausage into his mouth.

"I swear to God," said Christy, kicking him hard in the shin again. "What are you talking about?"

"Jesus. Watch those heels. They're really sharp."

Christy raised her eyebrows.

"All right, fine," he said. "I may have managed to get a look around Malcolm's room. Horrible mess. Blood everywhere. The killer must have been absolutely covered in it. Would have been hard to sneak around after that without being spotted. Plus, what did they do with the clothes? Stash them somewhere. Burn them? Run down to the beach and bury them?"

"I think you're straying off the point."

"Yes, right. Like I told you. I found other clues in the room. In the bin, to be precise. A little bottle of that vape liquid stuff. And two used condom wrappers."

"And what does that have to do with me? I don't smoke."

"No, but you do…"

"Fuck you, Freddie."

"Maybe you and Malcolm started up your little fling again."

"I certainly did not. My relationship with Malcolm is purely professional. Or, at least, it was. I'm with a new publisher now."

"And why is that, exactly?"

"What do you mean?"

"Come on Christy, everyone knows he fucked you… in more ways than one."

"What?"

"He fucked you over with your publishing contract. Shit terms. Piss-poor royalties. Tied you into a three-book deal which made you barely any money even though your books were flying off the shelves. That must have really pissed you off."

"I wasn't exactly ecstatic, but…"

"What did you think, he was going to publish your books, make you a millionaire and you'd settle down happily together? It must have really stung when you found out he'd stitched you up with the same crappy contract he screwed so many other writers with?"

"I… well, I…" she said.

"So, what happened? You decide he's not going to get away with it. How dare he treat you like that? But you know you can't do anything straight away. People will suspect you. So, you bide your time. A few years go by. You wait for the perfect opportunity. A literary festival in Spain. The ideal chance to seduce him. You shag him a few times to make sure he doesn't suspect anything. Then you wait for your moment, hide in his room, and stab him to death."

Christy stared back hard at him. Then she burst out laughing. "Holy fuck. You've lost it. Why the fuck would I want to kill Malcolm? Yes, I screwed him back in the day. And yes, he screwed me with a shit publishing deal. But not worse than he screwed anyone else. And he got me published. He got people reading my books. He made me famous, and that led on to better things. Like the million pound, two-book deal I signed just a week ago."

"Well, yeah, but…" said Freddie.

"And why would I want to kill Max? I think I may have met him four times in my whole life."

"Well, I mean, you could have been…" stumbled Freddie.

"Pathetic," said Christy, standing up. "You know, I was hoping we could be civil. When I heard you'd be here, I was looking forward to bumping into you. I really did like you. I know you thought I was just getting back at my husband when we… you know. But I really did like you. It's just a shame you never liked yourself. Deep, deep down inside, you can be a sweet, genuine, lovely man. It's just a shame you keep it buried and wrapped up inside a petty, pathetic, miserable dickhead."

She lifted her glass and went to throw it in Freddie's face. Then, thinking better of it, she gulped the rest of the wine and dropped the glass in the middle of Freddie's plate of food. She smiled, turned and marched off, her heels click-clacking on the stone floor.

Freddie lifted the glass from the plate, pushed a large forkful of chicken curry into his mouth, and sat there, thinking.

CHAPTER 13

THE MOON REFLECTED bright in the still water of the swimming pool. A faint smell of chlorine danced on a gentle breeze. The air was thick and humid, still warm from the fading afternoon sun. The distant drums of nightclub music throbbed somewhere inside the building.

Freddie perched on the edge of a sunbed, staring at the spot where Max Graves' dead body had lain less than 48 hours before. He scanned the background, looking for anything that stood out. Any slight clue. What was he missing?

"Who killed you, Max?" Freddie muttered to himself.

He'd already decided it must be someone that Max knew. Someone who could have lured him here and tricked him into drinking the spiked booze.

Had they sat there chatting and drinking together? Had the killer looked on as the poison took hold, watching as the light slowly faded in Max's eyes? Or had it been more clinical and detached? A simple sleight of hand, administering the poison unnoticed, then simply hoping Max would drink it?

No, Freddie didn't think so. The killer would have wanted to see Max take the drink, if even from afar.

Freddie scanned the pool area for obvious hiding places. They could have watched, concealed behind the pool bar. Maybe they stood on the other side of the pool, simply secreted in the shadows.

He gazed up at the hotel building. Dozens of rooms, reaching up into the dark, night sky. Lights flickered in some of the balconies. People sat drinking, chatting and smoking out in the warm night air. Other rooms lay in darkness, seeming somehow sinister with their lack of activity. Had the killer sat up there, looking down and watching as Max gradually stopped moving and faded into death?

Freddie sighed, anxious and angry. What was he missing?

He suddenly heard footsteps in the distance, the rhythmic clunk-thwap of flip-flops. He spun round to look. There was a man on the other side of the pool. He was wearing long shorts and a baggy jumper, the hood pulled up to conceal his face. It was the same man Freddie had seen around the hotel. And now he was standing there, gazing intently at the spot where Max had died.

"Hey," shouted Freddie.

The man lurched back in surprise, nearly tripping over his flip-flops.

"Hey, you," shouted Freddie. "What are you…"

The man dashed off, walking fast. Frantic and jittery, like a peeping tom who'd just been caught gazing through someone's window.

"Stop," shouted Freddie. "I want to talk to you."

Freddie jumped up to make chase. He dashed this way and that, slowed down as he traversed the intricate maze of sunbeds. He stumbled and skidded as the thin soles of those stupid deck shoes slipped in spots of water on the edge of the pool.

On the other side, the man in the hoodie dashed across the little wooden bridge that connected the main pool to a smaller one, then disappeared behind the hotel building. Freddie clambered over the last sunbed, slipped and scurried and made his way over the bridge. He rounded the edge of the building, readying himself to clobber the guy. But there was nobody there. Fuck.

Freddie ran to a side door, pulled it open and burst through. Nothing. Just a few old biddies sitting on a sofa playing cards and a young couple in the corner, casually groping each other as they played pool. Shit.

Panting and sweating, Freddie bent double as he fought to catch his breath. Then he dashed across the hallway, peering down the adjoining corridor. Nothing. Where the hell had he gone? And, more importantly, how did he know the hotel well enough to disappear so easily?

Fuck this, thought Freddie. He definitely needed a drink now.

******

The banging was loud and insistent. Fast, furious raps against the wooden door that echoed off the stone tiles in the hallway. They'd started off small and polite, then got louder, faster, more urgent. Now it sounded like someone was trying to burst through the wood with an axe.

"Who the bloody hell is that?" sighed Edward Cross, tutting as he placed his white wine on the table. "Can I not get a minute's peace?"

He stared at Marylin, as if expecting her to move and remedy the situation. Marylin sighed back, holding firm. Did he really expect her to get up and answer his bloody door for him? Cheeky sod. She already did more for him than any of her other clients. But she was damned if she was going to let him treat her like a maid.

She'd just spent the last 15 minutes listening to him whinge about how drinking wine out of those little miniature bottles was sacrilege… and didn't an author of his standing deserve a full-sized bottle… something of a decent vintage, from a decent country… not this piss-tasting New Zealand slop… and couldn't they have provided a decent sized wine glass and…

It was enough to make her scream. Instead, she managed to internalise it, smiling and nodding in agreement. It was a skill she'd mastered over the last 40 years of dealing with needy, immature man-children like this, constantly repeating that well-worn mantra in her head: *think of the money, think of the money*. But she had to draw the line somewhere. Besides, getting up from a sofa was becoming harder and harder at her age – a damn-near Herculean task that often needed several attempts to accomplish. No, let the lazy git answer his own door.

The two stared at each other, neither budging, eyebrows raising as the knocking grew more intense. Finally, Edward cracked, humphing and cursing under his breath as he stood and walked to the door.

"All right, all right," he shouted, yanking it open. "Oh, I might have known it would be you."

"Bloody hell, Edward," said Christy Collins, "I've been stood here knocking for 10 bloody minutes."

"You always were one for over-exaggeration," sighed Edward. "I should have known you'd turn up here eventually. What do you want?"

"Still the same charmless, arrogant prick I fell in love with," smiled Christy. "I want to talk with you. Why the hell else would I be here?"

"Very well," said Edward, retreating into the room. He sat back on the armchair, leaving Christy to close the door.

"Oh, I should have known you'd be here too," sneered Christy as she caught sight of Marylin. "I thought I felt a cold, dark, soul-sucking presence in the room. Tell me, how is hell these days? Still nice and hot?"

"You always were funny," said Marylin, coughing out a fake laugh.

Christy walked over to the minibar, pulled out two tiny bottles of vodka and poured them into a glass. She took a big mouthful, breathed heavily and said, "So, does one of you want to tell me what the fuck is going on?"

"You'll have to be a little more specific than that," said Edward.

"The murders? The fact that both Max and Malcolm have been killed – two people you've worked with for many years. And the fact that a copy of your book – *the* fucking book – was left at both crime scenes."

"Keep your voice down," said Marylin, looking around in case somebody was listening in.

"Oh, so there is something going on?"

"No," said Marylin. "Well, yes… I mean, obviously something has happened. Two people have been killed. It's a strange coincidence."

"More than a bloody coincidence," said Christy.

"We don't know that. All we know is Max and Malcolm have been murdered. And yes, we knew them and worked with them. But you could say that about half the people here. We've all worked together in some way or other over the years."

"And what about the book?"

"Yes, okay, that is a bit of an… anomaly. Anyway, how do you know about the book?"

"Freddie fucking Winters told me," said Christy, taking another swig of vodka. "And trust me, if that weasel knows about it, it won't be long before everyone else does."

"How the hell does he know?" said Marylin.

"You know what he's like. He has a real habit of being in the wrong place at the wrong time."

"Don't I know it," sneered Edward.

"Oh, grow up," snapped Christy. "That was years ago. And it's not as if you didn't have your own long list of indiscretions."

"Yes, I know, but… why *him*?"

"To put that look on your face," smiled Christy.

"Oh, you bloody conniving…"

"Children, please," shouted Marylin. "I can't listen to this argument again. And we have more pressing matters to discuss. So, how does Winters know about the book?"

"He's been talking with that Spanish Inspector," said Christy. "And he's been up to his old tricks, worming about, looking for clues. He was the one who found Max's body, and he even managed to sneak into the room where Malcolm was killed."

Marylin scrunched up her face, worry flashing in her eyes.

"So, what's going on?" asked Christy. "With the book, I mean. You don't think it could be related to…"

"We don't talk about that, do we, darling?" snapped Marylin. "How many times do I have to say that?"

"Yes, I know, but it's such a coincidence. And the words circled and scribbled on the pages. It has to be related."

"She has a point," said Edward.

"It's all in the past. It's done," said Marylin. "It's all just some kind of prank."

"A prank? Two people are dead," said Christy.

"Well, I don't know. I can't explain it. But it can't have anything to do with… well, you know."

"What if somebody's looking for revenge?" said Christy.

"I promise you it has nothing to do with that. Outside of this room, only two other people knew about it. And they're both dead."

"That's not entirely true," said Edward. "There was at least one other person that knew."

"Trust me," said Marylin. "Everything was taken care of at the time."

"Well, I hope you're right," said Christy. "Because only a few people ever knew. And now two of them are dead. What if we're next?"

"Let's not get hysterical," said Marylin. "There's nothing to worry about. We just need to be smart. Keep our eyes and ears peeled, and our heads down. Don't give anyone any reason to suspect anything."

"Why should anyone suspect anything?" said Christy.

"Don't start twisting my words, darling. You know what I meant."

"No, hang on," said Christy, a cold shiver of dread coursing up her spine. "What do you mean it was all taken care of?"

"What?"

"You said it was all taken care of. What did you mean?"

"Exactly that. The situation was dealt with."

"Yes, but how? And how can you be so sure the other person isn't behind this? What exactly did you do?"

"I'm not sure I like your tone, darling," said Marylin. "What are you accusing me of?"

Christy placed her glass on the table and started edging towards the door. "I don't know what you did. And, honestly, I don't want to. But you said it yourself, only a few people knew about what happened. And we're all here at the same time. Now two of them are dead, and the killer leaves *that* book at both murders, like a calling card."

"What are you getting at?" said Edward.

"It's far too much of a coincidence."

"That's all it is," said Marylin.

"No. Not buying it," said Christy. "Only three people left. And I know I haven't killed anyone. So that leaves two." She stared intently at them both in turn.

"You can't be serious, darling," laughed Marylin. "You really think I…"

"I'm leaving now," said Christy. "I don't know how long we're all stuck here for, but you two had better stay the hell away from me. As soon as they unlock this hotel, I'll be on a plane home. And I don't ever want to see either of you two again. Do you understand me?"

Christy continued edging her way backwards, keeping her eyes on the pair. She made it to the door, opened it clumsily and staggered out into the hallway.

******

Cursing his slowness, and fighting to catch his breath, Freddie made his way to the piano bar. The atmosphere was a little darker than the previous evening. A sea of moody faces. A beleaguered looking pianist was sitting in the corner of the room, trying to lift the mood with a jolly, jazzed-up rendition of *When You're Smiling* – but also clearly aware that people were neither smiling nor even paying him any attention.

Bill Pascale was sitting at a table in the corner with Austin James. Both had sombre expressions, and spoke quietly, slowly sipping at two pints of lager. Michaela Kemp was at a table on her own, staring into middle distance and nursing a bright yellow cocktail with a stick speared with fruit chunks poking out the top. She looked even more grizzled and battle-hardened than she had during her ill-fated panel talk. Freddie tried to catch her eye, thinking he might join her and carry on where they'd left off the previous evening. But she looked away immediately, lost in thought, and clearly not interested in company.

A soft hum murmured through the room as the UK's brightest and boldest crime writers hunched together chatting. Freddie knew there was only one topic of conversation –
the murderer roaming the halls of the hotel. He was sure they were all trying to fit the pieces of the puzzle together. All desperate to be the one to crack the case and catch the killer. Unlucky for them, Freddie was the only one who'd infiltrated the crime scenes. And only he was in possession of all the clues.

Freddie ordered a pint of lager and a whisky chaser.

"How's it going, Dan?" he said, sitting down at the bar next to the event's organiser.

"How's it going?" slurred Dan with a laugh. "I'm fucking ruined, that's how it's going."

Dan looked like he'd been sitting there for a while. He was slumped on a stool and leaning heavily against the bar. His eyelids hung down, and his eyes were glazed and bloodshot. Freddie could smell the booze emanating from him like a warm wave and his words were all melting into each other.

"Hmmm," said Freddie. "I guess having a murderer turn up to your event and start bumping people off isn't exactly ideal, is it?"

"We've had to cancel the rest of the events," said Dan. "The police are insisting. Too dangerous, apparently. You know, what with a fucking serial killer on the loose. But nobody's allowed to leave the hotel. So, everyone's knocking on my door, asking for a refund. That's why I'm hiding in here. I don't know how I'm going to pay them all back. They're saying I put their lives in danger. I mean, how was I supposed to know there'd be a madman going around killing people?"

"You must be insured, though?"

"Of course. But that's not the point. It's not the money. This was my baby. Years of planning. Do you know how hard is it to get all these crime writers in the same place at once? It's a nightmare. This was supposed to be the best event ever. We were going to do them every year. We already had people asking if they could pre-book for the next one and… well, that's all gone now, isn't it?"

"Hey, you just need to let the dust settle and you'll bounce back. You know what they say, there's no such thing as bad publicity."

"Really? Would you come to another one of these?"

"Depends how much you're paying," laughed Freddie. "But to be fair, I'm probably not the best benchmark."

"What the hell was I thinking, putting on an event like this?" said Dan, taking a large mouthful of whisky. "Things were so much easier when I was just doing the website."

"Yeah, Killerbooks.com, isn't it? How did that all start, anyway?"

Dan looked off into the distance, lost in a trance for a second. Then he said, "Do you know, I don't even know. I never meant to do it. It was just me at first, reviewing books on my blog. I guess people thought I was pretty good at it, because every month I'd get more likes and subscribers. Then people asked me for recommendations, so I wrote a few posts. You know, top ten of this... lists of that... my thoughts on... well, whatever occurred to me.

"I've always loved crime fiction and I just wanted a nice place where people could come and read reviews, recommend books, talk about the ones they liked. It was great. And it just blew up. I started doing video reviews and people liked those. I convinced a few authors to do guest posts, reviews, video posts. The odd giveaway. It all just snowballed. Suddenly I was making money from advertising."

"Sounds like a real success story," said Freddie, genuinely impressed.

"After I'd built up a decent following, I started getting emails from amateur writers wanting to find out how to break into the industry themselves. They'd ask me how to get an agent or how to get a book deal. They wanted to know the secrets of writing a bestseller, creating characters, structuring plots, that sort of thing. I'd already built up good connections with authors, publishers, editors... So, it was kind of a no-brainer to start the advice section for aspiring writers.

"I was an aspiring writer myself, once upon a time. So, I knew how popular it could be."

"Really, you wanted to be a writer?"

"Yeah. I even wrote a book. Thought it was pretty good, actually."

"Really? What happened?"

"Didn't work out. Usual story. So, I focused on the website instead. And the advice section really took off. I knew real advice from real authors could be a hit. And it was. Then this event seemed like the perfect next step. Let all these budding authors combine their week away in the sun with some interesting, productive learning and writing. Who wouldn't want that?"

"Seems like a good idea. Except…"

"Yeah," said Dan, downing the last of his drink, "except."

The two sat in silence for a few seconds as Dan ordered another drink.

"So, come on then," said Dan, "what's your theory?"

"Sorry?" said Freddie.

"Who did it? Who's the killer?"

"What makes you think I have a theory?"

Dan let out a small laugh. "Because you're a crime writer. And because everyone else in this room has a theory. I've been sitting here for hours, listening, and every writer in this bar thinks they've figured it out. Some are a bit more outlandish than others, of course."

"Sounds about right," said Freddie, looking around at the small clusters of writers. "I can't say I haven't thought about it. Nothing concrete yet. But I've got my eye on a few people."

"Really? Got your eye on people? Who?"

"Can't say just yet," said Freddie, winking. "Let's just say, a few clues have come to light. But I need to dig deeper."

"Goodness," said Dan. "You know, I reckon that Inspector thinks you might be involved."

"Tell me about it. Wrong place, wrong time. Story of my life."

"So, what did she say? What did she ask you? She won't tell me anything."

"Oh, the usual," said Freddie. "Ongoing investigations. Asked me a lot about CCTV and how well I knew the victims. She's clutching at straws. And she's leaning on me because she's got no other suspects."

"Really? No other suspects?"

"Not that she's told me, anyway. And she's completely blind to the fact that people here might be able to help. I mean, I've consulted with the police in the UK loads of times. But will she hear it? Will she bollocks."

"Right. No. That must be annoying."

The waiter appeared and placed another whisky on the bar. Dan went to drink it, then placed the glass back down.

"On second thoughts," he said, "I've probably had quite enough of that. God knows what horrors tomorrow will bring. I think, perhaps, I need some sleep."

"Well, I wouldn't usually advocate an early night over a drink," chuckled Freddie, "but in this case, I think you're right. I'm sure things will seem better in the morning. And if not, I've got a bit of advice for you." He leaned in close and whispered, "Fuck 'em. Fuck 'em all. It's a mantra that's worked wonders for me over the years."

Dan smiled for a second. "You seem like a good man, Mr Winters... despite what everyone else says."

"Hey, don't go telling people I'm nice," smiled Freddie, "I've got a reputation to keep up."

Dan patted Freddie on the shoulder, sighed and walked out of the room, stumbling and swaying as he went.

Freddie turned back to the bar, lifted his pint, closed his eyes and breathed, enjoying a few seconds of peace. He was just about to take a sip when he heard another voice calling out. "Freddie. Hey, Freddie."

Oh, for fuck's sake.

He turned to see Nick Foster at a table in the corner, grinning and waving at him. He was sitting with Lisa Smythe and Colin McMaster, and he was beckoning Freddie to join them. Freddie sighed, collected his drinks and ambled over.

"Evening," said Freddie. "No prizes for guessing what you're all talking about."

"It's the talk of the whole hotel," said Nick, grinning. He seemed to notice his own eagerness, then slowed his voice and said, "So tragic, though. Horrific."

"Come on then," said Freddie, "what's the current theory?"

"Wouldn't you like to know," said Colin, his gruff voice ringing with suspicion.

Colin used to be a police detective somewhere up north. Freddie wasn't entirely certain where. He'd come to writing later in life, fuelled by years of experience on the force, and it certainly showed in his work. His novels were clinical explorations of police work, with gruesome, vivid descriptions that put you a bit too close to imagining a crime scene than you wanted to be.

Freddie was unsure how old Colin was. With a short crop of brilliant white hair and a wrinkled face etched with a lifetime of stress, he could easily have been in his sixties. But the way he moved, spoke and carried himself suggested a younger man – in his forties and prematurely aged by the horrors he'd seen. He spoke with a deep, grizzled northern accent, filled with authority and more than a hint of anger. With the white hair, hunched back and quiet aggression in his eyes, he reminded Freddie of a silver-backed gorilla perched on a mountainside.

"It's not a competition, McMaster," chided Freddie. "I'm not here to steal your ideas and take credit. I was just wondering what you all thought."

"Crime of passion," said Lisa, throwing a handful of peanuts into her mouth. Freddie didn't know Lisa very well. They'd met at a few events in the past, but never spent much time talking. She was a good writer – clear prose, nothing too flowery or fancy – although she did go in for some particularly brutal murders. Sitting there in skimpy shorts and a vest top – and with Freddie still scoring zero on his holiday conquests card – she suddenly seemed more attractive than he'd realised.

"Max and Malcolm were caught up in some twisted love triangle," continued Lisa. "Something goes wrong. Maybe all three of them are shagging each other, but Max and Malcolm decide they're gonna run off together. The other party doesn't like this and thinks 'if I can't have you, nobody can' and bumps them off."

"So, who's the injured party?"

"Don't know yet. Still working on that. Could be a woman, could be another man."

"Hmm, I'm not sure," said Freddie. "Neither Max nor Malcolm ever struck me as gay."

"I'm not saying gay," said Lisa. "What an antiquated way of thinking, you old dinosaur. Sometimes people just fall in love, you know, whatever their gender. Why do you have to put a label on it? You know, Max and Malcolm worked together. He published Max's book, didn't he? Maybe things just sort of… happened. Next thing you know they're…"

"Involved in some mysterious, gender-non-specific, group sex love triangle that sees them both murdered?" said Freddie.

Colin McMaster coughed with shock, choking on his pint and spraying the table with tiny droplets of beer.

"I never said group sex. Although…" She seemed to drift off inside her head.

"No, not buying it. Sorry. Besides, don't you think that was all a bit strange in itself?"

"What's strange?" asked Nick.

"Malcolm publishing Max's book," said Freddie.

"Not really. Max was a good editor. He wrote a decent book. They'd worked together in the past, so why wouldn't Malcom publish it?"

"Yeah, but to give him such a big advance. You know Malcolm paid him a million quid for a first novel. That's, well… it's not exactly common. And it wasn't standard practice for Malcolm, was it?"

"That tight bastard? No way," growled Colin. "He'd steal his grandmother's nightdress if he thought he could flog it for a fiver. He was notorious for it. Fucked me over on my first book deal, the prick."

"Really, so you had a grievance against him?" smiled Freddie.

"I never said that, you cheeky git. True, he collared me with a shit deal on my first book. Tiny advance and you wouldn't even believe how low the royalties are. Plus, he had me contracted for a second book on the same shit rates. Nothing I could do to get out of it. But you know what it's like with your first book. I was just out of the force, I'd never written anything before, and I was desperate to get it published. So, when that slippery snake oil salesman offers to take me on, well… Just naïve, I suppose."

"So, you were genuinely upset with him?"

"Not enough to kill him. Don't start trying to twist things, Winters. I've got 20 years' experience twisting suspects' words in interrogations, so don't try that crap with me."

Freddie raised his hands in surrender.

"Yes, I was upset at the time. But it was my own fault. I could have checked the details in the contract. Could have held out for a better deal. But then, I might not have got one. At least Malcolm published my first two books. And he got people buying them. So, by the time I'd written book three, I got a far better deal with another publisher. And things have been much better since, as you can see." He waved his hands, first to highlight the expensive Hugo Boss t-shirt he was wearing, then around the bar to draw attention to the company he was now keeping. "I don't hold too much against him. He gave me my first break."

"Funnily enough," said Freddie, rubbing his chin, "you're not the first person to tell me a story like that tonight."

"Really? Who else?" asked Colin.

"Wouldn't you like to know."

"Wanker," said Colin, laughing and shaking his head as he lifted his pint.

Freddie smiled. He was actually enjoying himself. Enjoying the camaraderie. He rarely let himself get involved in conversations like these with other writers. He'd learned from bitter experience that it was far easier to keep himself closed off. Avoid people. Avoid friendships. That way, you didn't let your guard down, and that meant it was harder to get hurt and disappointed. But he had to admit, these guys were all right. And as he sat there, joking and chatting and theorising, he was having fun with them.

"Maybe not everyone else was as understanding as you, though, Colin," said Nick. "Malcolm did have a reputation for taking advantage of new writers. Perhaps they didn't all go on to have successful careers. The killer could be one of the ones who faded into obscurity. They never got that better deal. They spent years watching Malcolm get rich off their hard work, and they never got the reward for it. Then one day, they read about how Malcolm is paying Max an extortionate amount for a debut book. Well, that's not fair, is it? Not after what Malcolm did to them. They can't take the injustice. They snap and kill Malcolm in revenge. And they bump off Max out of jealousy for getting the deal they never did."

Colin, Freddie and Lisa sat there pursing their lips and nodding.

"Certainly plausible," said Colin.

"Bit harsh, killing Max, but I can see it," said Freddie.

"Nah, I still think it was a sex thing," said Lisa.

"But who, though?" said Freddie. "Malcom probably published books by half the writers here. And he probably rejected the other half. But I can't see any of them being angry enough to stab him to death with his own pen. Present company excepted, Colin."

"Very funny," growled Colin. "Hey, hang on, what do you mean, pen? How do you know the killer used a pen?"

Fuck. He hadn't meant to let that slip out.

"Yeah," said Nick, "how do you know what the murder weapon was?"

"Oh, erm… Perez let it slip when we were talking," said Freddie, begrudgingly. He wasn't going to let them know he'd sneaked into the crime scene and seen the pen in situ, protruding from the dead publisher's eye. And he wasn't going to tell them about the other clues he'd uncovered.

"Oh yeah?" said Lisa. "What else did she say?"

"Nothing," said Freddie. "She was more interested in hounding me about my movements. She wasn't giving away any details about the case or taking any help from me. She's very closed-minded, you know. Doesn't want any help, even though… well, you know." Freddie pointed towards himself with double thumbs. "I did recently thwart a potential murder. Just saying."

"Tell me about it," grumbled Colin. "I used to be a bloody DCI. I've investigated hundreds of murders. Some so horrific they'd give you nightmares. In fact, some did give me nightmares. Anyway, I went to offer my services. Miserable cow totally blanked me."

"You're thinking too literally, anyway," said Nick. "It could be a disgruntled writer that killed Malcolm, but it's hardly likely to be anyone on the bill. As you say, everyone's moved on to bigger, better things. If it was me, I'd be looking at the guests. The wannabes in the classes. The ones so eager to get that book deal they'd kill for it. Or in this case, maybe kill because they didn't get it."

"So, they come on this writers' retreat with ulterior motives?" said Freddie, scratching his head. "They lay in wait, hiding in plain sight, and wait for the perfect moment to strike?"

"Doesn't even need to be anyone on the course," said Colin. "Could be any of the guests here. Or someone in the staff. Lots of people would have known that Max and Malcolm would be here at the same time. Wouldn't be hard to book a room in the same hotel, or get yourself hired as a waiter, chambermaid or barman."

"Bar *person*," said Lisa indignantly.

The other three sighed together.

"So," said Nick, "it could be literally anyone here."

"I have seen a suspicious guy hanging around the place," said Freddie. "He caught my eye because he's walking about in a big, hooded jumper pulled right up over his head, even though it's hot enough to cook fried eggs on my bollocks."

"Lovely image," said Lisa, scrunching up her face.

"I actually saw him tonight, down by the pool, gawping at the spot where Max died. He was acting all shifty and when I tried to talk to him, he just bolted."

"Really?" said Colin, sitting up straighter in his chair.

"I chased after him, but he just sort of vanished."

"Hang on, yeah," said Lisa. "Guy in a hoodie. White one?"

"Yeah."

"He was at my talk today. Sitting at the back. I thought it was weird."

"Hey, come to think of it, I had a hoodie bloke at my panel discussion on self-publishing," said Nick. "He was constantly looking at his phone, not really interested in the actual talk."

"Well, that's no surprise, eh?" laughed Freddie, elbowing Lisa in the arm.

"Piss off, you dick," said Nick. "What about you, Colin? Ring any bells?"

"No, but it does seem strange. Some guy clearly trying to conceal his identity, hiding out in talks he's not interested in. Suspicious. Almost like he's casing the scene."

"Picking up intel," said Nick. "Staying incognito. Waiting for the perfect moment."

"Could be," said Colin.

"Definitely have to list him as a suspect," said Freddie.

"Yeah... no, I still think it was a sex thing," said Lisa.

The four carried on drinking, chatting, laughing and deducing for the next few hours. Over the course of five pints, three rum and cokes and one flaming sambuca, the group waxed lyrical on the state of the publishing industry, the unfortunate decline in book sales, their collective hatred of James Patterson and how the TV and film industry seemed determined to turn every crime novel into a movie – except for theirs.

They went through the list of authors at the event, outlining their potential motives, opportunity and likelihood for murdering Max and Malcolm. They then concocted several other reasons why someone might be running amok bumping off literary figures at a holiday resort in Malaga. And Lisa once again forcefully contended that it was all part of an outrageous sex scandal.

Finally, they called it a night, and each wandered back to their rooms. Freddie stumbled as he made his way down the winding corridors and, after spending three minutes trying to open his hotel room door with his Tesco Clubcard, he finally found his key card in his pocket and lumbered through the door.

He staggered down the hallway, pulling his t-shirt over his head, and nearly tripping over his feet as he dropped his shorts to the floor. He was just about to flop onto the bed when he noticed something on the other side of the room.

He squinted hard, trying to bring his double vision into focus. There was someone there. A dark figure, hidden in the shadows, sitting on the sofa and waiting for him.

"How the hell did you get in here?" said Freddie.

CHAPTER 14

THURSDAY

SUNLIGHT GLINTED THROUGH the balcony window. A single beam shone onto Freddie's face, creating a mellow, pink glow and bringing him gently out of his slumber. Outside, the distant rumble of waves crashed against the shore, soft and rhythmic, soothing yet insistent. As he drifted back to consciousness, he could hear people walking, chatting, laughing outside. The day was already in full swing. People down by the pool, draping towels over sunbeds, claiming their territory for the day.

Freddie shifted in bed and became aware of a sharp pain throbbing in his head. A dank, bitter taste in his mouth. A sickly rumble in his stomach. A sheen of sweat tickling his forehead. Oh, not this again.

Fearing even the slightest movement might exacerbate things, Freddie lay completely still, trying to hold his world together. Memories flashed like a series of distorted pictures. He saw Perez on stage, delivering the news about Max and Malcolm. He saw Max's dead body on the sunbed. He saw the bank of security monitors with images of rooms, hallways and corridors.

An image of Edward's book flashed into his mind, scrawled in and scribbled on. He saw the two different covers. Then an image of Christy and that strange look of recognition when he told her about it. He saw Malcolm laying on the floor, covered in blood, a pen protruding angrily from his face. He saw the image of the moon glinting in a swimming pool, then a stranger in a hooded top running away from him.

Freddie's memory flashed to his night with Malcolm, drinking in the bar. Then the strange juxtaposition of sitting in that same bar just 24 hours later, discussing the man's murder. He thought about the theories he'd discussed with Nick, Colin and Lisa. Then he remembered staggering back to his own room, too drunk to walk straight. Barely able to get the door open. And then...

There had been someone in his room. Waiting for him. Hidden in the darkness. He'd confronted them. But then what?

Why couldn't he remember?

Oh God, was it the killer? Had they sneaked into his room and waited to attack? Poison him maybe? Did that account for how he was feeling now? His head swam as another sharp jolt of pain crashed through his brain. His stomach flipped, nausea filling his mouth with saliva. He couldn't move, frozen in place, every joint and muscle in his body throbbing. He shivered, ice-cold sweat beading on his forehead.

Oh God, that was it, wasn't it? This was no mere hangover. He'd been murdered. Poisoned. And now there was nothing he could do but lie there and wait for the toxin to do its work. The death throes of another literary legend. The end of Freddie Winters.

He groaned as another sickly wave of nausea pulsed through him. He took a deep breath, building himself up to move. Then, just as he was preparing to lift his head, he felt something moving next to him. What the hell?

The bed rumbled with the weight of another person shifting. The unmistakable sound of bed springs squeaking, mixed with the soft, breathy sigh of somebody next to him. Wait, what?

Freddie's eyes snapped open. He lifted his head. His eyes stung as the bright light hit them. His head pulsed with pain. The room spun and wobbled as everything came slowly into focus. Empty beer cans tumbled on the table. A glass still half-filled with clear liquid. Clothes scattered on the sofa. His gaudy shirt and shorts. Those horrible deck shoes. And a pair of bright pink knickers.

Freddie widened his eyes, trying to look without moving his head. Then he saw it. The damning piece of evidence. The most terrifying thing he could have seen. Draped over the back of the chair, it hung there, taunting him. Crying out in cruel ridicule. A bright yellow t-shirt emblazoned with a large, blue picture of a cat.

Freddie Winters had not been murdered. It was far worse than that.

"Morning, sleepy head," said the voice next to him.

Oh fuck!

Freddie rolled over, his stomach flipping and churning. The room spun and shook as he saw her, laying there, beaming from ear to ear.

"Caroline?" he said. "What the hell are you doing here?"

"Well, I would have thought that was obvious," she snapped, the smile dissolving from her lips. "You know, that's not exactly the greeting a woman wants to hear in the morning. Especially after what we got up to last night."

"Oh God," sighed Freddie, "we didn't, did we?"

"Oh yes we did," said Caroline, lifting the sheets to reveal their naked bodies. "Several times. You were magnificent."

Goddammit. Why did he never remember these things? He was angry at himself for giving in to Caroline so easily. Ashamed and degraded, and all that crap. But he wished he'd at least been conscious enough to enjoy it at the time.

At least, he supposed, he'd broken his dry spell. It was just a shame he couldn't remember it. And an even bigger shame it had been with Caroline.

"It was you," said Freddie, "waiting for me in the dark last night."

"Yes, I wanted to surprise you. Did the trick, too. You were very pleased to see me."

"But how did you get in?"

"Easy. I told the guy at reception I was your wife and I'd lost my key card. He gave me another one."

"And he just believed you?"

"Yeah. To be honest, I was surprised how easy it was. He didn't bat an eyelid, just gave me an extra card. I think he was a little bit… you know," she said, pointing to her head.

"Jesus. There's a killer on the loose and they're just handing out room keys to any old fucking lunatic that asks for them."

"I know," said Caroline. Then, catching up with the second part of Freddie's sentence, said, "Hey, I'm not a lunatic."

"No, just a nutbag stalker who sneaks into people's rooms and seduces them when they're legless."

"I've told you before, I am NOT a stalker," said Caroline. "Besides, you weren't exactly complaining."

Freddie humphed and climbed out of bed, the world swimming as he fought back the urge to vomit. He grabbed a bottle of water from the minibar and downed it in one.

"Might explain one thing, though," said Freddie. "I've been wondering how the killer got into Malcolm's room to ambush him. I'd assumed they sneaked in behind reception and used the machine to create their own key card. But if the dimwits are handing out extras to any old psycho that asks for them, that would make things easier."

"Ooh, so you're investigating the case?" said Caroline, choosing to ignore his barb. "Any suspects?"

"Too early to tell," said Freddie. "Although, your recent devious actions could put you at the top of my list."

"Ha. Are you scared of me, Freddie?" She threw her head back on the pillow and laughed. "Besides, why would I want to kill those people? I don't even know who they are."

"True. There is a very personal element here," said Freddie. "I think it's connected to something in their past. But what?"

"Maybe it's a sex thing?" said Caroline.

"What is it with you women and your crazy sex murder theories?" said Freddie.

He tutted and staggered to the bathroom. He climbed into the shower, murmuring as hot, rejuvenating jets of water prickled on his aching skin. A few moments later, Caroline climbed into the shower with him and started soaping his chest and arms.

He really shouldn't. It was just going to encourage her. But he'd apparently already succumbed the previous evening. And he did have a sizeable boner. In for a penny, he thought, and he kissed her.

******

"Don't get carried away," said Freddie, spearing a sausage with his fork. "Just because I'm letting you have breakfast with me, it doesn't mean I'm your boyfriend. And what we just did in the shower is definitely not happening again."

"Yeah, we'll see," said Caroline, smiling and rubbing her foot against his leg under the table. "You can't resist me, Mr Winters. You might as well stop trying."

Freddie humphed and pushed a forkful of food into his mouth. The restaurant was bustling. The incessant sharp twang of knives and forks scraping against plates echoed around the room. The sound of people's chatter buzzed and swarmed, threatening Freddie's delicate brain with full sensory overload. The paracetamol he'd gulped down in the room had barely dented his hangover and the food was so far failing to soothe his queasy stomach.

"So, how is the investigation going? Who do you think the killer is? And why are they doing it?" said Caroline.

"Can't say," said Freddie, chewing. "Got my eyes on a few people. Few leads to follow up on."

"Ooh, exciting. So, what do we do first?"

Freddie was just about to shoot her down when an anxious Dan rushed over and sat down next to Freddie.

"Ah Mr Winters," said Dan, "good to see recent events haven't upset your appetite." He raised an eyebrow as he looked at the mishmash of food spilling off the edge of Freddie's plate.

"Gotta keep your strength up," said Freddie. "Especially after a night like last night."

"Yes," said Dan. "Apologies if I was a little worse for wear in the bar. It's all been a bit… stressful."

"No sweat. Happens to us all. So, what can I do you for?"

"Well, just to say that I've just spoken with Inspector Perez, and she's asked that we carry on with today's itinerary as planned. She wants to keep people active. Stop them from getting bored and drunk and misbehaving while the hotel's under lockdown."

"Is that a good idea?"

"I can see the benefit of keeping people occupied," said Dan. "Plus, if the events are taking place, that means we haven't officially been cancelled. So I won't have to refund people."

"Ah, so there's the real reason. And what do the other writers think about that?"

"I'm just doing the rounds now, letting people know," said Dan. "I'm also reminding them about the contracts they signed, and how I'd hate to withhold their appearance fees due to breach of said contracts."

"Of course," said Freddie, dipping a chocolate donut into the yolk of his fried egg.

"Anyway," said Dan, running a finger down his clipboard, "I have you down for the *Creating Effective Dialogue Workshop* at 12pm. That's by the small pool, so at least you won't be stuck inside. You've got plenty of time to finish eating and get ready. Might even squeeze in a little dip in the pool beforehand, eh?"

"I can't fucking wait," grimaced Freddie.

"Good, good," said Dan, standing up and rushing off.

"Oh, that's a shame," said Caroline. "I was hoping you'd be free today. I thought we might go for a romantic walk."

"I know. I'm crushed. So disappointing," said Freddie. "Still, duty calls. I'll tell you what, why don't we finish eating our breakfast, then I'll go and get ready for this dire workshop."

"And what will I do?"

"Well," said Freddie, taking Caroline's hand in his and smiling softly, "I was thinking you could sod off and never darken my door again."

Caroline snatched her hand back from his. "Still playing hard to get, eh? We'll see about that." She leaned in, kissed him hard on the mouth and said, "See you tonight then."

Then she stood up and walked away.

Freddie was just about to take a bite of food when he heard yet another sound that filled him with dread.

"Hello Mr Windows," said the annoying kid, appearing at his side.

"For God's sake," said Freddie. "You again? Can't a man get any bloody peace?"

"Ummm, you said another..."

"What the hell do you want, kid?" said Freddie, cutting him off.

"Could you get me a drink, please? I still can't reach the machine. My mum says I'll grow up big and tall one day, but I'm still too little."

Jesus, this kid was incessant. Another wave of nausea pulsed in Freddie's stomach and a sharp pain jolted in his head.

"I like the Coca-Cola and I like the Lemon Fanta, and..."

"For God's sake, kid," snapped Freddie. "Do me a favour and piss off, will you? I'm not your dad. I'm not a waiter. I'm not your bloody friend. I'm just a grumpy man, with a stinking fucking hangover, who wants to eat his breakfast in peace."

The boy's bottom lip started quivering. He looked like he was about to burst into tears, then he turned quickly and ran off.

Oh shit. Freddie instantly felt horrible, seeing the boy so upset. The nausea pulsed heavier in his stomach, and he only just about managed to keep from throwing up.

You've really done it this time, Winters, he thought to himself. Shouting at a little kid. Swearing. What an arse. Sometimes he even surprised himself with his bad behaviour. He'd have to find the boy and apologise. But first he had to get rid of this awful hangover.

******

Whichever idiot decided to hold the event outside needed shooting. It was at least 30 degrees and Freddie could feel himself melting away. Sweat coursed down his spine in rivulets. The armpits of his bright yellow Hawaiian shirt were damp and sticky, not to mention the state of his sweaty underpants. He could practically smell last night's booze leaching out of his pores. His head was still throbbing, and his dark sunglasses were only just dimming the brightness of the sun.

It had started out fine. He was on a little makeshift stage at the edge of the pool, directly under the shade of the main hotel building. However, as the sun shifted, so did all his shade, until he was left with the searing sun cooking his delicate, pink skin. Why hadn't he thought to put on some bloody sun cream?

When he'd first sat down, Freddie had scanned the crowd for anything or anyone out of the ordinary. No sign of Hoodie Man. No obviously deranged killers. He did spot the grey-haired man from the first night again, sitting at the back and scribbling away in a leather notebook. Freddie still couldn't place him, though. It was really frustrating. He was so familiar, but Freddie just couldn't figure out how he knew him.

Freddie was joined on stage by Helen Brennan, Austin James and Colin McMaster, all equally disgruntled and bemused the event was even taking place. After the first hour, the pain in Freddie's head was so bad he'd decided there was only one thing for it. While Colin was in full flow about the techniques for creating authentic voices, Freddie had hopped down from the stage and wandered off, returning a few minutes later with two pints of lager – much to the annoyance of the other panellists, who were just jealous they hadn't thought to do the same thing.

The beer helped take the edge off his hangover, but the longer he sat in the sun, the more he could feel his brain pickling inside his skull. The event dragged on, each author giving his or her tips on the need for creating distinct voices and realistic dialogue. Then came time for the Q&A section. Unsurprisingly, the topic shifted very quickly onto more recent events within the hotel.

"Do you have any theories on the murders?" asked an elderly woman with white hair and a bright pink t-shirt.

"Are you assisting the police with their investigations?" asked a pink-faced man with a thick moustache.

"Is there any truth to the rumour that the victims were caught up in a deadly love triangle?" asked Caroline, sitting at the back.

At first, Freddie had tried to steer the conversation back onto the topic of writing. However, the crowd wouldn't be dissuaded, and the event descended into a bigger, more elaborate version of the previous evening's conversation in the bar – with more than 50 people now joining in to speculate on their own bizarre, twisted theories.

One man was convinced the murders were carried out as part of Chinese censorship, silencing the men for their anti-communist opinions – although he wasn't sure what those opinions were. "Well, that goes to show just how effective the Chinese propaganda machine is," he said, when questioned on it.

One wild-eyed woman speculated about the possibility it was a time-travelling assassin, sent back to take out leading literary figures before they could write and publish a book that would eventually lead to the rise of the machines and the downfall of mankind.

Freddie wasn't convinced.

Another man, who'd clearly been reading too much Dan Brown, was certain it was all the work of the Illuminati – a secret society that runs the world from behind closed doors. Quite why they'd want to kill a publisher and a crime author, the man couldn't say, but he was sure it was all part of a duplicitous scheme, the scale of which was yet to be revealed.

The mad theories came thick and fast. They included everything from jealous ex-lovers to ninjas, killer robots, shady politicians, crazed psychopaths, disgruntled ex-employees, escaped mental patients and Russian spies. It was no great wonder none of these people had ever been published.

With the sun high in the sky, and the crowd buzzing with misplaced excitement, Freddie gazed at the clock on his phone, willing the last 12 minutes of the session to tick along. He was aching to jump in the pool and feel the refreshing cold water soothing his hot, tired skin. He'd spend a little time in the jacuzzi. Maybe have a spot of lunch and another drink or two. He'd grab a couple of hours sleep, just to refresh his brain, before carrying on with his investigations. He also really needed to set some time aside to sit and write something.

He was suddenly jolted from his reverie by someone in the crowd shrieking. Freddie looked down to see them pointing up at the hotel behind him. He followed their finger up to the bank of balconies that reached high into the sky. Then he saw it.

An object. Falling. Dark. Blurred. Travelling fast.

Freddie squinted, trying to make out the shape. But it was moving too quickly.

The whole world went into slow motion. Sounds echoing and elongated. People bustled, jolted, tripped over each other as they scrambled to their feet. The world seemed to throb around him. Panic behind him. Chairs scraping against concrete. People shouting in panic.

Then everything came rushing back to normal speed.

The falling object landed with a loud, squelching thud, just a few feet away from him on the hard patio floor. As it hit the ground, it exploded, bright drops of something red shooting out in a wide circle, splattering his leg, arm, neck and face. Stunned, Freddie looked out at the crowd. They stared back, open-mouthed and screaming, the first few rows equally covered in the strange, sticky, warm liquid.

Freddie spun round to look at the object. It lay there, distorted, splayed out, squished. Surrounded by a wide, splatter pattern of red, which was growing, pooling out around it. It took him a few seconds to realise he was looking at a person.

Long, dark hair arced out around the face. Christy's face. Staring back at him. Her eyes wide. Her mouth stretched into a silent scream.

Then Freddie was aware of something else. A fluttering sound, like thousands of butterflies flapping their wings.

He looked up to see paper raining down. Hundreds of pages, floating, drifting in the soft breeze. They filled the sky, dancing down like giant snowflakes. Eerie yet beautiful. Freddie reached up and grabbed one, pulling it down and inspecting it.

It was a page from a book. A novel. Someone had circled several of the words – *scandal*, *cheat*, *thief*. In harsh red pen, they'd scribbled the word *liar* across the page.

Freddie looked closer.

There, centred at the top of the page, were the words *The Terrible Bones*.

CHAPTER 15

"YOU SEEM TO be making a habit of this, Mr Winters," said Inspector Perez. "Every time somebody dies in this hotel, you're there."

They were back in the hotel manager's office, Freddie sitting across the desk from Perez. The bank of security screens flickered in the background as Freddie's heart beat fast. He was wearing a white, all-in-one plastic suit, the police having made him strip before placing his blood-soaked clothes in an evidence bag. The suit rustled every time he breathed or moved.

The swimming pool areas had been cleared with extreme efficiency once again. It had taken slightly longer to herd the event's attendees away this time – understandable, as they were all screaming, panicking and falling over each other, covered in various amounts of the dead woman's blood, hair and tiny bits of brain.

When you see someone fall from a building in a movie, they tend to land in a tidy, mangled heap. There might be a bit of blood on the ground. A little splatter here or there. In real life, things are a lot messier. People are essentially giant walking bags of liquid. And what happens when you drop a balloon filled with liquid from a great height?

Exactly.

So, when Christy hit the ground, she exploded all over the pool area, the stage, the patio and just about everybody in the crowd.

"Surely, you can't think I had anything to do with this?" said Freddie. His voice wavering with shock. "I'm covered in the poor girl's… well, you know."

"At the moment, we don't even know if a crime has been committed," said Perez. "My team are investigating the scene now. Nobody is pointing any fingers at you," she said, apparently not understanding the irony as she literally pointed a finger right at him. "But you have to admit, it's quite a coincidence you always seem to just be there."

147

"So, what do you think happened?" said Freddie. "Another murder?"

"I can't say," said Perez. "Not until I've had a chance to…"

"Oh, come on, Inspector," interrupted Freddie. "It has to be. You saw the pages. Pages from the same book that was left at the scene of the first two murders. The book that was written by Christy's ex-husband. Published by the same man who published her books – who's also now dead. It has to be part of the same thing."

"As I said, I can't say."

Freddie sighed, looking down at the specks of blood drying on the back of his hand. Why was this bloody woman so stubborn?

"So, what do you want from me," said Freddie, "aside from preventing me from having a shower?"

"I want to ask you about Ms Collins."

"Why?"

"I'm trying to learn more about her. Trying to determine what her mental state might have been at the time she died."

"Surely you don't think she jumped?"

"I'm looking at the evidence. Exploring every possibility."

"No," said Freddie. "Suicide? Sorry, but I don't see it."

"What was your relationship with Ms Collins like?" asked Perez.

"My relationship? We didn't really have one."

"That's not true, is it?" said Perez. "I told you, I've been doing my homework, Mr Winters. You and your author friends do like to gossip, don't you?"

"Okay, what?" said Freddie. "What have these fuckers been saying about me?"

"Why don't you tell me?" said Perez.

"All right, fine. I knew Christy. We had a bit of a fling a few years ago. But that's all it was. She was divorcing Edward at the time, and she only did it to piss him off. Me and Edward don't exactly get on, so it was a bit of a two fingers up at him. It only lasted a few weeks."

"So, you were intimate with her?"

"Yeah. She wasn't exactly a nun. After the divorce, she worked her way around a bit, if you know what I mean."

"So, you're saying there are lots of people who might have a motive to see Ms Collins dead?"

"I didn't say that exactly."

"A jilted lover, perhaps? Someone upset at the ending of a short affair?"

"Well, yeah… I guess so," said Freddie, "but…"

"How many of them are here, right now in this hotel? And how many of them were recorded on video having a heated exchange with her just last night?"

On cue, one of Perez's goons pressed a key on the computer and all the security monitors changed to one image. The video showed Freddie and Christy sitting together in the restaurant.

Freddie felt the heat grow in his face. He felt Perez's eyes boring into him as he watched Christy stand, shout at him, gulp down her wine, then drop her glass into his dinner.

"Very theatrical," said Freddie. "But what exactly was the point of showing me that?"

"What were you discussing?"

"Nothing much. Just catching up with an old friend."

"Doesn't look like catching up. Looks like you were fighting."

"That's just how I catch up with people. Believe it or not, I've been told by several people that I'm somewhat unlikeable. Tend to bring out the worst in them. I don't get it myself. I think I'm perfectly charming."

"What were you fighting about?"

"Something and nothing."

"Do you think I'm playing, Mr Winters?" shouted Perez, suddenly banging her hand down against the desk. "Is this a game to you? Three people are dead. And you are right in the centre of everything. Either you stop pissing me about, or I'll lock you in a cell you'll never get out of."

"Jesus," said Freddie, "you should have said you were on your period. I would have bought you some chocolate and a hot water bottle."

"That's it…" said Perez, her face purpling with exasperation.

"All right, all right. I'm only yanking your chain," said Freddie. "No need to go all CIA on me. Yes, I had a chat with Christy. Yes, it got a bit heated. She took offence at me accusing her of having something to do with Malcolm's murder."

"You accused her? Why?"

"I thought you'd been doing your homework?" he said. "You must know about Christy and Malcolm. Everyone in the industry knew. They had a little fling, then – surprise, surprise – he publishes her first book. Of course, he stitches her up with a terrible contract, completely ripping her off so she earns fuck-all money. Then he moves onto another woman. I just suggested she might have felt bitter about the whole situation and done something to get her revenge."

"And was she bitter?"

"Apparently not. All water under the bridge according to her. No desire to jab a pen into his throat whatsoever."

"That was it?"

"That was it."

"And you believed her?"

"She seemed pretty genuine," said Freddie. "Although there was one thing."

"What?" said Perez.

"Wouldn't you like to know?"

Perez sighed, looked at her feet and muttered something under her breath in Spanish. She signalled to her goon, who straightened and lifted a pair of handcuffs.

"Okay, okay," said Freddie. "Keep your knickers on. The book. She got all weird when I told her about the book."

"Weird? How so?"

"I can't say, exactly. Obviously, her ex-husband wrote the book. Malcolm published it and Max edited it. I pointed out the coincidence, and it was like I'd said something that really touched a nerve. And she tried to hide it."

"Hide what?"

"No idea. She got angry and chucked a glass in my dinner. But it has to be significant, right? Especially now she's dead and that book has turned up again. You see, isn't this better? The two of us working together."

"We are *not* working together," said Perez.

"Oh, come on, Inspector. Surely you must see I can help."

"Yes, you can help. You can help by staying out of my way. And for God's sake, don't be there when somebody else gets killed."

"You think somebody else is going to be killed?" said Freddie.

"You really are the most infuriating man," said Perez.

"Yeah, I hear that a lot," said Freddie.

"You can go now," said Perez. "Go and have a shower. Stay away from my investigations. And if it's at all possible, please try and stay out of trouble."

Perez sighed and placed a hand on her chin. The black-clad police goon marched over, unceremoniously helped Freddie up out of his seat and marched him out of the office.

*****

"The press are having an absolute field day with this back home," said Marylin, placing her phone down on the table. "Just spoke with the girls in the office. Front page news. *The Sun*'s headline is *Costa Del Killing Spree*. *The Mirror* is running with *Murders in Paradise*. Bit generic, I thought. And *The Star* went with *Murders They Wrote*. Kind of works, I guess. We've got practically every paper. Well, aside from the *Daily Mail* who are running a story about how Princess Diana would have given her full blessing to Brexit. Bloody idiots." She took a long puff on her e-cigarette and blew out a triumphant plume of vapour.

"Christ, Marylin, try not to sound too bloody happy about it," said Edward. He was sitting on the edge of his bed, holding his head in his hands.

"Of course, darling. It's an absolute tragedy. Just terrible. I'm completely torn apart. I'm just saying, there's no such thing as bad publicity. And all this press with the new book coming out… well, it's not going to hurt sales."

"When did you become so bloody callous?"

"I'm just a realist. A terrible thing has happened, but that doesn't mean we can't make something good out of it. And this callousness has helped me earn you a lot of money over the years. Don't forget that."

"Aren't you worried?"

"About what?"

"For fuck's sake, Marylin. Don't you see what's happening? Max, Malcolm and now Christy? Apart from you and me, nobody else knew about…"

"No, Edward," she said, cutting him off. "I'm not worried. How many times do I have to tell you, it was all taken care of?"

"But how do you know?"

"I know because I know. Let's just leave it at that."

"Well, how do you explain it, then? And how do you know we're not next?"

"Whatever's happening here, it has nothing to do with…" She stopped short, cutting herself off. "Besides, how do we know she was even killed? If you ask me, she jumped off that balcony."

"Well, how do you explain the book scattering down?"

"She probably did that herself. I bet she killed Max and Malcolm. Probably some kind of sex thing. Love triangle gone wrong. She gets jealous and kills them both. She leaves a book with each of them, then she leaps off a balcony with another one in her hand."

"You think?"

"Why not?"

"But why my book?"

"Probably just two fingers up to you. Or maybe she was trying to frame you. Who knows what goes in a deranged person's mind?"

"You really think so?"

"Stands to reason. Anyway, why are you so upset? That woman was nothing but trouble. I warned you about marrying her. Nothing but a bloody gold digger. She was bad enough when you were married. And then, when you finally saw sense and gave her the elbow, she was twice as bad."

"I know…"

"All that stuff in the press over the divorce. Publishing those dreadful, scandalous books. Nearly giving the game away with…" Again, she cut herself off.

"I know. It's just such a shock, though," said Edward. "And it's not as if things were always bad." He glanced off into the middle distance, his eyes glazed with a happier memory.

Marylin humphed and took another long drag on her e-cigarette.

"And such a horrible way to die," said Edward, looking solemn again.

"Looking for attention, as usual," said Marylin. "I'm sorry. I don't like to wish bad upon anybody. And I wouldn't wish her dead. But it's not the worst thing that ever happened."

"You're all heart," said Edward, burying his head in his hands again. "Anyway, how long are they going to keep us locked in this room? It's nearly dinner time and I'm starving."

******

Freddie needed to see inside that room. Whatever happened to Christy, he was sure it wasn't suicide – someone had pushed her off that balcony. When he'd spoken with her the night before, she'd seemed spooked. Pissed off, for sure. But suicidal? No way. There must be something in that room that would tell him how she really died.

He made a quick pitstop to his room to wash the poor girl literally out of his hair and change clothes. This time he opted for a pair of bright blue shorts and a shirt with tiny pictures of pelicans. He had to look reasonably smart to sneak past the police again, and this was the best he could do.

His head was still throbbing from sitting in the sun with a hangover, so he washed down some more paracetamol with another can of lager. He'd have loved to crawl back into bed, just for an hour, but time was against him. Perez was still interviewing witnesses in the manager's office but he didn't know how long she would be, so he had to be quick.

Finding Christy's room was a lot easier than finding Malcolm's had been. He already knew which side of the hotel it was on, having seen where she'd appeared from, and then where she'd landed like an overripe tomato. He headed to that part of the hotel, then went floor to floor until he found the room being guarded by police. There were two officers this time, but luckily his fake warrant card did the trick again, and he sneaked into the room with ease.

Freddie stepped over shoes scattered along the hallway and walked through to the main room. It was a mess. Clothes were strewn about the floor, hanging off the sofa and the backs of the chairs, spilling out of an open suitcase on the floor. It looked like the case had exploded, flinging bras, knickers, skirts, shorts and dresses all around the room like shrapnel.

The bed was completely unmade, sheets draped down to the floor. The little table was littered with empty miniature bottles – both white and rosé wine, plus vodka, gin and whisky. A dirty wine glass and a tumbler sat there, both smeared with Christy's red lipstick, next to a plate crusted with bits of dried food. It seemed Christy had eaten in her room the previous evening, ordering room service rather than coming down to the restaurant. And, considering the number of empty bottles, she'd put away quite a bit of booze. There were no signs anyone else had been there, Freddie noted, again talking to his imaginary Dictaphone.

It didn't add up. Christy was usually the life and soul of any party. In fact, she hated being alone, and she'd never spend the evening on her own in a hotel room when so many of her peers were just a few floors below, drinking and gossiping. But then, come to think of it, Freddie hadn't seen her last night.

"Why did you lock yourself away?" Freddie muttered. "What were you hiding from?"

Freddie reached under the desk on the far side of the room and pulled out the little bin. Empty. He scanned the room, looking for anything else that seemed out of place. Nothing obvious. He walked over to the balcony. The doors were still wide open. He took a deep breath and stepped out.

The sun was still high, blaring down from a cloudless, blue sky. A soft breeze whispered past him. The pool area was eerily quiet, completely abandoned apart from the two crime scene investigators stepping around a little white tent which had been erected to conceal Christy's mangled body.

Freddie got down on his hands and knees. He scanned the floor. Inspected the railings on the balcony. Again, nothing obvious.

To be honest, he wasn't sure what he expected to see. In the movies, the detective would always find some meaningful clue. Scuff marks on the ground, bloody fingerprints on the railings. Something that indicated a struggle had taken place. Something that showed the victim had to have been pushed rather than jump. But there was nothing. Just an empty balcony.

There was nothing to suggest Christy hadn't simply decided to end her life. But Freddie didn't believe it. He could feel it in his gut.

Freddie walked back into the room, feeling deflated. He sat down on the bed, sighing and glancing around. Then something caught his eye. Sitting on the bedside table was a book. Freddie hadn't been looking for one. The killer had already left that clue. Seeing one now, his heart started beating faster. He reached over and picked it up.

Hmmm, he thought, now that is strange.

He'd been expecting it to be another copy of *The Terrible Bones*, but this was Christy's own book, *The Contract*. It was the first one she'd had published. Weird. Who sleeps with a copy of their own book by the bed? Had she been reading it? Who the hell does that?

The cover was weathered and well-worn, the spine cracked and nearly falling apart from being read many times. Freddie had read it years ago, but he didn't remember much about the plot. He opened the cover and nearly dropped it when he saw the writing.

Scrawled in big red letters, the first page was covered by two words: *You knew.*

It looked to be the same red pen. The same manic handwriting. Freddie flicked through the pages to see the same message appear on every single page. No words circled this time. No other hidden messages. Just the same words repeating over and over again.

You knew.

"Knew what?" said Freddie. What did it all mean?

Was this why Christy had locked herself in the room all evening? Had she come back to her room to find it waiting for her? Had it unlocked some distant, hidden secret? Brought about feelings of guilt that drove her to suicide?

Or had the killer left it as another calling card, another hint at their motive?

"You knew," he whispered to himself. "Knew what? What did you know, Christy?"

This had to be connected. But how did the pieces fit together? Whatever the explanation, the killer was getting braver. They were seeking more attention now. Max was killed very much under the cover of darkness. Quiet, secret, hidden. Malcolm's murder was more explosive. A bout of extreme rage and violence, the body left doused with blood so everyone could witness the anger of the kill. And this new murder was much more brazen. The killer didn't just want the body to be found, they wanted everyone to see the death happen. Why else do it during the event taking place directly below? Maximum impact. Attention-seeking. Catch me if you can.

Someone with a very specific point to prove.

Freddie heard a sudden commotion outdoors. People talking. An argument. Rapid-fire Spanish. Then bursts of English. Angry. Incredulous. A voice Freddie recognised.

"What do you mean I'm already inside the room? I'm stood right here in front of you."

Oh fuck!

Freddie heard the door lock click. The handle grinding as it turned. The soft whistle of air as the door pushed open. He scanned the room. Panicking. Looking for somewhere to hide. He heard footsteps on the tiled floor, coming towards him. Was there time to climb under the bed?

"Oh, for fuck's sake," said Detective Inspector Richard Stone – the real Detective Inspector Richard Stone – as he walked into the room.

"Richard," said Freddie. "Fancy seeing you here."

CHAPTER 16

"WHAT ARE YOU doing in here, Freddie?" said Detective Inspector Richard Stone. "How did you get past those police officers?"

"I knew Christy," said Freddie. "There's no way she killed herself. I had to come and see what really happened in this room."

"Had to? Why? You're not a detective, Freddie. You're a second-rate writer who should know better and leave the police work to the real police."

"That's rich. I never heard you complaining when we worked together. A keen eye for crime, isn't that what you said I had? How many cases did I consult on with you?"

"We never worked together. I let you hang around and watch. And that was before you completely torpedoed my career, ruined my marriage and proved yourself to be the selfish, manipulative, inconsiderate weasel you really are."

"Oh, there's only so many times I can apologise for that. Besides, what are *you* doing here? Bit outside your patch, isn't it?"

"Believe me," said Richard, strolling around the room, snapping on a pair of blue nitrile gloves, assessing the items on the table and peering out onto the balcony, "it wasn't my first choice. When a bunch of British literary types started getting bumped off in a Spanish hotel, the local force here reached out to Scotland Yard for an assist. What with my previous experience with a crime-writing author wanker – in other words you – the top brass decided I was uniquely qualified to come and consult. Bloody joke, if you ask me. Proper stitch up. I get called to the Chief Superintendent's office and he tells me 'don't fuck it up' because the eyes of the press are all over it. They stick me in a taxi to Gatwick, bung me on a flight and three hours later I'm here looking at your ugly mug."

"It's hit the press?" said Freddie. "What are they saying? Have they mentioned me?"

"Same old Freddie," sneered Richard.

"Well, it's great to have you on board," said Freddie. "The old team back together. That bloody Perez has been a real pain in the arse. Won't listen to anything I have to say. She's even got it in her head that I'm a suspect."

"Yeah, I spoke to her on the phone. Bit of a hard arse, isn't she? I'm not surprised she took against you. You are quite a dickhead."

"Tell me something I don't know."

"So, what's going on here?"

"You mean the great Inspector hasn't filled you in?"

"Course she has. But I want to hear it from you. You generally tend to have a… unique perspective on things. Who's dead? And why?"

Freddie breathed deeply, savouring the moment. "Well, it's like this…"

Freddie told Richard all about the last few days. He explained the event and why they were all there. He told him about Dan the organiser, the other writers and the different guests he'd encountered. He told him all about Max, Malcolm and Christy – who they were, how they were connected and how they'd died. He held back from telling him every single detail. He didn't explain his own theories, or the madcap ones he'd been discussing in the bar with the other writers. He *forgot* to mention the clues he'd found in Malcolm's room. He did, however, tell Richard about the book on Christy's night table – partly because he'd find it himself anyway, but mostly because he suddenly realised he hadn't wiped his fingerprints off it.

Richard sat opposite him, gazing out the window as he listened. When Freddie finished, he looked up and said, "Right then. Thanks for the update. Now, do me a favour and piss off."

"What?" said Freddie. "I thought we were going to…"

"What? Work together? Team up?" chuckled Richard. "Why don't you go back to doing what you do best and just… I dunno… what is it that you do?"

"For God's sake, Richard," sighed Freddie. "You know how helpful I can be."

"Yes, but I also know what an odious, selfish, unscrupulous arse you can be. I wouldn't work with you if you had a signed confession from the killer."

"Well, that's a bit short-sighted."

"You're a witness, Freddie. And not a very reliable one, at that. You're not a detective. You're not needed. You're not wanted."

"I'm getting a bit tired of hearing that," said Freddie. "You know, I did solve a pretty big case last year. And save my friend's life. And help you make a significant arrest."

"Just go, Freddie," said Richard, his voice softening slightly. "Perez won't take kindly to you sneaking into another one of her crime scenes. I don't have to tell her, but she's on her way here now. Better not let her find you here."

"Fine," said Freddie, his face turning red like a toddler on the verge of a tantrum. He stood up, placed the book on the table and walked towards the door.

"Freddie, wait," said Richard suddenly.

Freddie spun round. A reprieve? Richard seeing sense and agreeing to accept his help?

"Hand it over," said Richard.

"What?"

"Come on, I know you've got another one."

Freddie humphed. "Fine," he said, fishing the fake warrant card from his pocket.

"Honestly, how many of these have I confiscated now?"

"Doesn't matter how many you take," said Freddie. "I've got plenty more at home." He dropped it on the ground like a petulant child, then marched out of the room, slamming the door behind him.

The two officers outside the room stepped back in surprise. Freddie shrugged. Then he heard someone approaching from the far end of the corridor, so he set off quickly, sprinting down the hallway as soon as he was out of sight.

He rounded the corner, trying to find his bearings. The hotel was noisier now. The sound of loud TVs and chatter in the rooms had transformed into the distant, low rumble of people talking, walking, congregating somewhere far off. Freddie looked out the large window and saw people milling about down by the larger pool area, dressed in their evening attire. It was dinner time. Perez must have released people from their rooms to go and eat.

Freddie was just about to head back to his own room when he bumped into Dan coming the other way and looking twice as flustered as usual.

"Mr Winters," he said, in a squeaky, rapid-fire voice. "Terrible what's happened. Absolutely terrible. Just when you think things can't... and then they do... and then..."

159

"Yes," said Freddie, "it's been quite the week. Where are you rushing off to?"

"Getting the main stage ready," said Dan. "Rounding people up. So much to do."

"What? The events are still going ahead? Surely not."

"Oh yes," said Dan. "Well, no. Not exactly. I spoke with Inspector Perez earlier. We've agreed to suspend the rest of the itinerary. Not much point carrying on. And it would be pretty poor taste, considering what's happened."

"Yes," said Freddie, doing his best to look solemn. "But what does that mean for… er…" He rubbed his thumb and forefinger together.

"Oh yes, not to worry," said Dan, placing a hand on Freddie's shoulder. "All our speakers will be paid in full. My lawyer assures me we're fully covered by insurance. He's already started the claim – you know what lawyers are like. He also thinks we've got a good case to withhold payment from the hotel. So, it's not exactly been the money-spinner I'd hoped. Should just about break even, but at least nobody's out of pocket."

"Well, that's something," said Freddie. "But if the rest of the event is cancelled, why are you setting up the stage?"

"Oh, that? I convinced Inspector Perez to let me set up an impromptu reading. A few authors doing a chapter or two from their latest books. Thought it might keep everyone entertained and save having to lock people in their rooms. Stop the masses revolting, and all that. And I don't know about you, but I always think there's safety in numbers. I know I'll feel a bit safer if we're all together."

"Makes sense," said Freddie. "So, when do you need me?"

"Need you?" said Dan, oblivious.

"On stage? And what should I read?"

"Erm…" said Dan, followed by an uncomfortably long pause. "Do you know, that's very kind. But I… in fact, you know… because I've already…"

"No problem," said Freddie. "Forget it."

"Oh no…" said Dan, "it's not because… I mean, it's just that…"

"Yeah, whatever."

Another uncomfortably long pause. Then Dan said that he really must dash off. And then he dashed off.

Dejected, Freddie trudged along the corridor to his room. He was just nearing the elevator when one of the bedroom doors opened ahead of him. A thick plume of sickly-sweet strawberry-scented vapour poured out of the room, followed closely after by a man in a white hooded jumper.

There he was. Hoodie man. This time with a thin, black vape pursed between his lips.

"Hey," shouted Freddie.

The man turned to look; his face partly obscured by the hood. A look of recognition flashed in his eyes.

"Hey," shouted Freddie again. "Hey, I want a word with you."

The man straightened, his hands twitching slightly. He stood there, frozen, staring at Freddie. Then he ran, darting down the hallway, the sound of flip-flops flapping against his feet.

Oh, for fuck's sake.

Freddie sighed loudly, grimaced and started running after him.

The man was fast, sprinting away as Freddie bounded after him, coughing and spluttering. Freddie's heartbeat was instantly racing. His ragged breath burst out in short, sharp gasps. A burning pain searing in his chest, just beneath his throat. His back ached and his knees crunched. His thighs burned with the effort. And he'd only run about 50 feet down a carpeted corridor.

Freddie saw the man barrelling ahead, turning a corner and disappearing out of sight.

Shit.

Freddie trudged along, sweating and wheezing. Trundling rather than running. His ankles throbbing with every step. His heart beating faster and faster until he felt like it might explode in his chest.

He reached the end of the corridor and turned the corner. Empty. Nobody in sight. The man was gone. Again.

"For fuck's sake," shouted Freddie, collapsing to his knees and gulping in large mouthfuls of air. Sweat beaded on his forehead, trickled down the sides of his neck. His face burned with heat. His chest throbbed. "Where the fuck did he go?"

Freddie leaned against the wall as tiny red and green dots sparkled in his vision. He rested there, catching his breath for far longer than a man of his age should really have to, wondering how Hoodie Man had pulled off another Houdini-style disappearing act.

Finally, he clambered back up onto his aching feet. He was just about to admit defeat when he heard a strange crashing sound. He looked up the corridor. Nothing. He gazed back in the direction he'd come from. No obvious signs of movement.

He tiptoed down the corridor, looking intently at each hotel room door. All closed. No sound coming from within. No signs of anything unusual.

Then he saw it. About 20 feet away, a door slightly ajar. From the sign, it looked to be some sort of janitor's closet. He stepped lightly, approaching slowly.

He reached out. Gripped the handle. Held his breath and prepared himself. Then he yanked it open, fast and confident.

A sudden gust of air whooshed out as Freddie pulled the door to reveal the hooded man cowering, jammed in against a stack of toilet rolls and cleaning products.

"There you are, you fucker," shouted Freddie.

The man grabbed a toilet roll and threw it at Freddie. It bounced off his forehead with a soft thud. Freddie remained firmly in place.

"What the hell was…"

Before Freddie could finish his sentence, another toilet roll came hurtling towards him, followed by another and then another, bouncing gently off his head, chest and shoulder. The man in the cupboard squealed with each throw, panic in his eyes.

"Could you stop doing that?" said Freddie. "I don't think it's having quite the effect you're hoping for."

"Please. Leave me alone," said the man. "Don't hurt me."

"Hurt you? I'm not gonna hurt you. Just put the loo rolls down and get the hell out of there."

The man seemed to think for a second. Then he climbed down off the bucket he was teetering on, unwedged himself from the stack of toilet paper, and stepped gingerly out of the cupboard.

"Jesus, are you all right?" he said, noticing Freddie's red, sweaty face and obvious difficulty breathing. "You look like you're having a heart attack."

"No thanks to you," said Freddie. "You know, there's a reason people aren't supposed to run. Firstly, it's a bloody stupid thing to do. Secondly, it makes you look like this."

"Not if you keep yourself fit," scoffed the man.

"Hey, I'm as fit as I need to be," snapped Freddie. "Anyway, why did you run off when I called out to you?"

"Why do you think? There's a killer in the hotel. I thought it might be you. I thought you might be trying to… you know…"

"You thought I was the killer? I was chasing you because I thought you were the killer."

"Me? Why?"

"I saw you last night. Hanging around the first murder scene. What were you doing there?"

"Murder scene? I was taking an evening stroll and minding my own business. Then you started shouting and running towards me."

"Oh yeah, so why did you run off?"

"Because you were shouting and running towards me. I didn't know who you were. I thought you might be… you know… a killer. Or the press."

"Again, I was chasing you because I thought *you* were the killer," said Freddie.

"Why would I want to kill a load of people in a hotel?" said the man, pulling his hood down to reveal his face. He was young, maybe 25 years old. He had short dark hair, a good week's worth of stubble and his eyes were bloodshot with big black bags hanging beneath them.

"That's what I wanted to ask you. Except you ran off."

"Of course I did. I thought you wanted to kill me."

"Jesus, we could go round like this for hours," sighed Freddie. "Look, can we both agree that neither of us are murderers, you're going to stop throwing things at me and, if I ask you a few questions, you won't run off again?"

"Well," said the man, thinking carefully, "so long as you promise you don't want to kill me."

"Good," said Freddie, "because I'm gasping for a beer. I'm Freddie, by the way. And you are?"

"Craig. Craig Mitchell."

The two men walked to the bar, Freddie panting and gasping all the way, while vehemently rejecting the strange man's assertion that he should seek medical attention. Maybe he had a point. Freddie couldn't keep up his unhealthy lifestyle forever. He should really cut down on the booze, start eating more healthily and, God forbid, exercising. But that was tomorrow Freddie's problem. He put it on his mental to-do list and ordered three pints – one each, plus an extra for himself – and they settled in at a corner table.

"Right, so who the hell are you?" said Freddie. "Why are you hiding out at this hotel and sneaking into literary talks you clearly have no interest in? And why do you keep running away from me? And why did you think I was from the press?"

"It's a long story," said Craig.

"Well, as long as I don't keel over from a heart attack, I've got plenty of time," said Freddie, taking a large gulp of beer.

"You were right about one thing," said Craig. "I am sort of in hiding."

"Why, what did you do?"

"Have you heard of Shawna Crawford?"

"Nope. Should I have?"

"She was this reality TV star. She's done all the UK reality shows. She started on *Love Castle*."

"What the hell is *Love Castle*?"

"You know, that show where they have a load of busty, pretty girls locked up in the tower of a castle. They have these muscle-bound, braindead 'Prince Charmings'." He held his fingers up in quote marks. "They do these 'Knightly challenges'…" Air quotes again. "So, they can free the 'Princesses'…"

Freddie winced as he made air quotes for a third time. He was going to wear his fingers out. Or have someone snap them off.

"…and win their fair hands, and all that crap. It's basically primetime softcore porn, with sexy people wearing next to nothing and shagging each other."

"Sounds awful," said Freddie. "People actually watch that shit?"

"You'd be surprised. Anyway, this Shawna was the star of the first series. Big boobs, blonde hair, typical reality type. After that, she was on everything else: *Celebrity Pole Vaulters, Singing in the Kitchen, Celebrity Long Distance Drivers, Superstar Drain Cleaners, Celebrity Bog Snorkelling…* You name it, she was on it."

"Right," said Freddie. "So, what about her?"

"Well, she became pretty famous. You know, famous for being famous. One of these social media influencers. Does nothing and gets loads of free stuff just because. Anyway, it hit the papers recently that she had cancer." The man hung his head and sighed with a doleful look. "A week ago, she passed away."

"Okay," said Freddie. "Sorry, are you gonna get to a point anytime soon?"

Hoodie Man looked back up, the start of tears glinting in his eyes.

"I was out with my mates after work. We'd had a good week, so we went out to celebrate, and before you know it, I was absolutely hammered. I remember getting the train home and I was bored and drunk and playing on my phone. I logged into Twitter and everyone was talking about Shawna's death. It had just been announced that she'd died."

"Okay."

"People were posting all these sycophantic messages, making out like she was some kind of Messiah figure. *A bright light has gone out today. The world will be a darker place without you.* All that sort of shit. I mean, only a few months earlier, they'd been slagging her off, calling her a talentless moron, and accusing her of shagging two footballers in the same team at once."

"So?"

"People were always slagging her off. The press were the worst. But now, they're all making out like she was a saint. It was ridiculous. It makes you sick how interchangeable these people are."

"I'm guessing you decided to air these views on social media?" said Freddie.

Craig took a deep breath, the tears glinting in his eyes. "I didn't mean it. It was only supposed to be a joke. I mean… you always think you're funny when you're drunk."

"What did you write?"

"I wrote 'The world has lost a great pair of tits today. But we won't miss the talentless twat they were attached to'. He said the words with genuine sorrow, each one seeming to burn on his tongue. He sighed and hung his head again.

"Jesus, that's harsh," said Freddie. "Even I wouldn't have said something like that."

"I know," said Craig. "I didn't mean it. I was drunk and… I just tapped it out, posted it, went home, ate a kebab and passed out."

"So, what's the problem?"

"I woke up the next morning, terrible hangover and no memory of what I'd done. I checked my phone and there's a text from my mate Paul saying, 'What the fuck?' I phoned him and he just says, 'Check Twitter'. I logged in and it was mental. I only have 67 followers but overnight my tweet had been retweeted 290,356 times. There were thousands of replies, calling me all the names under the sun, accusing me of abusing a poor dead woman. Celebrities were berating me, calling me out and asking all their fans to send me hate. I even had Piers Morgan claiming the moral high ground.

"I immediately deleted the tweet, but the damage was done. It was out there in the world. By the afternoon, people had tracked me down on Facebook and they're sending me all sorts of vile messages. Death threats. Telling me they're gonna come round my house and get me.

"The next day, the press had hold of it. They're writing articles about me. Calling me the most hated man in Britain. I get a call from my boss telling me not to come in for a few weeks, so I'm probably getting sacked. Then someone tracks down my phone number and address. I had to turn my phone off, it was just ringing constantly. Then people turn up at my door, throwing things, shouting at me, telling me I'm gonna burn in hell. I swear, I send one drunken tweet and I'm more hated than that dentist who killed the lion."

"Sounds like quite the overreaction. I take it that's what brought you here."

"Exactly. I managed to sneak out of the house, got a mate to drop me at the airport and booked the first package holiday that got me out of the country. I've been hiding here ever since, terrified the press might track me down. Or worse."

"Wow," said Freddie, taking another gulp of beer. "That's why you were acting all shifty, wearing a great big hoodie in 30-degree heat?"

"Have you seen the amount of people reading *The Sun* by the pool? I kept thinking someone would recognise me and start having a go. I'm just trying to keep my head down until I can go home."

"Makes sense," said Freddie. "No wonder you pegged it when I started shouting. Still, on a positive note, I can cross you off my list of suspects."

"Great news," said Craig. "That'll make everything better."

"No need to take the piss. It's not my fault you sent the world's least funny tweet. And it's not my fault you ran off to hide in a hotel with a serial killer on the loose."

"What's the score with that, anyway?" said Craig. "What's going on? The police aren't telling us much. Just stay in your room, then letting us out for dinner."

"Not sure yet," said Freddie. "I'm still piecing the puzzle together. Interviewing suspects and trying to figure it out."

"So, you're what… some kind of private detective? I figure you can't be a real cop, being that out of shape. No offence."

"Cheeky sod. I guess I'm a kind of private detective," said Freddie. "Actually, I'm one of the novelists here as part of the literary retreat."

Craig eyed Freddie for a few seconds, then burst out laughing. "You're a novelist?"

"Crime novelist, yes. You should know, you sat through two of my talks."

"Did I? Sorry, wasn't exactly paying attention. So, what are you doing interviewing people? Not exactly part of your job, is it?"

"Actually, my writing gives me a unique perspective. I'm very attuned to this sort of thing. I've helped the police solve lots of crimes."

"Pull the other one," laughed Craig. "Like what, missing dogs and cats?"

"If you must know, I was instrumental in preventing a high-profile murder last year. It was in all the papers. I wrote a book about it."

"Right. So, what, you're helping the local police here, are you?"

"Not exactly. They won't let me help. Bloody idiots."

"Oh, that's good," laughed Craig. "There I am running off, thinking you might be the killer. Or maybe the press has tracked me down. Turns out you're just a writer that fancies himself as some kind of bloody Poirot."

"That's not exactly…"

"No, seriously, that's brilliant," said Craig, standing up and taking a large mouthful of beer. "That's great. Just what I needed to cheer me up."

"No problem," said Freddie, shrugging and sighing.

Craig shook his head and pulled his hoodie up to conceal his face. "Do me a favour, will you? Next time you see me, just leave me alone."

With that, he turned and skulked out of the bar, moving quickly and keeping his head down.

Freddie drained the last of his pint and took out his notebook. He turned to the page where he'd made a shortlist of suspects. Christy's name had already been crossed out, hers having been added to the list of victims. Freddie scored through the words *Hoodie man*. Beneath that he'd listed out *Mysterious Writer*, *Hotel Manager* and *Nick Foster*.

Freddie had no reason to believe the hotel manager was involved in the murders; he'd made the list purely because he seemed a bit weird and Freddie's list needed bulking out. The same went for Nick Foster. Freddie didn't see him being involved. He had a borderline motive for wanting Malcolm and Max dead. But, to Freddie's knowledge, Nick didn't even know Christy. So, it seemed unlikely.

Besides, Nick was no killer – he was literally the nicest man Freddie had ever met. He was so damned friendly, enthusiastic and positive, Freddie found it impossible not to like him. And Freddie disliked at least 99% of the people he came across. So, no, Nick was not a real suspect.

Freddie had even added his own name to the bottom of the list, just for due diligence. He had to concede there was at least a chance that he was the killer – no matter how slim. After all, he had the temperament for it. And he certainly had motive to see them all dead, even if those reasons were somewhat spurious. Obviously, he didn't remember killing anybody, but that didn't necessarily mean he hadn't done it. He could have been suffering from an as-yet-unknown psychological condition that meant he'd blacked out during the murders and awoke with no memory of them. Perhaps he was suffering with undiagnosed dissociative identity disorder, and it was one of his multiple personalities carrying out the attacks, unbeknownst to him. It would make for an interesting twist, if nothing else.

On balance, Freddie decided he probably wasn't the murderer and scored through his and Nick's names. He focused on the words *Mysterious writer*. That still seemed the most likely fit. Someone in the industry who'd crossed paths with Max, Malcolm and Christy and was taking their revenge. But who? The place was packed with writers – both successful published authors and ambitious amateurs. The killer could be any of them.

There was, of course, one name that was very closely linked to all three victims. Someone with whom Freddie had had his own run-ins. And someone whom he was now very keen to speak with.

He wrote the name Edward Cross at the bottom of his list and underlined it three times.

CHAPTER 17

"HOW DO PEOPLE eat this slop?" said Edward, looking down his nose at the plate of food in front of him. "It's not exactly The Ritz, is it? More like The Pits, if you ask me." He smiled to himself, clearly pleased with his own wit.

Honestly, was there anything that man couldn't find to complain about, thought Marylin. The food looked perfectly fine to her. And he seemed to forget she'd known him for a very long time – since he was a penniless, starving artist who lived off jacket potatoes and tuna five days a week because it was cheap. Nowadays, he was so full of himself, flaunting his wealth and looking down on anyone with less than him. How quickly they forget. She'd seen too many like him come and go over the years. A little bit of fame and they couldn't stand being out of the spotlight. That first taste of critical acclaim and every negative comment or review they got thereafter – no matter how slight or innocuous – was like a dagger to their bleeding hearts. And, of course, as soon as they started making money, they forgot where they came from – the leaner times that made them what they were and fuelled their creativity.

Well, not her. She knew exactly who she was. She'd experienced her own lean times and knew just how hard they could be. Not something she liked to think back on. And she'd worked hard for what she had, always prepared to do whatever it took to get ahead. She'd told herself at a very early age that she'd never go without again, and it was a promise she'd managed to keep.

Now she was focused on putting aside as much money as she could, and in just a few short years she'd leave it all behind. And wouldn't that be a grand day, when she waved goodbye to all the whiny, needy men-children that she found herself mothering. Just think of the money. Just think of the money.

"I know, darling," she said, forcing enthusiasm into her voice. "Funny sort of place, isn't it? Still, looks very tasty."

"You not eating?" said Edward, shoving a large forkful of stew (or was it curry?) into his mouth.

"Honestly, darling, you know I don't eat. Have to look after my figure."

"Yeah, well, I can't wait to get the hell out of here." Edward winced as he watched people scurrying around the restaurant, wobbling about with big plates stacked high with food. "All these bloody mouth-breathers, shovelling chips and burgers into their faces like pigs at a trough. Oh, for a plane to rescue me and whisk me to Le Gavroche."

Marylin held in a sigh. "Well, hopefully that will be soon. The police can't keep us locked up in here forever. The event's officially cancelled now. And don't worry, I've had a word with the organiser. You'll be getting paid in full. Not that that's the point, but money is money. And I've got the girls contacting the Foreign Office, trying to grease the wheels and speed things up. But for now, we'll just have to bide our time."

"Well, couldn't we bide it somewhere with a few less psychotic killers on the loose?"

"I know, darling. But safety in numbers, eh? Nobody's going to do anything to us if we keep in big crowds like this."

"So you do think we're at risk?" said Edward. "You know something, don't you? What aren't you telling me?"

"Nothing, darling. Nothing. I don't know of any reason that we're at risk – no more than anyone else, anyway. I just mean we're better off with lots of people around. Certainly better than sitting in that room stewing over things."

"Hmmm, I guess so," grumbled Edward. "Safety in numbers."

"Speaking of which…"

"Oh God, what? What have you done?" said Edward.

"Nothing, darling. I just…"

"Marylin?"

"Just a little reading, that's all. Nothing major."

"A reading?"

"When I was speaking with the organiser, he said he was putting on a little reading tonight. Getting a few authors up on stage to read extracts from their books. Keep people entertained. Stop them going mad locked up here in the hotel. He asked if you'd be willing, and I said you'd be happy to read a few chapters for the crowd."

"Oh, did you now?"

"Think of the publicity, darling. We'll get it all up on social. *Hero Author Entertains Frightened Crowd in Murder Hotel.* The press will lap it up. Think of the book sales."

"Honestly, my ex-wife and two colleagues have been murdered, the killer's still on the loose, and you're thinking about book sales. You're bloody tenacious, I'll give you that."

"That's why you love me, darling."

"Still, I guess it's not the worst idea. Who else is doing it, though?"

"Don't worry, darling. It's all sorted. Just you and three other writers. Helen Brennan, Austin James and Colin McMaster. And you're on last. The headline act. Everyone else gets one chapter, you get to read three. Trust me, by the end of the night everyone in that room will be so hooked on the new book they'll have it on pre-order before they get back to their rooms."

"Yeah, all right, then," said Edward. He lifted another forkful of food, wrinkled his nose and shoved it into his mouth.

"Edward Cross, as I live and breathe." The voice came ringing out behind him – loud, whiny, annoying. Before Edward could do anything, it was next to him, in his ear. "Eddie, baby. Long time no see, eh?"

Edward closed his eyes for a second, seemingly hoping that if he just ignored the problem it might go away. It didn't. He opened his eyes again, looked at the man standing next to him and sighed. "Hello Freddie," he said.

"Great to see you," said Freddie Winters, sitting next to him and putting down a plate of the strangest assortment of food. It was stacked so high it looked like it could topple over at any second. "How long has it been? 18 years? Honestly, you don't write, you don't call. It's almost as if you don't want to see me." He laughed and shoved two onion rings into his mouth, chewing loudly.

"Whatever gave you that idea?" sneered Edward.

"What do you want, Winters?" said Marylin, her mouth pursed like she'd just swallowed a ball of ear wax.

"Marylin, daaaaaaarling," said Freddie. "Given your flying monkeys the night off, I see."

"Very droll. We're just in the middle of a discussion, if you don't mind," she said, making shooing motions with her hand.

"No problem. Don't mind at all. It's actually rather handy, because I wanted to have a discussion with you two as well."

"Really? What could you possibly want to discuss with us?"

"Oh, you know, the three murders that have taken place and how you two are clearly up to your necks in it. I was just wondering, how exactly are you both involved?"

Marylin snorted out a fake laugh.

Edward bristled slightly. His forehead tensed. He went to speak, then changed his mind and forced a forkful into his mouth.

"Don't be ridiculous, Winters," said Marylin, her voice whiny and high-pitched. "What are you doing? Don't tell me you're investigating this? You really are as deluded as ever. Still that same, sad, second-rate writer who's too big for his boots and drags chaos with him everywhere he goes."

Things between Freddie and Edward hadn't always been so acrimonious. In fact, some years ago, the two were very good friends. They started out at roughly the same time. Freddie was a young writer, having just received a decent level of critical and commercial success for his first novel. Not exactly setting the world alight, but the critics seemed to like it, and a reasonable number of people had bought it. He was working on his second novel when *The Bloody Dagger* magazine – the leading crime writing journal at the time – did a piece on him and a selection of other novelists. It hailed them as the new generation of crime writers and ones to watch – or *The New Bloods*, as they christened them. The magazine did an interview with him and his fellow writers and gathered them together for a photoshoot. That's when Freddie and Edward first met.

Edward was a debut author. His first book was still yet to be published, but critics had heaped so much praise on it, hailing him as the best debut crime writer for a generation, that he'd made the magazine's list before selling a single copy. Freddie had taken to him instantly. Freddie had actually been quite open and friendly in the early days, although he did hold particular disdain for anyone with whom he'd have to compete for book sales. But there was something about Edward – maybe he saw a bit of himself in him – that he couldn't help but like him. The kid was naïve. At 19, he was just four years younger than Freddie, but seriously innocent to the ways of the world. A real dreamer. The sort of rube Freddie could see being chewed up and spat out by the industry. So, Freddie took him under his wing.

He looked after Edward when they met at events, signings and literary festivals. He gave him pep talks before he went out on stage.

They spent hours emailing, swapping ideas and critiquing each other's work. And they spent many, many hours together in the pub, talking about books, women, and coming up with the most outlandish ways of killing people – in a purely literary sense, of course.

For nearly two years, the writers were as thick as thieves. However, as Edward's star ascended, Freddie's own popularity waned. His sales dipped. He stopped being invited to as many events. And he struggled to find the killer idea for a big hit.

Eventually, Freddie's publisher chose not to print his latest work and, soon after, his agent dropped him. Before long, Freddie found himself drunk, depressed, jealous of his friend's success, and at the start of a downward spiral that would see him penniless, perpetually angry and scrabbling about for whatever third-rate, poorly paid book deals and writing jobs he could get his hands on.

And then came the killer blow. During an interview in *The Bloody Dagger*, Edward was asked about his friendship with Freddie – specifically his opinion on Freddie's most recent book. Edward had apparently labelled it as 'derivative', 'obvious' and 'far from brilliant'.

The words were like ice in Freddie's heart.

Naturally, Edward pleaded innocence. He claimed the journalist had twisted his words. He'd never said those things, and what he had said was taken out of context – the writer was just looking to create a scandal to sell more copies.

Freddie didn't believe him. And the friendship instantly soured. Freddie stopped replying to Edward's emails. He refused to meet him for a drink when Edward pleaded for the opportunity to explain. And Freddie did what he did best – he went on the offensive, criticising Edward to anyone who would listen and any journalist who would interview him. Freddie even wrote his own vitriolic, expletive-filled reply piece which was published in *The Bloody Dagger*'s next issue.

Bad feelings abounded and the two soon became bitter rivals, bad mouthing each other, criticising each other's work and perpetuating one of the longest-running literary feuds ever. On the rare occasion they did cross paths, the men refused to speak. And with Edward now one of the darlings of the literary world, Freddie was always the one left out in the cold for events – the organisers fearing a no-show from Edward if Freddie was on the bill.

It wasn't until many years later that Freddie found out Marylin had been the architect behind the demise of their friendship. Fearing her client was spending too much time in the company of a bad influence, Marylin sought to split the pair up. She didn't like the way Freddie had Edward's ear. She thought he had too much of a controlling influence on her young prodigy. He was encouraging him to spend more time in the pub and less time writing the books that made her money. Freddie was introducing Edward to women that distracted him. Even worse, he was encouraging Edward to stand up to Marylin, questioning her decisions and encouraging her to argue with her over his book deals.

Then came the night the two of them were arrested for drunk and disorderly behaviour during the Cheltenham Literature Festival. Freddie had apparently thought it would be hilarious to storm the stage during a talk by Ian Rankin, moon the audience and then dump a bucket of ice over the writer. Edward, being equally drunk, and highly suggestible, had been cajoled into going along with it all. When the story hit the national press, and the two novelists were lambasted throughout the industry, Marylin had to work hard to maintain Edward's contracts, reputation and literary future.

No, that Freddie Winters was a disruptive factor. He had to go.

Having gained a certain level of power within the publishing world, and knowing how big a draw her favourite client was for literary events, she started turning down invitations unless the organisers promised Freddie wouldn't be there. When she heard that Edward was planning a trip to the pub to see Freddie, she'd create some last-minute meeting that Edward had to attend.

It was Marylin that put pressure on Freddie's publisher not to print his newest book, threatening to pull deals with several of her other clients as leverage. She'd amassed quite a roster of big-name writers by that point, and no publisher wanted to be on her naughty list, so they relented and cut Freddie adrift. The fact that Freddie's agent followed suit was less to do with Marylin, and more because they'd been looking to break free from him for years – Freddie was not the easiest, most accommodating client to work with and the lost publishing deal gave them the perfect excuse to part company.

The final nail in the coffin was the inflammatory interview. Marylin had set the whole thing up, paying the journalist to do a hatchet job, knowing the irreparable damage it would cause. Then all she had to do was sit back and watch the fallout.

By the time Freddie found out the truth, it was too late. Too many barbs had been fired over the years. Too much bad blood for the friendship to be saved. So, Freddie did the other thing he did best – he ignored it and let it fester.

Edward transformed from the friendly, happy, enthusiastic kid who just loved to write into an arrogant, egotistical, big-headed arsehole who looked down on everyone and everything. And Freddie turned into a bitter, jealous, overbearing hack who blamed the world for denying him everything he thought he was entitled to.

"Come on then, what despicable shit have you two been up to now?" said Freddie, grinning.

"You and your imagination, Freddie," grumbled Edward.

"Max. Malcolm. Christy," said Freddie, counting out the murder victims on his fingers. "Your former editor. Your publisher for the last 20 odd years. Your ex-wife. All murdered within days of each other, in a holiday resort where you just happen to be staying?"

"Are you suggesting I…"

"Killed them? Honestly, I don't know. I wouldn't put it past you. But then I also don't think you'd do the dirty work yourself. Her, on the other hand," said Freddie, pointing at Marylin, "now, she's more than happy to get her hands dirty, isn't she?"

"I'd be very careful if I were you, Freddie," said Marylin. "Accusing people when you don't have a single shred of evidence. That sort of thing can get you into big trouble. Besides, why exactly would I do it? Why would I want any of them dead?"

"Max was stealing your client's thunder. His was the biggest book last summer and that wouldn't stand, would it? How ungrateful of him, after all those years working with Edward. Learning from him. Earning from him. And how does he repay you? By stealing all your sales and pushing you down the bestsellers list."

Marylin laughed. "Poppycock. Max's sales were his own business. Edward didn't have a book out last year, so there were no sales to steal. If anything, the publicity around Max's success – especially the link to him being Edward's former editor – were only good for us."

"Malcolm, then," said Freddie, slightly deflated. "He's published Edward's books for 20 years or so. But the whole industry knows what a crook he is. Maybe after years of him taking the piss on Edward's deals, you both finally had enough and bumped him off."

Both laughed now.

"Honestly, Freddie," said Edward, "do you really think I'd have stayed with the same publisher for so many years if they were ripping me off? I'm not being funny, but I'm one of the most successful writers in my genre. Every book I write tops the bestsellers list. And you might not have noticed," he said, holding his hands out to indicate his expensive clothing and the £50,000 Rolex glinting on his wrist, "but I'm not exactly doing too badly. Do you really think Malcolm was skimping on my advances? And do you think I wasn't inundated with offers from other publishers?"

"Maybe he had something on you. Some sordid secret that kept you bound to him. You finally had enough, so you decided to get rid of him."

Edward froze. Just for a second, but there was something in his eyes.

Marylin quickly interrupted. "Complete nonsense, you utter buffoon. I've been in this business a lot bloody longer than the pair of you. Don't tell me you honestly believe I'd let Edward take anything but the very best deals for any of his books. Yes, Malcolm had a reputation for taking advantage of naïve writers. But do you really think I'd let him get away with that?"

She took a long drag on her e-cigarette, savoured it for a second, then glowered at Freddie as she blew a large white plume of vapour into his face.

"Really, Freddie," said Edward, "is that the best you've got? Wild speculation and baseless accusations?"

"Just because I haven't pieced together exactly what's going on," sneered Freddie, "doesn't mean there's nothing going on. And it's all too much of a coincidence for you not to be mixed up in it."

"You've got a few coincidences here, too, haven't you? Max rejected one of your books some years ago. Tell me, didn't you have a fist fight about that only the other night?"

"It wasn't a fist fight," said Freddie, stumbling onto the back foot, "it was…"

"I'm not sure how you knew Malcolm," continued Edward. "Chances are his company rejected several of your books over the years. Stands to reason. Every other publisher rejected you. Maybe you were bitter about that and looking for payback."

"Yeah, well," sneered Freddie, "we all know why my books got rejected." He threw a glance at Marylin, who stared back, unflinching.

Edward looked confused.

"Besides," continued Freddie, "I'd never even met Malcolm until a few days ago."

"Oh, and there's Christy, too," said Edward. "We all know about you and her. A rather sordid episode. Quite sad, really. I mean, everyone knows she only ever slept with you to get back at me. And when she was done with you, she moved on to the next conquest and then the next. Is that what happened? She broke your heart and you couldn't take it, so you snapped and killed her?"

"Broken heart? You sad, pathetic little…" said Freddie. "There was only one broken heart, and it certainly wasn't mine. That girl worshipped you. But you were the great Edward Cross. Too big for your boots to realise what an amazing woman you had at home. Too busy shagging your book groupies, or any pretty girl that turned up at a signing. And how many of your young, naïve writing students did you end up taking to bed? And all the while that poor girl was at home, loving you and wondering why she wasn't enough. What happened to you?"

"I got successful, Freddie. I did well. And I enjoyed everything that came to me."

"Yes, I shagged your wife," said Freddie. "A lot of times. I knew she was only sleeping with me to get back at you. That was part of the fun, knowing how pissed off it would make you. But that's all it was. Sex with a pretty woman and the opportunity to get back at you. No broken heart. No motive for murder. And none of that would even begin to explain the other two deaths. Sounds like you're the one clutching at straws."

Edward's face hummed with redness. Small beads of sweat glistened on his forehead as his jaw clenched and the corners of his mouth turned down. "What do you want, Freddie?"

"Exactly that," said Freddie, pointing at Edward's scarlet face. "Just getting under your skin. Just rattling your cage. Looks like it's worked, too. I know you didn't kill anyone. You don't have the bollocks.

"Now her," he said pointing at Marylin, "she's definitely cold and calculating enough to kill someone. I wouldn't leave her alone in a room full of puppies without expecting to come back and find her wearing a new fur coat. But she's also so skinny she's practically a skeleton. She can barely lift that bloody vape pen, let alone carry out a frenzied stabbing or throw someone off a balcony."

"We don't know that Christy was even thrown…" said Marylin.

"Yes, she was," snapped Freddie, cutting her off. "She wasn't suicidal. Her career was flying. She was happy. And she was getting back at you in the best way possible – showing you that she'd moved on from the great Edward Cross. There's no way she killed herself. She was murdered. And it's got something to do with you two."

"She was a second-rate writer – worse even than you – turning out that tawdry porn-crime filth," said Marylin, taking another big puff on her e-cigarette. "And she was far from the doleful, dutiful wife you paint her as."

"Marylin, please…" said Edward.

"No, darling, I'm sorry. I've bit my tongue for long enough. Now, I never liked her, I won't pretend otherwise. And if you want the truth, I think the world is probably a better place without her in it. I don't know how she died, but I didn't kill her. Neither of us did."

"I'm not sure how you're caught up in this," said Freddie, "but I'm gonna figure it out. There was something between you two, Christy, Malcolm and Max. Something to do with *The Terrible Bones*?"

Freddie said it loudly, like a magician's big reveal, expecting a reaction. Guilt. Panic. The two of them running out of the room, or breaking down in front of him and confessing.

But they just sat there, looking back at him blankly.

"Or maybe it has something to do with Christy's book, *The Contract*?" said Freddie.

Edward's eye twitched slightly. Then his attention darted to the floor, as he crossed and uncrossed his legs, clearing his throat with a cough.

"Some secret," continued Freddie, "that's come back to haunt you. Maybe you're covering your tracks, getting rid of everybody that knows about it. Or maybe the killer found out what you all did, and they're getting their revenge? Maybe you're next on the list?"

"Oh, you do talk bullshit, Winters," said Marylin, another giant plume of sickly-sweet fog pouring from her lips. "Honestly, it's worse than a plot in one of your books. Predictable, derivative and unbelievable. How do you even come up with this nonsense? One of the leading lights of the literary world is caught up in some scandalous secret that results in him carrying out a series of murders. Nonsense. If you ask me, the three of them were probably caught up in some sordid sex thing. I wouldn't put it past Christy. And everyone knows

Malcolm was a randy old goat. He'd sleep with anyone and, correct me if I'm wrong, he'd already ploughed that particular furrow."

Edward, still staring at the ground, clenched his jaw and gripped his fists tightly.

"How Max comes into it, I couldn't say," continued Marylin. "He was a sweet boy. Gifted editor. Not bad as a writer. He knew Malcolm and I guess he must have met Christy a few times at least. Other than that, I don't know. But their deaths have nothing to do with Edward or me. No conspiracy. No sordid past. Nothing."

"Sorry, not buying it," said Freddie. "But I'll figure it out eventually."

"Yes, well," said Marylin, standing, "good luck with that. Now, Edward and I have places to be."

Then Edward and Marylin stomped out of the restaurant.

CHAPTER 18

THE CROWD CLAPPED, whistled and roared as Edward Cross took to the stage. He walked slower than he needed to, taking his time, milking it and letting the applause carry on for as long as possible. He gave sycophantic thanks to the three authors who'd come before him, ensuring the crowd were in no doubt the main act was now here. The other three were merely his warm-up acts, there to get people ready for the real star, and nobody had better forget it.

Freddie sighed as he wriggled in his cheap, uncomfortable plastic seat at the back of the room. It was a decent turnout. The majority of the hotel's guests all crammed into one room. Although it wasn't as if they had anything better to do. They couldn't leave the resort. And the police had closed all the other bars in the hotel in an attempt to corral all the guests into one place. Easier to keep an eye on everyone. And if something unpalatable was going to take place, it would be easier to prevent – or at least catch the perpetrator afterwards.

Edward stood there in front of his microphone, chest puffed out and pretending to bashfully plead the crowd to cease their applause.

The wanker.

Eventually, he sat down, opened a proof copy of his forthcoming book and started reading. The crowd sat quietly, enraptured as he spoke.

Freddie had to hand it to him; he certainly had stage presence. Gone was the shy young lad who used to throw up before events like these and had to be literally dragged on stage. Now he commanded the crowd as well as anyone Freddie had ever seen. He read with confidence and poise. Rising and slowing as the action of the book demanded. And it wasn't bad, either. Well-written and engaging, with an intriguing, energetic start.

Jealousy coursed through Freddie's chest, ran down his body, into his legs and made his foot tap against the leg of the chair in front of him – much to the annoyance of the white-haired old lady, who spun round, stared daggers and told him to 'fucking well knock it off'.

"Hey babe," said Caroline, sitting down in the chair next to Freddie.

Oh, for God's sake. As if this evening wasn't bad enough, he now had to deal with Caroline as well. Although, he couldn't pretend he was completely unhappy to see her. Perhaps it was spending a day with people – Richard, Perez, Marylin, Edward – all telling him to go fuck himself. Or maybe it was down to the three glasses of wine he had with dinner, but he felt a warm glow when she sat down. It was nice to be with someone who wanted to be in his company. Of course, he couldn't let her know that.

"What the hell do you want?" said Freddie.

"Still playing hard-to-get, I see," she said. "You are funny. So, what have I missed?"

Freddie sighed. "Helen Brennan read the first chapter of her new book. Some crime romance thing, where a man gets killed on his wedding night and his new bride has to catch the killer. Pretty good first chapter, to be fair. Austin James came on next."

"Ooh, I like him," said Caroline. "He writes about that crime-fighting florist. Any good?"

"If you like that sort of thing," said Freddie. "I always find his prose a bit flowery."

Caroline overreacted, laughing heartily at his bad pun and grabbing his arm. Freddie knew she was just flirting – doing that thing women do when they laugh at all your unfunny jokes – but he couldn't help but smile back.

"Colin McMaster was on after him," whispered Freddie. "Grim story about prostitutes being strangled and disembowelled. Good writing, but so dark and gory. Honestly, there's something wrong with that bloke."

"Hmmm, not for me," said Caroline.

The old lady in front spun round again, her eyes clamped into thin slits and her mouth pursed tight like a dog's arsehole. Freddie raised a hand in surrender, and he and Caroline giggled like teenagers when she turned back.

"What about this guy?" said Caroline. "Any good?"

"This is Edward Cross," said Freddie. "Surely, you must know him."

"Never read him," she said. "Never really been into crime books. Not until I met a certain sexy crime author who changed all that." She squeezed his thigh and winked.

Freddie felt another warm glow in his chest and that unmistakable tingle in the end of his penis. What was wrong with him? Was he really that starved of affection that he was getting turned on by the first lunatic to show him the smallest amount of affection?

"Edward is one of the most successful crime writers in the country," said Freddie. "I used to be mates with him, but then he turned out to be a dick. He learned everything he knows from me. This new book seems okay. But, like I say, the man's a complete arse."

The old lady spun round again, her jaw clenched tight and her eyes twitching so fast Freddie thought she might be having a stroke. "Will you please shut the fuck up?"

She said it so loudly that Edward stopped reading up on stage and the whole crowd turned to see the commotion.

Freddie burst out laughing, followed by Caroline. He stood up, looked around the crowd who were now all staring at him, then gazed up at Edward on stage.

"Crikey, Edward," he said, "I don't think this old bag's enjoying your story, mate. Perhaps you should do as she asked and, you know…"

"No," implored the old bag, standing up on wobbly legs. Her face was bright red, her voice crackly, and she was really overdoing it with the poor old, confused grandma bit. "I didn't mean you, Mr Cross. I love your books. I was talking to this inconsiderate man. He was talking all the way through your reading and spoiling it for everyone."

She turned back to Freddie and glared at him with murder in her eyes. Perhaps he ought to add her to his list of suspects.

"I dunno, Ed," said Freddie, "I kind of feel like she was expressing the thoughts of the whole crowd. Perhaps it's time to wrap things up."

The crowd turned on Freddie instantly, with a loud, collective drone of disapproval.

"Sit down," shouted one man from the front row.

"Let him get on with it," yelled a woman on the other side of the room.

Freddie was sure he even heard a few people booing and hissing.

"Mr Freddie Winters," said Edward up on stage, addressing the crowd. "If you don't know, Freddie is one of the other authors here this week. I think he's a little jealous he wasn't asked to read tonight. But I'd urge you to read some of his books. They're not too bad. And the great thing is, you can usually find them in the bargain bin, so they're always nice and cheap."

A ripple of laughter worked its way around the room.

"Now, if you don't mind, Freddie," said Edward, "I'm pretty sure people were enjoying my reading. So, if you could keep it down, I think I'll crack on."

A round of applause erupted, a few people whooping and cheering. The old lady wrinkled her face with a big, smug grin and sat back down.

"Yeah, well," said Freddie, "I've got better shit to be doing anyway. Like trying to figure out who's been running round the hotel killing people. Remind me, Edward, the victims so far have been your former editor, your publisher, and now your ex-wife, haven't they? All seems a bit suspicious doesn't it? I wonder how you fit into it all exactly."

The crowd ummed and oohed, low conspiratorial whispers echoing around the hall.

Edward went to speak, but Freddie cut him off by simply holding up his hand. Then he turned and sauntered out of the room with a smug grin – Caroline running quickly behind him and Edward looking totally befuddled on stage.

Freddie walked through the door, passing Dan the organiser, who stood there with his mouth hanging wide open with shock. Marylin Sharpe was standing next to him, glaring at Freddie with a look that suggested she might just reach forward and rip his heart right out of his chest. He made it through the hotel reception area, round the corner and into the corridor before Caroline managed to catch up.

"Hang on, babe," she said, grabbing his arm and pulling him back. "Where are you going?"

"Eh? What? I dunno, back to my room, I suppose," said Freddie. "I need a large drink. I suppose you can come with me, if you like."

He knew he shouldn't encourage her, but he didn't fancy being alone – partly because there was an as-yet-unidentified murderer on the loose, and partly because he just fancied some company. Mostly, though, it was because Caroline was looking very attractive in a long, flowing, silk maxi dress and the end of his penis was tingling again.

"Ooh, Mr Winters," said Caroline with a flirty smile, "that sounds nice. But I've got a better idea. With everyone in that room, the rest of the hotel is pretty much deserted. Why don't we pop over to the spa centre? They've got a private pool, a jacuzzi… a very intimate little sauna?" She placed a finger on Freddie's chest and slowly worked it downwards, smiling.

"A sauna? Are you mad?" said Freddie. "I've just spent the last few days sweating my bollocks off in 30-degree heat, and you wanna go and sit somewhere even hotter?"

"The thing about saunas," sighed Caroline, raising an eyebrow, "is that people tend not to wear very much inside of them. Sometimes nothing at all…" She raised her eyebrow higher.

"Oh," said Freddie, the penny finally dropping, "I see what you mean." His penis tingled even more. "I suppose we could give it a look."

"Great. Why don't you head there? I'm gonna nip back to my room, I've got a bottle of champagne chilling. I'll meet you there in a few minutes."

It might have been the booze, but Freddie found himself smiling as he made his way down the long corridor, past the pool and into the spa centre. As Caroline had predicted, the place was empty. Even the grumpy woman who manned the little reception desk was away, replaced by a sign that reminded visitors the doors would be locked in just over an hour.

A wall of hot, humid air hit Freddie as he walked in. He'd only just about cooled off from the day's heat, and he could already feel a thin layer of sweat building. A strong smell of chlorine hung in the moist air, mixing with the thick perfume of massage oil. It was a little dark inside, minimal lighting used to create a mellow, dreamy atmosphere. Tedious ambient music played softly – plinky piano blended with nature sounds, annoying chimes and monks humming in the background.

How people found this shit relaxing, he'd never know.

Freddie made his way through the changing room, past the indoor swimming pool, and found the sauna at the end. He peered in through the glass door. Completely empty. He looked around again. Called out to make sure the place really was deserted. Then, when he was sure he was alone, he stripped, dumped his clothes on the floor, stepped inside and sat his bare bum down on the hot wooden slats.

Christ, it was hot. It was a sauna, so he shouldn't have been surprised. But still. It was horrible. The air made his mouth dry. His head swam as his skin prickled and turned bright pink. Within seconds, sweat was beading all over his body, running in gentle rivulets down his face and chest, and coursing the length of his spine into his arse crack. Where the hell was Caroline with that cold champagne?

A few minutes went by as Freddie sat there, sweating and waiting and growing more irritable by the second. He didn't like the heat at the best of times, but this was something else. Sweat was pouring off him now, his hair wet with it. The gentle warm buzz he'd enjoyed from the alcohol earlier was wearing off, replaced by the start of a heavy headache. Even his erection was beginning to fade.

Perhaps there was a way to turn down the temperature. He'd seen something on TV, where people ladled water from a bucket onto hot stones in a sauna. Was that to cool it down? It didn't matter, anyway. There were no signs of any water bucket, ladle or hot stones. Just wooden panelling covering the floor, walls and ceiling. Perhaps this was a more modern design. In fact, hadn't there been a digital display on the wall outside? Perhaps that was a temperature gauge?

Freddie stood, a horrible squelching sound echoing as he peeled his naked buttocks from the wooden bench. He stepped over, gripped the handle of the door and pulled. Nothing. It held firm, no movement at all.

He yanked it again. Still nothing. What the fuck?

Panic rising in his chest, Freddie placed both hands on the glass door, pulling hard. No movement. He pushed and pulled, rattling and clanking the door but nothing gave. It was wedged completely shut. He stepped back, his heart thudding quicker, and examined the door. There was no lock. Of course not. Why would there be? He scanned around the tiny room. No other doors, no escape hatch. Nothing but slat after slat of orange-brown wood.

"Hello," he yelled, stepping back towards the door. "Caroline?"

No response.

What the fuck? Where the bloody hell was she?

Again, Freddie gripped the door handle, pulling it as hard as he could. Still nothing. He wiped the condensation from the glass and peered out. Something caught his eye. Fuck. Thrust in between the handle on the other side of the door was a large pole. It was wedged right in there, holding the door firmly in place. This was no accident. Someone had placed it there to stop the door from opening.

"Caroline?" yelled Freddie. "Caroline? What the hell's going on?"

Freddie yanked the door, harder, harder, hoping it might somehow loosen the pole. No good.

Shit.

It was really hot in there now. His breathing was coming in short, panicked rasps, hot air rushing into his chest, burning his lungs. His skin prickled more, the hot pins and needles of sunburn dancing over his chest, arms and legs.

Just then he heard a noise outside. A footstep. Somebody there.

"Help," screamed Freddie. "Help, I'm trapped in the sauna."

No reply. Then another footstep.

Then Freddie saw a hand reaching out across the misted glass.

"Hello?" he screamed.

No reply. Instead, the hand pressed a button on the digital display. Freddie heard a series of bleeps. He wiped more condensation off the glass door. Peered outside. It was too dark out there, and too light inside the sauna. He couldn't see anything past the mist and the reflection of his own pink, naked body. The hand moved out of sight, then Freddie heard more footsteps. Fast, urgent, running away.

"Oi," shouted Freddie. "What are you doing? Hey, come back here."

The footsteps trailed off until Freddie could hear nothing but the soft hum of the swimming pool motor, his own ragged breathing and those fucking chanting monks.

Shit. Someone had locked him in there on purpose. And was it his imagination or was it getting even hotter in there? That explained the bleeping. The fucker was turning up the temperature. Holy crap, someone was trying to cook him alive.

Freddie stumbled backwards, collapsing onto the bench and burning his back on the hot wooden wall behind him. Sweat was running into his eyes. He felt dreamy, distant. Every inch of him was burning and he started to shiver with panic, like the worst fever he'd ever had.

The pain in Freddie's head grew stronger, thumping and pounding with each beat of his heart. His vision grew blurry, his eyelids heavy as he struggled to see just a few feet in front of him. He was so hot now it felt like he was on fire. He could practically feel his skin cooking as sweat covered every inch of him, trickling down and dripping onto the floor in great drops. His arms and legs felt heavier than they'd ever felt.

His breathing was slow, every hot intake of breath agony as his insides burned.

This was not good. He'd already been in there for five minutes before the heat was turned up. He knew he couldn't endure it for much longer.

One of Freddie's less successful novels featured a murderer who killed his victims by locking them in a freight container which he slowly heated, like a giant oven. He got the idea after reading about a tragedy at the World Sauna Championships, where two contestants had to be dragged out of a hot sauna after passing out. They'd both suffered third degree burns across their bodies, along with severe dehydration and many other things. One of them subsequently died. Freddie had taken the idea and adapted it, because what kind of idiot would try and kill someone by locking them in a sauna? It was completely unbelievable.

The two men in the world championships had lasted only six minutes. Freddie was already coming up to that time. He could feel his body starting to shut down. The pain in his head was getting worse, the dreamy feeling growing stronger by the second. If he couldn't free himself, he was going to die.

A wave of anger overcame him, and he lashed out, screaming and throwing a fist into the wooden wall next to him. He heard it crack. He punched it again and this time he felt it move. Just slightly, but it moved.

He looked closer, examining the wall. He pressed the wood, the tips of his fingers burning, as he felt it give. It was marginal, but it might just do. He pressed again, pushing the plank as hard as he could, managing to get the tips of his fingers underneath and pull. His arms ached, the muscles weak and drained of energy, but he pulled and pulled until with one loud, joyful creak, he managed to pull the plank right off the wall.

It came away with such force that Freddie stumbled backwards, bouncing off the wall behind him and tumbling to the ground. He took one big, burning gulp of air and hauled himself up, his head woozy and his legs wobbling. He lined the plank up against the glass door and thrust it forwards as hard as he could.

Thud.

Freddie's arms were so weak, his legs barely supporting his weight, and the plank just bounced off the glass with little effect. He pulled it back and swung again.

Thud. Nothing. Fuck.

Freddie steadied himself, lined up his plank and swung it forwards with all the energy he could muster. The wood crashed into the glass, shattering the pane as the plank went sailing out of Freddie's hand and through the broken door. A delicious gust of cool air sucked into the room, dousing Freddie's burning, sweaty body as he stumbled forwards.

With his eyes barely open, Freddie gripped onto the door frame and pulled himself out of the scorching room. Careful to step over the broken glass, he hopped and danced awkwardly along the cool, tiled floor. The swimming pool was there in front of him, glistening, shimmering. He managed the three steps towards it, reached the edge and fell forwards, dropping into the water headfirst.

The sensation was incredible. Icy cold water slapped him out of his slumber like an airbag going off in his face. Suddenly wide awake, he dropped down, sinking to the bottom, his burning skin cooled in an instant. Relief washed over him, his heart still racing, and he lay there for a second, looking up at the shimmering water above him, delighting in the cool sensation of it surrounding him.

Then he became aware of a far more urgent need. He pushed against the bottom, sailed up and burst through the surface of the water, sucking in a large, cool breath. He coughed and spluttered, his lungs adjusting to the much colder air. His feet found the floor and he managed to stand and make his way to the side of the pool.

His whole body was aching and tired, his head still swimming with shock and dehydration. His arms could barely support him, but with one gargantuan, groaning effort, he managed to haul himself out of the water, twist round and collapse onto his back on the pool's edge, wheezing and coughing and thanking the lazy workman who'd failed to adequately secure the wood panelling to the sauna wall.

He lay there for a few moments, his skin tingling and prickling all over. Gradually, the panting slowed, and his breathing went back to normal. His head still throbbed but his vision grew less blurry.

Fuck. Someone had tried to kill him. They'd locked him in there on purpose and tried to burn him alive. But who? And why?

He lifted himself onto his elbows and looked around. The place was still deserted, quiet and serene, the monks chanting away as if nothing had happened. Broken glass littered the floor outside the sauna. Heat poured out of the door in long, ethereal waves. Freddie sat up, looked more closely at the scene of destruction and... what the hell?

He hauled himself up, stepped over to the sauna and looked down at the book propped up against the wall. He gasped when he realised what it was. He tiptoed over the glass shards, bent down and picked it up. Another copy of *The Terrible Bones*, the same print as the one he'd found in Malcolm's room. He flicked through the pages. The same circled words. The same manic scribbling. The same clue that had been left with all the previous victims. But why?

What did it have to do with Freddie? He'd read the book, many years previously, but that was his only connection with it. He hadn't even paid for it; he'd pinched a copy off a shelf in Waterstones during an impromptu book reading, before the manager had found him and kicked him out with a stern warning. Other than that, he had no link to the book. He hadn't edited it. He had nothing to do with the publishing. He hadn't even read an early draft, like he had with several of Edward's earlier novels. At the point the book came out, Freddie and Edward had long since stopped speaking. So why had the killer left a copy here? How was Freddie caught up in it all? And more to the point, why had they tried to kill him in the first place?

Freddie wanted answers. And there was only one man who could give them.

Gripping the book tightly, he marched out of the spa, made his way past the swimming pool, through the courtyard and into the main hotel building. A young couple hanging around on the large sofas in reception looked at him open-mouthed as he strolled by. A man coming out of the large conference room choked on his pint as he saw Freddie walking towards him, coughing and spluttering and sending beer cascading down the front of his white Puma t-shirt. As Freddie stormed into the hall, Dan caught sight of him, his eyes wide and confused.

Edward was still on stage. He'd completed his reading and was now fielding questions from the crowd. A tall man with a thin, ginger moustache was in the process of asking Edward about his approach to dialogue.

"Edward Cross," shouted Freddie, holding the book high enough for everyone to see. "What in the name of fuck is the meaning of this?"

The crowd fell silent. All eyes turned to look at Freddie. Then to Edward.

Freddie didn't wait for a reply, he dashed up to the front of the room, climbed onto the stage and thrust the book into Edward's face. Edward sat there looking up at him, his eyes glazed with shock. Somewhere in the crowd, a woman let out a high-pitched shriek. The sound of a glass tumbling to the floor and shattering. Several loud, sharp intakes of breath. And then the crowd burst out into heavy fits of laughter.

It was at this point that Freddie realised he was still completely naked. He looked down at his sauna-burned, soaking wet body, which was glowing pink under the stage lights. How the hell had he managed that? He'd been so incensed and desperate to confront Edward that it hadn't occurred to him to cover up. He'd marched straight out of the spa, past a row of fluffy white robes hanging by the reception desk, and stormed through the hotel completely starkers.

"I don't know what you're all laughing at?" Freddie shouted at the crowd. "The killer has just struck again. They locked me in a sauna and tried to cook me alive."

The crowd laughed even harder.

"It's not fucking funny," shouted Freddie. "There's a killer in this hotel and I nearly became their fourth victim."

The crowd settled. Shocked silence hung in the room. Then they all burst out laughing again – possibly at the notion of somebody using a sauna as a murder weapon, or perhaps just at the site of an angry, naked man wobbling in all the wrong places. Perhaps they thought it was all just some bizarre comedy sketch to entertain them.

"I'm lucky to be alive. And this fucker," screamed Freddie, pointing at Edward, "is behind it all."

That shut them up. The crowd ceased laughing and turned their attention to Edward, who was still staring up at Freddie, open-mouthed and stunned.

"The killer locked me in the sauna and turned up the heat. Luckily, I broke out just in time. And what did I find? A copy of this fucker's book on the ground."

He held the book up for the crowd to see.

"Not just that," continued Freddie, flicking through the pages, "the killer has been quite busy, circling words throughout. Words like *cheat*, *liar*, *scandal*, *thief*… Oh, and here's a good one: *fraud*. Tell me Edward, what do they mean by that?"

190

"I… erm… I…" mumbled Edward, the confident man who'd commanded the stage just moments before receding into the shy, confused, panicked boy that Freddie used to know.

"Here's another thing you might like to know," said Freddie, "a copy of this book, with all these deranged scribblings, has been found at the scene of every single murder. Now, I don't know about you, but I'd say Edward is up to his eyeballs in all this. What do you think?"

The crowd mumbled and muttered. A low hum of conspiratorial coughs and whispers echoed along the rows.

"Tell me something, Edward," said Freddie. "Are you behind all this? Why did you want your publisher, former editor and ex-wife all dead? More to the point, why did you try and kill me?"

"I… no… what?" said Edward, his voice cracking, his eyes pleading.

"Or if you're not behind it, who is? Why are they killing people close to you?"

"All right, that's enough," said a voice from the back of the room. Detective Richard Stone marched up the aisle and climbed up onto the stage. "Show's over."

A collective sigh of disappointment echoed around the room.

"But it was just getting good," someone cried out.

"Be that as it may, let's call it a night, shall we?" said Richard. "If everyone could head back to their rooms, please? Off we go, eh?"

The crowd grumbled, chair legs scraping against the floor, as people stood and walked slowly out of the room. Richard turned to Freddie, sighed and raised an eyebrow as he looked up and down Freddie's glistening, scarlet, naked body. He took the book from Freddie's hand and flicked through the pages.

"Right then," said Richard, "I think you two should tell me what's been going on. And cover that up, Winters. It's enough to give a ghost a fright."

CHAPTER 19

"TELL ME EXACTLY what happened," said Detective Richard Stone, walking into the hotel manager's office. He was followed into the room by Inspector Perez, who perched in front of the large bank of security monitors. She crossed her arms, squinted at Freddie, and gave Richard a small nod.

Was that his cue to continue? Had the two of them been stood outside the room, discussing interview tactics, assigning the roles of good and bad cop? From the look in her tired eyes and the way her jaw was clamped shut, Freddie assumed Perez had opted for the latter. Richard might be asking the questions, but she was firmly in charge.

Freddie was sitting in the hotel manager's chair again. He'd been there for nearly an hour, as Richard went to check the sauna and summon Inspector Perez. From the crabby look on her face, Freddie guessed she'd been interrupted in the middle of a meal — or maybe something more intimate.

Someone had been to fetch Freddie a hotel robe, which prickled against his hot, pink, aching skin. A paramedic had also been called to check him out. He'd roughly poked Freddie's skin, taken his temperature and blood pressure. Freddie was deemed to be dehydrated, exhausted and, what with all the adrenaline and anxiety, his heartbeat was still a bit fast.

While his skin was tender and red, he'd managed to escape the heat before he'd suffered any permanent damage. He'd recover well enough, he just needed fluids, plenty of rest and he should stay out of the sun for a few days — easier said than done in a Spanish bloody holiday resort.

A glass of water sat on the desk, small beads of condensation rippling down the sides. It was the fourth one they'd brought him, the first three having been gulped down in seconds. He felt less woozy now, the dehydration easing and the sharp pain in his head subsiding, but he could feel the water sloshing uncomfortably in his stomach and he really needed to pee.

"Where the hell is Edward?" snapped Freddie. "He should be here for this. Either he tried to have me killed, or he knows something about who did? You should be interrogating him, not me. In fact, leave me in a room with him for five minutes and I'll find out exactly what that smug prick knows."

Perez shifted against the desk and rolled her eyes.

"Don't worry about Edward Cross," said Richard. He pulled a chair out and sat down across from Freddie. "We'll be talking to him. But first I want you to tell me what happened."

"Fine," said Freddie. He took Richard through the events of the previous few hours. How Caroline had lured him to the sauna. How he'd been locked in and nearly cooked to death. He recounted his heroic escape and how he'd found the book.

"That's another thing," said Freddie, when he'd finished, "where the hell is Caroline? Maybe she had something to do with this. She used to be a stalker, you know. Still is actually. You remember her from Dylan's case? She was stalking him and I thought she might have been involved in the plot to kill him. Now that I'm famous…"

Richard coughed out a small laugh. Lifted a hand to his mouth to cover the smile he couldn't hold back.

Freddie winced. "Now that I'm *famous*… she's started stalking me. Always texting me. Turning up at book readings. Coming all the way here just to see me. It's mental."

"Doesn't really sound like the actions of a killer, though," said Richard.

"You never know what's going on in a nutbag's mind. Maybe she figured if she can't have me nobody can, so she tries to off me?"

"But she could have you, though, couldn't she?" said Richard, tilting his head in that annoying way he did when he thought he'd caught you out.

"Eh?"

"She *could* have you. You've just told us you went there to have sex with her. And, in fact," he said, pulling a little notebook from his pocket and flicking through the pages for dramatic effect, "you slept with her last night, didn't you?"

"What? Eh… erm…"

"I've just spoken with Caroline. One of the officers found her in her hotel room, locked inside a wardrobe. She says she went to collect a bottle of champagne. That ties up with your story." He flicked through the pages of the notebook again. "She says someone snuck up behind her, bundled her into the wardrobe and locked her in. It all happened so fast, she didn't see who it was. Probably the same person that locked you in the sauna."

"Hmmm… maybe," said Freddie. "Sounds a bit fishy, though. I'd keep an eye on her." Then, with a deep breath, he looked at his hands and said, "She's all right, though, yeah? Like, they didn't hurt her or anything?"

Richard smiled. "My God. Freddie Winters expressing concern for another person. Will wonders never cease?"

Freddie grimaced.

Perez cleared her throat impatiently.

"Have you been to see the crime scene?" said Freddie. "You should get your people over there and dust for fingerprints. Especially on the heat control. They turned it up after they locked me in."

"Don't worry, we've got people checking it out. Looks a real mess. Wood panelling pulled off the wall. Glass door smashed." Again, Richard flicked through his notebook. "A store cupboard was broken into. Looks like that's where they got the mop to wedge the door closed. Not sure if anything was taken, but it doesn't look like it. Other than that, there's very little to go on."

"Almost like there was no attempted murder at all," said Perez, piping up from the back of the room.

"Oh, here we go," said Freddie, "so the bad cop routine starts. Tell me, do you rehearse this shit? Is that what you were doing outside? Come on, then, what exactly are you accusing me of?"

"I'm just saying," said Perez, "all we have is your story and some circumstantial evidence?"

"Circumstantial?" scoffed Freddie, pulling open his robe to reveal his bright pink chest. "Somebody just tried to boil me alive like a lobster."

"Well, technically, it would have been steaming, not boiling," said Richard, again failing to hide a smile. "Or, actually, no. If it's a dry heat, what would that be…" He turned to Perez, "Dehydrating?"

"Yes, dehydrating, I think," she said.

"Very funny," said Freddie. "You're a regular fucking Morecambe and Wise."

"Morecambe and Wise?" said Perez, confused.

"They were a famous comedy duo from England," explained Richard. "Kind of like an old school version of Ant and Dec."

"Oh, I love Ant and Dec. They're so funny. I used to watch them when I lived in London. That show where they make celebrities eat all those bugs and things. My God."

"Yeah, they're good," laughed Richard.

"All right," snapped Freddie, "I think we might be straying off the point. You were just accusing me of something?"

"Not accusing," said Perez. "Just making an observation. You say you were heading to the sauna to meet your girlfriend."

Freddie winced at the sound of the last word, his jaw clenching tightly.

"But nobody else knew you would be there. The sauna has been heavily vandalised, but there's no evidence anybody was locked inside."

"So, you're saying I did this to myself? Why the hell would I?" said Freddie.

"To deflect attention," said Perez. "Currently, you're a person of interest in the deaths of three people. Maybe you thought that if you were a victim as well, then we'd stop looking at you as a suspect. How could you be the killer if someone is also trying to kill you?"

"What? I…" said Freddie, stunned.

"But there's one big difference, isn't there? The other people are all dead, but you're still quite alive. A bit pink and sweaty, but definitely not dead. And there's no real evidence that anybody tried to kill you."

"So I sat in a deathly hot sauna, burning my skin and nearly dehydrating myself to death just to throw you off the scent?"

"I'm just looking at the evidence," said Perez. "The evidence tells me it's possible that somebody tried to kill you. But it's also equally possible that you arranged to meet your friend in the sauna. You followed her to her hotel room, pushed her into a wardrobe and locked the door. You then headed to the sauna, ripped a piece of wood from the wall, turned the temperature up and sat there just long enough to create some physical evidence of your supposed attack. You then smashed the glass door to make it look as though you had to escape.

And then, for full dramatic effect, you run naked into a crowded room. At least, that's one other possibility."

Freddie sat there, stunned, his skin prickling and his mouth suddenly dryer than before. "My God," he said, "I can't... I mean, do you really think... Are you hearing this, Richard?"

"Inspector Perez makes a fair point," said Richard coldly, sitting up straight in his chair. "There's no actual evidence that anybody tried to kill you. And yes, I know it sounds a little far-fetched, but... well, you're a fiction writer. Far-fetched is what you do. If you were behind the other murders, don't tell me it wouldn't cross your mind that the best alibi would be to make yourself a victim too."

"I can't believe this," said Freddie. "I've done nothing but try and help. And then, when I become victim number four, you accuse me of making the whole thing up."

"You have to admit," said Richard, "you and the truth don't exactly have the closest of relationships."

"What's that supposed to mean?"

Richard sighed. "All right, if you're going to make me say it: you're a liar. I know from personal experience, that you, Freddie Winters, are a distrustful, manipulative, fucking liar, who will say anything to get what you want." There was real anger in his voice, years of betrayal and bad feelings bubbling up to the surface. "I mean, for Christ's sake, you say you've been trying to help with the investigation. But that includes sneaking into crime scenes with a fake warrant card and impersonating me, doesn't it? Forgive us if we call your trustworthiness into question."

"But do you really think I'm making this all up? That I'd fake an attempt on my life?"

Richard looked at him with heavy eyes. "Honestly, Fred, I wouldn't put it past you."

Freddie slumped back into the chair. He'd been accused of doing some terrible things over the years. And, in fairness, a lot of the time he had done them.

Yes, he did once trick a pidgin-English-speaking tourist into paying him £250 for a private tour of the Queen's secret hideaway residence, where she'd go to escape the rigours of ruling the Empire. Of course, the residence Freddie gave them a tour of was his own tiny one-bedroom flat and, wouldn't you know it, it looked like they'd just missed Her Majesty by a few minutes.

And okay, yes, he had once slept with three different writing students in a week, when he taught on a creative writing retreat. And, yes, maybe they had only slept with him after he told each of them the same white lie that he was going into business with his good friend James Patterson (yes, *that* James Patterson) to start their own publishing company, and although he couldn't prepare the paperwork right then and there, he was sure Patterson would sign off on the five-figure advance he'd promised. Little did they know that, far from being future business partners, he actually hated James Patterson and, in return, Patterson didn't even know who Freddie was.

So, yes, Freddie had done some reprehensible things. But he'd grown up since then. And being accused of faking his own attempted murder? Okay, it wasn't outside the realms of possibility, but come on.

"Okay, then," said Freddie, something pinging to the front of his mind, "what about the book? The killer left another copy of the book, just like the ones at the other murders."

"All circumstantial again," said Perez, yawning. "There's nothing to suggest who left it there. And you picked it up and carried it around the hotel, covering it with sweat and fingerprints. Even if there were any other prints or DNA on it, we'd be lucky to find it."

"But it had the same scribbling throughout it. The same words circled and the same mad writing."

"Easy enough to fake, if you wanted to. Aside from the police, you're the only person to have seen the books at the crime scenes. Funny fact, they have them on sale in the hotel shop. You could have bought one, copied the same writing and left it as a clue to tie your whole story together."

"But... but... I..."

"Even then," said Richard, "you said it yourself: how does it relate to you? There's nothing connecting you to the pattern. You didn't work on the book. You didn't have anything to do with Mr Cross when it was written or published. So, why would the same killer want to kill you?"

"The only way it makes sense," said Perez, "is if the whole thing is a fake, made up by a second-rate crime novelist to try and throw the police off the trail."

The heat grew in Freddie's face. Rising up his neck. Pulsing in his cheeks. Apoplectic at the injustice. "Well, what about the fucking video cameras? There must be footage of the killer going in or out of the spa building."

"Nothing," said Richard. "We've checked the cameras and the only person we can see going anywhere near the place is you."

"Well, the killer knows their way around the hotel. They know how to move around without getting spotted by the cameras," said Freddie.

"That's one theory we're working with, yes," said Perez. "But then, after a long time investigating cases like this, there's one thing I've learned. The simplest explanation is usually the true one. And in this case, the simplest explanation is…"

"That I faked the whole thing? I can't believe it. Somebody just tried to kill me and, not only do you not take me seriously, you accuse me of making the whole thing up. It's no wonder nobody trusts the police. You should be out there trying to catch the killer, not accusing me of… Oh, do you know what? I give up. What's the point? If you want something done properly, you have to do it yourself."

"What is that supposed to mean?" said Perez.

"If you lot aren't going to find the killer, I'll do it myself."

"Come on, Freddie," said Richard, "there's no need for…"

Perez cut him off, her bad cop routine in full swing. "Stay away from my crime scenes, Mr Winters. My officers are working hard to catch a killer and I still haven't ruled you out as a suspect. So I suggest you go back to your hotel room, stay there and keep very quiet. If I even think you're interfering with my investigations, I'll have you locked up. Do you understand me?"

"Perfectly," said Freddie. "Now, if you don't have any further questions, I think I'll do just that."

"That's a good idea, Fred," said Richard, overdoing the Good Cop bit. "Keep your head down. Feel better."

"Fuck off, Richard," said Freddie. He stood up, wincing as the fabric of the dressing gown grated against his tender skin. Then he stomped out of the room and walked gingerly back to his hotel room.

"Fucking wankers," he muttered to himself, as he slammed the door behind him and sat on the freshly-made bed, the skin on his buttocks tingling with the contact.

How could they think he'd done this to himself? What kind of lunatic would lock himself in a sauna, burning his skin and risking death like that? And what was Perez's deal? It was like she didn't want to catch the killer. Had she even spoken with Edward? That fucker knew more than he was saying. Freddie would have to confront him. Put the screws on him. Find out what he was hiding.

He also had to do a little extra research. Dig into the past. And he knew exactly the right man to talk to.

He grabbed his phone, opened the text app and found a stream of messages from his friend, Dylan, saying he'd heard about the drama at the hotel and asking if Freddie was okay. Freddie ignored them all. He scrolled through his contacts until he found the number of his former agent, then typed out a new message:

Need a favour. Urgent. Need you to dig around and find out everything you can about Edward Cross. All the nasty, dirty, sordid secrets. Call me when you have it. Wouldn't ask if it wasn't vital.

If the police weren't going to take this seriously, Freddie would do it for them. First, though, he might just close his eyes for a few minutes. He eased himself back onto the bed, his whole body singing with white hot pins and needles, and laid his burning face on the cool pillow.

******

"This is not good, Marylin," said Edward Cross, walking into his hotel room and perching on the edge of the bed. "This is really not good."

Marylin was sitting at the table in the corner, puffing away like a demented dragon, plumes of white candyfloss-scented vapour dancing in the air around her.

"What did Inspector Perez say?" said Marylin.

"Say? She didn't say anything."

"Come on, darling, you've just spent the last hour chatting with her. She must have said something."

"Chatting? I've spent the last hour being interrogated," snapped Edward. "She didn't tell me anything. She asked lots of questions, but she said nothing about what's going on."

"Okay then, what did she ask you?" said Marylin. "What's got you so worried?"

"What's got me worried? Three people are dead, another person nearly dead, and a copy of my book – *the book* – has been left at the scene of each. I know you said it can't have anything to do with it, but come on, Marylin. Open your eyes. It's coming back to haunt us. What we did. What *I* did. There's no denying it."

Marylin shifted slightly in her chair, scratching the back of her hand with her long, red fingernails. She took another long puff, blowing out the sickly, sugary scent. "What exactly did she ask you?"

"Lots of questions about Freddie. How do I know him? How was he connected to Max, Malcolm and Christy? There was another detective there this time. English. That guy Freddie used to consult with." He walked over to the minibar, pulled out two tiny bottles of whisky and poured them both into a glass. He gulped down half the contents, placing the glass down heavily on the side with a shaky hand.

"Yes, I heard about the English detective being sent over to assist. He's good for us. Absolutely hates Winters," said Marylin. "What else?"

"Obviously, Perez asked me about the book again. Going over everything we've already discussed; all the same questions she asked the several hundred other bloody times she's questioned me this week. Then she goes back to Freddie, asking if he might have any reason to harm me."

"And what did you say?" Marylin scratched and puffed again.

"I told her I didn't know. I said the guy's a dickhead. That we used to be friends, a long, long time ago, and that he got all bitter and twisted when I became successful. That he's a sad, spiteful loser who shagged my wife to get back at me, along with countless other mean-spirited pranks over the years. But do I think he's a killer? No."

"Good, good," said Marylin. "You did well. Perez is clearly clutching at straws. That's why she was going back over the questions she's already asked. That's what they do, especially when they don't know what's really going on. They ask you the same questions again and again, hoping you might slip up, forget a lie, change your story or accidentally drop yourself in it. You know this, Edward. You've written it a hundred times."

"I know," said Edward, "you're right. Standard probing questions."

"It's good that she's fixated on Winters. It means they don't really suspect you."

"What does that mean? Why would they suspect me?"

"Well, no, they shouldn't, darling. But you know what the police are like. They get hold of something, convince themselves it's true and then they're like a dog with a bloody bone. I'm just saying it's better if they're looking in Winters' direction."

Edward walked back over to the bed and sat down with a loud sigh. He swirled his glass, gazing at the dark brown liquid, seeming to get lost in it. "I knew this would come back and bite us in the arse. I told you at the time. I said it would never work and one day..."

"Calm down, darling. It's just a demented fan, thinking they're funny and..."

"It's not a fucking fan, Marylin," snapped Edward. "This is not a joke. It's them, isn't it? They've come back."

"It's not them, darling, I can assure you of that. It's not possible. Everything was taken care of at the time."

"What does that mean?" said Edward. "How did you 'take care of' things? I assume there was a contract, preventing them from suing us or even talking about it."

"Standard non-disclosure agreement, yes," said Marylin, again sucking hard on her e-cigarette and disappearing behind another large, white cloud. "Everything was watertight."

"Well, what if it wasn't enough? Okay, they get their money, they sign the contract and go away. But then maybe a few years down the line they're feeling bitter about things. I mean, they weren't best pleased at the time."

"Hmmm," said Marylin.

"Maybe they stew on it for ten years. They get more and more angry. They decide they're not gonna put up with it any longer. They know they can't get us financially. Can't go to the press; our lawyers would shut it down within seconds."

"Quite right," said Marylin.

"So, they snap. They follow us here and run around killing people. I'm sure there was nothing in the NDA that prevents them from carrying out a massacre."

"Hmmm, no. Perhaps I should get the lawyers to work in something like that in future?" said Marylin, smiling.

"It's not bloody funny," said Edward.

"No, it's not, darling," replied Marylin, "but please trust me, it's not them. I told you: everything was taken care of. It can't be them."

"What does that mean?"

"Darling, as your agent and your friend, sometimes I need to keep things from you. It's for your own good. What do they call it? Plausible deniability? It really is better if you don't know certain... details. But please believe me, it was handled. There's nothing to worry about."

"But how can you be sure?"

"I'm sure because I'm sure," said Marylin, tersely. "Now, let's just leave it at that. I won't be drawn on the subject any further."

Edward drained the last of his whisky and flopped back onto the bed, looking up at the ceiling. "Christ, how much longer are they going to keep us locked in this hotel?"

"Sorry, darling, I'm not sure. My contacts in the UK have been utterly useless thus far. And I fear this latest development might stymie us even further. Don't worry though. Marylin's on the case. When have I ever let you down, eh?"

Edward rolled his eyes and breathed out a heavy sigh.

CHAPTER 20

FRIDAY

FREDDIE WINCED AS the hot coffee passed over his dry, aching lips. He tried to blink the tiredness out of his eyes, his head throbbing with a dull ache. He felt like he was moving in slow motion compared with the manic bustle of the other buffet diners. At least the coffee tasted good; strong and dark and sweet, thanks to the four sugars he'd heaped into his cup. And it was having the desired effect, slowly bringing his groggy brain back to life.

He looked at the plateful of uneaten pastries in front of him. His stomach turned over at the thought. Unusual for him not to be hungry. Or at least not to be able to shove something down. But he had no appetite whatsoever. Another side effect of someone trying to cook you to death in a sauna, he thought.

He hadn't slept. Not for more than a few seconds at a time. He'd spent a frustrating night in bed, hot pins and needles dancing over his seared skin and his mind whirring with thoughts of murder and conspiracy. Every time his brain succumbed to the sheer exhaustion and he drifted off, he'd shift in the bed, the sheets tugging at his aching flesh, and he'd be jolted back awake, squirming and sighing with pain. Finally, as the morning sun flooded the room, he'd given up and come down for coffee.

He'd avoided showering, fearing his skin might literally melt off him under the water. Even the brief dash he'd made through the courtyard had felt like fire ants crawling all over him, nipping and biting, as the sun's rays burned into his reddened skin. How he was going to spend a day in this heat, he had no idea. Perhaps the chef might let him set up a bed at the back of the walk-in fridge?

He took another mouthful of coffee, watching the other diners piling food onto their plates, as if it was any other morning and they had no idea the hotel was under siege to a maniacal killer. He watched a fat man in a pink t-shirt push half a sausage into his mouth in one bite. A petite, blonde woman was tucking into a foul-looking bowl of yoghurt and prunes. An elderly woman with bright white hair tutted loudly as another woman took the last fried egg from the tray. What kind of murderous spree would it take to put these gluttons off their food?

Freddie studied their faces. Any one of these people could be the killer. Any one of them could be the vindictive fucker that locked him in that hot, dry hellhole. He'd only caught the briefest glimpse of his attacker. An arm moving quickly behind a fogged-up pane of glass. Freddie switched his gaze. He started looking at people's hands. Checking for any familiarity in shape, size, skin tone, movement. But it was no good. Nothing recognisable at all.

Again, his mind drifted back to the investigation. The clues swirled around his mind. The connection between the victims. The ways they were killed. The potential motives. And Edward's book. Another thing that connected them all. But it didn't connect to him. How was he mixed up in this? It didn't make sense. He had no link to that book, no real connection to the other victims – or at least as a group. So why had the killer targeted him?

Was it a case of mistaken identity? Had the killer been meaning to lock someone else in the sauna and they'd got Freddie by accident? Maybe Freddie was getting too close to the truth and the killer was trying to silence him? Or maybe the connections between the other victims were just coincidence? Maybe the killer was picking his victims at random, bumping off authors and industry figures in no particular order.

But then why leave the book? The whole thing was like an itch deep in the centre of Freddie's brain, which he was desperate to scratch but he just couldn't reach.

"Not hungry?" said Nick, sitting across from Freddie and pointing at his untouched plate of food.

"Couldn't quite face it, this morning," replied Freddie, smiling. Usually, he'd have preferred to be alone, but he found he was pleased to see Nick. The feeling didn't last for long.

"Christ, you look awful," said Nick, grimacing at Freddie's pink face. "Like the last saveloy in the chip shop."

"Thanks."

"Honestly, you're redder than a post box. I don't know whether to say hello or slip a letter between your teeth."

"You're all heart."

"No, seriously, though, mate. I heard what happened. Well, everyone heard what happened. And saw quite a lot, too, when you burst up onto the stage. Are you all right, though? What's the score? Any idea why someone would want to do that?"

"Yes, I'm okay, thanks. A bit tired and tender, but otherwise fine. And no, I've no idea who did it. I spoke with that fucking Perez last night. Far from taking me seriously, she accused me of faking the whole thing."

"You're joking," said Nick, his eyes widening. "Why would she say that?"

"She's still got me down as prime suspect. She reckons I could have faked the whole thing to draw attention away from myself."

Nick sighed, gently nodding his head. "To be fair, she's got a point. Good way to point suspicion away from yourself."

"Oh, not you as well," said Freddie.

"Hey, I'm not saying I agree. I've seen you do some mental stuff, but that's beyond even you. And hey, you might be a crotchety, miserable, foul-mouthed, grumpy, irritable…"

"Please, don't hold back," said Freddie.

"Stroppy old git," said Nick. "But you're no killer. You've got a good heart buried in there somewhere, even though you do a good job of hiding it."

"Seriously, mate, you should get a refund from the charm school you went to."

"So, what's next?" said Nick, picking up a pastry from Freddie's plate and taking a bite. "How's the investigation going? Any hot leads?"

"No. Nothing. If anything, this," said Freddie, pointing to his pink face, "has confused me even further. None of it seems to connect. I mean, why would the killer want to kill me?"

"Despite the obvious?"

"Seriously, do you want some more salt to rub in my wounds?"

"Hey, I'm just winding you up," laughed Nick. "It's what friends do."

"And who the hell says we're friends, anyway?"

"Right. Got it," said Nick, his face straightening, the mischievous smile disintegrating as he looked at the pastry in his hand.

Freddie instantly felt bad. He'd been experiencing that feeling a lot recently. A lot more than he liked. What was wrong with him? Was he growing as a person or something?

"But they left a book outside?" said Nick. "Edward's book?"

"Exactly."

"So, what does he have to do with all this? Is he behind it? Is he the next victim?"

"Fucked if I know."

"Goes to show though, no matter how big or successful you get, just one person can come along and destroy your life in a second. One minute you're the great Edward Cross, and the next it's going all kinds of wrong."

"What does that mean?" said Freddie.

"No, nothing. I just mean, I... erm..."

Freddie eyed Nick suspiciously.

An awkward silence hung between them.

"Still no word of when they're gonna let us out of this place?" said Nick finally. "I've heard there's an English detective over here now. Here to help. Didn't you know him?"

"Richard Stone. Yes. We go way back, although things aren't all that amicable between us."

"Why doesn't that surprise me?" said Nick. "Anyway, I'm gonna see if I can track him down. Try and find out what he knows."

"Good luck with that."

"And listen, me and some of the other guys are getting together in a bit. You know, see if we can't put our crime-writing minds together and figure this whole thing out. You should join us. We'll be up in the bar."

"Well, I certainly won't be sunbathing," said Freddie. "I might see you there later."

"Cool," said Nick, the eager puppy look returning to his eye.

Honestly, no matter how mean or rude Freddie was, the guy always came back for more. And, experiencing a second anomaly for the day, Freddie found that he was glad Nick's feelings didn't appear to be irrevocably harmed. Christ, maybe they actually were friends.

Nick stood up, pinched another uneaten pastry from Freddie's plate and headed out of the restaurant. Freddie poured more coffee from his pot, added another four sugars, and was just about to take a sip when Caroline sat down opposite him.

"Oh baby," she said, the start of a tear in her eye. "Oh, you look awful."

"Yeah, that seems to be the general consensus," said Freddie.

"They wouldn't let me come and see you last night," she said. "And I was so shaken up, I… Oh, are you all right? Are you in pain?"

"Only when I move, breathe or think."

"Oh, poor darling. Why don't you come back to my room and I can make you feel better?"

"No, I don't think so," said Freddie. "For one thing, I suspect your idea of making me feel better includes a lot more skin-to-skin contact than I can take."

Caroline winked with a sultry smile.

"And secondly, the last time I agreed to go anywhere with you, someone tried to kill me."

"You don't think I had anything to do with that, do you?"

"I don't know. All I know is, you asked me to meet you in the sauna, then you conveniently buggered off. You're the only one who knew I'd be there. And then before I know it, I'm locked in and nearly gasping my last."

"You can't honestly believe I would have…"

"Really?" he snapped. "You don't exactly have the best track record for sane behaviour. You're a bloody stalker, Caroline. You followed me here, seeming to be under the impression we're in some sort of relationship. Newsflash: we're not. Never have been. Christ, I only know you because you latched onto me so you could get a peek inside my friend's flat – someone else you happened to be stalking at the time."

"I am not a stalker," said Caroline. "And correct me if I'm wrong, but I didn't exactly have to twist your arm to get you in that sauna last night."

"No… but… well…"

"For your information, I popped back to my room to get some champagne so we could have a lovely, romantic evening. Then someone attacked me and locked me in a wardrobe. I was in there for about two hours, shouting and screaming, before someone found me."

"So you say."

"Yes, I do bloody well say. I don't want to kill you. We've got a good thing between us. I just want to be with you. And deep down, I know you want to be with me, too."

"Yeah, well… maybe you thought 'if I can't have him, then nobody can'?" Freddie said. "So you try and kill me out of spite."

"That doesn't even make sense," said Caroline, screwing up her face. "I was on my way to meet you for sex. I was literally about to have you."

"Yeah… well…," said Freddie, "that could all have been an act. How do I know you're not behind the other murders? Maybe I was just next on your list, and you lured me there to kill me."

"Why the hell would I want to kill those people? I don't even know them."

"Maybe it's all part of some twisted scheme to get back at the industry and… maybe you wanted to kill Max because… I mean, it's possible that you knew I'd slept with Christy and… well, there's Malcom too, you see, because he's…" Freddie's voice drifted off, like a machine running out of battery power. He knew how ridiculous he was being. He squinted at the coffee in front of him, scratching his head, his eyelids feeling heavy and the throbbing in his brain getting worse.

"I think you're clutching at straws there, darling," said Caroline, reaching forward and taking his hand in hers.

"Yeah. Sorry, Caroline," sighed Freddie. "I haven't slept. It's been a funny few days. I know you didn't really try to kill me. And I didn't mean any of that about you being a… you know…"

"That's okay, baby," she said, rubbing the back of his hand with her thumb. "Honestly, what are you like? Being your girlfriend is hard work. You and your crime-writer's brain. Is this what it's going to be like going out with you? You accusing me of murder every five minutes?"

Freddie smiled back. Did she really call herself his girlfriend? His usual instinct would have been to bang his hands on the table and loudly refute it. But he didn't. Surprisingly, he found himself quite liking the sound of it. His girlfriend.

After the events of the previous evening, Freddie found himself feeling more than a little contemplative. Someone had tried to kill him. At one point, he really did think his number was up. It was scary. It was depressing. And if he was honest, it was making him question a lot about himself and his life.

What if he had died? Would anybody care? Would anybody miss him? He doubted there would have been a mass outpouring of grief on his behalf. In fact, he wondered whether more than a handful of people would even notice.

Freddie knew what he was like. He knew what a cantankerous, rude, obstinate, snidey, devious grump he could be. And that was on a good day. He wasn't sure quite how he'd ended up like that. But after a life filled with regret, disappointment, heartbreak and failure, he found it was far easier to close himself off. Never let people get close and they can't get close enough to break your heart. So, he'd adopted this prickly demeanour as a defence mechanism, pushing people away with his bad behaviour.

But now, following such a close brush with death, he couldn't help but wonder whether he'd got it wrong all these years. Don't let people get close and who'll miss you when you're gone? Plus, he had to admit it was all a bit lonely.

When it came to Caroline, he knew he wasn't easy to put up with. But somehow, it didn't seem to put her off. She just kept coming back for more. Perhaps she really did care for him. And perhaps he was starting to develop feelings for her. When they spent time together, he had to admit he did enjoy her company. She was attractive, intelligent, warm and kind. And once you got over the weird obsession with cat-based clothing, he found that maybe he actually did like her. And maybe he liked the idea of her being his girlfriend.

Christ, what was happening to him?

"Listen, I think they're opening the pools again today, so I'm gonna go and sunbathe for a bit. And I think Mr Grumpy here needs to get some rest," Caroline said, putting on a silly, girly voice and pressing the end of his nose with her finger. "Why don't you go back to your room and get some sleep. I'll come by later and cheer you up. And I promise I'll be gentle."

"Yeah, that sounds nice," said Freddie.

"Honestly," laughed Caroline, standing and looking down at him, "as if I'd try to kill you. What are you like?" Then she walked off, giggling to herself.

Freddie took a sip of the acrid coffee that had gone cold in his cup and nearly spat it back out again. This wouldn't do. And he couldn't be bothered to queue up for more. The restaurant was at full capacity now, people bumbling and tutting and chatting. Knives and forks clanging and scraping. The anxious snapping of parents pulling their annoying kids close to their sides – the presence of a killer in the vicinity proving strangely useful in making them stop the little shits running around like tiny hooligans.

The skin on Freddie's arms, face and neck pulsed with heat. His head throbbed as his annoyance levels rose. He had to find somewhere more peaceful.

He didn't want to go back to his room. Sleep would be the most beneficial thing for him, but he still didn't fancy his chances of getting any. His burned skin meant he couldn't relax by the pool. He didn't even fancy going to the bar. He still felt completely dried out from the night before, and booze would just exacerbate his dull, pulsing headache. So, for the third time that day he found himself experiencing a wild inconsistency in his character – he didn't even fancy a drink.

Besides, he still had a mystery to solve. He had clues to find. Motives to uncover. Suspects to weed out. And he couldn't do any of that if he was asleep or drunk.

He was just about to stand up and leave the restaurant when he noticed the annoying kid from the plane on the other side of the restaurant, walking cautiously with a plateful of food. The two caught eyes. They paused for a second. Looking at each other. Then a look of fear came over the boy and he rushed off, walking quickly to get away.

Good work, Winters, Freddie thought to himself. The kid seemed genuinely scared of him. He really needed to apologise. And he would. But probably best to wait just a little while, until his scarlet skin died down and he looked a little less like an angry lobster.

Besides, he needed to check out the scene of last night's attack before it was too late. He headed to the spa, where he found the doorway closed off with plastic police tape and a couple of Perez's foot soldiers stood guard outside. There was a good chance they'd been warned Freddie might try and sneak in. And they'd no doubt been told to look out for his fake warrant card. He could probably have found a way to outsmart them and get inside, but he was still tired and needed more coffee. So, he headed to the little café opposite instead, where he could watch and wait for the guards to leave.

It was dark inside, a pleasing contrast to the bright sunshine outside. Brown, wooden floorboards stretched out to a mahogany bar at the end, with a glass cabinet that contained a selection of cakes, pastries and cookies. Behind the counter stood a large, shiny coffee machine. Professional. Expensive. The kind you see in any decent coffee shop. Eight wooden tables were dotted around the place, each with four chairs, and an old, comfy leather sofa sat in the corner. The whole place contrasted wildly with the rest of the hotel. It was as if Freddie was stood in any standard boutique coffee shop in London. A delightful oasis of calm plonked in the centre of the chaotic holiday resort. Freddie couldn't help but smile.

The air hummed with the scent of freshly brewed coffee. Thankfully, the place was quiet, the rest of the hotel guests either still stuffing their faces with breakfast or scrabbling over sunbeds.

There were only two other customers. Sitting at a table in the corner was the mysterious salt-and-pepper-haired guy Freddie had noticed at the party on the first night, and who had popped up at several events. Freddie still couldn't place him. The face seemed so familiar. He knew he'd seen it before. Or perhaps he just looked like someone Freddie had known.

The man had a large coffee in front of him and was scribbling away in a big, leather-bound notebook. He glanced up, caught eyes with Freddie, then looked away furtively, twisting his body to cover the notebook with his arm.

Nice one, thought Freddie. Are you trying to hide your masterpiece from me? As if Freddie could give a shit what the idiot was writing. Bloody amateur novelists. Although it was refreshing to have someone hide their work, rather than thrust it in his face and ask for feedback.

A young man was fussing away behind the counter, unloading glasses from a dishwasher. Freddie stopped for a second to take in the array of baked goods in the glass cabinet. Then, turning to decide where to sit, he saw the only other customer in the place.

"Oh great," he said, noticing Detective Inspector Richard Stone sitting at a table in the other corner.

Richard glanced up and sighed. He, too, was writing in a notebook, which he quickly slammed shut.

"Christ, what is it with people trying to hide their writing from me today?" said Freddie. "Do you really think I care?"

"Morning, Freddie," said Richard, more sympathetically than Freddie expected. "How are you feeling after your ordeal last night?"

"Well, I ache all over. I've barely slept. My head is pounding and my mouth is constantly dry. I've been described as looking like a saveloy. Oh, and despite having been nearly killed last night, the local police accused me of making the whole thing up. Other than that, I'm fucking peachy."

"Saveloy," said Richard under his breath, failing to hold in a laugh. "Mind if I join you?"

"No, go ahead," said Richard, pushing a chair out with his foot. "I was hoping to speak with you. I wanted to apologise. Perez went a bit hard at you last night. Seems to have a bit of a bee in her bonnet when it comes to you. Can't imagine why…"

"Hey, all I've done is try and help that woman. I don't know why she's taken against me."

"Yeah, well, that's debatable. Sneaking into crime scenes? Trying to wedge yourself into the middle of her investigation? You're lucky you're not behind bars."

"Oh, come on, Richard, you know how useful I can be."

"That's debatable too," sighed Richard. "I'll admit you used to add a unique perspective when we worked together. But that's in the past. I just wanted you to know that although Perez was needling you last night, we're taking it very seriously. And if someone tried to kill you…"

"They did fucking try to kill me," snapped Freddie.

"If they did try and kill you," said Richard, raising his hand along with his voice, "we will find out. And we'll catch them."

"You're being nicer than usual," said Freddie.

"I don't have to be," said Richard.

"No, it's nice. I was just wondering why the sudden mellowing."

"Oh, I still hate your guts, Freddie, don't worry about that. You're an arsehole. You'll always be an arsehole. I'll never forgive you for what you did to me. But…"

"But?"

"Christ, you're like a bloody tapeworm. Or one of those parasites that burrows under your skin and you can't get rid of. Or Brexit. Eventually, you realise there's nothing you can do about it, so you just have to make the best of it."

"That might be the nicest thing anyone's ever said to me," said Freddie, wiping fake tears from his eyes.

"Yeah, well, truth be told, I did actually want to pick your brains."

"Really?" said Freddie, his eyes widening and a large grin spreading across his face.

"Hey, you can cut that out, for a start," said Richard, "or this conversation ends now."

"Cut what out?"

"That fucking annoying, smiley, 'I-told-you-so' excitement plastered across your stupid face."

"I'm just pleased. It's nice. The old team back together."

"That is absolutely not what I want," snapped Richard. "Don't go thinking anything's changed between us. I just want to get your spin on things. See what you know. This is your world. Your people. You clearly have a different... perspective."

"You've changed your tune. The other day you told me..."

"The other day I was winding you up. You got so upset that I wouldn't even hear your side of things. That was just a bit of fun for me. But, as an investigating detective, I'd be a fool not to at least hear you out."

"Well, I'm glad you've finally seen sense. Although, if we'd done this yesterday, we might already have caught the killer, and I wouldn't be sitting here looking like a roast bloody chicken. So, what do you want to know?"

"Tell me about Edward Cross," said Richard, opening his notepad to reveal pages of scribblings.

Freddie signalled for the guy behind the counter to bring him a large cappuccino, then he set about telling Richard everything he'd discovered over the last few days and the details of the conversations he'd had with everyone involved. He explained some of the wild theories the other writers were bandying about the hotel, and his own, more plausible conclusions.

Freddie told Richard how Max had worked as editor on *The Terrible Bones*; how Malcolm's company had published it; and how Christy had been married to Edward at the time of publication. He speculated about Max's recent rise to literary success and the questionable sum of money he'd been paid for his debut novel. A sum particularly suspicious, he said, on account of the rumoured nefarious business dealings of his publisher, Malcolm – a man known throughout the industry for taking advantage of authors and paying unfeasibly small advances and royalties.

He failed to disclose a few minor details, like some of the clues he'd found at the crime scenes. It was only sensible to keep a few bits of information for himself, and Richard could get all that stuff from the police reports anyway. He also downplayed some of his own interactions and relationships with the deceased. Perez already thought he was guilty of something and he didn't want to point further fingers of suspicion at himself.

When Freddie was finished, Richard sat back, put his pen down and looked more confused than ever.

"So, let me get this straight," said Richard. "You think Edward's book has something to do with the murders, but you don't know what. Edward is mixed up in it, but you don't know how. Edward's agent, Marylin, is a…" he referred to the notes he'd taken as Freddie spoke, "…a 'vicious, nasty, wily old crone who'd swap her grandmother's kidney for a fancy, designer handbag'. She's also up to her eyes in it, but you're not sure to what extent."

Richard paused to take a breath. Then he continued: "The murderer could be a disgruntled former employee of Edward's, a former lover of either Edward or Christy, or someone who'd worked their way around all the people involved in some bizarre sex game. Alternatively, it could be someone who'd been ripped off by Malcolm. Or it could be an angry writer whose work had been rejected by Max or Malcolm or Edward. Or it could be a deranged fan like…" again he referred to his notes, "…like that 'fucking loony from the Stephen King book, *Misery*'. Or it could just be some psycho picking people off at random."

"In a nutshell, yes," said Freddie, sitting back and taking a large sip of coffee.

"Christ," said Richard. "Clear as mud, eh? Let's start rounding up the suspects."

"Hey," said Freddie, looking hurt, "I never said I knew who the killer was. But there are some good leads in there. And we're getting closer to finding out the truth."

"So, what's this book about?" said Richard, again flicking through his notes. "*The Terrible Bones.*"

"Standard crime thriller," said Freddie. "It was the first in a new series for Edward. Word was at the time that he'd been struggling with writer's block. Couldn't produce anything decent. You see that, sometimes. Writers get so full of themselves and their success. The weight of expectation for the next book hangs heavy, and they get inside their own heads. Can't write anything decent. It was a few years since he'd published anything, and he was past his deadline to produce a new one. I heard rumours the publisher – Malcolm – was demanding Edward repay the advance he'd been given. Then he comes up with this new book."

214

"Really? Is that usual?"

"It's not unheard of. Nothing sharpens the mind like a deadline. And nothing gets you writing quite like someone asking you to pay back a huge sum of money that you've probably already spent."

"But you don't buy it?" said Richard.

"At the time I thought it was all a PR stunt. You know, leak all these stories to the press about how this famous writer can't now write for shit. Not only that, but his publisher is so pissed off they want their money back. Then, lo and behold, said struggling writer suddenly comes out with not only a new book, but it's a new direction to his writing, with a new lead character. And the critics absolutely lap it up, heaping praise on it. All sounded a bit fishy at the time."

"But you think there might be more to the story?"

"I don't know. Like I say, at the time it just seemed like marketing guff to generate a few extra sales. But that's before three people were murdered."

"So, what then? What happened with this book and why is it resurfacing now?"

"Fuck knows," said Freddie, shrugging and taking another large swig of coffee.

"Brilliant," sighed Richard, scribbling something in his notebook. "As illuminating as ever, Freddie."

"Trouble is," said Freddie, "knowing what happened or why, doesn't really get us any closer to knowing who did it. Say it is a disgruntled writer looking for revenge. Just look around you. The place is full of wannabe novelists, the majority of whom have probably had books rejected left, right and centre. Any one of them could be behind it."

"I don't know," said Richard. "The book is too big a thing. The killer's leaving them on purpose. He wants us to find them. He wants us to see the connection between it and the victims."

"Exactly. I'm not saying it's not a part of it. But we don't know why. It could be that it's just a trigger for the killer."

"How so?"

"Say you've written this book. You think it's amazing. Better than anything that anyone's ever written before. Your wife says it's amazing. Your mum says you're a genius. I mean, they're always going to say that, aren't they? Doesn't make it true, though."

"Is there a point in there somewhere?"

Freddie sighed. "So your book is the best thing ever. But try as you might, you can't get an agent or publisher to even look at it. Worse than that, maybe they do look at it and they slate it. They tell you to give up your dreams. Your book is shit. You'll never make it. But you don't believe them because, like some tragic contestant on a talent show, deep down you know you're an amazing writer. And at the same time, there's this other author who's being lauded for his amazing new book, which you've read and didn't like. How is this fucker doing so well while you're being trodden on? What makes him so special?

"So, you stew on it for 10 years. And all that time, you never get your big break. You write and write but nothing is ever good enough. No matter how many writing courses you go on, and how many publishers you send your work to, nobody gives you a chance. It eats away at you. And all that time, you've got Edward's book in your head. Why him, not you?"

"You think that explains the scribbling in the book?"

"What am I, a fucking psychologist?" shrugged Freddie. "Who knows what goes on in a lunatic's mind? But 'thief', 'cheat', words like that. It all fits, doesn't it? Maybe he sees Edward as the man that stole his chance? The man who has the life he thinks he deserves. I mean, it's just a theory…"

"So, the killer is one of the event attendees? They're upset about their work being rejected, so they're taking it out on the people who snubbed them. And they leave the book as some kind of… what? Political statement?"

"Could be," said Freddie, glancing around the deserted coffee shop, checking for anyone listening in. He gazed at the mysterious writer in the corner, who again looked away as soon as they caught eye contact.

"Since I got here," said Freddie, turning back to Richard, "I can't tell you the number of times people have tried to foist their lame, poorly written, nonsensical crap upon me. They think if they just get the right person to read it, they'll be the next J.K. Rowling overnight. As far as they're concerned, the manuscript in their hand is as good as anything that's ever been published. So why aren't they being offered book deals? Why don't they get to live the dream? It could drive people to do some pretty drastic things."

"Yeah, but murder?"

"You know as well as anyone that people have killed over far more trivial things."

"Okay, so who? You've been mixing with these people for a few days. You've been teaching classes, signing their books, watching them around the hotel. Do any of them stick out as potential suspects?"

"That's exactly what I'm saying," said Freddie. "None of them do. And they all do."

"Fuck me, that's helpful," sighed Richard.

"Have I seen someone walking round the place with a big knife dripping with blood? No, obviously not. Nobody stands out as a killer. But almost everyone here has that same desperate look in their eye. They're all chasing that same dream. Any of them could have snapped and started bumping people off. Look at the murders. They're not exactly that well planned out."

"How do you mean?"

"Max was poisoned. But they didn't use some rare drug they bought off the dark web or extracted from an exotic plant. It was antifreeze. They probably syphoned it out of a car in the car park and slipped it into Max's drink."

"How would they know to use antifreeze as a poison?"

"That's what I'm telling you," said Freddie. "You're looking at hundreds of amateur crime writers. They spend half their time reading about this stuff in their favourite books and the other half coming up with their own murder plots to emulate it. They've got this stuff floating around in their heads. At any given point, they can probably think of a dozen methods for murder. They come to this event, they get that last devastating bit of rejection that pushes them over the edge, and they snap. They remember something they read about different kinds of poison. They realise how easy it would be. And before they know it, they're syphoning antifreeze and killing someone."

"It's possible," said Richard, making another note in his book. "But what about the others?"

"They were even less planned. Real spur of the moment. Stabbing someone with the first thing that comes to hand, pushing someone off a balcony and locking someone in a sauna. You could argue they weren't even premeditated."

"They'd have to have known where the people would be, or how to get them alone."

"Sure. But we're all cooped up in a hotel. It's not like tracking someone around London. Wouldn't take too much effort to find out which room people are staying in. And the schedule of events would tell you where most of us would be."

"Which brings us back to who," said Richard.

"Take your pick," said Freddie. "I've seen a few bloody wackos this week. A few faces I've seen before at events like this. Nutbags that turned up at readings and tried to get me to take their manuscripts. A few unwelcome blasts from the…"

Freddie froze. A sudden jolt of recognition hitting him. Synapses firing in his brain. A memory deep within his subconscious bursting through. His eyes widened.

He looked back at the man in the corner. Staring. Studying him. Squinting as he scanned every inch of the man's face.

"Fuck," said Freddie, turning back to Richard and trying to act nonchalant.

"What?" said Richard.

"I know," said Freddie, grinning widely, his eyes sparkling with excitement.

"Know what?"

Freddie leaned in close, so his face was only inches from Richard's and whispered. "I know who the killer is."

CHAPTER 21

"QUICK, GIVE ME your phone," said Freddie, reaching across the table with an excited, panicked look.

"What? Why do you want my phone?" said Richard.

"Come on, quick," said Freddie, flapping his hands in a gimme gesture. "I need to google something."

"Why don't you use your own phone?"

"Are you having a laugh? I don't wanna get stung with all those roaming charges."

"What?"

"You hear about it all the time. People take their phone on holiday, go online for five minutes and come home to a two grand phone bill."

"That's absolute crap. You get free data in Europe now. Unless Brexit fucked all that up," laughed Richard. "And even if it were true, why's it okay for me to get a huge bill?"

"Look, I'm trying to do you a favour," said Freddie, his voice dropping to a gravelly whisper as he looked around. The man in the corner was still head down, scribbling away in his notebook. "This is a matter of life or death, Richard. Stop being a tight arse. Besides, the police pay your phone bill."

"Yeah, but I still have to justify all the charges. And Sharon in Accounts can be a real bitch about that sort of thing."

"Oh, wind your neck in. I thought you were a big, scary detective."

"Yeah, well, you're not the one who has to fill in all the bloody paperwork."

Freddie snapped his fingers and held out his open palm.

Richard sighed and tutted. He pulled out his phone, typed in the unlock code and handed it to Freddie.

Freddie went to work, tapping away at the touchscreen. He ummed and aahed. He sighed and groaned. He scratched his head and pursed his lips and squinted with frustration.

He scrolled and swiped until he finally found it. A news story from 20 years ago on the website for *The Bloody Dagger* magazine. The headline read *The New Bloods: Meet the next generation of crime writing stars.* A picture featured a group of 12 young men and women, all huddled together in a staged living room and looking uncomfortable in each other's company. Their clothes were typical of the era, though they would have been considered crimes against fashion in any decade. It was as if they'd all been told to dress as much like a stereotypical author as they could. The women wore jeans, big baggy jumpers and enormous scarves that were either wrapped around their necks to create that 'woman rolled up in a carpet' effect, or trailing to the floor. The men mostly wore boot-cut jeans and trainers, paired with blazers or sport coats with leather arm patches on the elbows (a look which Freddie still hadn't quite been able to retire). And there were more roll-neck jumpers than seemed safe in such a confined area.

The stars of the picture had also clearly been told to act moody and 'literary'. However, these were far from trained actors and, with not a single smile between them, the resulting effect was 12 people looking pissed off, bored, melodramatic and, in one case, borderline psychotic. Freddie was in the middle of the group, hands planted firmly in his sports coat pockets, glancing ominously into the camera and doing his best 'ooh, aren't I mysterious' face. Edward Cross was next to him, grimacing with staged disinterest. He wore a flowery, pink shirt which contrasted horribly with his brown corduroy trousers.

The rest of the group stood at strange angles to each other, making them look like a group of melancholic strangers at the world's most boring party. It was not a good look for any of them and they came off as the rudest, most elitist, unfriendly bunch of pricks you could ever want to avoid. Quite how they'd thought it would endear people to buy their books, Freddie had no idea.

A young Bill Pascale stood to Freddie's right, doing his best to look smouldering, but instead looking constipated. A fresh-faced Helen Brennan, drowning in the collar of her oversized jumper, perched on the edge of the sofa with a look that suggested she'd just eaten a spoonful of her own earwax. And Patrick Marcombe, with a ludicrous beard and a mop of jet-black hair, looked off into the distance – presumably for dramatic effect but just making him look like he'd missed the photographer saying 'cheese'.

Freddie winced as he scanned the rest of the faces. While his career had floundered in the years following the photoshoot, the rest of the group had gone on to achieve the success the magazine had predicted. Staring back at him from Richard's phone were now the cream of modern-day British crime writing. All apart from one of them.

On the far right of the picture, wearing a tweed jacket and sand-coloured trousers, stood Ronnie Fraser. Ronnie had made the list having written one of that year's best, most intriguing courtroom thrillers with a twist so devious and clever that Freddie had sought him out during the photoshoot to congratulate him on it. It was a terrific book and, along with being hailed as a star in the making, people were keenly awaiting his next big smash. But it never came. Like so many one-hit wonders, Ronnie never published another book.

For a while, his fans were outspoken about the writer's tardiness. Critics wondered what he was doing. The consensus was that he was taking so long to craft his follow-up novel that it must be a work of absolute genius. But no such work ever manifested.

People soon forgot about the new Ronnie Fraser book they were waiting for. And then they forgot about the writer. Freddie himself hadn't thought about Ronnie for a very long time. And now, if he wasn't very much mistaken, he was sitting on the other side of the coffee shop, acting all shifty and hiding his notepad with his elbow.

"It's him," whispered Freddie, pointing out Ronnie in the picture, then nodding his head in the direction of the man in the corner.

"What?" said Richard, brow furrowed as he looked at the picture.

"The guy in the picture," said Freddie, now talking out the side of his mouth, "is the same guy sat over there."

"I dunno," said Richard, squinting. "How can you tell?"

"It's him. I know it's him."

"Okay, so what?"

"This picture is of a group of writers. Look, that's me. That's Edward. At least half of the others are here this week, too. And that guy is sitting over there."

Richard looked at the picture again, then at the man.

"Don't make it too fucking obvious," said Freddie, louder than he intended.

The man in the corner looked up from his notepad to see the two of them gawping at him. He gave an embarrassed, uncomfortable smile. Then he closed the cover, put his pen in his pocket, drained the last mouthful of coffee and, without making eye contact again, he got up from his table and walked out of the room.

"Shit," said Freddie, turning back to Richard. "Fucking well done, Mr Inconspicuous. Why did you have to go and look right at him? Do they teach you that at detective school? How to stand out like a sore thumb and scare the suspects off?"

"What suspect? What the hell are you talking about?"

"Him," said Freddie, again jabbing his finger against Richard's phone. He pinched the screen to zoom in on the man's face. "He's the killer."

"Where the hell are you getting that from?"

"It's obvious," said Freddie. "This picture is from 2003. These are the most successful new crime writers of the year, and the ones predicted to go on to big things."

"So?" said Richard.

"So, he never went on to big things. He never went on to anything. He disappeared off the face of the planet and never published another book. And now he turns up here, 20 years later, acting all suspicious, just as people are being murdered. I knew I recognised him. I've seen him around the hotel all week, hiding at the back of my classes, mingling with the amateurs. I didn't recognise him until I saw him in here, but now it's all clicking into place. He's the killer. He has to be."

"It's a bit thin, Fred."

"Thin? It's highly fucking suspicious, that's what it is."

"Circumstantial is all you've got. He just happens to be here at the same time a crime has been committed. What evidence do you have?"

"He's hanging around with a load of writing students, pretending to be on a writing course. Why's he doing that? He's already a professional writer. It's bizarre behaviour."

"Maybe, but it doesn't make him a killer."

"Open your eyes, Richard. 20 years ago, that guy wrote an amazing book. He's tipped for success, but he's never heard of again. What went wrong? Maybe he was conned somehow and he's back looking for revenge. Or maybe he failed to find the success he wanted. He's spent years stewing over it, blaming everybody but himself, and now he's here to take it out on those who did find fame."

"Sorry, but it's a bit of a reach," said Richard.

"No, it's him. I can feel it. All the pieces fit together. And you've just tipped him off. He's probably making a run for it. We need to stop him."

Freddie launched himself up, knocking his chair backwards and spilling his coffee all over the table. Then he dashed out of the coffee shop. As soon as he stepped outside, he could feel the heat of the sun cooking his skin. He winced with pain as he scanned the area, looking for Ronnie. He dashed past the entrance to the sauna, down the path and round the corner of the building at the end. He burst out into the main pool area and stood there, scanning the crowd, looking for any signs of the man.

The pool was busy now. People languished on sunbeds, rubbing cream onto each other, reading books and chatting loudly. The previously neat rows of sunbeds had been dragged into a higgledy-piggledy mess around the edge of the pool. Freddie ran his eyes across the assembled sunbathers. Then he spotted him, in the distance, walking briskly with his notepad tucked under his arm.

"Ronnie!" shouted Freddie. "Ronnie Fraser!"

People stopped talking and turned to look at him.

"Ronnie!" Freddie shouted again, louder this time.

Ronnie glanced back at him, a flash of recognition on his face, then he turned and continued walking away, much quicker.

Shit. He was trying to run.

Freddie dashed after him, his tired legs aching and the sun scorching his fragile skin. "Ronnie," he shouted again, "I want to talk to you."

The man in the distance sped up, almost running as he went. Freddie rounded the edge of the pool, skipping around sunbathers, hopping over sunbeds. People gawped as he passed them, tutting and moaning as he barrelled through their perfect sunbathing setups.

Up ahead, Ronnie stumbled upon a dead end. A group of sunbeds had been pulled together so the family of occupants could block off a whole corner of the pool just for themselves. There was no way past.

Freddie could see the panic in the man's body language as he shifted this way and that, trying to find a way through. The people in his path weren't moving. Quite the opposite. They held their ground, glaring at Ronnie with menacing stares, allowing Freddie to make up precious ground as his prey floundered.

Finding no way through, Ronnie doubled back, searching for a new route to the hotel building. Freddie continued moving towards him, closing in, getting near enough to see the fear in the man's eyes.

Ronnie shuffled left, gripping his notepad tight as he tiptoed through a narrow space between two sunbeds and found his way to the edge of the pool.

"Ronnie," shouted Freddie, hurdling a sleeping sunbather. He leapt over a large pot plant, nearly tumbled into a bin, and staggered his way to the edge of the swimming pool until he was just feet away from Ronnie. "Give it up, mate. I just want a word."

"Leave me alone," shouted Ronnie, spinning around and darting off in the other direction.

Freddie sprinted after him. He hopped over abandoned flip-flops. Fought to keep upright on the slippery tiles. He got close enough to reach out. Grabbed the back of Ronnie's t-shirt. Tugged it hard, pulling the man off balance.

That was enough to startle Ronnie and upset his movement. His feet slipped in the water slurping up out of the pool. His legs caved in under him. His body jolted wildly. He lost his footing. And in one fluid movement, he tumbled sideways, lurching headfirst into the pool and dragging Freddie with him.

The two men splashed into the water, bucking and shaking, their arms and legs flailing as they struggled against each other. The cold hit Freddie like a shock of electricity, stunning his body and making all his muscles tense. His burnt skin tingled, his eyes blurry as he struggled to see where he was. He sunk further, hitting the bottom as his lungs burned and ached with the pressure. Stunned and unable to move, he lay there dazed, looking up at strange shadows dancing above him and golden patterns of light rippling on the surface of the water.

And then he was moving. A hand gripped tight to the front of his t-shirt, pulling, yanking, dragging him upwards. Ronnie's hand. Saving him.

Freddie burst up through the surface, coughing and wheezing. He spluttered and gasped, sucking in huge, panicked breaths as he flapped about in the water. Ronnie dragged him over to the side of the pool and, with great effort and little grace, both men pulled themselves up and out, collapsing onto the tiles in two soaking, dripping heaps.

"What the fuck did you do that for?" shouted Ronnie, sitting up and panting as he tried to catch his breath.

"Do what?" said Freddie.

"Push me in the fucking pool."

"Push you? I was apprehending you."

"Apprehending me? What the fuck for?"

"Because you wouldn't stop."

"I didn't want to stop."

"Exactly. That's why I had to apprehend you."

"You keep saying that, as if it's supposed to make some kind of sense," said Ronnie, looking down at his drenched clothing.

"I wanted to talk to you."

"About what?" said Ronnie.

"I wanted to question you about the murders," said Freddie.

Ronnie stopped and gazed at Freddie with a quizzical look. "Have you lost your damned mind?"

"If anyone's lost their mind, it's you. Running around a hotel murdering people. Trying to murder me."

"What the fuck are you talking about?" said Ronnie.

"You *are* Ronnie Fraser, aren't you?"

"Yes," said Ronnie. "I never said I wasn't."

"The same Ronnie Fraser who wrote *The Midas Files*?"

"Yes."

"The same Ronnie Fraser hailed by *The Bloody Dagger* magazine as one of the most promising new crime writers of his generation? The same Ronnie Fraser who subsequently disappeared and failed to publish anything else?"

"If this is a new direction for *This is Your Life*, I have to say the format needs help," said Ronnie.

"Just answer the question," said Freddie.

"Yes, that's me. So what?"

A small crowd had gathered round to gawp at the two lunatics who'd just leaped into the pool fully clothed.

"Well, why the hell are you here?" said Freddie. "On a writers' course? Bit mysterious, isn't it? You just happen to be here, and then people start getting killed. It's obvious. You're upset you never got the success you wanted, now you're getting revenge on those of us that did. You're jealous. You're warped. And now you're a killer."

Ronnie's mouth gaped wide, water running down his face, dripping from his nose. He closed his eyes and breathed deeply. Then he lowered his head, his whole body slumping with defeat.

And then he burst out laughing. Great, big, body-shaking, belly-wobbling, thunderous cackles.

"You're still a complete dick, aren't you, Freddie?" said Ronnie, still giggling.

"What?"

"You really think I'm here carrying out some murderous revenge because I'm... what? Jealous of you?"

"Yes, that's exactly what I think."

"You couldn't be more wrong if you tried."

"Really?" said Freddie. "Well, what are you doing here?"

"What do you think? I'm on a bloody writers' course."

"Why the hell would you need to do a writers' course? You were one of the best crime writers of your generation."

"Yeah, 20 years ago, maybe. Christ," he said, picking up his sodden notebook and shaking it, "you've done a real number on this. Thanks for that." He looked up at the crowd of people still staring down at them. "What do you say we go and chat somewhere a little less... conspicuous?"

The two men returned to the coffee shop and ordered more coffee. They sat down at Richard's table. Freddie made brief introductions. Ronnie then set about giving the men a rough account of the past 20 years of his life and everything that had led to him being there in Spain that week.

He explained how, far from being enamoured with his newfound success, he found his literary superstar status rather unhelpful and limiting. With the publishing world and a legion of fans waiting for his next big masterpiece, Ronnie found his creative muse suddenly went silent on him. The weight of expectation was crushing. Try as he might, he couldn't think of an idea for a new book – nothing that seemed good enough anyway.

"Call it writer's block, I guess," said Ronnie, "but all of a sudden, I couldn't write for toffee. I couldn't get through a paragraph. Nothing seemed to work."

Following several years of trying, and many abandoned manuscripts, Ronnie still had no success. His publisher soon forgot about him. His agent stopped calling. And with his fans moving onto the next big thing, he just stopped trying.

"So, what have you been doing for the last 20 years?" said Freddie.

"The money I made from *The Midas Files* has kept me going. It went to number one in about 30 countries, I think. And I got a decent sum for the movie rights. Did you see it? Not great, I thought. And why they cast Tom Cruise, I've no idea, but still… Every now and then the publisher does another reprint, and the book gets a bit more buzz, so I've been comfortable enough not having to work. So, I've just been… chilling, I guess."

Freddie pinched the bridge of his nose between his thumb and forefinger, forcing himself not to reach over the table and slap the man. Nice work if you can get it, he thought. The cheeky bastard. What he wouldn't give to have a book successful enough that he could live off the royalties and just 'chill' for 20 years.

"None of that explains why you're here now, though," said Freddie.

"Well, I was just getting to that. Like I say, I spent years trying to think of an idea for a new book, but nothing was good enough. Then about six months ago, I wake up and it's there. It's just there."

"What is?"

"The idea. The new book. Fully formed in my head. Plot, characters, subplots, twists. It's all there. It's like my subconscious has been working away in the background for the last 20 years, and suddenly, I have a new book. So I start to write it, but then I start panicking. What if I've lost my touch? It's been a long time since I wrote anything decent."

"Right?" said Freddie.

"I sent an outline and a few pages to my agent. I tell you: he was more surprised to hear from me than anyone. He said he loved it, but I still wasn't convinced."

"So you thought you'd pick up a few lessons? Attend a writing course incognito and dust off the old skillset? Maybe share a few pages and see what response you get?"

"Exactly. I saw this thing advertised and I thought, why not have a little holiday in the sun and pick up a few new writing tips."

"Yeah, must be nice to have a break from all that 'chilling'," said Freddie.

"I wanted to surround myself with writers," continued Ronnie. "See what people are working on. Attend a few classes. Get my brain back into writing mode. Or at the very least, get a peek at other people's work and reassure myself I haven't quite lost it after all."

"And how well did you know any of the victims," said Richard, again referring to his notebook, "Max Graves, Malcolm Alexander and Christy Collins?"

"Barely at all. I'd never met Christy. I knew Edward, of course, but that was a long time ago, before he'd even married his first wife." Ronnie took a large swig of his coffee. "I never worked with Max. I heard he was a good editor. Didn't really think much of his book, if I'm honest. Tad derivative. Lots of bits of other books all stitched together."

"That's what I said," laughed Freddie, slapping the table and making the coffee cups judder.

"And how about Malcolm Alexander?" said Richard.

"I knew of him, of course. But never worked with him. Funnily enough, I did have a conversation with him this week. My agent set up a meeting with him. We had a drink in his room."

Freddie's mind flicked to the piece of paper he'd found in the bin in Malcolm's room: *Tuesday 11.30. Meeting with RF. New book? Opportunity?* Of course, RF was Ronnie Fraser. It was a reminder about an upcoming meeting.

"And what did you discuss?" asked Richard.

"He wanted to know about the new book. He was interested in publishing it. I told him I hadn't even finished the first draft, but he was keen to talk about advances. Told me he wanted to lock me down before anyone else made me an offer."

"And what did you say?" said Freddie, failing to hide the bitterness in his voice.

"I told him I wasn't ready to talk about it. I'm concentrating on getting the words down first. Or at least I was, until some dickhead pushed me into a swimming pool and soaked my notepad," said Ronnie, glancing at the book he'd left to dry out in the sun. "Luckily this was just thoughts. I've got the actual work on my laptop."

"So you wouldn't be too interested in killing him?" said Richard, talking to Ronnie but raising his eyebrows in Freddie's direction. "In fact, it would be counterintuitive to kill a man who was so keen to publish your new book and, I assume, for quite a lot of money?"

"Exactly," said Ronnie. "Truth be told, the book will probably go out for auction. I think my agent was just trying to cause a stir. You know, let everyone else know Malcolm was interested and see what other offers came in. But I'd be stupid to reduce the number of people bidding, wouldn't I?"

Freddie shuffled in his chair, partly due to his soaking shorts clinging to his legs and partly with the frustration of seeing his brilliant theory crumbling in front of him.

"Doesn't prove you didn't kill him, though," said Freddie, sneering. "This could all just be bullshit. How do we know you really have a new book in the making?"

"I'm sure my agent will confirm it. He was the one who booked my ticket for this week. And I'm sure Malcolm will have called him after we spoke the other day."

"And can you account for your whereabouts at the times of the murders?" asked Richard.

"Yes, let me see," said Ronnie. "I mean, obviously I don't know the actual times people were… you know… But on the first night, I met a lovely young lady at the opening party, and she came back to my room with me for a drink and… well… you know. We didn't get much sleep and neither of us left the room.

"The night Malcolm was killed I… well," he grinned and blushed slightly, "I met another young lady in the hotel bar, and we spent the night in her hotel room. I'm sure she'd vouch for me."

"Fuck's sake," said Freddie, not even trying to hide his jealousy. "And what about Christy? Where were you when she took a tumble off her balcony?"

"About four rows directly in front of you, listening to your talk. And, before you ask, last night I was in the auditorium listening to Edward's reading. I was there the whole night, until you burst onto the stage, naked and screaming."

"And can anyone corroborate that?" snapped Freddie.

"Actually, yes. I was sitting next to a charming woman. We hit it off and when the room was cleared, we retired to my room for a drink and… well…"

Freddie shook his head with disbelief. "So why did you run, then?" he said.

"What?"

"When I called you just now. You ran away."

"Of course, I did," said Ronnie. "You spent 20 minutes staring at me when I was sitting here trying to write, then I get out the door and you start shouting at me. Then you start running towards me, screaming like a lunatic."

"I just wanted to talk to you."

"Well, it didn't seem like that. And in case you've forgotten, there's a killer loose in the hotel. Is it any wonder I didn't want to hang around?"

"You thought I was the killer?" said Freddie.

"I didn't know you *weren't* the killer," said Ronnie. "And, in my defence, you were acting a bit… homicidal. Besides, word travels fast. It's no secret that Spanish detective has you as her main suspect."

"But… but… but…" said Freddie.

"Well, thank you, Mr Fraser," said Richard, cutting in. "That's all been very helpful. I will need to double-check with the witnesses you've mentioned, if you could let me know their names. But otherwise, I don't think I have any other questions for you."

"Very well," said Ronnie, standing up from his chair. "Any idea when they're going to let us out of this place?"

Freddie sneered up at him, sulking like a child who'd just been told he wasn't getting any dessert.

"Can't say for certain, I'm afraid," said Richard. "I'm not leading the investigation, I'm just consulting. You'd have to check with Inspector Perez, but I'm hopeful we can release people soon."

"And how close are you to finding out who's behind all this?"

"I'm afraid I'm not at liberty to discuss any of the details of an ongoing investigation."

"Spoken like a true police officer," said Freddie.

"Well," said Ronnie, picking up his sodden notebook, "I've got some work to do, and some notes to try and salvage, so…" He let a silence hang between them for a second, then turned and walked out of the coffee shop.

Freddie slumped in his chair; his mouth stretched downwards in a grimace. "Fuck's sake," he said.

"Don't sulk, Freddie," said Richard.

"I was so sure, though," said Freddie. "All the pieces were fitting. What if he…"

"He didn't," said Richard, cutting him off.

"But maybe he…"

"He couldn't," said Richard.

"But what if…"

"Give it up, Freddie. He's not the guy."

"No," said Freddie, breathing out heavily, "you're right. He didn't do it. So who the fuck did?"

"Don't be so downbeat," said Richard, standing up and gathering his things. "You might not have cracked the case, but we've eliminated a suspect. And it might not all seem clear just yet, but we're getting closer."

"Yeah, I guess so," sighed Freddie. "I just thought…"

"Listen," said Richard. "I've got to check in with Inspector Perez. Just let us take it from here, eh? Let the real detectives do the detective work. Go and get some rest. No offence, but you really look like you need it."

CHAPTER 22

FREDDIE TWISTED AND wriggled on top of the bed, the cool, rough sheets scratching his delicate skin. An army of red-hot pins and needles danced over every inch of his burned body, and he found himself becoming painfully itchy in some rather delicate places – but too scared to scratch them.

His attempt to follow Richard's advice and get some rest was not going well – partly due to the agony of simply laying there, and partly because he could hear Richard's voice in his head: "*Let the real detectives do the detective work.*" The words repeated on a loop, the voice becoming more condescending each time.

Who the hell did he think he was? Cheeky sod.

But then, maybe Richard had a point. How had he got it so wrong? And how stupid had he looked bundling an innocent man into a swimming pool?

More to the point, what the hell was he thinking doing that in the first place? What if the dangerous killer he'd thought he was apprehending had turned around and tried to kill him? Again. Had he learned nothing from the last time he'd tracked down suspected murderers and was subsequently battered senseless by a lunatic killer?

Try as he might, Freddie couldn't help but turn the details of the case over in his head. He'd been so sure Ronnie was the killer. All the pieces fit. His past career as a writer that had been cut short. His strange appearance at the festival. His shady behaviour, guarding his notebook and lingering in the shadows. The motive fit so neatly, too, until Freddie discovered that Ronnie was motivated by none of the things he'd assumed. In fact, all those reasons – outrage for being slighted by the industry, jealousy at others' fortune, craving revenge for being denied the success he so desperately wanted – seemed to fit himself much more closely.

It was no wonder Perez still saw Freddie as a suspect.

The more Freddie tried to breathe deeply and push the details of the murders out of his mind, the more vivid the images became. He saw Max's prostrate figure laying on the sunbed. Malcolm's blood-soaked, punctured corpse collapsed on the floor, the silver pen twinkling where an eyeball used to be. The flattened, oozing pancake of what had previously been Christy Collins thwacked on the poolside, and the stunned, screaming, blood-spattered faces of the crowd next to her. And, of course, the image of those books, scribbled all over – the words circled with such menace.

Freddie thought about the clues he'd uncovered. He thought about the different methods for the murders – seemingly opportunistic in design, but still somehow carefully plotted. He considered all the possible motives. Then he spun through the faces of the various people he'd encountered during the week, picturing them in his mind's eye, analysing them for the merest hint of guilt. But he kept coming up blank. He was no closer to solving the case than day one. All he'd done was rule two people out and make himself look like a fool.

Richard was right. Freddie wasn't cut out for this. Maybe he never had been.

If it was the plot for one of his books, he'd be able to see the killer instantly. He'd scan through all the clues, assess the various suspects, determine the motive and have the whole thing wrapped up by lunchtime. But that was because he'd come up with the whole story in the first place. He could easily spot the killer because he'd decided who the murderer was right at the outset.

He'd always thought his powers of deduction went both ways. He was good at setting up an intricate murder plot, with lots of twists and turns, so surely he'd be able to pick out those same details in a genuine murder case. The detectives he wrote about were able to spot the clues that led them to the truth, so it stood to reason that he'd be able to do the same. But in the real world, it wasn't working like that. Of course not. Freddie's detectives were able to spot clues because Freddie put them there for the detectives to find.

Christ, what the hell was he thinking? He was no detective. He was just playing at it. And if he was making such a mess of it in the real world, was he actually any good at it in the literary one? He'd always thought of his books as brilliantly intricate, with fiendish plots and twists that smacked you right between the eyes. But what if they weren't? Maybe his plots really were 'obvious and lazy' as several readers had pointed out in the Amazon reviews he tried to ignore. What if his characters were 'paper thin and creaky'? What if his killers really were 'easy to spot from page 7'?

What if he was so bad at solving puzzles in the real world because the formidable puzzles he thought he'd been creating in his books were actually very easy to crack? He could see now that he'd been fooling himself all these years – walking around like the world just didn't understand his genius and thinking readers were idiots for not buying his books. It wasn't that he was a bad writer, he was just ahead of his time. Everyone who criticised him was wrong – they were just too stupid to understand what he was trying to do.

But now he could see the truth. All those publishers, editors and agents had been right to reject him over the years. He was a talentless loser who didn't deserve to be in print.

And then it hit him, like an ice-cold arrow right through his heart: he was no better than the second-rate, clueless, overly ambitious amateur writers he'd spent the whole week – no, his whole career – mocking, condescending and ignoring.

Oh fuck!

God, he needed a drink. More than that, he had to get the hell out of his room, away from the silence where the little voice in his head was able to run riot. That voice needed to be drowned with booze as quickly as possible.

He eased himself cautiously off the bed, his aching body creaking and stinging. He slipped on the ridiculous deck shoes. He winced and sucked in great mouthfuls of breath as he dragged a gaudy yellow and lime green shirt over his scorched, pink shoulders. Then he marched grumpily out of the room.

He stomped through the hotel, muttering under his breath, castigating himself for being so blind to his own lack of ability. The hotel was still strangely busy. People milled about here and there. They chatted in the corridors. They sunbathed by the pool, read Kindles in the lounge, drank coffee, laughed, joked and behaved in every way as though they were just enjoying any other holiday.

How could they continue to frolic as though the place wasn't currently overrun with killers and armed police? More to the point, how dare they enjoy themselves when he was going through the mother of all existential crises?

Freddie sneered as he bounded past them. He acted like an angry toddler, stamping loudly to disrupt their peace. He purposely walked in the sun to cast a shadow over sunbathers. He petulantly slapped the out-hanging branches of the big pot plants as he walked. Two young boys were enjoying a tense game of pool and as he passed them, Freddie kicked the edge of the table to send the balls out of position.

If he was feeling this unhappy, he was taking as many of these annoying, smiling fuckers down with him as he could.

He marched into the bar like an angry gunman in a shoddy Western movie, slapped his hand on the bar and demanded a pint of Stella, much to the chagrin of the three people who were ahead of him in the queue. To make their outrage even worse, the barman jumped straight to his request and served him first.

Pub rules, dickheads, thought Freddie. You don't have to be first; you just have to be loudest.

Freddie took a long swig of the cold, refreshing drink, necking nearly half of it in one go. He gasped loudly as the cool liquid chilled his insides and released those familiar, calming sensations in his brain. He raised a hand to order another and, by the time he'd gulped down the rest of his drink, the barman was placing a second pint on the bar – much to the annoyance of one customer, who tutted loudly and marched out in protest.

"Freddie," called Nick from a table in the corner. "Freddie, come and join us."

Freddie looked over to see Nick sitting with Colin McMaster, Lisa Smythe and Bill Pascale. Judging by the number of empty glasses on their table, they were several drinks into a lively discussion. And from the grimace on Colin's face, they were clearly not all in agreement.

Freddie wandered over and slumped down into an empty chair at their table. They each had their notebooks open in front of them.

"Christ, you look awful," said Nick.

"Thanks," said Freddie. "It's been a fucking awful day."

"Yeah, I heard about you bundling some poor bloke into the pool," said Colin, the serious, gravelly timbre of his voice contrasting with the smirk on his lips.

"Not just some man," said Freddie, wriggling in the uncomfortable chair, "Ronnie Fraser."

"Ronnie Fraser?" said Lisa, with a star-struck glint in her eyes. "*The Midas Files?*"

"The one and the same."

"I didn't know he was here," said Lisa.

"I didn't know he was still alive," chuckled Colin.

"I haven't seen his name on any of the speaker line-ups," said Bill.

"That's because he's not here as a speaker," said Freddie. "He's here as a punter. He's got a new book coming out and, after 20 odd years, he wanted to make sure he hasn't lost his touch. So he's been hanging out incognito at the back of classes."

"A new book?" cooed Lisa. "Oh, how exciting."

"And why exactly did you push him into a swimming pool?" asked Colin, his smirk growing wider.

Freddie told them about his reasons for chasing down Ronnie: the suspicious behaviour, the potential motives, his relationships with the victims. He then explained how his theory had collapsed after just a few minutes of talking with the man. When he looked up, Colin's smug, self-satisfied grin had stretched across three quarters of his face.

"Hey, don't worry about it," said Nick. "Easy mistake to make. I probably would have come to the same conclusion. In fact, some of the wild theories we've come up with in the last hour are twice as laughable."

"Didn't bundle anyone into a swimming pool, though," laughed Colin.

Freddie flashed his best 'go fuck yourself' smile.

"So, come on then," he said, pointing at Colin's notebook, "who's the killer? Sounds like you've got the whole thing figured out."

"Er… well… erm," said Colin, backtracking faster than a Tory MP.

"Yeah, that's what I thought," sneered Freddie. "Anyone else?"

"Lots of observations," said Nick. "A few theories. We thought it might be interesting to think about what our own fictional detectives might do in this situation. How would they look for clues and question witnesses? What observations might they come up with?"

"And?"

"Well, taking a step back and putting my Milton hat on, I wonder whether there's some kind of government conspiracy going on."

"Of course, you do," sighed Freddie, rolling his eyes and taking another swig of lager.

Milton Beck was the protagonist in all seven of Nick's books. He was a stereotypical former police detective sergeant, drummed out of the force for getting too close to a criminal conspiracy at the highest levels of the establishment and those in charge wanted to silence him. He now worked as a private detective, taking on random cases for a collection of eccentric characters, but in each book Milton Beck also continued to investigate the conspiracy that ruined his career – getting closer but never quite putting all the pieces together.

Naturally, Beck had all the standard formulaic character attributes: a mild drinking problem, an ex-wife that hated him, and an inability to either play by the rules or cede to authority of any kind. It was all a bit clichéd (and not miles away from Freddie's greatest literary creation – the fictional detective Dick Stone), but it worked. And Freddie could see why Nick's books had proved popular.

"Let me guess," said Freddie, "Edward's holding some sordid secret over one of his hoity-toity cabinet minister friends, which he's using to blackmail him. For what? I dunno… Edward's richer than Jesus, so it can't be money. Maybe Edward wants this minister to push through some kind of legislation. Or maybe he wants to buy an island in the Caribbean, and he needs this friend to grease a few wheels. Maybe it's not the first 'favour' Edward has asked for and said friend gets the hump with it. He sends a hitman out to Spain, to bump Edward off and make the blackmail go away?"

Nick leaned forward to cover his notebook with his arm, nearly tipping over his drink in the process. "Stranger things have happened," he shrugged.

"Yes, I suppose they have," said Freddie with a resigned indifference.

Nick, Colin, Lisa and Bill all looked at Freddie with surprise.

"Come on then," said Nick. "Where's the joke? Where's the ribbing?"

"What?" said Freddie.

"Where's the piss-taking?" said Colin. "You're not just going to let him get away with that? Where's the ten-minute tirade on what a stupid idea it is? No offence, Nick."

"Yeah, you wouldn't usually let anyone off that easy," said Lisa, placing a caring arm on Freddie's shoulder. "Are you feeling okay, babe?"

"All sounds plausible, I suppose," said Freddie. "Besides, what the fuck do I know? My theories this week have all been horse shit. Much like my books."

"Ha, he finally admits it," said Colin, chuckling and slapping the table.

The other four stared at him.

"What? He's always taking the piss out of us," said Colin.

"Freddie's had a rough couple of days," said Lisa. "Somebody did try and kill him. And then he ended up on stage all… naked. He's obviously not himself. So, just lay off."

"He wouldn't lay off us, would he?" sulked Colin.

"No, you've got a fair point, Colin," said Freddie. It was true. Normally, Freddie would have been relentless, mocking them, laughing at them. Never letting up until they felt stupid and he felt slightly better about himself. But looking around the table, he suddenly realised how poorly he'd treated them over the years. These were probably some of his closest friends. People he did actually enjoy spending time with. People who he could definitely benefit from letting get just that little bit closer.

"I'm as much of a dick as the next man," continued Freddie. "And I've been known to throw the first stone. And the second. And the last too, probably. I haven't been a very good friend over the years. I haven't been a very good person, really. And it's dawning on me that I've never really been a very good writer, either."

The other four sat back in shock at the sudden candid outpouring.

"And you lot," continued Freddie, raising his drink in salute, "you lot are brilliant. You're good people. You never give up on me, Nick. Even when I send your calls to voicemail, or hide from you at events, or pretend I'm too busy to read your latest book and give you a quote for the cover… you always make time for me and you're a good friend."

"Erm… well, I didn't actually know you did all of those things," said Nick, "but… er… you're welcome?"

"You, Lisa," said Freddie, placing a hand on hers, "you're a terrific writer. Your plots are considered and careful. Your characters are intriguing and well formed. And you always keep me guessing until the end."

Lisa smiled back, not quite sure how to respond.

"You're also a lovely person, and like… seriously fit," said Freddie with a wink.

Lisa blushed and raised her eyebrows. "Goodness, I honestly don't know whether to be flattered or deeply offended," she said, smiling.

"Don't worry," said Freddie, "I get that a lot when I talk to women."

Lisa smiled again, then slowly moved her hand away from his.

"Colin, you're a gruff old bastard," said Freddie. "And you give a whole new meaning to the term grizzly murder. I mean, seriously, how you come up with some of that shit is... disturbing. Like, I suspect something bad probably happened to you as a child. But I always enjoy your books. You have a keen eye for detail and your former life as an actual detective – although it can make you come across as a bit of a prick – gives you such insight."

"I'm flattered?" said Colin.

"And you, Bill," said Freddie. "I just think you're brilliant. Just a great writer and such a nice guy."

Bill's face flushed even redder than Lisa's and Freddie would have sworn he saw the glint of a small tear in the man's eye.

"I guess what I'm trying to say is that I feel honoured to be in your company. And if we ever get out of this fucking hotel... I hope we can continue to be friends."

He raised his glass again in salute. The others joined in.

"Jesus, it's worse than I thought," said Nick, finally breaking the tension. "I think all that heat in the sauna must have melted Freddie's icy heart."

******

At a table on the other side of the room, Edward Cross was jabbing at his smartphone, sighing and cursing under his breath. Marylin was sitting opposite him, sighing even louder as she thumbed buttons on her e-cigarette then pressed it to her lips and sucked hard. This was followed by a dissatisfied grumble and the release of a tiny outpouring of vapour. Then the whole routine started again.

"Will you stop pissing about with that bloody sonic screwdriver?" said Edward.

"Sorry," she said, paying him less than half her attention, "I think this thing's on the fritz again. I swear, I'm refilling the liquid at least once a day. That can't be right, can it?"

"Maybe if you put it down every once in a while, rather than continuously puffing away like a Chinaman in an opium den," said Edward sneering.

"Don't say Chinaman, darling. That's one of the ones you can't say anymore. And it's hardly opium, is it? Just my little vice."

"Little?" scoffed Edward. "You're practically surgically attached to it. In fact, you should see if they can do that. Get it grafted onto your face. That way you might actually be able to concentrate on other things."

"Oh, is someone feeling left out?" she said.

Edward crossed his arms and poked out his bottom lip, looking every bit the sullen child.

Honestly. Marylin had never had her own children. She couldn't bear other people's snotty-nosed, snivelling, knee-scraping little turds at the best of times, let alone having to put up with any of her own. But she sometimes felt like, having decided to leave all that maternal stuff behind, she'd ended up trading it in to become the honorary mother to a group of useless, male writers who could barely dress themselves without her organising every aspect of their lives.

Just think of the money, she thought. Just think of the money.

"Are you even supposed to be smoking that in here?" said Edward.

"This is Spain, darling," laughed Marylin. "You can do whatever you like. I probably *could* sit here with an opium pipe and nobody would say boo to a goose. One of the few good things left about this country, if you ask me. Besides, it's not even real smoke. It's just vapour."

Edward grimaced.

Marylin sighed and started again, poking buttons and twisting knobs.

"Anyway, what are you whinging about now?" said Marylin, finally giving up and slamming the device down onto the table.

"Look at this," said Edward. He thrust his phone into Marylin's face. "Halfway down the page on *The Sun* website. You have to scroll for five minutes to find anything on *The Mail*. Hidden away in the Culture section of *The Guardian*. And not even a single mention on *The Telegraph*. I mean, it could be hidden behind the pay wall, and I'm fucked if I'm paying for that, but you'd expect something, wouldn't you?"

"Sorry, darling, what am I looking at?"

"The press, Marylin. The press. We're getting sod all coverage. Barely a mention. Three people are dead, I've been locked up in a hotel for days – with a killer, I might add – and I'm not even front-page fucking news. Has anyone even been in touch for a quote?"

Marylin tried but failed to hide her sigh. Honestly, trust this man-child to direct all the attention back on his own imagined plight. He'd said it himself; three people had been killed – one of whom was his own ex-wife – and the thing he was most worried about was his own dented ego. If he only knew what was really going on.

Besides, with Malcolm now dead, she had bigger things to worry about. His company was responsible for publishing more than half of Marylin's clients. With him out of the picture, the future was uncertain. Rumours back in the UK were that Malcolm's number two – a testy old bitch called Janet McGuire – would likely take over running the company.

This caused Marylin several problems. She and Janet didn't really see eye to eye – partly on account of Marylin making no secret that she disliked Janet, and partly because Janet had fallen foul of Marylin's devious ways in the past and she was still upset about it.

The two women started their careers together as Junior Agents at the same firm. At first, they'd been quite friendly. Marylin liked the young Janet. They had similar interests, similar ambitions and, being the two new girls, they quickly banded together and formed a little union – taking lunch breaks together, helping each other avoid the lecherous advances of the senior partners and generally looking out for one another. The problem was that Marylin realised early on that Janet was very good at her job, with a keen eye for spotting debut writers. This talent was already impressing their bosses. Janet was destined for great things. And that would just not do. Because, unfortunately, Marylin also suffered from that most unfortunate of plights that still affects many people even today – she'd been brought into the world by a pair of complete dickheads.

Her mother, Jean, had been generally fine. A quiet woman, who seemed happy simply being at home, she lacked gumption or any real opinions of her own. She just adopted those of her husband, let him make all the decisions, and allowed him to treat her like a dinner-making, house-cleaning, baby-producing doormat. A typical trophy wife. A lovely, loving woman, but in no danger of having any real impact on the world. And certainly not someone to look up to.

Marylin's father, Maurice, was the real problem. He was a fast-talking, arrogant, deceitful wretch who valued money more than anything else in life. A small businessman with an overly ambitious mindset, he wasn't scared about breaking the odd law here and there, or screwing over colleagues and competitors in the pursuit of amassing as much money as possible. He loved his wife and daughter, of course, and treated them to all the fine things his money could buy: a nice house, fast cars, expensive holidays, fancy clothes and jewellery, and anything else extravagant that he could show off about. But, of course, it wasn't long before his dishonest business methods caught up with him. One dodgy investment too far and Maurice saw his business go bust. His empire collapsed, his life fell down around him, and he was lucky to avoid a lengthy stay in prison.

Almost overnight, Marylin saw her family's circumstances dramatically reduced. The grand five-bed detached house became a poky two-bed flat in the roughest part of town. Marylin was unenrolled from her expensive private school and found herself shoulder to shoulder with the common kids she and her former classmates had so enjoyed looking down their noses at. Gone too were the fancy holidays, the nice clothes and all the little treats and gifts she'd become accustomed to. They weren't entirely destitute, but Marylin had enjoyed all those finer things and was distraught that she now had to do without them.

Worst of all, she saw a great change in her father. His swagger transformed into a slow trundle. His permanently smug grin slunk into a look of constant worry and embarrassment. His fight was completely gone. He just totally gave up.

Well, not her. She made a promise to herself that she was going to get back everything she'd lost – and more. And God help anyone who stood in her way.

She quickly adopted the attitude: *the only way to get on in life is to fuck over everyone else and take what you want.* And so she set out in life determined to never be left behind, settle for second best, or allow anyone to achieve more than her.

When she saw Janet doing so well – and making Marylin look inadequate in comparison – she couldn't allow it to continue. There then began an illicit campaign of deceit, lies, manuscript-stealing and general bad behaviour. Marylin would find out which authors Janet had a 'great feeling about', then contact them for secret meetings in which she'd badmouth her colleague and lure them to sign with her instead. She contacted several of the illiterate, talentless idiots who had sent her dreadful books, posing as Janet and pretending to be interested. She drafted fake contracts in her young colleague's name then sneakily showed them to senior board members, pretending to be worried that her friend was losing her touch – and likely to cost the company money. And of course, her pièce de résistance, she spread a series of inflammatory, contradictory rumours throughout the industry. The lies detailed the various people Janet had confessed to hating, different executives she was sleeping with to get ahead, authors she'd badmouthed and colleagues whose jobs she was actively campaigning to steal from under their noses. And naturally, Marylin made sure the rumours always got back to the people they were about.

Within just a few weeks, Janet was drummed out of the business, uncertain as to how things had gone so wrong for her so quickly. And with a decent roster of well-performing authors on her books, Marylin soon rose to the heights Janet had been destined for.

It didn't take long for Janet to figure out what Marylin had done, and she vowed revenge. Thankfully, once the dust had settled, people still recognised how talented Janet was and she found a new job as a junior editor with a major publisher. She then rose through the ranks in a career that saw her holding several senior positions with big-name publishers. Her relationship with Marylin continued to fester, with the two barely speaking and never once working together.

And now, with that bitch taking over at Darkhouse Publishing, she would finally be able to get her revenge and tear down everything Marylin had worked so hard to achieve. Several of the deals Marylin was currently negotiating for her writers would be in jeopardy. Worse still, Janet had made no secret over the years that she was no great fan of Edward. She'd tried to convince Malcolm several times to drop the author from their roster, but considering the huge amount of money Edward's books made, Malcolm was never in agreement. And should that financial impetus ever disappear, Marylin still had a very juicy piece of scandal up her sleeve that she could use to blackmail Malcolm and ensure Edward stayed a Darkhouse author.

Edward's latest book was already printed and scheduled for release. There was nothing Janet could do to stop it now. But she could easily pull the marketing budget, postpone the release date, cancel the PR, and see the book flounder at the bottom of the charts. And the chances of getting another big money deal for Edward's next book were dwindling by the second. Which meant Marylin's long overdue retirement in that French cottage was suddenly feeling like a dim and distant dream again.

And this deluded, sheltered, crybaby of an author was more concerned that he wasn't getting enough column inches in the tabloids? It was enough to make her scream. And worst of all, she couldn't even do what she'd normally do and quell the rage in her chest by sucking down lungfuls of delicious, sweet, calming nicotine.

"Hmmm," she said, drumming her nails against the table as she looked at Edward's phone. "Yes, you'd think they'd have a bit more interest. Could really help push up pre-orders if we bagged a bit more coverage. Tell you what, I'll get the social media team to fire out a few more posts. See if we can't get it trending."

"Hmmm," grumbled Edward, placing his phone on the table and taking a swig from his glass of whisky.

Marylin lifted her bag from the floor and started rooting around it, reaching her bony arm right in, like Mary Poppins searching her magic carpet bag but with a far less cheery face and a lot more expletives.

"Ah ha," she said, finally, pulling out her hand and glancing lovingly at a small bottle of vape liquid. She lifted it to her ear and shook it, smiling as she confirmed it was not just another empty. "I knew I had one in here."

"Thank God," Edward humphed.

"Weird, though," said Marylin, lifting the small bottle and inspecting the bright pink label. "Strawberry Candy Floss. I could have sworn I'd already had this one. Well, never mind. That is what I call a definite bonus."

"Absolutely," said Edward. "Life can go back to normal. Never mind the dead bodies and the bloody lockdown. Marylin has her nicotine fix, so we're all saved."

"Oh dear," sneered Marylin, "sounds like someone's getting a bit hangry. Don't worry darling, we'll get you something to eat soon."

Edward sneered back. Marylin raised her eyebrows, grabbed her vape machine and started twisting, unscrewing, pulling off parts and laying them out in a neat row on the table. She looked like a soldier disassembling his rifle. She then picked up the little bottle of liquid and unscrewed the cap.

"Hmmm, strange…" she said, looking down at it with a frown.

"What?" said Edward, staring at his phone screen again.

"No, it's just… no click."

"No what?"

"No click. There's usually a safety twist on these things. You know, it clicks the first time you open it. Did you hear a click?"

"No idea," said Edward, jabbing at his phone.

"Well, never mind," said Marylin, placing the bottle to the little liquid tank and filling it up.

Finally, she went back into soldier mode, slotting, screwing, twisting and assembling the thing back together. She practically giggled with excitement as she adjusted the gauge to allow the maximum output of vapour. She then raised the device to her lips and sucked as hard as she could.

She felt the warm liquid vapour rush through her mouth, down her throat and into her expanding lungs. She breathed in, sucking down as much as she could. But something didn't feel right. The taste was harsh, acrid and chemical-like. Instead of the soothing, relaxing feeling she expected, suddenly her mouth and throat were burning with an intense heat, like she'd just bitten into the world's hottest chilli pepper.

The pain grew, stretching down the back of her throat, permeating into her lungs until her whole chest was on fire. Panic filled her eyes. She looked at the machine in her hand. She tried to breathe out. Tried to breathe in. Nothing happened. It was like her lungs were solid blocks of burning pain.

Tears ran down her face. She twisted and writhed in her seat, dropping her vape machine onto the floor with a loud thud. Edward looked up to see what the noise was. He jolted back, his eyes filling with surprise as he saw the obvious distress in hers.

"Marylin? Marylin, are you all right?"

She clutched at her throat. She tried to breathe. Tried to gasp for some air, any air, but it was no good. The burning in her chest grew worse. Pain unlike anything she'd ever felt. She looked at Edward, pleading with her eyes, imploring him to somehow read her mind and understand what was happening. He just sat there, open-mouthed.

She tried to stand, but her legs gave way and she tumbled to her knees. All the time, the burning pain grew worse and worse. She wanted to scream, but she couldn't summon the breath to make even the slightest sound. She looked up at Edward, darkness creeping in at the edges of her vision. She felt woozy, the lack of oxygen making it hard to see, hard to think. She reached up and gripped the edge of the table with her bony fingers.

People had turned to see what was happening now. Every eye in the bar staring at her. Mouths gaping. Eyebrows raised. Everyone motionless, not knowing what to do.

Suddenly, she felt something shift in her chest. Burning, swirling, uncomfortable. She tried pulling herself up to her feet, but she had no strength. The pain in her lungs grew even more intense. Then she felt something pop. Deep inside. She lurched forward violently, involuntarily, the force of it nearly breaking her back. And finally, she let out a loud cough, great spurts of dark, red blood spattering out, covering the floor. It splatted over the table, over her hands, and drenched a shuddering Edward.

She tried to suck in a breath, but still nothing came. The pain throbbed in her chest. She lost her grip on the table and tumbled forward, landing face first in a small puddle of her own blood. She lay there for a few seconds, wheezing and listening to the commotion around her as people screamed, chair legs scraped on the ground, and panicked voices danced around the room. Darkness crept in from the edges until everything was black. And then the burning pain stopped.

CHAPTER 23

"WHAT THE HELL?" said Freddie, looking down at Marylin.

Her thin, bony frame looked even more gaunt than ever. She wasn't moving anymore. The violent, quaking, coughing shakes had ceased and she was now laying there completely motionless.

The room had fallen silent. A small group of people gathered around behind Freddie to look, standing there like meerkats, heads spinning round with shock. Colin McMaster edged up to the front, looked down at the body, barked in his loud, gruff voice that he was going to get the police and call for an ambulance, then ran out of the room.

Freddie kneeled and placed a finger on Marylin's throat. He wasn't entirely certain what he was supposed to be feeling for. But he'd seen it done in countless movies, and he'd always fancied giving it a try should the opportunity arise.

"Well?" said Nick, who'd shuffled up behind him.

Freddie glanced up with a solemn look. "Dead."

The crowd took a collective intake of breath, their dazed meerkat faces going into overdrive, looking all around them with worry.

Freddie wasn't qualified to make that pronouncement. He'd never had any medical training, unless you counted his unhealthy obsession with hospital dramas, A&E-based reality shows, and those lurid documentaries that feature the horrendous results of botched plastic surgery. However, Marylin's skin was turning greyer by the second and she'd just coughed several pints of blood all over the floor, table and a petrified-looking Edward. He thought it was a safe bet that she was a gonner.

Freddie grabbed a napkin from the table, used it to pick up Marylin's vape machine and lifted it close to his face to inspect it. Nothing obviously strange or unusual, but then he had no idea what he was looking for. He placed it back on the floor and used the same napkin technique to pick up the little bottle of liquid from the table.

247

He gazed at the pink label. Again, he had no idea what he was looking for, but with everyone watching he felt a strange duty to put on a show of investigating – squinting and hmmmming and nodding his head as if he'd just uncovered something key. And if he was completely honest, he quite liked the feeling of acting like a real detective.

He carefully unscrewed the bottle's lid, lifted it to his nose and sniffed. He then recoiled instantly, screwing up his face and coughing.

"Fucking hell," he said.

"What?" said Nick, leaning over him.

"Smells like a fucking swimming pool," said Freddie, "but a thousand times stronger."

"Chlorine," said Nick, a little too impressed with himself.

Freddie took another, more careful sniff to confirm. "Yep," he said. "Chlorine. Jesus Christ, if she's just sucked in a mouthful of this stuff… it's no wonder she's coughed up half a lung all over the room. Why the fuck would she put chlorine in her…"

Freddie cut himself off, the realisation hitting him. Small sighs and waves of sound jostled through the crowd of onlookers as they slowly reached the same conclusion.

"She's been murdered," said Freddie, looking up and squinting for extra dramatic effect. "The killer has struck again."

Bollocks. That was a shit line. *The killer has struck again?* What was he thinking? He could have done way better than that. He hadn't even worked in a clever pun, or anything. Had he learned nothing from the countless hours of *CSI Miami*, *Castle*, *NCIS*, *Criminal Minds* or the other cheesy cop shows he'd watched over the years? He wished he could go back and come out with something pithy, but it was too late.

Freddie's proclamation sent the room into overdrive. The assembled crowd looked this way and that, glaring at each other. They all slowly moved away from the person next to them, edging into as much of a safe zone as they could make for themselves, fearful that they might just be next on the list. The whole time, Edward Cross remained fixed in his seat, completely motionless. His face was a deathly shade of white, dappled with Marylin's blood and stretched out into a look of horrified shock.

Freddie glanced back down at Marylin's body, scanning the scene for anything that stood out. Her clothes seemed like the normal expensive tat she'd wear – nothing strange or different there. The vape machine was standard, as far as he could tell. The little bottle of liquid seemed inconspicuous. It just looked like a normal bottle; the same ones he'd seen in the shop next to reception. Marylin's hands were…

Looks like smoking really can kill. Fuck. That was the line he should have used. Why do these things always pop into your head when it's too late? Dammit. There'd be no way to work that into the conversation now. The moment was gone. Typical.

Freddie was just about to lean down and start rifling through Marylin's handbag when Richard came running into the room, followed closely by two of Inspector Perez's black-clad goons.

"Richard," said Freddie. "Thank God. It's Marylin Sharpe. She's dead. I think she…"

"Okay, sir," said Richard, waving Freddie off without even having the decency to look him in the eye. "The police are here now. If you could all just get back and let us do our jobs."

"Yes, but…" pleaded Freddie.

"Please, sir," said Richard, with cold impassion. "Take a step back."

What the fuck? Why was he acting like such a dick? If he'd just listened, Freddie could have told him what had happened.

Richard kneeled over the body and placed a finger on Marylin's throat. He then went through the same routine Freddie had carried out only moments earlier.

Freddie watched, seething inside, shaking his head as Richard inspected the pool of blood emanating from Marylin's mouth. Richard then pulled a pair of nitrile gloves from his pocket, put them on and carefully lifted the vape machine.

Freddie tutted loudly inside his head. Honestly, he'd just done all this.

Richard moved onto the small bottle, unscrewing it and taking a sniff. He recoiled with a grimace, just as Freddie had done.

"It's chlorine," shouted Freddie, more so that the crowd could hear him than Richard. He wasn't letting that wanker take all the glory. Richard ignored the outburst and continued inspecting the scene. He rooted around in Marylin's bag, pulling out various items, squinting at them, then placing them back.

No book, thought Freddie, studiously monitoring every item that Richard lifted and placed back. No copy of *The Terrible Bones* at this scene. Was that significant?

Finally, Richard stood and placed the small bottle with the pink label back on the table. He looked out at the crowd, tilted his head to one side and said, "Well, I guess smoking really can kill."

Freddie balled his hands into tight fists and screamed inside his head.

"What happened?" asked Richard, turning to Edward, who was still sitting there, motionless. Freddie could have sworn the man hadn't even blinked once in the last five minutes.

Richard reached forward and snapped his fingers twice in front of Edward's face. That shocked him out of his stunned silence. He looked at Richard, focused in on his face, but it was as if he wasn't entirely there – the shock keeping him one step removed from reality, like he was sleepwalking.

"I... erm, I... er," said Edward, with tears in his eyes and a shaking bottom lip. "She was smoking that thing. And then... then..."

"Talk me through it," said Richard. "Every small detail could be important."

"We were just chatting. She was fiddling with that thing. Couldn't get it to work and she was getting really wound up."

"And then what happened?" said Richard.

"She was rooting around in her bag and she pulls out that bottle. She used it to fill up the vape thingy. She takes a great big suck on it and then... then... the next thing she's gone all red in the face and thrashing about and... then she's coughing and spitting blood all over the place and... then she's on the floor... dead... I mean... is she? Is she dead?"

"Yes, I'm afraid so," said Richard.

Edward's quivering bottom lip went into overdrive as two big tears rolled down his cheeks.

"You said she'd only just filled this up," said Richard, now holding the vape pen. "Using this bottle?" He pointed at the bottle on the table.

"Yeah."

"And was there anything else? Anything she said?"

"I don't know," said Edward. Then suddenly remembering, he said, "The click."

"The click?" said Richard.

"She was asking me if I heard a click. You know, the click you hear on the security cap when you open a bottle?"

"Go on."

"She fished that out of her bag. She opened it. Then she was asking me if I'd heard a click. I said I didn't know."

"Hmmm," said Richard. "Looks like the bottle's been tampered with. From the smell of it, someone's filled it with chlorine. If she breathed in a big lungful of that stuff, then, well… Obviously, we'll get forensics to check, but it looks like the killer has struck again."

As if on cue, Inspector Perez marched into the bar, flanked by another handful of police officers, who quickly formed a semi-circle around the corpse. Perez walked over and looked at the body. Then she and Richard stepped over to the far wall, where they quietly conferred.

"What do you reckon?" said Nick, sidling up to Freddie and whispering in his ear.

"Doesn't look good," said Freddie, shaking his head slowly. "I definitely suspect foul play."

"Foul play," said Lisa Smythe, appearing on Freddie's other shoulder. She had a perverse grin on her face, her eyes sparkling with intrigue.

"Jesus, Lisa," said Freddie, "not exactly the best time to be sneaking up on people. Tensions are high. I could have lashed out and clobbered you."

"Yeah, try it," she said, smirking. "Then there'd definitely be another murder. So the killer's struck again?"

"It certainly seems that way," said Freddie.

"Shit," said Nick. "So you think your theories might have been right after all?"

"What?"

"Your detective skills? They're coming back to you?"

"What the fuck are you talking about?" said Freddie.

"You know… it's just that you've spent the last 20 minutes doubting yourself and…"

"Well… I mean… I might have been…"

"And saying how… like… what the fuck did you know about it anyway… and all your theories are horse shit, much like your books…"

Freddie stopped, stunned. Nick stared back like an inquisitive boy scout. Lisa smirked again, wondering what fun she'd missed out on.

Finally, Freddie said, "What the hell are you trying to say?"

"No, nothing," said Nick, "I just meant, it's good to see your confidence back up."

"Well, you've got a funny way of showing it."

"No, I just think it's good that you're investigating again. Working through the clues. It's exciting. So, what's the latest theory?"

Freddie sighed. His shoulders dropped. "Come on, man," he said. "You've put me right off my flow now."

"Sorry, I was just... getting into it, I suppose. So, do you think the killer could be in the room now?"

It was a thought that hadn't really occurred to Freddie. He was slightly embarrassed to admit it. So, he didn't.

"More than likely," said Freddie. "This killer likes to be there to see his victims die."

Freddie had nothing to back that up, other than it sounded good. And more importantly, it made him sound like he knew what he was talking about. "Look at the previous victims. The killer had to get close enough to Max to poison his drink. It's likely they hung around to make sure it worked."

"Hmmm," said Nick, joining in.

"They lay in wait for Malcolm, then stabbed him to death. They had to get close enough to Christy to push her off that balcony. And they snuck right up on me and locked me in that sauna. I didn't see where they went, of course. I was too busy freeing myself. But they probably hung around, just out of sight, waiting and watching."

"Do you think so?" said Lisa.

"Stands to reason. Trouble is, I outsmarted them, didn't I?" said Freddie, pushing out his chest. "They didn't count on me escaping. And when I did, they probably scarpered as quick as they could. But yeah, this killer likes to see their handiwork."

"Oh Jesus. Oh God. Oh Jesus..." said Dan, sidling up behind the group. His face was grey and gaunt, like a man who hadn't eaten in a week. "Oh my God. Oh, I can't believe it..."

"Dan," said Freddie. "Jesus, you look like you've just sucked off a dead horse."

"Fuck's sake, Fred," said Lisa, her face screwing up like she'd just eaten a lemon. "You really have a way with words, don't you?"

"I'm just saying," said Freddie, "the man looks absolutely fucked."

"What... eh?" said Dan, half lost in a trance. "Erm... oh, it's just the... you know... I can't believe this is happening again."

"Yeah, the body count really is racking up," smiled Freddie. "I'll say this for you, you certainly put on an entertaining week. As far as murder mystery writing retreats go, you've over-delivered on the murder and the mystery."

"Oh God," said Dan, wringing his hands as his body juddered with shock. "Oh, I'm ruined. This is just… I mean, three murders was bad, but… this is the end of me."

"Hey, I'm sure it's not that bad…" said Freddie. "Things will soon blow over… and… actually, no sorry, that's bollocks. You're fucked mate. This is really, really, really bad."

"Who the hell is doing this? And why?" said Dan, suddenly angry.

"That's what we were just talking about," said Nick. "We've come up with a few different theories."

"Yeah, you all have your wild theories," smirked Freddie. "Of course, some of us have built an investigation based on actual facts."

Nick was right, Freddie did feel his confidence rising again. Sod Richard and sod Perez. Freddie did know what he was doing. He'd investigated the clues every bit as well as they had. And he was just as close to figuring out what was really going on. Compared with the other writers' theories, he was the only one even close to cracking the case – all built on solid detective work. Why had he ever doubted himself?

"Really?" said Dan. "You think you know who's behind all this?"

"Too early to say," said Freddie. "I've eliminated some suspects. And I have a few more leads to work through. But I'm getting close."

"Freddie thinks the killer could be in this room right now," said Nick, peering around at the rest of the crowd.

"Really?" said Dan. "What makes you think that?"

"I didn't say that. Not exactly. But it's a fair bet they're not too far away," said Freddie, smirking with a 'don't you wish you were as smart as me' grin. "This is all very personal. Connected. The killer knew the victims well enough to get close to them. This isn't some stranger to them. They would have trusted them – certainly enough to be alone with them, or close enough that they could slip things into their drinks or handbags."

"Of course," said Nick, with a conspiratorial whisper. "A close friend, maybe. Someone that knew them all. Someone from their past?"

"Do you think so?" said Dan.

"Possible," said Freddie.

The group turned to scan the room.

"So, who then?" said Lisa. "I know it wasn't me. I barely knew any of the victims. And it certainly wasn't Dan here. Just look how grey his bloody face is."

Lisa, Nick and Freddie laughed. Dan didn't.

"Well, it wasn't me," said Nick. "And I'm pretty sure it wasn't Freddie. Not unless you faked the whole sauna thing as a clever…"

"I didn't fake the fucking sauna thing," snapped Freddie, cutting him off before he could finish the thought. "You're not the first person to suggest that, and I can promise you I didn't nearly boil myself to death as a ruse to avoid detection."

"Hmmm, would it be boiling, though?" said Nick. "More like steamed. Or baked."

"Not you as well," said Freddie, shaking his head. "Can we focus on the more important matter at hand?"

"Yes, sorry," said Nick. "So, who's the killer?"

"Someone that hates Edward, that's for sure. Somebody with a real grudge against him."

"How do you know that?" said Lisa.

"It's his book left at every murder. And they're bumping off people close to him. Taking them out one by one. People who all shared a secret."

"A secret? How do you know that?" asked Dan.

"Oh, there are a few things I know that the police don't," said Freddie, winking.

"Really? Like what?" said Nick.

"Yeah, like what?" said Richard Stone.

Freddie spun round to see the detective standing behind him, accompanied by Inspector Perez. They'd closed in and listened to the last 30 seconds of their conversation. And now they were frowning.

"Oh," laughed Freddie, "now you want my help, do you? You didn't want it a few minutes ago."

"Seriously, what do you know that I don't?" said Richard.

"Yeah, you'd love that, wouldn't you? Sorry, but why should I share my leads with you?"

"Because if you don't, I'll arrest you for accessory to murder, wasting police time and anything else we can think up to charge you with," said Perez.

Freddie sighed and shook his head. Just as he went to speak, he was interrupted by a voice on the other side of the room – high-pitched, panicked, shouting.

"Detectives! Detectives!" yelled Edward Cross. He was standing up now, looking down at the dead body, his face bright red and a look of utter dread in his eyes. He'd finally snapped out of his trance, like he'd woken to find himself in a strange place with no idea of how he'd got there.

Freddie, Nick, Dan, Lisa, Richard and Perez all turned to see the source of the commotion.

"Detectives!" shouted Edward again, small strands of spittle flying from his mouth. "I demand protection. Someone is trying to kill me. They've killed everybody close to me, and they'll be coming for me next. You have to protect me."

The crowd in the bar jostled again. Worried. Twitchy. The police officers straightened, poised to jump into action.

"Okay, okay," said Richard, raising his hands and addressing the room. "There's no need to panic. The police are here to protect you and I promise we will find out who the killer is. But for the time being, I need you all to head back to your rooms and stay there until further notice."

"How can you be sure we're safe?" cried a voice from the back of the room.

"Any one of us could be next," shrieked another.

"You're all safe," said Richard, his voice sounding confident but his eyes suggesting otherwise. "The police are here, and we have more officers on the way. Please head back to your rooms and await further instructions."

Another troop of police officers appeared at the door and wordlessly started shepherding people out of the room and down the long corridors.

"Right," said Richard, turning back to the group. "You lot and Mr Cross over there are all heading back to his room with us now. I want to know what you three have been saying and what the hell it is you think you know. One way or another, we're getting to the bottom of this."

Freddie felt his phone vibrating in his pocket. He pulled it out. The caller ID revealed it was his former agent calling.

"You lot go ahead," said Freddie, nodding to Richard and raising his eyebrows. "I need to take this."

CHAPTER 24

"ARE YOU HAVING a fucking laugh?" said Freddie, walking into Edward's hotel room. The two police officers guarding the door had waved him in, his eyes widening with surprise as he saw the sheer opulence laid out before him. It took him a full 30 seconds to walk down the hallway from the door to the main room. On his way, he glanced into a giant, shiny, white-tiled bathroom which featured a toilet, bidet, shower cubicle, huge bath and a separate whirlpool spa. There was even a bloody sofa in there.

The bathroom was easily as big as Freddie's whole hotel room. And that wasn't the worst of it. As Freddie continued down the corridor, he looked through a series of doors that revealed a huge walk-in wardrobe, a kitchen big enough to contain one of those large American fridge-freezers with an ice dispenser built into the front, and another room which housed two large sofas, a giant TV on the wall and a cabinet of Blu-Rays. He was already huffing and tutting as he reached the end and turned the corner into the largest bedroom he'd ever seen.

A giant bed – the size of two doubles pushed together – sat in the middle of the room, pressed up against the wall, with four pillows lining the top in a neat row. Another two sofas sat facing each other by the furthest wall, with a large coffee table nestled between them, and in the far corner was a full-sized dining table with eight chairs. Across from the bed, lining the whole far wall, was the largest set of bi-fold patio doors Freddie had ever seen, opened and leading out to a giant balcony. But not just any balcony. This one had its own built-in infinity pool, another private whirlpool spa and two sunbeds – with another table and set of chairs for good measure.

Freddie could barely breathe. If his face wasn't already pink from having nearly been cooked to death, it would have glowed red with indignation. And that was before he saw the worst of it.

Nestled under a long dressing table, beneath another 60-inch flat-screen TV, was not just one, but three separate minibars. Freddie gazed through the glass-fronted doors to see that one of them contained different kinds of beers (both canned and bottled), one held a large array of mini bottles of wine, and the third one featured a selection of miniature spirits and cans of soft drinks. Freddie had to hold onto the wall to stop himself dropping to his knees with shock.

"Holy shit," said Freddie, walking over to the sofas where Nick and Dan were sitting opposite Lisa and Edward. "It's like a bloody aircraft carrier."

The group looked up at him. Richard Stone and Inspector Perez glanced over from where they were standing by the open patio doors, then quickly turned away and continued a hushed, private conversation.

"I know," said Nick, beaming like an excited child whose parents had finally taken him to Disneyworld, "it's incredible isn't it? Way bigger than my room."

Freddie had been more than happy when he'd checked into his room. Delighted, in fact. He couldn't believe the size and luxury. He'd felt a like a spoiled prince. But that was before he found out how much better everyone else had it. And now, seeing the luxury afforded to Edward, he felt genuinely aggrieved. He was just about to unleash all his pent-up anger, but he stopped short when he saw the look on Dan's face.

Dan was perched on the edge of the sofa, staring at his hands and gently mumbling to himself. His eyes were wide open and dark, glistening with tears, like someone who'd just seen his own parents having sex. The man was clearly in a state.

"Oh, wind your neck in, Freddie," said Edward. "Yes, I've got a nice big room. And yes, it's probably nicer and bigger than yours. Big fucking whoop, mate. There's a very good reason for it. I'm a bigger name than you. I'm a better writer. I sell more books. And there are more people here hoping to get my autograph than have ever even heard of you, let alone read any of your books."

Edward spoke slowly and calmly. There was no anger. No hint of condescension or cruelty. Just a man stating the facts that everyone else in the room already knew and that Freddie didn't like to admit.

Freddie just stood there, open-mouthed and, for once, seeming humbled.

"They give me the big room because I'm the star draw. That's it. I don't ask for it. I never even think about it, to be honest. It's all down to my agent. My…" Edward's voice cracked, emotion flooding his throat, making the words harder to speak. "My… friend. Who only moments ago I saw die in front of me, coughing and spluttering and panicking. And now she's gone."

Two large tears rolled silently down Edward's cheeks as his shoulders gave an involuntary shudder. He looked vulnerable. Broken. And suddenly he was no longer the man who'd enraged Freddie so much over the years. The one who betrayed and deserted him. The man with whom he'd spent the past two decades in a bitter feud. Instead, Freddie once again saw the confusion, innocence, and naivety he'd first seen in that scared young man he'd befriended all those years ago.

Freddie walked over, placed a hand gently on Edward's sobbing cheek and looked him in the eye. "I'm sorry, mate," he said. "I know how much Marylin meant to you. I really am sorry for your loss."

Edward smiled through glistening eyes, the two men looking back at each other, lost in a strange, bitter moment of condolence and regret.

"Nice of you to finally join us," said Richard, his secret conversation with Perez now over. They both took a couple of steps towards the group, still maintaining a cautious distance.

"Apologies," said Freddie, stepping back from Edward. "I've just had a rather illuminating conversation with somebody back home in England."

"Yeah," said Richard, "I'm sure chatting with whichever bookie or prostitute was phoning to demand payment was the highlight of your week, but we're trying to solve a murder here."

"Very droll," said Freddie.

"Seriously, though. Don't forget there's a killer on the loose. We can't have people wandering off alone."

"I didn't know you cared," said Freddie, pretending to fan fake tears out of his eyes. "But not to worry. After the phone call I've just had, you don't need to be concerned about me. In fact, you can stop trying to figure out who the killer is. I know exactly who they are. Even better than that, I happen to know they're in this room with us, right now."

Everyone looked at him with surprise. Then they slowly scanned around the room, eyeing each other suspiciously, a strange mix of fear and curiosity dancing over their faces.

"Bollocks," said Edward, finally breaking the silence. "You know fuck all."

"Is that right?" said Freddie, walking over to the row of minibars. He opened the door to one, pulled out a small bottle of gin and teeny can of tonic, and poured the contents into a glass. He took his time, pouring slowly, smiling to himself as he savoured the tension in the room. "Hmmm… ice. Ice. Now, where would I find ice?"

"Never mind your sodding ice," snapped Richard. "What the hell do you mean you know who the killer is?"

"Exactly what I said. You see, while this lot," said Freddie, pointing at the other writers on the sofas, "having been coming up with unrealistic, wild, fiction-based theories, I've been doing some actual detective work. Interviewing witnesses. Chasing down leads. Hunting for clues. Eliminating suspects. Digging into people's pasts."

"And we haven't?" said Richard, pointing at himself and Inspector Perez, indignation ringing in his voice.

"Hey, no offence meant. No disrespect, Inspector. I know you've both been doing the same. I'm not criticising you or questioning your police work. I've just got a little advantage over you, that's all."

"Are you going to tell us what you're talking about?" sighed Inspector Perez. "Or do I have to get my men to take you back to the police station? Believe me, I can make the rest of your time in my country a lot less comfortable than this hotel."

She clearly wasn't enjoying Freddie's theatrics. But he wasn't going to let that ruin his Poirot moment. He literally had a roomful of people assembled, hanging on his every word, as he planned to outline his findings and reveal the identity of the killer. He might never have this chance again.

"I'm sorry, detective. Please bear with me as I explain what I've discovered."

Perez narrowed her eyes and growled softly under her breath.

Freddie took a large sip of his drink, turning to look ominously out of the large window for effect. He could feel Edward rolling his eyes as he did so, but he didn't care. He was enjoying himself way too much.

"As I said, you've both done a valiant job in your investigations," said Freddie, turning back to address the room. "But I have one advantage that you don't. I'm a writer." He let the words hang in the air for effect. "I'm part of the writing community. And that affords me certain insights that you don't have. Insights, for example, that helped me determine the motive for these murders and the very methodical, elaborate way in which they were plotted."

Freddie took another sip, savouring the crisp, bitter taste on his tongue almost as much as the attention he was getting.

"Because these murders, and the reasons behind them," continued Freddie, crossing the floor slowly to look down at the group on the sofas, "are very much related to this industry we all work in."

Perez huffed impatiently on the other side of the room.

"Sorry Inspector," said Richard, "he gets like this. Trust me, it's easier to let him put on his little show rather than trying to rush him. Otherwise, he'll get all huffy and it'll take twice as long."

Freddie tutted.

Perez sighed and shook her head, making a 'carry on then' gesture with her hand.

"As I was saying," said Freddie, "this case is very much rooted in the publishing world. Dreams. Hope. Rejection. Betrayal. Deception. Dishonesty. These are the things that drove our killer to carry out these murders. Angry murders. Violent. Brutal. Seemingly random and spur of the moment, but actually quite calculated and carefully planned. All part of an intricate web of revenge."

He was really going for it now. Elongating words, adding in long pauses, speaking in a strangely formal accent and staring off into middle distance to hit the points home.

"The killer is taking out their anger on a small, connected group of people. People all connected to Edward. Hence the book left at the scene. But why him, exactly?"

Everyone in the room turned to look at Edward, then back to Freddie.

"First we must consider the book. The same book at each scene. The same manic scribbling inside. But why? The killer is leaving us a message. This is someone who feels slighted. Betrayed. And they want us to know why.

"But it's not just these people the killer is angry with. They hate the whole publishing world. They feel let down, cast out. They've spent their life feeling like they're not quite good enough. But who?"

On the other side of the room, Richard cleared his throat noisily, with a look that said, 'I've bought you a bit of leeway, but don't take the bloody piss'.

"Once I realised why the killer was doing this, I had to look at who might have reason to feel this way. Who might want to take revenge on the industry that shunned them? Someone who'd spent years being mercilessly rejected. Someone rebuffed so many times they resorted to publishing their own books. And even when they started to get a few sales, they still never really felt like they'd made it. Someone who only a few days ago told me how they'd grown up admiring a certain Mr Edward Cross. How they dreamed of achieving his level of success. Someone whose favourite book was *The Terrible Bones* – the very book that inspired them to become a writer in the first place. The book that, no matter how much they tried, they were never able to emulate and always made them feel second best."

"Oh… hey… wait a second," said Nick, suddenly bustling on the couch. "What the…"

"Yes, Nick. You hated Edward for that, didn't you?"

Everyone in the room turned to look at Nick.

"Eh? No. What are you trying to say?" said Nick.

"The pain of rejection burned away at you, didn't it? Toiling for scraps while the great Edward Cross lived in his mansion, churning out bestseller after bestseller. And all the while people looked down their noses at you, because you're not a real published writer."

"What? I never… That's not what…" said Nick, exasperated and confused.

"Isn't that what you told me? That no matter how successful Edward became, just one person could ruin his whole life?"

"Well, yes," said Nick. "But you're taking it out of context…"

"You hated Edward for his success. You hated that it all came so easily to him. That anything he wrote would be snapped up and sell millions of copies, while you spent your days doing your own publicity, working all hours just to make a living."

"I… I…" said Nick, his face turning red as small beads of sweat formed on his forehead.

Edward squinted at Nick and slowly edged away from him on the sofa. Perez and Richard both straightened on the other side of the room, listening intently as they subconsciously prepared themselves to subdue a criminal.

"You hated Edward. You couldn't let him get away with it any longer. So, you plotted your revenge on him and everyone close to him. When you heard he was going to be here at the same event as yourself, you suddenly had the perfect opportunity. And not only him. It was also the perfect chance to take your revenge on Malcolm, the publisher who'd rejected your books time and time again. On Marylin, the agent who never replied after you sent her all those submissions. On Max, the agent who belittled your work and said you weren't cut out to be a writer. And on Christy, who scored a major publishing deal not on the quality of her writing, but just because of who she used to be married to. You spend years toiling away, trying your hardest, facing rejection at every turn, and she just snaps up a publishing deal. It wasn't fair, was it? And by God, you were going to make them all pay."

"Wait, no… bollocks…" said Nick, his hands trembling in his lap and his face now so red he looked like he might have a heart attack at any second. "That's complete crap. I never hated Edward. And I've never considered myself second best. Yeah, I self-published my first couple of books but, in case you forgot, they were good and loads of people bought them. That's why I got a publishing deal for my last three. So, yes, I am a properly published author. And I sell a lot more than you, you cheeky prick."

Nick's breathing was hard and ragged, his voice filled with fury. Freddie stood quietly, pursing his lips and tenting his fingers against his chin.

"And as for that other shit, yeah I sent submissions to Marylin. And no, she didn't reply. Just like the hundred other agents who rejected me. I haven't bloody murdered them, though, have I? And what's all that shit about Max belittling my work? I've never even met him. Or Malcolm. And I didn't want to kill Christy Collins. None of it makes any sense."

Freddie stepped over and looked down at Nick. He reached out and placed a hand on his shoulder, like a priest pardoning a sinner.

"Don't worry, Nick," he said. "I know you're not the killer."

Everyone in the room let out an exasperated sigh.

Richard raised his hands and shook his head.

Nick collapsed back into the sofa cushion and said, "Prick!"

"No, that would have been far too easy, wouldn't it?" said Freddie, turning and crossing the floor to where Richard and Perez stood, scowling. "Far too neat. But this case is anything but neat. Is it, Lisa?"

Freddie spun round to look directly at Lisa.

She sat back, startled. "What the hell?" she said.

"You hated Malcolm, didn't you?"

"What, no… I…" she gasped.

"You and Malcolm were having an affair. Don't deny it. You've been seen flirting and hanging out with each other in the hotel. When we were having drinks the other night, don't think I didn't notice all the secret glances you were giving each other."

Lisa stared back. Silent. Her eyes wide with confusion.

"And I found the crucial piece of evidence that points to you. The used condom wrappers in the bin in Malcolm's room."

Everyone in the room turned to look at Lisa. She pressed back into the sofa cushion with surprise.

"Sales of your last book haven't been great, have they, Lisa? Rumour is, your publishing company is thinking of dropping you. No home for your new book. No guarantees anyone else will pick it up. So you come to this retreat to lick your wounds and think of a new plan. And then you see that Malcolm's here. Head honcho at Darkhouse Publishing. Hmm, there's a good opportunity, you think. If you can work your womanly wiles on him, get him into bed and get him wrapped around your finger, your next book deal is in the bag. But it doesn't work, does it? Everyone knows what Malcolm was like. As soon as he's had his way with you, he ditches you. And you couldn't stand for that, could you, Lisa?"

Perez took a small step forward, looking closer at Lisa, examining her.

Richard uncrossed his arms.

"That night in the bar, there was clearly tension between you. You just couldn't believe how he'd used you, and then you saw your chance to get back at him. You made your excuses to leave but, instead of going back to your own room, you went to Malcolm's. You still had the spare key card he'd given you the night before, so you let yourself in and waited. Then when he walked through the door, you unleashed all that fury and hatred against him, stabbing him to death with the very pen you'd hoped he'd use to sign your contract."

Silence hung in the room. Everyone eyed Lisa cautiously. Then she burst out laughing.

"Jesus Christ, Freddie," she said, still chuckling, "where the hell are you getting all that from? No wonder people don't read your books, if that's the loose, erratic, assumptive drivel you come up with. It makes no fucking sense."

Richard and Perez both sighed loudly again.

Freddie clasped his hands, pressing both forefingers against his lips, as he listened to Lisa's mocking.

"For a start, where do you get that my publisher is dropping me? If you must know, I had a call from my agent this morning, telling me she's putting the finishing touches to a new three-book deal. And I wasn't sleeping with Malcolm. How dare you suggest I'd shag him to get a contract? You might resort to that sort of thing, but I bloody wouldn't. I don't know who he was using those condoms with, but it certainly wasn't me." There was real anger in her voice now. "And apart from anything else, it doesn't explain anything to do with the other murders. Why the hell would I want to kill them? Tell me that, you bloody cretin."

"All right, all right. Christ, who dipped your tampons in chilli sauce?" said Freddie, smiling. "Don't worry, I know you didn't kill anyone. I was just busting your chops." He laughed and winked at her.

"Fucking dickhead," she hissed.

"Christ's sake, Freddie," said Richard, "are you taking the piss?"

"Easy there, tiger," said Freddie. "Just trying to lighten the mood."

"That's it," said Perez. "I've had enough of this." She began marching towards the door.

"Inspector, please. I'm sorry. I'll behave. I really do know who the killer is."

Perez breathed out through her nose and shook her head. "Get to the point," she said. "Fast."

"You're on thin ice, Freddie," said Richard.

Freddie nodded and took a deep breath. "As I was saying, this is a complex case with many parts. We know all the victims are linked to Edward. All the crime scenes are linked to him, with his book left as a calling card. Now we're all holed up in this room protecting that very same man, because nobody can deny the killer is very carefully, meticulously targeting him."

Freddie paused and took another deep breath, slowly turning to look each person in the eye. "Or at least, that's what we're supposed to think. Isn't it, Edward?"

Freddie snapped round to look at Edward. He was hoping for a sharp intake of breath to echo around the room. A real mic-drop moment. Instead, everyone shrugged and remained silent, waiting to see where he was going. Perhaps he'd overdone it with his first two accusations.

"Edward Cross," continued Freddie, "you're a decent crime novelist. Not the best, but… you know, some people seem to like your stuff."

Edward sighed and rolled his eyes.

"You know better than anyone that plotting a good murder mystery is all about misdirection. You lead the readers down the wrong path. Get them looking in the direction you want, to keep them from seeing what's right in front of them. That's how you hide what's really going on."

Nick and Lisa couldn't help but subconsciously nod in agreement.

"If you don't want people to suspect somebody, you make it look like they couldn't possibly have been the killer. You make it seem so implausible that they're involved that the reader doesn't even think about them. And who could be less likely to be behind everything than the person who's being targeted in the first place?"

"Oh, what the hell are you suggesting now, Freddie?" sighed Edward. "What is this, Inspector? Are we really going to sit here and listen to this bloody claptrap?"

"No," said Perez, "I think I want to hear where he's going with this?"

"You worked so hard to make it look like you were the victim, didn't you?" said Freddie. "Leaving those books lying around. Your books. Filled with mad scribblings and insults that could only have been directed at you."

Freddie pulled his phone out of his pocket and started flicking through pictures of the scribbled-on pages, showing them to everyone in the room.

"Hey, where did you get those pictures?" said Richard, incredulous. "Did you take those yourself? I could charge you with tampering with evidence."

"Hush, Richard," said Freddie, tutting and darting the phone back into his pocket. "I'm building to something of a climax here, and you're putting me right off my stroke."

Richard shook his head and raised his hands in disbelief.

"Anyway, where was I…" said Freddie. "Oh yes, the books. I mean, who would suspect you of leaving them there? You'd have to be a complete imbecile to leave such incriminating evidence that links directly back to you."

"Or an imbecile to think it's a double bluff," sighed Edward.

"You wanted everyone to think you were the real target. The one the killer is working their way up to. But that was all nonsense, wasn't it? Nobody's trying to kill you. Because you're the one killing everybody else."

"What? That's preposterous," snapped Edward. "Why the hell would I want to kill any of these people?"

"Jealousy. You couldn't take it that Max had the biggest-selling book last year. Your former editor. The man who used to work for you. Suddenly, he's the new big star in town, and nobody's looking at poor Edward anymore. He's the one in the press. He's getting all your interviews. His book takes top slot in the Richard and Judy club. The great Edward Cross suddenly overshadowed. You couldn't stand for that, could you?

"Except it gets worse, doesn't it? Not only is Max stealing your sales; he's being lined up as the big new star at Darkhouse Publishing. They're putting all their marketing resources behind him, not you. He's in, you're out. Even worse, you find out that your agent has been having secret meetings with him and Malcolm. I found one of those bottles of vape liquid in Malcolm's room, proving she was there. She was going to take Max on as a client and leave you behind."

Edward sat there, incredulous, his face turning white.

Perez and Richard were staring at him now, watching intently.

"And then the final piece of the puzzle clicks into place. The person behind it all. Your ex-wife, Christy. She's been having secret conversations with all of them. She talked Max into trying his hand at writing in the first place. She convinced Malcolm to publish the book. She was the one Malcolm used those condoms with," said Freddie, smiling and winking at Lisa. "She used her connections in the industry to promote the book and make it a success. And when sales really soared, she reached out to Marylin and Malcolm, setting the scene for them to focus on the new wunderkind and leave you out in the cold. She hated you for the way you treated her. She knew this would be the best way to get back at you. And she spent years planning it."

"That's not..." stumbled Edward. "What even... where are you getting this from?"

"Once you figured out what they were all up to, you had to put a stop to it. And being here together at the same time was the perfect opportunity. You could kill them all and make it look as if you were the real target all along. Nobody would ever suspect you. So, you left the trail of evidence pointing away from yourself, then went about getting your revenge."

Lisa and Nick eyed Edward suspiciously.

Richard and Perez both stiffened again, standing slightly more to attention.

"Whoa, fucking wait a minute," said Edward. "Where's your proof? What makes you think any of this is even remotely plausible?"

"Oh, I don't need any proof," said Freddie, strolling over to the open balcony windows and staring out at the gently rippling sea in the distance. "I don't need to prove any of it. Because none of it's true, is it?"

Again, a wave of annoyed sighs floated around the room.

"For fuck's sake, Freddie," growled Richard.

"What the fuck?" said Nick.

"Are you having a laugh?" said Lisa.

"Please," said Freddie, holding up a hand without turning around. "I'm not quite done. Yes, that was all a load of bollocks. It sounded plausible, didn't it? But then that was the point. As I said at the start, this is a complex case. Made even more complex by a very clever mind. Someone who knows this world of intrigue like no other. Someone not only able to construct an intricate murder mystery, but someone who's been the victim of one themselves. Someone who understands plot and misdirection. Someone who's suffered at the hands of the very industry they love so much. Someone able to get close enough to the victims while still avoiding suspicion. Someone who not only benefited from the victims being in the same place at the same time, but in fact spent years orchestrating a vast number of moving parts to make sure they all would be.

"Someone, as I said before, who appears to be completely above suspicion. Someone who's spent the past few days seeing their livelihood being destroyed. Someone who couldn't possibly be guilty, because they're as much of a victim in this whole charade as anyone else.

"Someone," said Freddie, turning around and looking at the group, "who for the whole time I've been pacing about, throwing around wild accusations has barely moved, or spoken or even looked up from the ground."

"Fucking hell," said Dan, glancing up at Freddie with a mischievous grin, "it took you long enough."

CHAPTER 25

DAN JUMPED UP from the sofa, grinning with a manic look in his eyes. He leapt over the coffee table, grabbed Edward by the collar and pulled him up to his feet with one strong yank. Edward squealed with surprise, his feet scrabbling around on the tiled floor. Then he was coughing and spluttering, his shirt collar riding up into his throat and cutting off his breathing. In one fluid movement, Dan spun around, shifted in behind Edward and pulled a small, shiny, silver knife from his pocket. He pulled Edward close to him and moved the knife up to rest against Edward's throat.

As Dan hopped across the table, Lisa and Nick tried diving to safety. Unfortunately, they both leapt in the same direction, colliding mid-air, banging their heads together with a loud thud, and landing in an awkward pile of limbs. Lisa looked down at Nick, her body pressing down on his and their faces just millimetres apart, embarrassment momentarily overtaking the dread of imminent death. Then they remembered the real threat, pushed away from each other, and crabbed back across the cold, tiled floor to relative safety.

"Jesus," said Richard, stunned into action. He scrabbled around, nearly falling over his own feet, and just managed to hold himself up on the edge of the minibar.

"What the…" said Perez, instinctively reaching to her hip for the gun which she had unfortunately neglected to bring. When she realised it wasn't there, she screwed up her eyes and cursed herself.

The only person who didn't move was Freddie.

"Ladies and gentlemen," he said, pointing at Dan with a smug grin. "And the killer is…"

"Well done," said Dan, "I knew one of you would get there eventually." He pulled harder on Edward's collar. Edward wheezed and spluttered again, a confused look in his eyes. "Although, I have to say, I'm surprised how long it took you. The greatest crime writing brains in Britain, apparently. I didn't think I'd get away with it for this long."

"You played your part well," said Freddie. "I definitely believed the whole snivelling, drivelling, pathetic wreck thing. And the other night in the bar. Were you even drunk at all?"

"Sorry, no. Just pretending."

"Well, you had me fooled."

"So, what finally gave me away?"

"You did," said Freddie. "But then, that was the whole point. You've been leaving clues, challenging us to catch you. You wanted to get caught. You want the world to know why you're taking out your revenge on Edward."

"Yeah, but I haven't given that much away," said Dan. "I've been saving it for the grand finale."

He pressed the knife a little harder into Edward's throat, eliciting another high-pitched squeal as he nicked the skin and a small rivulet of blood trailed down Edward's neck. "And before you think about signalling to your men outside, Inspector, just think how long that corridor is. They won't make it halfway here before I can cut his throat and he bleeds out all over the floor."

Perez raised her hands to signal her compliance, her lips pursed into a hard ball and her eyes filled with anger.

"What the bloody hell is going on here?" said Richard. "Who is this man?"

"Do you want to tell them," said Freddie, "or shall I?"

"Oh no, please, be my guest," said Dan, smiling. "I'm keen to see how much you've figured out."

"Very well," said Freddie. "It all starts about 11 years ago. A young man with a dream. A dream to be a published…"

"Oh, not this again," said Perez, raising a hand to her forehead. "Do we really have to…"

"Trust me, Inspector," said Richard. "It really is easier just to let him."

Perez sighed and shook her head, then gestured for him to continue.

"Thank you," said Freddie, "Now, where was I? Oh yes, a young man with a dream. You see, I've just had a rather illuminating phone call with my former agent, John. Lovely guy. Well, not lovely exactly. More of a deceitful, morally bankrupt old rogue. And he never exactly got me the deal of a lifetime – hence why he's my former agent. But he does have his uses.

"He's very well connected in the industry. He knows everyone and he's not exactly shy about poaching clients, ruining other people's deals and swooping in to undercut them, and working just outside the limits of the law. In other words, a bit of a scumbag. Seriously, he makes Rupert Murdoch look trustworthy. And if there's a dodgy publishing deal to be done, you can guarantee he'll be there in the thick of it. I mean, he did represent me for years, so it's not surprising, really.

"Anyway, I was assessing the facts of what's been going on here. Authors being murdered. Strange scribblings in books left at the scene. An obvious literary connection between the victims. There was clearly something connecting it all. Something from the past. And then I thought of John. If there was ever a scandal in the publishing world, pound to a penny John would either be up to his neck in it, or he'd know all about it. You know, I heard he once had three publishers bidding for the rights on a book from some old call girl who'd apparently slept with the Prime Minister at the time – except not only was this woman not actually his client; there wasn't even a book to sell in the first place!"

Richard cleared his throat loudly, raising his eyebrows to nudge Freddie back on track.

"Anyway," said Freddie, taking the hint. "I contacted John and asked him what he knew about Edward, and what he thought about the situation here. Unsurprisingly, he's been watching it unfold in the tabloids. We're big news back home, you know. Getting lots of coverage. Can't be hurting sales, eh?" he said, smiling and winking at Lisa and Nick.

They didn't smile back.

"So, where was I…" continued Freddie. "Oh yes, John's heard all about it. Knows who the victims are. Then I told him about the bit the press doesn't know – the book that Dan's been leaving at the scenes. That was it. Real lightbulb moment. Everything fell into place for him and he tells me about a rumour he heard about *The Terrible Bones* and how Edward Cross didn't actually write it."

Sharp intakes of breath echoed around the room as everyone looked at Edward. Dan shifted behind him, pulling him closer and pressing the knife a little harder against his throat. The panic in Edward's eyes fell away, replaced by a strange mix of sadness and relief.

"You see, John was close with Marylin Sharpe back in the day," continued Freddie. "Unsurprising, really. Pair of unscrupulous villains. It's well known that before that book was published, Edward had a touch of writer's block. Hadn't published anything in ages. Marylin was always in the pub, whinging to John and their other publishing cronies, bemoaning this useless writer who'd lost his touch and was on the verge of having to pay back a hefty advance. She's fretting because there's no money left and doesn't know what to do. And then lo and behold, just a few months later, *The Terrible Bones* comes out.

"Well, that seems a bit fishy," continued Freddie. "It certainly didn't add up. Then one night, one of the junior agents at Marylin's firm gets drunk in the pub and starts telling this story about how Edward didn't write the book himself. She's seen secret documents. They bought the book off some unknown and they're passing it off as Edward's work."

Freddie paused for dramatic effect, looking around the room, before turning back to stare at the man with the knife to his throat. Edward's body was slumped back against Dan, like a half-deflated balloon. His face was sallow and gaunt. His eyes dark, staring at the floor and filled with shame.

"Everything was denied, of course. Marylin laughed it off as a joke. But the junior agent was quickly reassigned to the queue at the job centre and never heard of again. And nobody ever found out the truth behind it. Until today. It was your book, wasn't it, Dan?"

Dan smiled back, anger in his eyes, as he whispered something into Edward's ear.

Edward closed his eyes as a single tear rolled down his cheek.

"Once I'd heard about that rumour, everything else fell into place. And I realised you had to be the killer."

Dan didn't speak. He just smiled back at Freddie, a similar look of relief in his face, like he was pleased the truth was finally being spoken.

"We spoke the other day. You told me about your ambitions to become a writer. How you'd written a book, tried to get it published and the industry had totally fucked you over. But you weren't just talking about rejection, were you?"

"Very good, Mr Winters," said Dan. "Yes, it was my book. I wrote it. I used to be a big fan of Edward Cross. I'd read all his books. I dreamed of being like him. His writing inspired me to have a go myself. So, I wrote this book, but of course I didn't know if it was any good. And I thought, why not go to the source of the inspiration for some advice? I sent the book to him and never really expected to hear back. But a few weeks later, I get this call."

A strange melancholic smile played across Dan's lips. The glimmer of tears forming in his eyes.

"It was Edward Cross's agent, asking me to come in for a meeting. You can't imagine how excited I was. So I travelled down to London, went to the office, and next thing, I'm sitting there with literary agent Marylin Sharpe and Edward Cross himself. And they're both telling me how great my writing is and how much they love my book. It was like a dream come true," said Dan, his voice cracking.

"They told me they wanted to publish my book. Apparently, Edward had read it and loved it, and took it to his agent for her thoughts. She said it was exactly the sort of thing they'd been looking for and it was going to be a bestseller. I couldn't believe it. Marylin starts talking about percentage share and royalties and how they were going to put it out to auction. And then she gives me a scotch, and I drink it. And then she gives me another. And we're all drinking and laughing and toasting the future.

"Marylin starts talking about contracts and sales strategies, and marketing budgets and… then she starts pushing all these forms at me to sign. And like a fucking idiot, I did. I just signed away. She's talking ten to the dozen, and I'm excited like a little kid who's just been told to help himself to anything in the sweet shop. And I just signed without properly reading anything. I just signed them."

He paused, looking down at the floor and shaking his head.

"And then what happened?" asked Freddie.

"We all go out for dinner together. Edward is the perfect host. The two of them spend the whole evening blowing smoke up my arse and telling me how well the book is going to do, and then I get the train back home. A few weeks pass and I hear nothing. I try and call Marylin, but she doesn't answer. A few more weeks go by and I still hear nothing. Then a few more weeks and a few more. Marylin never answers the phone. I travel down to London and go to her office, but I can't get her to meet with me. I just get fobbed off by her secretary who says Marylin's busy, but she'll be in touch soon.

"A few months go by and to be honest I've given up hope. I figure they've changed their mind about the book. And then one day I walk into a book shop and it's right there. The book. *My* book. *The Terrible Bones*. Already published. A great big table of them, right there at the front of the shop. Except it doesn't have my name on it. It has Edward's."

Another symphony of gasps echoed around the room.

Edward squeaked slightly, his eyes closed now, as Dan tightened his grip.

"I couldn't believe it. I bought a copy, got straight on a train to London and marched into Marylin's office. And do you know what? She wasn't even surprised to see me."

"Jesus," said Lisa, "what did she do? What did she say?"

"She offered me a drink. A fucking drink. I couldn't believe it. She just acted all calm and business-like, as if there was nothing strange about me barging in there and throwing the book down on the desk. Then she just says how great it looks, and tells me that early sales and reviews are good. And I say, 'What the fuck are you talking about?' and she pretends like she doesn't understand why I'm upset."

Edward's hands fiddled nervously at his side. Dan's grip was the only thing holding him up now. He looked like he might collapse to the floor and disintegrate into a big puddle.

"So I call her a thief and a crook," continued Dan, "and I say, 'How could you do this to me?' and she just sits there pretending to be baffled. Then this cold, hard look comes over her and she says, 'I'm sorry if there's been some confusion. Were you under the impression we were publishing the book in your name?'

"I told her of course that's what I thought. That's what we'd agreed. And then she says, 'Oh, did you not read the contract you signed?' And that's when I knew she really was expecting me to barge in there at some point. Because she reaches over and there's a copy of it right there on her desk."

"Shit," said Nick, still sitting on the floor next to Lisa, "what did it say?"

"She hands it to me, already opened up to the right page, with the relevant passage highlighted. And it's right there in the small print. The contract states that I'm signing over all the rights to my book. They would have total ownership of it, to publish however they saw fit, under whoever's name they wanted. And right there at the bottom is my signature.

"I said, 'You can't do this. This isn't what we agreed!' And she just laughs and says, 'I think you'll find I can do whatever I want.' And then she hands me a cheque for two grand and shows me where in the contract it said that's what I'd agreed to as payment. I couldn't believe it. I felt so stupid."

"So, what did you do?" asked Freddie.

"I told her I was gonna sue. And then she just laughs even harder and hands me another piece of paper with my signature and tells me it's the non-disclosure agreement I signed. If I even think about telling anybody about what she's done, or disclose any information about the book whatsoever, she'll sue me for everything I've got."

"Jesus, what a bitch," said Lisa. "I mean… fucking hell, Edward."

Edward didn't respond. He just stood there, slumped against Dan with the knife to his throat and his eyes tight shut.

"So, then what happened?" asked Richard, scribbling down notes.

"I went to see four different lawyers and showed them the papers I'd signed. Nobody would take me on. They said the contracts were watertight and I couldn't possibly win. Even then, I couldn't let it lie. I couldn't bear it. Every time I picked up a newspaper, or turned on the telly, I saw this prick taking credit for my work. Not only that; they're saying it's the best thing he's ever done. A bold new direction. Changing the face of crime fiction."

"Fucking hell, Edward," sneered Freddie. "You arrogant fuck. You've been lording it all over everyone for years, and you don't even write your own stuff."

"Only that one," said Edward, opening his eyes and straightening up. Tears were running down his face now and he spoke with a sniffly, snotty croak. "It was only that one. Everything else I wrote myself."

"But it was all based on that character," laughed Freddie. "Your next six books all featured the same main character. The same style. You stole it. And then you copied it. You're a fucking fraud."

"You don't know what it's like," said Edward snivelling. "All that pressure. All that expectation. Publishers, readers, all demanding another bestseller. It all got too much, and I couldn't write. I didn't know what to do and I couldn't see a way out. Then this book arrives in the post. This brilliant, amazing book and I think, fuck me, I wish I'd written that. And then I showed it to Marylin, and she said, 'Well, what if you could have?' Then she comes up with this scheme to buy the book and publish it under my name. It was all her idea."

"Oh well, that's all right then," laughed Freddie. "It wasn't my idea, guv. Don't blame me."

"It wasn't like that. Everything happened so fast and before I knew it the book was being published and… and…" Edward started sobbing again.

"So, then what happened?" said Lisa.

"I was powerless to do anything," said Dan. "But I couldn't let it lie. I thought maybe I could give the money back and we could come to some agreement to put my name on the book as co-author. Or maybe if they liked my writing, we could chalk this down to experience, and I could get Marylin to help me publish something else. But she wouldn't see me. I tried calling, but she ignored me. I went to her office, but she'd hired some giant security guard and I couldn't get close to her.

"I tried reaching out to this prick here," said Dan, scraping the knife against Edward's throat, "but he wouldn't respond either. Then I found out he was going to be at the Cheltenham Literary Festival. I thought, that's my chance. I could corner the pair of them and make them listen. Only I never even got within 50 feet of them. They obviously figured I might try and do something, because they had people looking out for me. I found out where Edward was doing a talk and waited for him to come out but, before I got the chance, these two thugs grab me, bash me over the head and throw me in the boot of a car."

"Really?" said Freddie. "What thugs?"

"We weren't exactly on first name terms," said Dan. "But they did tell me they worked for Frank Mcleod."

"Shit," said Freddie.

"Shit," said Richard, looking up from his notebook.

"What?" said Perez. "Who is this Frank Mcleod?"

"Local gangster type back in London," said Richard. "Had a few run-ins with him over the years. Put him away last year, after we caught him laundering money."

"So what happened next?" asked Richard.

"They drove me around for a few hours," said Dan, "then finally we stopped in the woods in the middle of nowhere. They dragged me out of the car and kicked the crap out of me. They told me I was causing problems and they'd been hired to get rid of me. Didn't take much to figure out who'd hired them. They punched and kicked and stamped on me. I knew they were going to kill me and the only way to stop them was to play dead. So, that's what I did. I went limp and they stopped. Then they dragged me over to this shallow grave they already had waiting and threw me in.

"Have you ever been buried alive?" said Dan, anger flashing in his eyes. He gripped Edward's hair. Pulled his head back and pressed the knife even harder against his throat. "It's not very fucking nice, I can tell you."

Edward said nothing. He just closed his eyes again and whimpered.

"So, what did you do?" said Freddie.

"Honestly, I'm not sure," he said. "It's all a blur. I was barely conscious, just trying to stay still and make them believe I was dead. I can remember stuff being chucked on top of me. Earth. Mud. Then… I don't know… I guess, somehow, I managed to dig myself out when they were gone. I think I must have been there in the woods, shivering for at least a day. I managed to walk to the nearest town, where some people helped me get to the hospital. I had four broken ribs, a dislocated shoulder, a broken nose, a fractured humerus, three broken fingers, a fractured skull, my eyes were so swollen I could barely see out of them and I had a serious concussion. On top of that I had a bruised liver and the doctor told me that if I'd got to the hospital even an hour later, I would probably have died."

"What did the police say?" asked Richard.

"Police?" laughed Dan. "I didn't tell the fucking police. I'm not stupid. I knew who Frank Mcleod was. And if he wanted me dead, I knew it was far better if he thought his men had succeeded."

"But he tried to kill you," said Richard. "A crime was committed. You have to tell the police."

"Yeah, right," said Dan. "What, so the word can get back to Mcleod and he sends his thugs to finish the job? No thanks. I gave the hospital a fake name, told them I'd had an accident while out walking and fell off the side of a mountain. They didn't believe me, but they didn't push me on it. They kept me in for a few days, then I signed myself out and got the fuck out of there."

"I had no idea," said Edward. "I promise you. Marylin just told me she'd taken care of things."

"Really? And what did you think that meant?"

"I don't know. I thought she'd just paid you off or something."

The room went quiet as everyone looked at Edward and collectively shook their heads with disappointment.

"So, where did you go?" asked Nick. "What did you do?"

"Like I say," said Dan, "I knew I was fucked. If Frank Mcleod wants you dead, you're better off dead. So, that's what I did. I didn't really have anything keeping me in my life anyway. Poky rented flat, no girlfriend, a job I hated. So I left it all behind. I had a cousin living out in Spain, so I sneaked back home, grabbed my passport, cleared my bank account and went out to stay with him. Seemed like the perfect opportunity to reinvent myself."

"And start planning your revenge?" said Freddie.

"Fucking right," said Dan, smiling.

"So, you started your website, Killerbooks.com, as a means for revenge?"

"What? No, of course not. That was just a bit of luck. No, my original plans were far less intricate. I was going to save up and hire someone to kneecap Edward. You know, like that ice skater who had someone clobber her rival."

"Hmmm, yeah," said Freddie, nodding with approval.

"Or I was going to sneak back into the country, get a job working in the kitchen at Edward's favourite restaurant, then slip something into his food when he came in for lunch."

"Ooh, yeah," said Lisa, a little too excitedly, "that's a good one."

"I had one plan where I was going to pretend to be a foreign publisher, lure him to a secret meeting and push him in front of a train. One where I'd sneak into his bedroom at night and stab him to death while he slept. And one where I'd burn down his house, with him and all the others inside."

Freddie, Nick and Lisa all nodded along.

"Believe me, I wasn't short on ideas for how to kill this prick. The website thing was just something I did while I was hanging out at my cousin's place. Everything I told you about that was true. I started it for fun, to keep me entertained while I plotted my revenge. It really did just grow organically. People liked it. And soon I was making money out of it."

"So you were living well," said Richard. "Why not just let the rest of it go? Live a happy life and leave it behind?"

"You know, I actually did think about that," said Dan, smiling and looking off into the distance, as if remembering a happier time. Then the smile fell from his face, instantly replaced with an angry grimace. "I thought about it. But the more popular the site became, the more I got requests from publishers to feature stuff on their site. All wanting to use me. Offering me money and free stuff to feature their titles. And then it comes. The email. A request from Darkhouse Publishing to feature the new book by Edward Cross. A book featuring the character he stole from me."

Dan stopped talking and again everyone stared at Edward.

"And then it hit me," said Dan, "the website was the answer. That was how I could get them all in the same place at the same time. So I carried on working, building it up, increasing the reader base. I reviewed book after book, and it got so popular I had to take people on to write reviews and articles for me. As we got bigger, I started featuring guest posts from authors. Then we started up the advice section, with tips and hints on how to write and get published.

"I got to the point I could start putting on small events – signings, workshops, that sort of thing. But if I was going to get the likes of Edward, I knew I'd have to put on something special. Something he couldn't possibly turn down. Do you know, it's taken well over a year to organise this little reunion?"

"So, you came up with a plan," said Freddie. "You lured all your victims here. Then you just set about killing them. You were perfectly placed. You'd set the agenda for events, so you knew which rooms people were staying in and where people would be at any given point. You chose the location, so you had plenty of time to come in weeks or months in advance and scope the place out, find every nook and cranny, every hiding place, every security camera. No wonder you were able to move about the place undetected."

"I told you, when I left England, I came to live with my cousin. His house is just a few miles away. That's why I chose this place. I knew all these authors would never be able to turn down a free, fancy holiday. Not even Edward. I got a job here last year for a couple of weeks, working as a kitchen porter. I could move about in places you wouldn't expect and really get the lay of the land. And on an unrelated note, you would not believe how filthy those kitchens are, or some of the unsanitary things they do there. Gordon Ramsay would break a rib screaming at them."

Everybody grimaced and their hands instinctively went to their mouths. All except for Edward, who was still sobbing and looking at the floor.

"That's how you got close to your victims," said Freddie. "You were the event organiser, so they had no reason not to trust you. And you always had the perfect excuse to pay them a visit or drag them away for a quick chat. That's how you killed Max. You lured him down to the pool for a conversation and slipped the poison into his drink."

"Sort of," said Dan. "Remember, I couldn't afford to be seen with him. I laced his drink upstairs in the main party. I sneaked out to the car park earlier in the day and syphoned some antifreeze out of one of the cars. I had it in a little bottle, so I could pour it in his drink when he wasn't looking. I was nervous about getting caught, but he was so drunk at that point he didn't notice what I was doing, or taste anything wrong with his drink. Then I told him a female fan wanted to see him by the pool, and he wandered down there. The rest took care of itself."

"But why kill Max?"

"Why? He was as guilty as the rest of them. He edited that book. Don't tell me he didn't smell a rat. He knew Edward's writing. He would have known instantly that he hadn't written it. He should have done the right thing, but instead he went along with it. Why do you think he got such a big advance on that crappy book he wrote last year? He held onto that secret until he needed it, then when he'd written his own book, he used it to blackmail Malcolm Alexander into giving him a generous contract."

Freddie nodded. "Yep, makes sense. So, then you killed Malcolm?"

"That one was pretty easy. I saw you all talking in the bar and I knew I could sneak into his room and wait for him. It's funny, I've been here organising things behind the scenes for long enough that the staff almost don't even notice me moving about the place. Hiding in plain sight, you know? I've been able to watch them and see how they do things."

"That's how you managed to get into the hotel manager's office and turn off the security cameras," said Freddie, talking to Dan but looking at Perez with a 'told you so' expression. "And you used the check-in computer to create a duplicate key card to get you into Malcolm's room?"

"Gold star to Freddie Winters," said Dan, smirking. "I turned off the cameras, got myself a key card, then went to hide in his room until he came back. I didn't know how I was going to kill him, to be honest. Then I saw his silver pen on the table, and I knew it was perfect."

"The special pen Malcolm used to sign all his contracts," said Freddie with a knowing smile. "Very clever. The pen is mightier than the sword, eh?"

"What? No, it just looked like it would do a lot of damage. Really good for stabbing someone with. I didn't know it had any significance. But yeah, let's go with your thing."

"You must have been covered with blood after an attack like that," said Perez.

"Yeah, that was a bit of a worry," said Dan. "Luckily, Malcolm and I were about the same size, so I stole some of his clothes. I cleaned off in the shower, got changed then sneaked down to the big furnace in the basement to burn the evidence. Didn't want you lot catching me too soon."

"Okay," said Richard, "but why kill Malcolm Alexander?"

"Shared guilt, for a start," said Dan. "He published *The Terrible Bones*. Made a lot of money out of my work. Plus, he was the one with connections to Mcleod. Remember when I said Mcleod's men told me they been hired to kill me? I asked them who wanted me out of the way and they just told me. Marylin Sharpe and Malcolm Alexander. I guess they thought why not give me the satisfaction of knowing who wanted me dead. After all, who was I gonna tell? I'd be dead. Only they got that wrong, didn't they?"

"Stands to reason, Malcolm being connected with a gangster like Mcleod. He was dodgy enough, so it's no surprise he had connections in the underworld. Probably worth looking at Darkhouse Publishing's books," said Freddie, nodding at Richard. "I wouldn't be surprised if there are a few irregularities there."

Richard smiled and nodded, scribbling away in his notepad.

"Okay," said Freddie, "so you killed Max because he knew about the book, and you killed Malcolm because he not only knew about it, he was involved in the plot to get rid of you. And you murdered Christy because of the other book."

"Very good, Freddie," smiled Dan. "You found my other clue. There's hope for you yet."

"Other book?" said Nick. "What other book?"

"The other book he left when he killed Christy," said Freddie. "Her own book. *The Contract*. I saw it when I went to investigate her room."

Perez tutted and crossed her arms.

"Yes, sorry about that, Inspector. Anyway, Dan went to Christy's room and she unwittingly let him in. He got her out onto the balcony, pushed her over the edge and then scattered pages from *The Terrible*

Bones to come fluttering down after her. And on his way out, he left a copy of her book on the bedside table.

"I thought it was weird at the time. Why would she be reading a copy of her own book? Then I opened it to find more scribbling. Only it was different this time. Just two words: *You knew*. It didn't make sense until I downloaded a copy onto my phone and reminded myself of the story. Then after speaking to John just now, the motive all fell into place."

Nick, Lisa, Perez and Richard all looked on, intrigued.

Dan smiled with satisfaction.

Edward let out a soft whimper.

"You see, Christy's book tells the story of a young man – a keen writer – who gets involved with this older, female writer. She's down on her luck. Hasn't written anything decent in years. He shows her his book, she sees that he's written something good, and she offers to help him with it. They get into a relationship and there's fifty shades of torture porn thrown in for good measure. Then, at the end of the book, even though this older woman has fallen in love with the younger man, her ailing career still means more to her. So, she betrays him, steals his book and publishes it under her own name."

More sharp intakes of breath echoed around the room.

"Jesus," said Nick. "Christy knew about it too?"

"She was married to Edward," said Freddie. "She was bound to know something. Her grumpy, depressed husband who hasn't written anything decent in years suddenly has a hit on his hands? Maybe he confided in her. Maybe she figured it out. And a few years later, when she'd finally had enough of his cheating and left him, she figured what better revenge than to use his biggest, dirtiest secret against him and publish the whole thing in a book."

"That was the icing on the cake," said Dan. "First, they steal my work and try and kill me for it. Then they publish the story in a book. Laughing at me."

Edward again squealed as Dan pressed the knife harder against his throat.

"Making money out of me again. The lot of them, taking the bloody piss. So, yeah, I killed her."

Freddie smiled with a smug, satisfied grin. He caught Richard's eye, who looked back, tutting and shaking his head.

"And Marylin, of course," said Freddie. "Her murder was the easiest. All you had to do was buy a little bottle of that vape liquid from the hotel shop. You swapped out the contents for chlorine, which you stole from the storeroom at the spa centre, slipped it into her bag and waited for her to find it. She was always puffing away on that thing, so you knew you wouldn't have to wait long."

"Right again," said Dan. "I didn't know exactly when she'd use it, so I missed the main event. Shame. I would have loved to see that old bitch coughing her last. And I didn't get to leave my little calling card, either. I couldn't risk her finding it before using the vape stuff. Still, I figured by that point people would see the connection."

"She must have been in agony," said Richard, anger flashing in his eyes. "Her lungs would have been literally burning. Her throat inflamed, her chest seizing up. And all that blood. That's no way to go, I don't care what she did."

"I disagree," smirked Dan. "That old cow was the ringleader. She deserved everything she got. And you know the worst bit? The thing that really pissed me off the most? She didn't even fucking recognise me. I've been around her for the best part of a week. We had drinks and a meal together. We've had several chats and meetings. And she didn't even recognise my face. Neither of them did.

"I sat in a restaurant with them as they lied through their teeth. And then I sat across a desk from Marylin a few months later as she ruined my life like it was just some business deal. And 10 years later, she didn't even know who I was. Not even a flicker of recognition.

"They ruined my life, got rich off the profits of my work, and tried to have me killed. And they didn't even have the decency to remember my face."

Dan's eyes were wet now. He sniffled back tears, forcing anger into his voice. "So, yeah, she got what she deserved. They all did. I even left them a great big bloody clue, staring them right in the face. My name."

"Your name?" said Freddie.

"Yeah, you don't think I've been using my real name all week, do you? Dan Josham? It's fake. It was just another clue to see how self-obsessed they were. And unsurprisingly, they never even noticed. My real name is John Adams. You'd think they'd have remembered a detail like that, from the forms they had me sign."

All around the room blank faces stared off into middle-distance. Thinking. Like they were trying to solve a cryptic crossword. Freddie got there first.

"Fuck. It's an anagram, isn't it? Dan Josham. John Adams. Holy shit. God, how did we miss that? I mean, what the hell kind of name is Josham? You're right, you know," he said with an appreciative smile, "it was staring us in the face."

Nick nodded with a wry smile. Lisa, getting there a second later, pursed her lips and squinted. Richard still looked confused, like a dog staring at itself in a mirror. Perez just looked angrier than ever.

"Come on guys. Seriously?" said Freddie, looking over at Nick and Lisa. "An anagram? How did none of us spot that? That's the oldest trick in the book. Hiding the real name of the killer in the name of someone else? That's lesson one in bloody crime writing. I really thought better of us." He tutted and shook his head.

"To be fair, nobody really does that anymore, do they?" said Lisa.

"Yeah, it's a bit hackneyed, isn't it?" said Nick.

"Fuck you," said Dan. "Took me ages to come up with that. The old hiding in plain sight bit. It's genius. Plus, I've had to live with a different name for fucking years."

"No, it's fine," said Nick. "Very clever. Just a bit... you know... Agatha Christie, isn't it? Modern readers want something a bit smarter."

"Yeah, not sure this is the best time to critique the man, Nick," said Freddie. "Not when he's holding a knife to someone's throat."

"Fair point," said Nick, as Edward grizzled and whimpered.

"One thing I don't understand," said Freddie, "is why try and kill me? What have I got to do with any of this? I didn't know anything about it until today. I'd never even met you before this week."

"Yeah, sorry about that," said Dan. "You were just a bit of a red herring."

"A what?" said Freddie, heat tingeing his cheeks and reminding him of the sauna.

"Red herring," said Dan, shrugging, behind Edward's quivering frame. "You know, something to throw the police off. Stop them getting to the truth before I had time to finish this prick off."

"Yeah, I know what a fucking red herring is," said Freddie. "I just mean 'what?!' Like, seriously? You tried to kill me for no reason? I was just a fucking distraction?"

"Yeah, sorry about that."

"So, it was all just, what… spur of the moment?"

"Yeah, kind of. I was standing at the back of the room, watching Edward on stage. I heard you and that Caroline woman talking about going to the spa and I saw an opportunity. I followed her to her room and locked her in the wardrobe, then I ran down and locked you in the sauna. All completely off the cuff. Then I sneaked back to the main hall and nobody even noticed I'd been gone."

Freddie threw his hands up. "Unbelievable."

"You know as well as anyone that you need a decent red herring or two thrown into every plot. Same reason I left the empty vape bottle and used condom wrappers in the bin in Malcolm's room. Distraction. Something to throw the police off the scent and look in the wrong places. You don't wanna make it too easy," said Dan, looking a little too pleased with himself.

"For God's sake," said Freddie. "I feel so… used. But it is good to get an answer to those other clues I couldn't figure out."

"What can I say? No hard feelings, eh?"

"Actually, no," snapped Freddie. "Quite a lot of hard feelings, if you must know."

"Well, I mean, I didn't succeed, anyway. So, you know…"

"Oh yes," snapped Freddie. "How rude of me. Where are my manners? Thank you. Thank you for not managing to murder me."

"Well, there's no need to be a dick about it," said Dan.

"Hey, when you two quarrelling lovebirds are done," said Richard, cutting in. "I'd say there are a few more important things to focus on here."

Freddie tutted loudly, shaking his head.

"What exactly is the plan, Dan… or John… or whatever your real name is?" said Richard. "You can't expect to get away with this. You won't make it out of the room. Why don't you just put the knife down and let us take you into custody, eh?"

"Put the knife down?" laughed Dan. "When we're so close to the end?"

"Come on, seriously. You've proved your point. The truth will come out now. There's no need for anyone else to get hurt."

"Oh, I disagree, detective. There's a very great need for Edward to get hurt. This is what it's all been about, don't you see? I had a really spectacular finale planned," he said, pulling Edward hard back against

286

him and talking directly into his ear. "What a show that would have been. I wasn't exactly counting on this, though. So, looks like I'm gonna have to improvise a bit more."

Dan tightened his grip on Edward's collar, keeping the knife tight against his throat. He pulled him upright, so he was on tiptoes and started walking him backwards, making sure to stay tightly concealed behind him. They rounded the edge of the sofa and moved slowly backwards, inching towards the open balcony windows.

"What are you doing?" said Perez, again instinctively reaching for her gun only to find it missing. She held up her hands in a calming gesture. "Stop this now. Give yourself up and we'll take it into consideration."

"Give myself up? What, so I get a shorter prison sentence?" laughed Dan. "You don't get it, do you? I never planned to get away with any of this. I'm already dead. I'm in a shallow grave in the woods back in England. I just came back for long enough to make sure people found out the truth, and that Edward's life ended as miserably as mine did."

He continued edging closer to the window.

Lisa and Nick stayed planted on the floor, looking up with a mix of intrigue and terror, like bystanders unable to look away from a car crash.

Perez held her arms up, trying to stay in control of the situation but not sure what to do.

Richard remained still, his eyes flitting around the room, clearly assessing all possible options.

"Shame I won't be able to give Edward the death I had planned for him," said Dan, stepping through the door and out onto the balcony. "It was a real doozy."

Slowly, carefully, Richard, Perez and Freddie edged towards him.

"And I really hate to repeat myself," said Dan. "Always seems lazy doing something you've already done. But, like I say, I'm improvising now. And a tumble off this high balcony will still have the desired effect, won't it?"

Dan continued moving until his back hit the guardrail at the edge of the balcony. Richard, Perez and Freddie shuffled forwards until they were in the doorway.

"I dunno," said Freddie, "seems like a bit of an anti-climax to me. Why don't we have a brainstorm? See if we can't think of another, more interesting way to kill him. Nick, Lisa? If you were in this situation, how might you do it?"

Nick and Lisa looked up from the ground, confused.

Edward's eyes went wide as he whimpered again.

Richard raised his palms to Freddie, as if to say, 'What are you doing?'

"Nice try, Freddie," said Dan. "But there's no use trying to stall for time."

"Oh, I disagree," said Freddie with a smug grin. "I'd say it's worked out pretty well so far."

"What the hell are you talking about?"

"Stalling. I've been stalling for time ever since I walked into the room. What do you think all that waffle was about, earlier? Accusing Nick, Lisa and Edward of being the killer. I knew they had nothing to do with it. When I got off the phone with John, all the pieces fell into place and I knew it had to be you. But I also knew you were all trapped in a room together, camped out to protect Edward. I figured you'd realise this was your last chance to do something.

"So, I spoke to the police. Deputy Inspector Garcia," he said, nodding at Perez. "I told him what was happening, and we came up with a plan. Everything since that has been about wasting time until he could get his men into position and I could get you to exactly where I needed you to be."

"What the hell are you talking about?" said Dan.

Freddie raised both hands, like a magician showing they were empty, then very slowly went to his pocket and pulled out his mobile phone.

"The police have been listening in to the whole thing," said Freddie. Then talking into the phone, he said, "He's in position now, Inspector."

Everything that happened in the next few moments seemed to go in super slow motion.

A loud bang sounded at the far end of the suite as the door flew open. People shouted. Loud, sharp sounds on the tiled floor as heavy-booted policemen surged into the room. Dan's face contorted with confusion as he looked to the source of the commotion. He was so stunned, he dropped the knife and it hurtled to the floor, clanging loudly as it hit the ground.

Then there was shouting outside on the adjacent balcony. Everyone turned to see a policeman in full, black combat gear, his face hidden behind a helmet and big, dark protective goggles. His arms reached out towards Edward, holding a square, black pistol.

A sharp, snapping sound as his finger clicked against the trigger. A small explosion in the end of the gun as two thin wires burst out, with sharp, shiny spikes glinting on the ends. They flew across the gap between the balconies. Bit into Dan's shoulder. Making him squeal out loud. He tensed immediately, his whole body stiffening as he growled and groaned.

Then Dan was shaking. Up on tiptoes. Bucking wildly. His jaw clenched tight. Surprise in his eyes. His face pale. He shook and juddered as the volts of electricity surged through him, unable to move, unable to break free. He was still gripping tight to Edward, who juddered along with him, his own jaw clenching as the Taser's powerful voltage transferred through to him.

Then Dan fell to the ground, landing on top of Edward as the two men continued writhing in a confused heap.

The world jolted back to normal speed as armed police officers flooded the room, shouting in Spanish, thrusting big machine guns into everyone's faces. They grabbed Freddie, Nick and Lisa, forcing them to the ground and restraining them in place. One overzealous officer thrust a gun into Richard's face until an angry Perez pushed him away with a strong rebuke. Two officers surged onto the balcony, secured the knife, and dragged Edward away, still shivering and convulsing.

Three of them grabbed Dan, pushing him hard into the ground so that he couldn't move. He squealed and shouted as they lifted him, flipped him onto his front, dragged his arms behind his back and secured his hands with zip ties. The whole thing took less than 15 seconds.

"Take that man away," said Perez, pointing at Dan as she took control of the situation. "And let these people up." She pointed at Freddie, Nick and Lisa, who were still being pinned to the floor by police officers.

They all clambered up from the ground and looked over to see Dan being held up by two officers, laughing loudly with a crazed look in his eyes as he was dragged from the room. He was staring at Edward, who was sat up now, perched against the balcony railing. Tears were streaming down Edward's cheeks, snot bubbling in his nose, as his body shook not with the volts of electricity but with the force of his sobbing. He was a man who knew his world was about to come crashing down around him.

Perez walked over to Freddie, reached out a hand and helped him up to his feet. "Well done, Mr Winters," she said. "It seems I may have misjudged you. Your detective skills are clearly better than I thought. But I wish you'd come to me with any suspicions."

"Yes, sorry. In fairness, though, you weren't exactly responsive when I tried to help. And by the time the penny finally dropped, you were already in the room. I only had a few moments to act."

"Yes, well," said Perez, through gritted teeth, "it was very clever reaching out to my men and stalling until they had time to get into position. Thank you."

Freddie smiled and nodded, feeling a new level of mutual respect between them. Two detectives acknowledging each other's abilities. Revelling in a job well done.

"But if you ever pull any shit like that again," she said, "I'll have you behind bars quicker than you can blink."

"Honestly," said Freddie, "I don't know why I bother."

CHAPTER 26

10 MONTHS LATER

FREDDIE GRIMACED AS he swigged a mouthful of a cold latte. He looked up to see Marta, the grumpy Polish barista, sneering at him as she wiped tables on the other side of the coffee shop. It was busy today and she was making no secret of her annoyance at him hoarding a table to himself while languishing over the same coffee he'd bought one hour and twelve minutes ago.

A low melodic hum echoed around the room as people clinked spoons, scraped chair legs across the floor, and chatted at the tables around him. A long queue of people lined up at the counter to order coffee. And they were all eyeing up the spare seat at his table.

He'd already had to ward off three interlopers who'd attempted to join him. In the first case, simply wielding his evil eye had been an adequate deterrent. The second time he'd been forced to pretend he had a companion joining him imminently. And in the case of the insistent woman who'd suggested she'd perch there until his imaginary friend got back from the toilet, he'd had to really stand his ground and tell her to bugger off. Honestly, what did he have to do to get a little peace and quiet?

He was in no mood for people today. He was in no mood for people most days, but today their presence was particularly irksome. They were breaking his concentration. He'd had a good idea for a new book, and he was desperately trying to get it written and sent to his agent as quickly as possible. And while he usually found the buzz of people around him stimulating, today it was just distracting.

A light rain drummed against the large glass window next to him. Freddie peered out at the grey London sky and the gleaming road and pavement. It was a world away from the sun, sea and luxury accommodation he'd been enjoying just 10 months previously. True, there was presently less risk to his life, and fewer lunatic killers in the

291

close vicinity, but he was really missing the warm climate, the relaxing sea breeze, the extra-large portions of food and the free minibar.

Being back in his cramped London flat, with the wind whistling through the cracks in the window frames and the depressing lack of daily replenished free booze, was a stark reminder that the life he really wanted was still eluding him. And if things continued as they were, there was still little chance of life getting a great deal better any time soon.

Meanwhile, Edward Cross got to return to his mansion in the Surrey countryside, with its indoor swimming pool, acres of land, cinema room, bowling alley and private chef. The fucker. And Freddie was sitting there drinking cold bloody coffee.

He didn't think it was unreasonable to have expected Edward might have gifted him some kind of monetary reward. He had saved his life and caught his would-be killer, after all – putting his own life at risk in doing so, and very nearly ending up dead himself. Any half-decent private detective could have expected a sizeable payday for that. And Edward certainly had the ill-gotten gains to spare. But, to that day, the ungrateful prick hadn't sent so much as a thank you card.

As he sat there, looking down at the dregs in his cup, Freddie couldn't help but slightly regret saving Edward's life. If he'd waited just a few more minutes, or failed to tell the police about his suspicions, Dan would have launched Edward off that balcony and at least some level of justice would have been delivered.

The events following Dan Josham's arrest were carried out quickly and efficiently. The police dragged the murderer away and cleared the room within seconds. Once the officers determined Freddie and the other writers to be no threat, they were released and shepherded to another room where they were checked over by medical staff and a group of less senior detectives took their statements. They were then escorted to the main hall, where they were reunited with the other hotel guests, who had also been released from captivity.

Caroline came running up to Freddie with anxious tears in her eyes, threw her arms around him and peppered his face with kisses. He'd usually have baulked at such public displays of affection – especially considering who was displaying them – but, after the ordeal he'd been through, he found he really was pleased to see her. And he felt safe and reassured in her embrace.

Perez got up on stage to announce that the killer had been apprehended. Everyone then remained cooped up in that room for the next few hours as the police took further statements – without even so much as a gin and tonic or a heaped plate of food to calm Freddie's nerves.

Freddie noticed Johnny, the bellboy who'd shown him to his room on the first day, hovering at the back of the crowd and looking rather beleaguered.

Freddie walked over to him and pressed a 20 Euro note into his hand.

"What's that for?" said the man, looking shell-shocked.

"Long overdue tip," smiled Freddie. "I reckon you've probably had a hell of a week, what with all this going on. And I have to hand it to you," he said, looking down at his ridiculous outfit, "you got me good. Really made me smile... once my eyes got used to these horrible clothes."

"Thank you, Mr Winters," said Johnny, smiling, and just for a moment looking slightly less stressed.

Finally, Freddie and Caroline were ushered onto a waiting coach, delivered to the airport and then spent four hours hanging around the departures lounge. Which was annoying, but it gave Freddie the chance to right another wrong from that week.

Noticing the annoying kid from the plane sitting with his mother on the other side of the lounge, Freddie took the opportunity to nip to several shops. He then approached the young boy, rather sheepishly, and presented him with a child-sized sombrero, a large stuffed donkey, a two-litre bottle of Coca-Cola and a giant bag of fun-size chocolate bars.

Seeing it all, the kid's face lit up with a huge, beaming smile.

"Sorry for being such a meanie," said Freddie.

The boy's mother looked up at him, totally flummoxed.

"Don't worry," said Freddie, "I'm not a... you know. Your kid kept bothering me at the hotel."

"Charlie," she said, turning to the boy. "What have I told you about bothering strangers?"

"It's no problem," said Freddie. "You've got a good kid there. Anyway, I was stressed, I might have been a little short with him, and I felt bad. Hence the gifts."

"Well, that's very kind. What do you say, Charlie?"

"Thank you, Mr Windows," said the boy, smiling at the big bag of chocolate.

"You know, you might want to pay him more attention," said Freddie. "Then maybe he wouldn't be bothering strangers. Although, once he's had all that sugar, I get the feeling you won't have much choice but to pay attention."

The woman's face pinched into a mortified look. Freddie walked off smiling, a strange warm feeling buzzing in his chest. God, what was happening to him? Maybe his icy heart really was melting.

Finally, everyone was packed into the first available budget flight to take them home. At least Freddie didn't have the hassle of checking in luggage, having chosen to leave his garish replacement clothing at the hotel.

The flight home was a melancholy affair, partly because Freddie found himself reflecting on the traumatic events of the past few days, and partly because he was incensed at the criminal amount of money the airline was charging for a single can of lager.

Finally, they touched down and Freddie, surprised at having enjoyed Caroline's company during the flight (even though she insisted on holding his hand and talking to him), surprised himself further by inviting her back to spend the night at his flat. He'd never been a particularly needy person, or minded his own company, but he suddenly found himself not wanting to be alone. And as much as he hated to admit it, he was growing quite fond of his crazy stalker.

Freddie clicked the clicker on his pen and was just about to press the nib against the paper, when he looked up to see a familiar face.

"Thought I'd find you here," said Detective Inspector Richard Stone. A light dusting of rain glistened on his greying hair and the shoulders of his jacket. He scraped the chair legs on the floor as he pulled it back and sat down opposite Freddie.

"Richard," said Freddie. "Don't usually see you over this side of town."

"No, I suppose not," said Richard. "So, how are book sales? I picked up a copy the other day. I had to see what you've written about me this time."

"And?" said Freddie.

"Actually, I didn't hate it."

"Wow. High praise indeed," said Freddie. "Although, sales aren't great to be honest. But what do you expect? Those fucking backstabbers."

Freddie was referring to Colin McMaster, Lisa Smythe and Nick Foster.

Upon his return to England, Freddie had quickly set about capturing the events of the fateful week in a new novel – much as he had done following his previous investigations, into the attempted murder of his good friend Dylan. It had proven very lucrative previously, and he knew it would work again. With such a high body count, and with several notable figures having lost their lives, the story had really captured people's attention. It had featured on the front page of all the British tabloids, and was still getting lots of coverage several weeks after the event.

As soon as he'd turned on his mobile phone once his flight home had landed, Freddie found four voicemail messages and a series of texts from his agent, all expressing an interest for him to "strike while the iron's hot" and get straight to work on a manuscript.

Freddie also found himself inundated with journalists looking to get his side of the story. This time, however, he refused their requests. People were clearly desperate to learn what really happened during that week in the resort. So, it was a no-brainer that he was better to keep the juicy details to himself, ensuring readers had something to look forward to in his fictionalised version of events.

It had been his quickest book to write yet, racing through the first draft in just two and a half weeks. He'd worked long into the nights, drinking gallons of coffee to keep his fingers dancing over the keyboard, then resting for just a few hours' sleep before getting straight back to it. Naturally, his agent loved it – especially as it filled the contractual requirements of the book he was already late delivering. The advance wasn't quite what Freddie had hoped for, but it would do. And the publisher was equally keen to get the book out as soon as possible, so there followed a flurry of activity as covers were designed and revealed, and a whole campaign of pre-publicity was thought up, cranked out and posted.

Finally, Freddie's latest book, *Death on the Beach*, was published and found itself on the new releases table in bookshops up and down the country.

The problem was, he wasn't the only one to have the same idea. Within a week of being published, three other very similar books also hit the shelves.

Having seen the success of Freddie's previous book, Nick, Colin and Lisa also saw the opportunity to capitalise on their shared experience. Freddie should have known something was up when the other writers also refused to talk to the press – claiming to want peace and quiet to privately process the trauma they'd endured. Secretly, they also wanted to keep as many details out of the public eye as possible, to drum up interest for the books they were also sneakily working on.

Nick Foster captured the story in a novel, telling the events pretty much as they'd happened, but with his regular protagonist Milton Beck in his role. Naturally, in his version, Nick (or Milton) was the one to foil the plot, with Freddie's role reduced to little more than grumpy, clueless comic relief. Otherwise, the story was close to the real events and, as such, very similar to Freddie's book – although obviously a far inferior version.

Lisa Smythe followed a similar tactic, retelling the story in a fictional guise but making the lead protagonist a streetwise, sassy waitress who worked at the hotel. True to her style, Lisa made the murders far more gruesome than they had been in real life. In her version, the character based on Max was kidnapped, restrained and pegged out on a secluded beach, then left out for several days in the baking heat to sunburn to death. Her Malcolm character died as the result of a somewhat unbelievable exploding pedalo debacle.

Lisa stayed true to the motive behind the killings and kept in most of Dan Josham's backstory, so again the book was similar to Freddie's – except that she, too, fudged the truth to make her female protagonist the one who caught the killer.

Colin McMaster had taken a different approach. Rather than using the story as a basis for the plot of a novel, Colin instead chose to write a true-crime, biographical account of the week's events. He also cast himself as the hero of the piece, over-inflating his role, suggesting he'd uncovered the truth and captured the killer. Freddie had coughed beer across the room when he read the passage in which Colin used his police training to scale the hotel walls, climb over the balcony, burst into the room where Dan had the rest of the group captive, then single-handedly subdue the killer, wrestle him to the ground and knock the machine gun out of his hand. If only the reading public knew that

McMaster's biographical account of events was more fictionalised than the other three books put together.

Freddie's first instinct had been to run around badmouthing Colin to everyone who'd listen, then call the major newspapers and let them know exactly how much of a fraud the man was. But that was the old Freddie. The new one was trying to be a bit calmer and more forgiving. And he had to admit, he rather admired McMaster's bold-faced cheek.

Whilst Freddie's book had started off with a decent run up the charts and plenty of positive reviews, people were soon spoiled for choice. And much to his chagrin, Freddie quickly found his book floundering against the other three.

"Cheeky bastards," said Freddie. "It was my fucking story to tell. I figured out the motive. I caught the killer. And I'm the one who nearly died. But they copy me and they're getting all the sales."

"Well, like I say, I thought it was actually okay," said Richard.

"Jesus. It gets better," sneered Freddie. "Already up from a 'didn't hate it' to an 'actually okay'. You wanna calm it with the compliments, you'll give me a big head."

"Oh, don't worry, I've got plenty of mean things I can say, if you'd rather."

"Perhaps not, eh?" said Freddie.

"I thought the story was good. And thanks for changing my name. I can't go through all that again."

"I told you: I've learned my lesson. That character's retired for good."

"Not sure Inspector Perez will give you such a good review, after what you did with her character," said Richard, smiling a cheeky, boyish grin.

"Well, she had it coming," said Freddie. "Miserable cow. Have you spoken to her?"

"Not for a while. I'm due back out there in a couple of weeks to follow up on a few bits. I'll take a spare copy, just in case she hasn't read it yet."

"So, what's happening with Dan Josham, or John Adams, or whatever his bloody name is?"

"Still banged up in a Spanish prison. The Spanish want to prosecute him, seeing as he did all the killing in their country. We've got a vested interest, too, considering it was British citizens he killed. So we want to extradite him. And now his lawyer's pitched in, saying he wants to be tried in Britain, as he won't get a fair trial over there. Bloody human rights. So it's all a bit of a legal nightmare. But he's behind bars. And he won't be getting out any time soon. You'll be called to testify, just as soon as they figure out when and where the whole circus is gonna take place."

"And what about Edward? Any joy bringing charges against him?"

"So far, no," said Richard, with a disappointed sigh. "There's still an open investigation, but I'm not hopeful. As far as we can tell, he wasn't behind any of the really bad stuff. It seems Marylin Sharpe and Malcolm Alexander were the real villains there. We might still have a shot at a conspiracy to murder charge, but it's very difficult to prove what he knew about, if anything. And it was all over 10 years ago, so people's memories are more than a little fuzzy. But we're still looking into it."

"And what about the rest of it? Stealing John Adams' book?"

"Nah. Technically, he didn't do anything illegal there. Adams himself admitted he signed the rights away in a contract. Our lawyers have dug into it and it's watertight. Adams agreed to the deal, signed his name, and from that point on Edward Cross was free to do whatever he wanted with it. Morally reprehensible? Yes. Illegal? Sadly not."

"Even if they got him so drunk he didn't know what he was signing?"

"Again, like I say, it was 10 years ago. Practically impossible to prove. And it's just his word against theirs. He had every opportunity to read the small print."

"Yeah, I guess," said Freddie. "Just annoying that fucker Edward gets away with it. Still living in that mansion, enjoying the high life."

"Maybe. His career's in the toilet, though. Can't see anyone publishing another book by him. Or anyone wanting to buy one. Not now you and your friends have so effectively got the word out on him."

"Yeah, that was pretty sweet," said Freddie, smiling. "Certainly took him down a peg or two."

"He might have a big mansion to live in," said Richard, "but as I understand it, he's become a complete recluse. Hasn't left the building once since he got back from Spain. We might not be able to arrest him, but he's pretty much put himself in prison."

"Pretty fancy prison, though," sneered Freddie. "I wouldn't mind doing a bit of time there myself."

"Hey, you can't win them all," said Richard. "But not a bad result, all in all."

The two men smiled awkwardly at each other, as the slightest hint of the friendship they used to enjoy flashed between them. Then it disappeared as another figure approached the table.

"Thought I'd find you here, babe," said Caroline, leaning down and kissing Freddie on the top of his head.

"Yeah, I like the peace and quiet," said Freddie, "and how I can get loads of work done without anyone bothering me."

"Cheeky," said Caroline, bopping the end of his nose. "I'm gonna get a coffee. Richard?"

"Nothing for me, thanks," said Richard. "Just a flying visit."

"Anything for you, babe?" she said, placing a hand on Freddie's shoulder.

"Yeah, I'll have another latte," said Freddie. "Oh, and maybe get me a couple of those chocolate croissants… and a bacon roll…"

Caroline raised her eyebrows and gave him a disapproving look.

"Yeah, maybe not, eh? Just the coffee."

Caroline smiled and ruffled Freddie's hair. His right eye didn't spasm and his top lip didn't curl into the hint of a sneer. He was getting better at public displays of affection.

"Babe?" said Richard, smiling and winking at Freddie as Caroline joined the back of the queue. "You two an item now?"

"Kind of," said Freddie. "Call it Stockholm syndrome. I figure she'd probably be stalking me anyway, so I might as well let her hang around."

"Well, I think you make a lovely couple. Really dreamy," laughed Richard.

"Mock me if you want," sighed Freddie. "She's a good girl. You know, once you get past all the crazy."

"Well, good for you."

Freddie smiled.

"And what's with the food? You watching your weight or something?"

"Something like that. Caroline thinks I need to be a bit more healthy," said Freddie. "To be fair, she's got a point. She's got me eating all this bloody rabbit food. Granola and vegetables. And salad. She's even had me out…" he took a second to steel himself, "jogging!"

"Oh my God," said Richard, with a loud snort. "Oh, I have to see that. Tell me where and when."

"Yeah, you wish," said Freddie. "Anyway, why are you really here? I'm sure you didn't just pop in to ask about my book sales and love life."

"Actually, no," said Richard. "I'm investigating a new case. Series of grisly murders. Looks like a possible serial killer and…" he breathed out a long, exasperated sigh, "I can't believe I'm saying this, but… I could use your help."

Freddie clicked his pen and rested it on his notepad, a large grin forming on his lips. "Tell me more," he said.

ACKNOWLEDGMENTS

Thank you so much for buying and reading my book. I really hope you enjoyed reading it as much as I enjoyed writing it. How early on did you figure out the who the killer was? Or did I keep you guessing until the end? Get in touch at alastairpuddick.com and let me know.

Writing a novel is a pretty solitary affair. However, bringing that book to life takes a whole team. So, there are a few people I'd like to thank.

First and foremost, a huge thanks to the amazing team at Raven Crest Books for believing in me and helping me bring another one of my wacky tales into the world. They're a fantastic bunch, and they've been great to collaborate with at every stage of the process. Thanks also to my editor, Alice Smales, for her advice and suggestions, and for helping me make the book even better than it was.

Thanks must go to the usual collection of early readers, who gave up their valuable time to read rough drafts and share their thoughts. That's you, Elizabeth Puddick and Peter Stephen. And, of course, my good friend Helen Brennan, who not only insists on being thanked in every book I write, but this time she even lent her name to a character. She also continues to be a constant source of support, advice and encouragement.

Thanks to my long-suffering wife, Laura, for your helpful comments and insights. And for all the time you let me sneak out of the house to spend countless hours in coffee shops, hanging out with imaginary characters and trying to think up even more horrible, ridiculous things for Freddie Winters to do.

Finally, thanks again to you (yes you) for buying my book. It really does mean so much to know that people are out there buying and reading my books. I hope it made you laugh.

THANK YOU

Thank you very much for deciding to buy my book. In a world where there are so many books being published on a daily basis, it means a very great deal that you decided to buy mine.

This is my fourth novel. If you've enjoyed the first three and come back for more, then thank you so much. If this is the first book of mine that you've read, then why not check out the others: *The Unexpected Vacation of George Thring, Killing Dylan* and *46% Better Than Dave*. All books are published by Raven Crest Books and readily available in the same place you probably found this one.

If you have enjoyed this book, please feel encouraged to leave a review or a few good words on Amazon, Goodreads, Facebook, Instagram, TikTok, X or any social networking sites you regularly use… or even good old word of mouth.

And make sure to come and say hello or sign up for my newsletter at alastairpuddick.com. It would be great to hear from you.

Alastair Puddick

OTHER BOOKS

Murder All Inclusive is Alastair Puddick's fourth novel. If you enjoyed this, check out his other books:

The Unexpected Vacation of George Thring
Killing Dylan (Freddie Winters Book 1)
46% Better Than Dave

CONTACT DETAILS

Visit Alastair's website:
www.alastairpuddick.wordpress.com

Visit Alastair's Amazon author page:
Author.to/APuddick

Follow Alastair on Twitter:
www.twitter.com/HankShandy

Follow Alastair on Instagram:
www.instagram.com/alastairpuddickauthor/

Like or join Alastair on Facebook:
www.facebook.com/alastairpuddickauthor

Cover designed by:
László Zakariás

Published by: Raven Crest Books
www.ravencrestbooks.com
www.ravencrestbooks.co.uk

Like us on Facebook:
www.facebook.com/RavenCrestBooksClub

Follow us on Instagram:
www.instagram.com/ravencrest_books

Printed in Great Britain
by Amazon

55787592R00175